The Journal of THE NEW ALCHEMISTS—7

The Journal of
THE NEW ALCHEMISTS—7

The New Alchemy Institute

The Stephen Greene Press, Brattleboro, Vermont

This book has been produced in the United States of America. It is published by The Stephen Greene Press, Brattleboro, Vermont 05301.

LIBRARY OF CONGRESS CATALOGING IN PUBLICATION DATA

The Journal of the new alchemists. 1–

Woods Hole, Mass., New Alchemy Institute, c1973–

v. ill. 31 cm.

Key title: The Journal of the new alchemists, ISSN 0162–833X

1. Human ecology—Periodicals. 2. Environmental protection—Periodicals. 3. New Alchemy Institute—Periodicals. 4. Organic farming—Periodicals. 5. Fish culture—Periodicals. 1. New Alchemy Institute.

GF50.J68   301.31'05   78–645501
ISBN 0–8289–0406–5

Editor	NANCY JACK TODD
Membership	CHRISTINA C. RAWLEY
Cover and Divider Artist	JEFFREY PARKIN
Drawings	JAN ADKINS
	J. BALDWIN
	EARLE BARNHART
	RICHARD C. BARTLETT
	HENRIKE KROEKER
	BOBBIE FORTUN LIVELY
	MAIA MASSION
	JEFFREY PARKIN
	PAUL SUN
	VAN RYN, CALTHORPE & PARTNERS
	MALCOLM WELLS
Photography	HILDE MAINGAY
	RON ZWEIG
	DENISE BACKUS
	RICK BECK
	BILL McNAUGHTON
Typing	CYNTHIA KNAPP
	JANE RUNGE

CONTENTS

To Restore the Lands, Protect the Seas, And Inform the Earth's Stewards

THE NEW ALCHEMY INSTITUTE is a small, international organization dedicated to research and education on behalf of humanity and the planet. We seek solutions that can be adopted by individuals or small groups who are trying to create a greener, kinder world. Our major task is the development of ecologically derived forms of energy, agriculture, aquaculture, housing, and landscapes that will encourage a repopulation and revitalization of the countryside. The Institute has centers in several countries in the hope that our research and experience can be used by large numbers of people in diverse regions of the world.

The Institute is nonprofit and tax-exempt and derives its support from private contributions and research grants. Grants for the scientific research are usually available, but adequate funding for general support remains uncertain. The success of the Institute will depend upon our ability to address ourselves to the genuine needs of people working on behalf of themselves and the earth, and on the realization by our friends that financial support of our research is essential if the task ahead is to be realized.

The New Alchemy Institute has an Associate Membership ($25.00 per annum, tax-deductible) which is available to those interested in helping support our work. Upon joining, Associates receive the current annual *Journal of the New Alchemists*. Newsletters and other special interest mailings sent throughout the year keep Associates further informed of the work in progress. Over the years, the support of our Associates has been critical to the continuance of the Institute and its work.

Associate Membership
for Individuals and Families $25 *per annum*

Contributions of larger amounts are very much needed, and if you can afford more that would be beautiful.

Sustaining Membership $100 *per annum*
Patrons of the Institute $1000 *or greater*

Friends wishing to have their membership payment qualify as a deductible contribution under the tax regulations of Canada should make Canadian dollar payments payable to the New Alchemy Institute (P.E.I.) Inc. All other membership contributions should be made payable to New Alchemy Institute. Because of the costs involved with collection charges and currency exchange, we ask that all payments to the New Alchemy Institute, except for Canadian membership, be in the form of United States dollar instruments, preferably International Money Orders.

We invite you to join us as members of the New Alchemy Institute. A company of individuals addressing themselves to the future can, perhaps, make a difference during these years when there is waning reason to have hope in the continuance of human history.

THE NEW ALCHEMY INSTITUTE
P.O. BOX 47
Woods Hole, Massachusetts 02543   U.S.A.

For information about obtaining back issues of the Journal, please write to:

The New Alchemy Institute
237 Hatchville Road
E. Falmouth, Massachusetts 02536

This Journal of The New Alchemists, our seventh, perhaps more than any of its predecessors reflects a tension between the actual and the conceptual, between the present and the future, between being and bringing into being. Were one searching for a descriptive thematic title, something like "New Alchemy and Beyond" would be fairly accurate. The journal remains, as it always has been, an on-going report by New Alchemists on our most recent work in various fields of ecological research. Still, journal is a better name than report for such an eclectic collection of writings because in the journal we have always tried to avoid the fallacy of much of orthodox science and not to overlook the fact that we, as people, with our various insights, priorities, and prejudices are a part of the paradigm. In sum, the Journal offers its readers not only the song but its assorted singers as well.

That explains the present, or "New Alchemy," part of this issue. The "and Beyond" is a bit more complicated, involving, as it does, two roughly definable categories or stages. We have, of course, always been conscious of the larger picture, knowing that our work had little meaning in a vacuum and that without our fellow travelers in the antinuclear, disarmament, alternative technology, environmental, and eco-feminist movements, our activities, however rewarding to ourselves, were largely esoteric. Still, that horizon is rather removed and part of processes less in one's own hands. It has only been within the last few years, and the last year in particular, that we have formulated a tangible effort in outreach. What began long ago with Farm Saturdays has evolved into an active educational program. Besides our own efforts in outreach we have joined forces recently with the Community Action Committee based in Hyannis, Massachusetts, and three other local groups to form the Cape and Islands Self-Reliance Cooperative. Should the co-op be a success, we shall have become part of a decentralized regional political network, as we always hoped to be. We have begun to be consulted in our area on other issues like waste treatment and energy policy as well. If in the beginning we were somewhat isolated from our community, we no longer are.

Now New Alchemy, which began as a concept, or vision, and became embodied in a physical reality that had a context in its time, sixties born and seventies bred, has a context of community, of place, as well. It becomes increasingly difficult to set precise boundaries between New Alchemy and that which is beyond it.

Perhaps it is because we live in such an extraordinary and dangerous time that we are constantly being tugged at to envision our work still further

into the future. Having encapsulated our discoveries in energy collection and storage, aquaculture, soils, and organic vegetable production in the bioshelter, we began to ask ourselves, What next? It was in response to such mental questing and more specifically to prompting from Margaret Mead that New Alchemy convened a conference entitled "The Village As Social Ecology: A Generic Design Conference." The entire Explorations section of this journal is devoted to ideas engendered by the conference and written by many of the participants.

So it is that although we continue to live and work in the present, adding solar greenhouses to our houses, tending gardens and fish, recording and analyzing data, and searching for underlying patterns and connections with the natural world, watching our trees and our children grow and mature, we are at the same time living in a dialectic with

Henrike Kroeker

Hilde Maingay

the future, fantasizing and planning our Platonic village of the sun, knowing that the vision will both form and inform us.

There are times in this decade of escalating militarism, frequent outbreak of war, the arms race, and the omnipresent nuclear threat, not to mention the continuing devastation of the natural world, when we see our efforts as quixotic at best, or even as absurd. But Gregory Bateson has written that a fantasy is made real or validated by the actions that it dictates and that in such a process the fantasy can then become morphogenetic, and as such a determinant of society. A tenuous hope perhaps, but reassuring coming from a mind with the stature of Bateson's. Richard Grossinger, writing in Plant Medicine of our work and that of others, observed, ". . . healing and farming have tended to take on a small piece of the cosmic vision and for many

involved in the transition, it seems natural and smooth."*

According to Gary Snyder, Coyote, Old Man (old with the oldness of once upon a time), who was the wonderful archetypical trickster of Native American myth—when myth was, as it should be, a way of understanding life and our place in the universal pattern—spoke of a Dream Time that is outside of history. Dream Time surrounds us, and out of Dream Time comes the healing. In this journal we have included a description of the time that is now and a glimpse of the Dream Time.

N.J.T.

*Richard Grossinger. 1980. Planet Medicine: From Stone Age Shamanism to Post Industrial Healing. Garden City, N.Y.: Anchor/Doubleday.

The Journal of THE NEW ALCHEMISTS—7

Ron Zweig

New Alchemy

A long time ago, when I first wrote about New Alchemy as it was just beginning, it wasn't too difficult to give a rendering that rang fairly true. There were so few of us then, and we had taken only a few cautious steps around the edges of the vast idea we were exploring. Each aspect of our work, every fish and garden crop, every new wind gadget, could be remembered, named by all of us. We had all taken part or at least been present for part of the activity surrounding each one of these.

But slowly at first, and then more rapidly, the group expanded, the number of projects increased, new fields of work were incorporated, and some of the sense of the turning seasons and years was lost; some of the harvests began to blur together a bit. Even then it was possible when writing of an event or particular period of time to convey a feeling of the place, of the people and what it felt like to be together, of the various projects, and of the underlying intellectual framework in which it all took place.

It has become much harder to do so. So many of the areas of research; the computer modeling of solar design, the analysis of the water chemistry in the solar-algae ponds, the details of suitable tree management, have reached a level of complexity requiring expertise well beyond that of the amateur. It has become challenging for any one of us to give a comprehensive explanation of all facets of our research. The range of subject matter in this Journal testifies to this. The report on toxic chemicals in the Ark, for example, or the one on modeling algal growth and decline in solar-algae ponds, is highly technical and while still of interest to nonexperts, could not have been generated by them. Clearly, in spite of our best intentions, we have had to give way to a degree of specialization. It is frequently essential that we have subgroup meetings in addition to the regular weekly meeting of the complete group. Five definable categories of work have evolved: agriculture, aquaculture, bioshelters, the National Science Foundation team, and administration and outreach. Each of these requires informed decisions, and although all meetings are open to everyone, none of us can possibly find the time to go to many that don't directly concern us.

With this unavoidable separation of work and, spatially at least, of people, it's harder to summon a phrase that encapsulates a feeling of a time common to all of us. A summer of great productivity in the garden may be one of mishaps in aquaculture. The windmills may be behaving commendably during the same period that the office staff or outreach people are running constantly just to stay in the same place. I used to write paragraphs that began, "It was a summar of sunflowers, marigolds and cabbages, tilapia and midges, weeding and picking . . ." and feel that such phrases gave a summary and essence of that time. I don't think I could do so now. It is so much harder to extract and distill a commonality from a more complex and diffuse reality.

And yet, at base, the fabric remains a whole. New Alchemy is not made up of departments, the work and goals of which are unrelated. We are conscious most, if not all, of the time whether some one of us is running the computer, or cleaning out a fish tank, or hoeing the soil, that we are working physically and conceptually to help make possible a sustainable future. Inching slowly forward, always falling short, that is the reason, the hope, and the ethic in which we work. So most of the time the prevailing psychological climate, although more disparate than it once was, is not one of disunity.

And then there are still the wonderful times like communal work sessions, or gatherings, or feasts like the weddings of Colleen Armstrong and Sheldon Frye, and Susie Hoerchek and Jeff Parkin, or Harvest Festival, or even a good Farm Saturday. Then it's all still there, an unshakable sense of what it is we set out to do, and why, and a sense that we would not have our collective life other than it is.

In this section, devoted somewhat loosely to events at the center on Cape Cod and its affiliate in Costa Rica or to various activities of New Alchemists, we have included a sampling of doings in the office, an account of apprenticeship, a description of our outreach program, some observations of a traveling New Alchemist, and Bill McLarney's saga of the eventful life in Costa Rica.

Hilde Maingay

N.J.T.

Hilde Maingay

Hilde Maingay

Adventures in the Mail Trade

Denise Backus

In October 1979 New Alchemy appeared on ABC's "Good Morning, America." The film crew arrived just days before Harvest Festival weekend. We were swamped with preparations for that, in the middle of reglazing the Ark, and talking with a writer doing a cover story on us for *New Roots*. The film crew was easy to have around, the weather cooperated, and to our surprise we enjoyed it.

On October 23 the three- to four-minute segment appeared on TV and our address was flashed on the screen for a split second at the end. I suppose we did discuss what the publicity might do to our already heavy mail load, but we were unprepared for the deluge of letters. Fifty the first day, then a hundred, and more in the days that followed. By the end of the third week, the numbers dwindled, but we had received a total of about 1,350 letters. Our small office staff couldn't handle the job, so we farmed it out to another person, who put all names and addresses on labels and helped us send out the letter John and Nancy Jack Todd composed along with a brochure and a bibliography.

Some wonderful versions of our address arrived at 237 Hatchville Road in East Falmouth:

Biotransition, Etc., Hatfield Rd.
Solar Living, Hatchmore Rd.
Solar Research Farm, Hatchenow Rd.
The Academy Corp, Hatchfield Rd., MA
Food Farm TV, Hackford Rd.
Organic Life Farm
Scientific Thermiology
Alchemy 2000
Hatchmill Institute of Solar Energy
New Way of Living
Food Without Fertilizer
Alcohmey Society, Homestead Project, Hatchmouth, Facemouth, MA

and my favorite:

Solar Energy-Windmill Power-Fish Raising-Vegetables (with nonchemical humis fertilizer) Experimental Farm, Hatchville, RFD, MA

Not bad for a quick flash on the screen. And hats off to the post office that brought it all to us. The mail hasn't been quite the same since.

Reflections on Apprenticeship

Scott Stokoe

"Volunteer." "Apprentice." "That new guy working with Ron."

All these epithets point to the meaning of being a volunteer at The New Alchemy Institute. But each of these categories alone is incomplete.

Volunteer. This definition touches the basic nature of our position here. We receive no pay, no benefits, no board or housing. We have come to donate our time, energy, and ideas. Yet our role runs much deeper; we do, in fact, receive so much.

Apprentice. We have come to learn, to practice under a skilled and learned person. And from our contribution of time and support we receive invaluable hands-on experience and an opportunity to study the basic research and information for which New Alchemy is noted.

"That new guy working with Ron." This third label points to our individual relationships with our work, our sponsors, and the institute as a whole. We are placed in one-to-one encounters with our mentors; this is rare in traditional higher education. The hours we work, the information we research, and the work we do in the field are all a part of these personal relationships. And we have the opportunity to pursue our own areas of interest within our research.

A final consideration is the simple opportunity to be present and involved with The New Alchemy Institute. From eating fresh out-of-season greens and vegetables to meeting and interacting with some of the innovators and thinkers of the alternative movement, the extracurricular experiences are many and varied. Conferences, lectures, gardening (for instruction and for eating), field trips, readings, and socializing with Alchemists and fellow volunteers are part of the extra bounty.

These terms roughly define the position of a volunteer. This is the basic experience common to us all at the farm. And yet this is only the foundation for each individual's experience. The substance of each apprenticeship is as varied as the personalities involved. Some of us work full time, some part time. Some are here as a part of their academic program, others have blown in on winds of discontent. Some have specific research directions, others are gaining broad exposure to the huge range of opportunities. Some have related skills and experiences to apply to the ongoing work here, others are acquiring new skills and information to apply to efforts beyond New Alchemy. Some of us have families here with us, others are single. Some of us are inclined to the theoretical and ideological, while others emphasize the practical and the concrete. And yet nearly every personal facet finds an avenue of expression. Truly, our experiences here reflect the character and goals of each of us.

Volunteers have a wide range of expectations when they arrive here and their experience to date indicates that those expectations are met and shattered throughout their time here.

John Q.

I came to New Alchemy out of a need to explore and discover. Feeling isolated and confused, I was challenging my own inherited axioms and the social structures that expressed them. My intuition and personal experience presented intellectual options, directions that ran counter to the values and ways with which I had grown up and that were currently dominating the culture in which I was immersed. I remained firm in my belief that positive, life-affirming, ecological, and humane alternatives were viable and it was possible to replace the wasteful, destructive cycles of our society. But my blindered search revealed no avenues, no options. Because my alignment with an alternative culture movement came solely from an internal intellectual grappling, it was not clear to me that many other people were searching for ways to create a sustainable future. It took some readings of William Irwin Thompson's work and a radio program about The New Alchemy Institute to bring me in touch with some alternative activities. From this little input, I knew that I was coming to New Alchemy.

Armed with a hardy idealism and buoyed by the knowledge that there was a place that was actually putting alternatives into physical form, I delivered myself to the Cape Cod institute, determined to "fit in." I had no idea that there was a volunteer program, nor what input I might have in the research. All that was clear was that New Alchemy was proceeding in directions I believed in and to which I wanted to contribute.

My limited background with citrus and avocado trees in Israel seemed to match a need expressed by Earle Barnhart for a yearlong volunteer (the maximum time allowed) to help in the tree crops program. I am now halfway through this program, picking up skills and information daily, while working in the field and in research. I offer this brief account of my own experience only as one example of the many different experiences and backgrounds of apprentices at The New Alchemy Institute. Each volunteer who comes has her/his own story to tell. The diversity of backgrounds, goals, and directions of New Alchemy apprentices seems as continuous as the flow of folks coming to exchange time, labor, and caring for information, skills, and sharing.

> . . . we formed our Volunteer's Group out of a basic New Alchemy principle of self-reliance. We wanted to increase the vitality of our experience; we wanted more and we created it.
>
> Mick G.

The diversity of the individuals in the fall 1979 group became evident in our early, limited contact. Working on different areas at the farm and pursuing different lifestyles away from the farm, communication and sharing were at a premium. And yet it became clear early in our collective tenure as apprentices that we did have some common goals. We all sought a context greater than our own minds to contemplate the issues raised at the farm within the general movement in which we found ourselves. We all felt a desire to get together socially, to take time to chat, to share our daily activities and the general progress in the fields in which we were working. And finally, we had a very pointed admonition from our predecessors: to pull together, to communicate, and to support each other.

Some of the volunteers from the previous summer had had some difficult times through that bustling, demanding season—insufficient contact with their sponsors and a heavy work routine without the desired information exchange. This summer group also recognized that a regular meeting of volunteers would be useful both for socializing and information exchange.

This is how meetings began. There were nine or ten of us in the fall and all but two were new. For the structure, we chose the traditional New Alchemy potluck supper. For the function, we chose to study together, in greater depth, the various areas of research at the farm. Since then speakers have been invited from the core group of the New Alchemists as well as other people knowledgeable about alternative lifestyles, philosophies, and technologies.

Our regular meetings, our organization, and our earnestness all combine to create a special place for volunteers at New Alchemy. It is a foundation, newly evolved for apprentices here, that can offer support and depth to the demanding and rewarding life of a New Alchemy apprentice.

Hilde Maingay

Valentine Season: Riverdale

It's Night
Upon the River
Mid-February
Venus shines
Out of the wintry Sky
From the distance
The Palisades
Loom starkly
Over the world
Such a night
Sends the mind
Back into
Those billion years
It took
To frame all this
The ancient Red Oak
Itself a newcomer
Here by the imbedded rock
With its long glacier striations
It's all here
Too overwhelming
For human endurance
Were it not
For radiant memories
Of the Willows
Seen earlier today
Yellowing
In the late
Evening Sunlight.

   Thomas Berry   February 1980

The stage is bare now. We are between theories. We are in the last period of the fossil fuel era— and the so-called nuclear era is already aborting.

What we miss is something as simple as a vision of how we will live in the future.

No one sees the future; we have no clear images—as a culture, as a nation, as the Western world.

When the stage is empty there is unprecedented opportunity.

When the stage of the future is unoccupied, when there is not one strong vision of which we are all in the process of working out, we don't have to fight against either the established vision or the rebels. There is no enemy. The empty stage is the rarest of opportunities. Then build a future, make it work, and let the world steal it.

Tyrone Cashman

Reprinted with permission from *Rain* magazine, November, 1977.

Reaching Out

Robert Sardinsky

In May 1978, New Alchemy celebrated Sun Day, an international day of recognition and festivities on behalf of a solar future. Over a thousand people visited New Alchemy that day, half of them students from local schools. I showed two elementary classes and one high school class around the farm. My first two tours were with a group of first and third graders who were as excited as Mexican jumping beans, curious about almost everything and full of thought-provoking questions (at least from their perspective). I was challenged to explain all that we were doing at New Alchemy in a simplified, yet thorough way. We played, talked, touched, and sang together. New Alchemy took on a completely different perspective for me as I saw it through their eyes. My energy level skyrocketed, and my spirit danced with the kites flying high overhead. I was hooked. Later that day my experience with the high school class was very different. They were a gum-chewing, radio-toting, disinterested and apathetic bunch, no fun at all. What had occurred in the process of growing up? This passage in Rachel Carson's *The Sense of Wonder* gave me some insight into what had happened.

> A child's world is fresh and new and beautiful, full of wonder and excitement. It is our misfortune that for most of us that clear-eyed vision, that true instinct for what is beautiful and awe-inspiring, is dimmed and even lost before we reach adulthood. If I had influence with the Good Fairy who is supposed to preside over the christening of all children, I should ask that her gift to each child be a sense of wonder so indestructible that it would last throughout life, as an unfailing antidote against the boredom and disenchantments of later years, the sterile preoccupation with things that are artificial, the alienation from the sources of our strength.*

Socialization and schooling was smothering young people's "sense of wonder." Thinking back to my youth I could sympathize with the high school students I had worked with. School had a stifling impact on my development, as did my best friend at home, the television set. Somehow my own deeply ingrained sense of wonder had endured. The beauties, mysteries, and excitement of my childhood experiences in the wilderness gave me this inner strength. My own negative schooling

Hilde Maingay

experiences combined with my initial exposure to working with young people at New Alchemy motivated me to search for more humane approaches to educating young people that foster an appreciation and respect for all life on earth. Our Sun Day celebration sparked many requests for tours from school groups. There was clearly a strong interest and need for us to begin catering to young people.

In the fall of 1978, I began building the foundations for a New Alchemy school group education program. It was decided to set it up as a one-year pilot project to determine its long-term feasibility. We wanted to know if the farm could be used as a classroom for school groups without their interfering with people's work and whether the program could sustain itself financially. My first year's experience working with school groups at New Alchemy was very successful and we decided to adopt the program.

---

*Rachel Carson. 1965. *The Sense of Wonder*. N.Y.: Harper & Row.

Over three thousand students, preschool pupils through graduate students, have participated in our educational programs during the past two years representing public and private schools throughout New England. The tremendous diversity in age, residence, and socioeconomic background of these students gave us an opportunity to try many different approaches to educating young people about living lightly on the earth. Such immensely challenging work has been both energizing and exhausting. In the half to full day we spend with each group, we attempt to open up each person's eyes and mind to the destructive, nonsustainable nature of human sustenance today and to ecologically sound means of building a solar-based society for tomorrow. Our twelve-acre farm/classroom offers an ideal environment in which to carry out this exploration. I begin each program by trying to find out where the group is "coming from" and where they "are at." To communicate with them effectively, I need to know what their interests are to best explain how New Alchemy's work applies to their own lives. I often use noncompetitive, representational games to break the ice and to build a community spirit through cooperative group play. I often turn again to these games later in the day to communicate concepts of ecology and energy that are otherwise difficult to conceptualize. Games like the "Web of Life," "Lap Sit," and "Knots" help develop an appreciation and understanding of the interdependence of life. We build "People Pyramids" while discussing the pyramidal structure and energetics of food chains, and use the "People Pass" for a working definition of energy.

I liked how you put the net over the plants so the birds and animals couldn't get them. It was better than killing the birds and animals.

The fertilizer they used was fish and leaves. They don't use the stuff you get in the store because it contains chemicals that kill the soil after a long period of time.

Inside the Ark our group did a play. The play was about two people and their realizing that wind power is a better source of energy than electricity, money-wise and energy-wise.

I liked New Alchemy and the things there like the ark and the dome and the solar structures. Because you are trying to make the world a better place to live.

When I went into the Ark and the door was kept open for a second I thought it was a waste of energy, then I thought the sun's power will never run out!

I thought it was interesting when you said to put our orange and banana peils in the bucket and this year I'm going to make a compost pile.

I liked having lunch in the dome and learning how you can work a garden with only natural stuff. I think it is really neat the way you can get energy from the sun, store it and grow all those nice vegetables and pretty flowers.

One theory that I found to be interesting and important was that nothing was done w/o an understanding of its effect on the environment.

Like most people I take our natural resources for granted.

The important thing they are doing at New Alchemy is looking to nature as a guide.

As I begin a farm tour, my role progresses from that of greeter to that of artist/interpreter. I try to weave the purposes of and meanings behind the various appropriate technologies demonstrated at the farm into a cohesive picture. The greatest challenge for me involves putting New Alchemy's work into perspective. An understanding of why we are doing what we are doing is essential to seeing the gardens, windmills, aquaculture ponds, and bioshelters. Without this emphasis, the day would be little more than a "show and tell," as most of the students that visit us are far removed from their life-support networks. Distant farmers, miners, manufacturers, and utility companies provide their needs. Few of them realize the devastating consequences of modern technology or how ultimately dependent they are upon the health of the natural world for their well being.

At each stop on our journey through the farm, we explore the relationship between meeting human needs and maintaining a healthy ecological balance. We play, experiment, eat together, perform skits, paint murals, and engage in group discussion. All are encouraged to use their senses as much as possible. We feel the steaming-hot compost pile and slimy worms, smell the fragrant herbs and vegetables, watch the fish and bees, and taste

The compost pile was interesting in the way that the sticks and junk turned to fertilizer.

I did not feel saturated with facts as I usually do after a day at a museum. Everything was part of an integrated system and what you didn't absorb when touring the garden you were given again in the Ark, but from a different perspective.

If the whole world visited New Alchemy then we could make the earth a better place to live.

I really like the way you never waste anything, not even waste.

I think you conserve a lot, that's great. If all the people in the world were like you and conserved so much and used the sun for energy the world would be so much nicer.

New Alchemy has the best gourds!

Hilde Maingay

some of the garden fruits and vegetables. After the tour, groups with special interests may participate in one of a number of the more focused workshops that build on what has been seen. We have given workshops to students from elementary school through college age on computer modeling of ecosystem dynamics, food politics/vegetarianism, solar greenhouse design, integrated pest control management in bioshelters, "living lightly" on the earth, and appropriate technologies in third world countries. Whenever possible, a hands-on job such as planting trees, building a compost pile, raising a windmill, preparing a vegetarian feast, or assisting in a fish harvest is included. By the end of their time with us we hope to have given the students a greater sense of their interdependence with the natural world and an increased awareness of the impact of their own lives on it.

Most of all we want them to leave realizing that there are healthy, sustainable means of providing for humanity's needs and feeling that they as individuals can make an important contribution in helping bring this about.

My work with school groups has given me a sense of hope for the future. Looking at their art, I have seen the perceptions of reality of many young people dramatically restructured at New Alchemy. In the short time we spend together most of them are able to grasp the essence of what we are doing, why we are doing it, and what it means to them.

I never thought the sun could do so much.

I was thinking on the way back I would like to make a fish farm this is my dream. Also I was thinking that if you can feed thirteen people for a year in green vegetables if they could do that in India people would not die from famine.

Thank you very much for the tour of NIA. I enjoyed my visit very much. Especially the dome because it didn't take any electricity to heat it which proves that solar energy works. The ark I really liked, because of the way you raised the fish with energy from the sun.

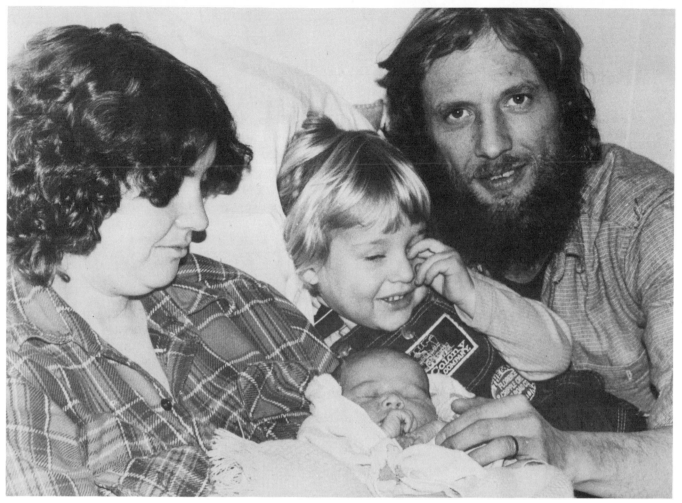

Another Earth Gypsy

Tyrone Cashman

Tyrone Cashman chose the title for his article that follows in reminiscence of one that appeared in our first journal. It was about earth gypsies and was by Laura and David Engstrom. Earth gypsy was a rather romantic term that John Todd had coined for those of us who chose to be wanderers for a while, taking with them, as part of them, the ideas and dreams of all of us. At first Laura found the term amusing but later confessed to finding it evocative of the time of her traveling with David.

We have almost all been earth gypsies at one time or another. John Todd's idea for the Margaret Mead, a great sailing bioshelter that would be a sort of ecological Hope Ship, carries the idea a step further.

Of those who have written of their experiences for this Journal, Ty has settled in California, where he has worked for Governor Brown, and has been president of the American Wind Energy Associa-

tion. As for David and Laura, their period of wandering has given way to a more settled period of parenthood, a task they share equally. David is still with New Alchemy. His meticulous analysis of water chemistry is indispensable to the National Science Foundation sponsored aquaculture research. In whatever other time he can find, he is an artist, working in precious metals and stones. Laura, in training to become a midwife, is bringing her gentle nature into the service of returning childbirth to the woman-defined, woman-controlled, and joyous experience it is again becoming.

In the article that follows, Ty apprises the movement of events since his time at New Alchemy, interweaving them with his own experiences, beginning with the time when he was nomadic—an earth gypsy.

N.J.T.

I put down my ancient copy of the first *Journal of The New Alchemists*. I sit on the edge of the West, in a house clinging to a cliff above the surf of the Pacific just north of San Francisco. Red-tailed hawks, buzzards, and kestrels soar and hunt around my cliff dwelling. Gulls in ragged flocks do barrel rolls in the spiraling winter storm winds. Fog flows inland in summer, coastward in winter. The sun heats the all-glass house by day and the star-flecked universe draws at it by night with an infinite hunger for heat. We sleep summer and winter in an open-doored cabin higher up the slope. Wrapped in fog and sea sounds.

As Laura said in 1973 in that first journal, "Earth gypsies we were called (in the previous *New Alchemy Newsletter*) and at the time I had to smile at the ultra-romanticism of it all. Yet now as I feel my way back to these days on the road the inevitable nostalgia makes the term seem appropriate after all."

I guess I relate strongly to this note, written at the moment in space-time when I became a New Alchemist. Looking back, over recent years I felt very much like a gypsy.

I too set out from New Alchemy in a VW van in the spring of 1977 to cross the continent, heading away from home on a voyage with no long-term destination.

I had only the first step mapped out. I had been invited to Green Gulch Farm on the northern California coast to design and help build a water-pumping windmill for garden irrigation. It was during the great California drought. I was a missionary, a traveling Alchemist, sharing in other gardens the skills, the vision, and the techniques we had wrestled with on Cape Cod. It was an appropriate work. Although we had up to that time hosted tens of thousands of visitors to our Cape Cod farm, the Prince Edward Island Ark, and Costa Rican Center, we had no outreach program to plant the seeds in other places. I was not sure that was what I was doing. But I was preparing to plant a New Alchemy sailwing on other soil.

When New Alchemy was young, the world was far from what we wanted it to be. Our act was a shot in the dark, a stab into a future we wanted and cared for enough for us to do an absurd thing—try to build it.

In the late sixties there were thousands of young people protesting the world as it was. It was Important Work. But we saw another important work to be done: quietly, creatively to nurse the seedlings of a *new* world.

When the Green Gulch Sailwing was up and we had set it free to do its work, I wandered again. I wandered to the East Coast, Long Island briefly, and New York City, to the midwest to connect with the clan, and back to California. Sim Van der Ryn, the founder of the state of California's Office of Appropriate Technology, had seen the windmill and asked if I might want to work for him in state government.

I was still ranging the world, an earth gypsy haunted and inspired by the New Alchemy vision: we can create a new world in place of the one we have recently inherited, a world more true to natural systems, gentler, greener, and longer lived, based on an energy and agriculture that will sustain our grandchildren as it sustains us.

I drove through the coastal hills by the Pacific trying to articulate this vision in the context of a whole continent that was leading a whole world along its technological path. It was the fall of 1977. Looking into the future I suddenly realized that it was blank. By the side of the road overlooking valley and sea I put my typewriter on the plywood bed in the back of the van and tried to describe what the emptiness must mean.

I recalled a course many years ago with Margaret Mead; a phrase of hers had struck me then: "We are between theories in anthropology now." Again I recalled an early image, as a theater major at St. Louis University, sitting before an empty stage with a spotlight lighting the bareness. Bateson's "random space" essential to all creativity; Lao Tsu's empty bowl and wheel hub; the void of the Zen Masters. The power of the emptiness of that bare stage has stayed with me.

Out of these images, the vision of our unique historical place came home to me. As it emerged I remembered Dick Gregory's comment during the Vietnam War: "If our democracy was what we claim it to be, we wouldn't have to force it on people with rifles. They would steal it for themselves."

I went to work for the state of California as a member of Sim's Office of Appropriate Technology. There I met young men and women from various parts of the country most of whom had come from small alternative groups: *Tilth* magazine, Ecotope, Turkey Run Farm outside Washington, Institute for Local Self Reliance, United Farm Workers Union, *Co-Evolution Quarterly*, Farallones. It was an odd assortment for a governmental office. Our mandate was to serve the other state agencies helping to implement energy-saving architecture and equipment, to be critics, designers, and proponents. We were to help as we could within this vast structure to show the way for small-scale, environmentally benign systems.

We were another culture. The traditional system tried to eject us with an immune reaction. Both our idealism and our unfamiliarity with how things get done in great bureaucracies got in our way. But we slogged on. And things began to happen. A passively heated and cooled office building was built. A first-cut design for a mixed-use, energy- and water-conserving neighborhood for downtown Sacramento was developed. The Water Resources Control Board was influenced. Drought-tolerant gardens were created in Sacramento. Solar heating training programs were initiated. On-site sewage systems were proposed and implemented. Large tax credits for solar and wind energy systems were passed. Another way of doing things had begun to be recognized in the mainstream of California culture.

And this is our task. I feel that New Alchemy remains as a tuning fork, setting a tone of holistic food and energy systems on a small scale. That tuning fork needs to continue to be heard; that research must continue to develop.

Here we are now in the 1980s. Our original vision of running low on oil and the possibilities of armed conflict over what is our present world's life blood, is on the horizon. We saw this ten years ago. We gave our nerve and sinew to getting tooled up, to preparing another path down which a nation and a world could go instead of seeing only the narrower options of war, national emergency, and martial law.

We saw that by the time the nation perceived its own energy bind it would be too late unless there had been those who had seen it early and prepared the path. The time for strong labor was early. Either we would make it or we wouldn't. We didn't know.

And here we are. Did we do it, we along with the other individuals, small groups and associations from coast to coast? I think we've come close. I think the original courage and audacity to attempt such a transformation of culture has paid off more than could have been expected.

Just look at the core alternative food and energy complex: homes-solar-wind-gardens. We know that America is a nation of TV watchers. It is our number-one recreational pastime. But now the second most common off-work pastime is gardening. The Gallup organization found in 1979 that out of 78 million American households, 68 million watch TV and 61 million practice some sort of horticulture. Of these, 33 million raise food—carrots, cabbage, cantaloupe, etc.—in backyards or community gardens. Food gardening is practiced by more people than vacationing, fishing, home workshop using, bicycling, jogging, bowling, photography, and on and on. As we've always said at New Alchemy, knowing how to garden is the best skill-base for holistic self-reliant food and energy systems.

We cannot credit New Alchemy, nor all the alternative organizations put together, for the spread of gardening, but it is a very encouraging sign for the future that the American people are already practicing the key skill that the addition of more commonland space and solar greenhousing can turn into decentralized, partial support systems. Even the economics are already good. The total retail value of produce from American gardens was $13 billion. The average cost per garden was $19. The average dollar yield per garden was $367.

The most widely available home energy resource is conservation. Then come solar and wind. Many states have introduced programs to encourage the use of solar and wind energy. The federal government has passed tax credits for this kind of equipment. These credits are being increased. Two major pieces of federal legislation have dictated that the nation's major utilities must offer energy audits to their customers and arrange for financing of solar and wind energy equipment, if, after the audit, the family decides they would like to use these renewable resources. In addition, utilities now *must* buy power from small power producers who use renewable resources, and must pay reasonable rates for that power. This greatly aids the economics of the household wind energy system, since the utility will now act as a storage battery.

In 1974 at New Alchemy I would not have expected changes this radical in so few years. And I have no doubt, after my peregrinations as an earth gypsy, that New Alchemy, standing as a tuning fork, sending out this pure note into the world around, has had a lot to do with this. That note has been heard in Congress, often to the consternation of the Department of Energy. Nearly everywhere I go the name of New Alchemy is known and respected, and often generates that spark of life and enthusiasm that even a small beginning that brings hope can elicit. These tiny notes we've been humming in different spots around the nation are resonating.

But now is the new era. Shortages are upon us. Swords are rattling. Let us take heart again, take another deep breath and join with all those who have heard and will carry forward the refounding of America.

Bill McNaughton

New Alchemy and Ecodevelopment in Costa Rica

William O. McLarney

Who knows where the work of writing begins? Certainly not at the precisely definable moment when pen first touches paper, but earlier, in some process of thought or perception. This piece may have begun one evening as I lay in the hammock on the elevated porch of our house in Gandoca, Costa Rica.* The rhythmic sound of the Caribbean surf, often wild, or even menacing when heard

---

*The New Alchemy Institute has a small sister organization in Costa Rica. Founded by Bill McLarney with the official and working title of NAISA, it is conducting small-scale, local experiments in aquaculture, agriculture, and tree crops. NAISA's primary motivation is to be useful to the people of its community and protective of the resources of the area, particularly the forests.

from the beach, seems peaceful and reassuring from just a few yards inland. It merges with other familiar sounds of nature—the song of the *paraque* (a sort of tropical whippoorwill), the sarcastic voice of the night heron that raids our fish ponds, the electric call of the toad *Bufo marinus*. The sounds integrate with the visual images—silhouettes of the feathery coconut frond, the almond tree with its branches "stacked" in layers, the proud new and tattered old banana leaves, the bamboo with its own whispering sound and its constantly dropping leaves, which spin or oscillate like coins sinking in water. The exotic, yet tranquil, mood of such hours touches all our time here.

Or this piece of writing may have been conceived a few hundred yards from the hammock, on the beach, where Susan and I discovered the first small globs of crude oil that appeared for a while along the coast between Puerto Viejo and Gandoca Bar, and maybe farther. It was a small "spill" of unknown origin, and the only discernible victims have been our tempers, as we cleaned our shoes. But it is a reminder that we are not so isolated as we might like to think and that delightful as meditation in the hammock may be, it is not my work.

An hour and a half by foot from where the hammock hangs, in the magnificent virgin forest that covers half of our new inland farm, one does not hear the sea. But if one listens carefully, one can hear bulldozers at work destroying natural forest, harvestable cacao, and, perhaps most significantly, Costa Rican topsoil in hope of financial profit. That sound is another reminder.

These reminders are not pleasant, but they serve to put our daily efforts in a context; the importance of what we are attempting to do becomes clear. We are attempting to work together with our *campesino* neighbors in the faith that the environmental problems we have been trained to see and worry about and the survival problems they confront daily have a common solution. They said, "*Donda no hay problemas, no hay vida. El gusto de la vida es resolver problemas.*" (Where there are no problems, there is no life. The fun of life is in solving problems.) I hope some of that attitude will emerge in this article, that it will help inspire some other worrywart conservationist or developer to see a particular problem in a greater context and small solutions merging in a greater solution.

The article will draw on my piece on Latin America in the fifth *Journal of the New Alchemists*. In that piece, I expressed some concern that Latin American *campesinos* could become "totally alienated from the ecology movement." I am pleased to report that, in our part of Costa Rica at least, the opposite has happened—*campesinos* are becoming more sensitive to ecology issues. Elsewhere I see the appropriate technology movement starting to reach the *campesino*. And a recent visit to Nicaragua suggested that a government more oriented to public welfare on a broad basis will also be a more ecologically sensitive government. But that is a larger context.

In my previous article I also invoked the single issue that has most concerned revolutionaries, reformers, and reactionaries in Latin America—land distribution. Here, making reference to a portion of Costa Rica that I shall define as "Coastal Talamanca,"[1] I shall examine present and possible future patterns of land tenure and use and their probable effects on ecological and social conditions.

For our purposes, Coastal Talamanca may be divided into three parts of roughly equal size. The Sixaola River valley, to which the Bribris fled after their conquest by Spaniards and Mosquito Indians, is, or was, the most fertile land in Coastal Talamanca. The last conquest of the Bribris saw them driven from the Sixaola valley by the United Fruit Company. Today the Indians live in the mountains, and various offshoots of the conquering multinational still control all but the lowermost portion of the valley.

A second portion of flatland, mostly along the coast but extending up the Sixaola valley to Mata de Limón, is almost entirely in the hands of small farmers. The nearer reaches of the hills separating the coastal plain from the river valley are also in the hands of *campesinos*, but the more remote portions are in large blocks owned for the most part by absentees. By virtue of their inaccessibility they have remained in natural forest.

The history of the fruit company lands since the ouster of the Indians has been one of intermittent agricultural activity and abandonment, with occasional episodes of violence. The valley has not seen the last of violence; in 1980 a group of *precaristas* (squatters) invaded company land near Margarita, erected makeshift houses and had to be forcibly expelled. This promises to be just the first of a series of confrontations.

What is the value of *La Compañia*'s 11,000 hectares to present-day Costa Rica? No one had ever tried to claim that the dominant crops (traditionally bananas and now African oil palm) contribute directly to the nourishment of Costa Ricans. Formerly it could be said that some employment was provided, though it was often tantamount to enslavement.[2] (In the 1950s the United Fruit Company realized more profits in Central America from sales to its workers at its commissaries than from sale of its products.) Today the operation is much less labor intensive than before, and such stoop labor as exists goes to poverty-stricken Panamanian Indians, who will work for less than Costa Ricans. The arguments usually made for the continued presence of the fruit companies in Costa

[1] "Talamanca," a Bribri Indian term meaning "place of blood," inspired by the aboriginal inhabitants' early contacts with European "civilization" and given added weight by the behavior of the fruit companies in the early part of this century, is variously applied in current usage. Politically, it implies the *cantón* (county) of Talamanca, a component of Limón province. In popular use, it is often restricted to the Talamanca mountains and valley, inhabited primarily by Bribri and Cabecar Indians. My usage of "Coastal Talamanca" roughly indicates that portion of Costa Rica bounded by the Rio Estrella, a line drawn from Pandora to Bribri, the Rio Sixaola, and the Caribbean Sea.

[2] If you read Spanish, the classic fictionalized account of life on a fruit company farm in Coastal Talamanca is Carlos Luis Fallas's *Mamita Yunai*. 1978. San José, Costa Rica: Libreria Lehmann, 222 pp.

Rica are couched in terms of "balance of payments" or "foreign exchange." These arguments have been attacked many times as apologies for economic colonialism; perhaps the best case is made by Galeano.[3]

For my part, I would like to submit that in the long run the current fruit company project will prove to be an economic liability for Costa Rica. To understand why I believe this, one must know a bit of the history of the region, and one really should see modern fruit company agriculture. I shall try to convey the essence of it.

I leave Mata de Limón on foot, headed to Sixaola, which happens to be the location of the nearest phone. Just across Quebrada Mata de Limón I pass a battered orange metal sign that declares, "Chiriqui Land Company." At that point I enter abandoned company cacao lands. The shade trees customarily planted with cacao have grown tall; the understory is filled in. Howler monkeys bellow from the treetops. The whole incredible array of tropical birds, insects, and flowering trees is on display.

Mature cacao farms are not only productive and attractive agricultural land, they are a seminatural environment that conserves soil, moderates climate, and supports a great diversity of other plants and wildlife. These abandoned cacao lands are a joy to walk through. With the investment of a certain amount of hand labor they could be made productive; they could produce an export crop, provide employment, be harvested for wood and food crops and protect the land for generations to come. But someone has determined (I suppose) that bananas and African palm oil will be even more "profitable" in the short run. And I can hear the bulldozers.

Soon I enter the desert. The bulldozers are at work removing cacao trees, overstory, understory— every living thing. Only a few of the largest trees are left for the chain saw and the ax. Smash! At a place called Bananera one of the last survivors, a lovely old *nispero*, bedecked with orchids, comes crashing down on a still-livable house, formerly the home of an ancient lady, Doña Nena, who dealt in herbal remedies.

A few hardwood trees are set aside, but most of the vegetation is pushed into windrows. The process inevitably results in scraping away most of the topsoil, especially where the terrain is uneven. When it rains the creeks run full and red, especially since the bulldozer operators pay no heed to the Costa Rican law that prohibits cutting any tree

within fifty meters of a watercourse. Further drainage is achieved by ditches; where it is more convenient, the natural watercourses are straightened.

As I walk on in the broiling desert sun, a howler monkey calls his defiance from the edge of the woods. Tonight, when I return, the tree in which he sits will be gone; when the weather is dry, the bulldozers work from dawn to dusk. Between me and the forest there is literally not a living leaf of vegetation to be seen, just hot, dry earth.

A little farther on, I enter a zone that had been cleared earlier. Seedlings of African oil palm have already been set out in monotonous files. Miraculously, a fair growth of grass is sprouting from the subsoil between the palm rows. Juan Lopez, the 12-year-old son of neighbors in Mata de Limón, has enterprisingly driven his father's small herd of cattle into this temporary "pasture." Perhaps later it will be eliminated with herbicide.

Still later, I enter a more established agricultural zone, planted to bananas. Taller monotony, punctuated by mountains of perfectly edible but "substandard" bananas, rejected to rot in the sun or be recycled by vultures.

As of this writing (April 1980) the destruction has stopped; rumor has it that it will resume when the profits start rolling in. For now perhaps three-fourths of the company lands remain in one or another form of second growth and abandonment. From a *campesino* viewpoint, mass invasion seems logical—to let the land stand as it is, with second growth gradually choking out the untended cacao, seems a waste. To "develop" it company style may prove to be a greater waste.

There is much in what I have described to invoke tears, frustration, or anger. The people of Gandoca and Mata de Limón are concerned that deforestation will exacerbate the cycle of flood and drought, already presumed to be worsening because of deforestation in the Talamanca valley and a dike, built by the fruit company, that extends along the Panamanian side of the Rio Sixaola from Guabito to California and tends to deflect floodwaters to the Costa Rican side. They are also worried that in the future company use of pesticides and herbicides could adversely affect their own crops, natural environments, or health. The environmentalist must be moved by the destruction of wildlife and natural vegetation at a scale and pace that should not be accessible to humans. The landless peasant sees the abandoned seventy-five percent and dreams of occupation. The aesthete need only contrast the abandoned cacao land or the farms of Mata de Limón and Gandoca with the monotony of company agriculture. The nutritionist might point out that African palm oil is one of the least desirable cooking oils and that company

[3] Edurado Galeano. 1973. *Open Veins of Latin America: Five Centuries of the Pillage of a Continent.* Translated by Cedric Belfrage. New York and London: Monthly Review Press, 313 pp.

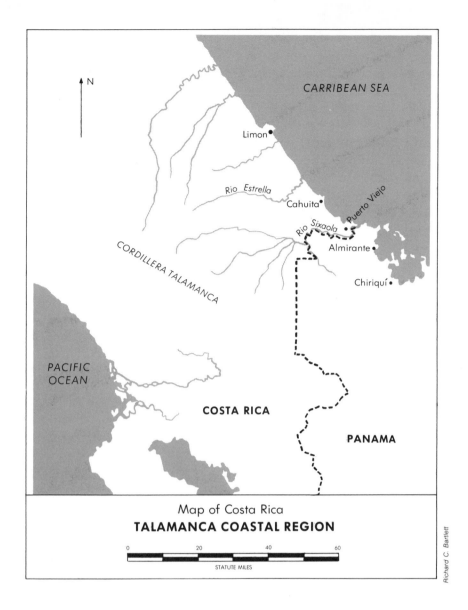

Map of Costa Rica
TALAMANCA COASTAL REGION

Richard C. Bartlett

bananas are destined for overfed *gringos*. Any person with a moral sense would protest the apparent impunity of the fruit companies before Costa Rican law and the waste of edible bananas in a poor country. Any thinking person should deplore the lopsided emphasis on short-term profits that permits the destruction of an ecologiclly benign agriculture (cacao) in favor of a depleting one (monoculture of bananas or African oil palm).

But for me the greatest outrage is the destruction of topsoil. This case need not be presented on aesthetic, legal, or moral grounds, though it could be. It can be argued in purely economic terms. A concept that is scarcely original but needs to be invoked is that topsoil is capital. Granted that as in business one *can* replace lost capital; so one can sometimes restore topsoil. But even a conservative estimate of the amounts of time, energy, and money necessary to accomplish some sort of restoration should dictate that topsoil be guarded even more zealously than financial capital, especially in the tropics, where even on virgin land the topsoil layer is dangerously thin.

The largely uneducated and sometimes illiterate *campesinos* of Gandoca and Mata de Limón would not commit such folly. Are we to suppose, then, that they are possessed of a degree of ecological comprehension unattained by company agronomists? Unlikely. Certainly among the company's staff are some who know something about topsoil; certainly they understand better than the *campesino* the long-range risk of trying to maintain crops with chemical fertilizers. One simply must believe that a decision has been made to sacrifice much of the productivity of the Sixaola valley in the long run to achieve financial profits in the short run.

Such a policy has precedent. The present company lands have previously been abandoned for long periods due to various combinations of disease, exhausted soils, and labor problems that made banana operations uneconomical. That this history is being allowed to repeat itself is evidence of the lack of concern by certain powers that be for real human needs (nutrition, soil conservation, environmental health, and stability), and of the economic bind in which countries like Costa Rica find themselves. Judged on their own terms, the banana and oil palm projects may turn out to be profitable; the same lands returned a profit in the thirties. But where are the cost sheets showing that profit balanced against the virtual lack of production on the same land for periods of twenty-five years or more? Has any economist attempted to allow for the probable eventual demise of the project and to put a value on the topsoil that is being lost? Has anyone ventured to compare the boom-and-bust economy of the early fruit company days to what might have been achieved by a stable agriculture, perhaps cacao based, over the same period of years? What about the social costs of the *peón* system compared to the family farms of which Costa Rica is so proud?

What can be done about this misuse of land? Not much, it seems, in the short run. Perhaps with legal help some sort of injunction could be obtained against clearcutting water courses. Perhaps our ecologist friends will help us monitor chemical pollution in the regions bordering the company lands. But these are popguns against cannons.

The prospect is this: the project will yield a certain amount of benefit to Costa Rica for an indeterminate number of years, which benefit will be at least partly offset by ecological and social problems created by the project. Eventually, Costa Rica will be left with one of her best pieces of agricultural land virtually useless. Granted, it may be possible to "restore" such land to a degree; the cost at that time will almost certainly exceed any short-term economic gain to the country as a whole. And the Costa Rican people will have that much less chance to secure their own nutrition; they will be that much more dependent on outside aid and investment, and the cycle will continue.

Even if we discount the aboriginal inhabitants, the history of small farming in Coastal Talamanca is longer than that of the companies; it has also been more stable. In communities like Cahuita and Puerto Viejo, farms go back seventy years in the same family. During this time, the land has remained productive, if not yielding cash crops then producing locally needed foods.

The dominant agriculture, from Penshurst to Gandoca, is cacao. Although cacao is an export crop, offering no nutritional benefits to the Costa Rican people, it has the considerable advantage of being eminently manageable by the small farmer. Furthermore, cacao farming as conventionally practiced produces an environment very analogous to that of the natural forest. For those unfamiliar with cacao, let me elaborate. Cacao is planted in fairly dense stands, with the trees three to four meters apart. The trees, which can survive up to ninety years, spread to provide nearly total shade,

and produce a continual "mulch" of fair-sized leaves. Cacao is said to do best with about forty percent shade above it, so it is customary when starting a cacao farm to leave other desirable trees in place, or to plant lumber or food trees. The end result is close enough to the natural forest that according to local wisdom the soil in an established cacao farm is equivalent to virgin forest soil.

Cacao has served the inhabitants of Coastal Talamanca well, enabling them to enjoy a standard of living somewhat above that of the *campesinos* in other parts of Costa Rica. More important, it has enabled local farmers to maintain soil fertility and pass their lands on in the family.

But for almost as long as there has been cacao farming in Coastal Talamanca, farmers have worried about the economic and ecological hazards of a monoculture. This concern became more than conjectural in December 1978, when the first cases of the fungus disease moniliasis were reported from Fortuna, in the Estrella valley above Penshurst. In October 1979 the disease was discovered in Mata de Limón; it can now be said to be ubiquitous in the zone. Moniliasis does not kill the tree, but renders the fruit worthless for chocolate production.

The local farmers' cooperative, Coopetalamanca, has provided expert advice and technical assistance, and through a combination of physical and chemical control, losses may be minimized. Nevertheless, a "best case" projection for most farmers is a twenty-five percent drop in production, that with greatly increased intensity of management. The problem is exacerbated by the fact that some farmers, unable or unwilling to maintain the necessary vigilance, have left their cacao in a state of semiabandonment, thus providing foci of infection for neighboring farms. (By far the greatest expanse of neglected cacao is of course the fruit company's.) Some farmers are already talking of selling out. The next few years will determine whether cacao will continue to play a major role in the life of Coastal Talamanca.

Even before the advent of moniliasis, it was clear that part of the key to the future lay in diversification. One of the forms of diversification most frequently discussed has been a more formal approach to interplanting hardwood trees with cacao. NAISA has devoted some energy to this project, but characteristically certain of our neighbors are ahead of us. The most commonly planted hardwood tree is laurel (*Cordia Alliadora*), the most popular local wood for construction, but various farmers are also working with *manú* (*Guarea hoffmaniano*), which yields posts that may last fifty years in the ground; *cedro reál* (*Cedrela fossilis*), second to laurel as a construction wood; *jenizaro* (*Pithecolobium saman*), a high-quality cabinet wood; *melina* (*Gmelina arborea*), a rapid grower imported from Africa, *cedro amargo* (*Cedrela mexicana*), and *cativo* (*Prioria copaifera*), particularly suited to low, wet places.

All ages are involved in hardwood planting, from teenagers to senior members of the community. Matute, at 62, has chosen to plant *manú*, which may take thirty years to produce a harvestable tree. He says he does so for his children, and because the aspect of agriculture he most enjoys is watching the young plants. This is the attitude of husbandry, which, if nourished and encouraged, will preserve and develop the lowland tropics as no corporate or governmental effort can.

Hardwood cultivation, while it may contribute to the economic development and stability of Coastal Talamanca, is ultimately a labor of love. Now that the theoretical perils of monoculture have become real, there is a need for more immediate solutions to economic problems. These solutions can take three forms:

1. Development of alternative cash crops.
2. Development of means of transport and processing for products that are available but presently unmarketable.
3. Greater emphasis on individual and regional self-sufficiency in food production.

Hardwood trees represent the most long-term solution conceivable to the cash-crop problem. Many of our neighbors are working at the opposite extreme, with quick-yielding annual food crops. Exploration of intermediate options is the subject of a proposal submitted to the Dutch government by NAISA and Coopetalamanca. We have taken the position that a "solution" that yields profits in the short run while degrading the land in the long run is no solution at all. The great majority of local farmers concur. For instance, conversion of cacao land to cattle pasture might be economically advantageous in the short run, but as Costa Rican *campesinos* elsewhere have learned from bitter experience, it would create poverty in the long run. We speak of ecology and conservation; our neighbors worry about their children. It comes down to the same thing.

In the more remote communities of Coastal Talamanca such as ours, the possibilities of economic diversification are sharply limited by the difficulty of transport. (We estimate that 500,000 oranges rot on the ground annually in Gandoca and Mata de Limón.) The conventional approach to this problem is to construct farm-to-market roads, a subject that will be taken up later in this article. A less conventional approach taken by the community development association of Mata de Limón and Gandoca with the help of NAISA was to secure a grant from Catholic Relief Services to construct a motor launch to serve the coastal communities. Construction of this launch has suffered a series of setbacks, partly due to the shortage of suitable wood, but it may yet assume an important role. A partial solution to the transport problem could be effected by establishment of processing facilities for perishable products in a central location like Puerto Viejo. The NAISA-Coopetalamanca proposal includes funds to begin this work.

In the short run, with the decline of cacao the most critical task becomes subsistence. This challenge is being met more successfully in Gandoca and Mata de Limón, the newest and poorest of the Coastal Talamanca communities, than in the established cacao towns farther up the coast, where young landowners in particular are more apt to think of selling out than of growing food or seeking alternatives. "They've been too rich too long," laugh the farmers of our community as they plant a few more beans or a field of pineapples, or dig a fish pond.

NAISA's original *raison d'être* in Coastal Talamanca was to aid and participate in ecologically oriented development, hence the cash crop diversification proposal, the aquaculture project, the struggle to construct the launch. These efforts will continue, but we and our neighbors see that no matter how much success we achieve in development projects, the future of the coast depends on what happens in the forested and sparsely populated hill lands. That in turn depends on the development strategies adopted by the national government and the fruit company. And so we have had to acknowledge another facet in the struggle for ecological development and modify our work strategy accordingly.

Much of that portion of the hill land that belongs to *campesinos* is untouched or lightly used. Where it has been cleared, it is a reflection neither of physical need nor pecuniary greed but of Costa Rican law. In Costa Rica, as in most Latin American countries, ownership of land is established by "improvement." (The alternative is an expensive process involving surveyors and lawyers, which *campesinos* simply cannot afford.) "Improvement" implies visible modification of the natural environment. Thus deforestation becomes virtually a prerequisite for security of tenure. In the more remote communities boundary lines are drawn and maintained on a basis of neighborly respect reinforced by community pressure; the need for "improvement" is less. But as frontier regions open up, community control breaks down and the pressure on the *campesino* to deforest land, even though he has no immediate plans to use it, increases. The other great impetus for deforestation is, of course, the cash value of lumber.

Until a couple of years ago, neither factor was of great moment in Coastal Talamanca. But the re-entry of the fruit company has altered the equation. Among the projects undertaken in the wake of the reactivation of agribusiness in the Sixaola valley was the construction of a highway from Bribri to the Panamanian border at Sixaola. With the completion of this highway, Coastal Talamanca is now linked with the Panamanian port of Almirante and with Limón, San José and the rest of Central and North America. In 1970, to travel by land from San José to Sixaola required taking a train to Limón, passing the night there, catching another train to Penshurst, crossing the Rio Estrella in a canoe, catching a bus to Bribri and finally boarding a third, sporadically scheduled and exasperatingly slow train to the border. Today the journey can be accomplished in six hours by car or in a single day by bus.

One of the first tangible results of opening up the new road was the utter deforestation of the hills between Puerto Viejo and Bribri; a beautiful piece of countryside was converted into a series of sterile and unstable slopes.

Naturally, in the wake of the new road those communities not yet served by roads began to petition for them. Manzanillo asked for a road from Puerto Viejo. The first response was to project a "tourist" road along the beach, which would have destroyed many of the coconut plantations of that area and cut the people off from their own beaches. Manzanillo people would prefer a service road, not a tourist road, passing well in back of their houses.

Gandoca and Mata de Limón are actively supporting the construction of just such a road on the site of the footpath connecting these communities with the existing highway. This could be done easily and without disturbing a square meter of natural or agricultural land.

At present the "official" plan, as far as anyone can learn, seems to be to concede Manzanillo's wishes for a road back from the sea, but to extend this road on into Gandoca and Mata de Limón, although the land in between is virtually uninhabited and no one is greatly concerned to be able to travel by highway between Gandoca and Manzanillo. (People I have talked with in San José insist this is "important." No one in the communities that would be affected expresses any desire for it.) The only "reason" for the road is to provide an alternate route between Sixaola and Puerto Viejo. Unless one looks at the forest, that is. Presumably the forest is also a factor in the road now being pushed through from Margarita to Punta Uva, despite the lack of even one house or farm in that stretch.

Are these roads inevitable? And if they are, will they inevitably lead to deforestation on a massive scale? Theoretically, deforestation can be prevented, since the Forest Service of the Costa Rican Ministry of Agriculture has the power to issue or deny permits for timber sales. In the past year they have let it be known that they do not wish to issue permits to cut and sell timber in the Coastal Talamanca region. Despite the lack of enforcement personnel, the *campesinos* have honored this prohibition; of some hundred landholders in our area, I know of two who have participated in illegal cutting.

Yet timber contractors are active in the region, and lumber is being sold, in some cases through the fruit company. The company has built a sawmill near Mata de Limón and a timber contractor

Bill McNaughton

was recently seen in Gandoca asking about possible sawmill sites in places remote from any road and at least three miles from the nearest tree that could legally be cut. It is fairly obvious that some of the large landholders nearby are either illegally obtaining permits or cutting in defiance of the government.

The ecological threat thus posed is immense; we are talking about no less than every last inch of watershed for all the Coastal Talamanca communities from Cahuita to Gandoca. We are also speaking of a considerable wildlife and aesthetic resource. For instance, the swamp behind Manzanillo and Punta Mona is, according to Dr. Joseph Tosi of the Tropical Science Center in San José, an *orey* (*Campnosperma panamensis*) swamp—the only one of its kind in Central America and perhaps the last haunt of tapirs in southeastern Costa Rica. The Rio Gandoca may be the only major spawning ground for tarpon in Costa Rica; not too long ago manatees were seen there.

The citizens of the coastal communities care about watersheds and wildlife. They care that development proceeds in a way that includes them and their children, rather than rendering their lifestyle unsustainable. They ask why the fruit company can clear every last vestige of vegetation from a streambank, when the *campesino* is restrained to leave the trees on either side. It is not that they question the wisdom of the forestry laws, but they do question the wisdom of a legislature that debates banning the importation of chainsaws while companies and contractors destroy expanses of virgin forest with bulldozers. All they ask is that, as the community development association of Mata de Limón and Gandoca put it in a letter to President Carazo, "*La ley debe que ser egual para todos.*" (The law should be the same for everyone.)

Who knows if the *campesinos* will triumph in the essentially political battle against the company, timber contractors, and large landholders. At least, you might say, they can act on their own convictions and preserve that portion of forested land that belongs to them. Not necessarily.

To illustrate the complexity of the problem, let me refer to NAISA's new property in Mata de Limón. Two years ago, we purchased 110 hectares, located directly behind Matute's farm, from a man well known in the community and resident in the neighboring village of San Miguel. Back in the good old days before roads he had made minimal "improvements," including clearing a portion for pasture, planting a few fruit trees, fencing a small piece, and constructing a makeshift house. Much of the land is still in virgin forest. Our plan was and is to leave that forest intact as a wildlife reserve for our own enjoyment and because it constitutes a major watershed area for two creeks. We have the backing of the local community in this goal.

At the time of purchase NAISA had next to no money, so we planted a few more fruit trees and cleaned the *trochas* (paths cut through the forest and planted at intervals with a brilliant red plant known as *sangre de drago*, used to delineate boundaries, to indicate possession while awaiting funding of projects for the cleared portion of the farm.

In August 1979 Elena Matute noticed a group of strangers passing through the Matute farm on their way to our land. When her husband went to investigate, he found eleven men hard at work clearing part of the farm. They declared that the land was abandoned. Matute insisted it was not, that he himself had been planting trees there on behalf of NAISA. The upshot of the encounter was a long series of visits to the police station in Sixaola, phone calls to San José, and so forth. In the process both Jim Lynch and Matute were offered bribes to look the other way while the farm was lumbered. Our fruit trees were destroyed, fences cut, *trochas* cut through the farm, and so forth. We learned that a neighbor (the proverbial bad apple in the Mata de Limón barrel) was offering logistic support to the invaders, who were directed by a timber contractor. (He is now trying to get at the Manzanillo swamp.)

We were forced to hire a full-time caretaker, Rafael Mora Sosa, to live on site, though we can scarcely pay him. (Rafa has turned out to be a gem, the silver lining to the situation.) One day Rafa encountered our bad neighbor, the timber contractor, several people from the sawmill, and an agent for ITCO (more about ITCO in a minute) walking around the property, obviously sizing up the lumber potential. The ITCO man ordered Rafa to stop work. More phone calls, visits to lawyers, and so on and so on. Today, ten months later, the problem remains unresolved.

In a way, the community is fortunate that this happened to us first. Poor as NAISA is, we can at least afford to go to town to complain or talk to a lawyer. And regrettable though it may be, the fact is that we can open doors in San José that might be closed to the *campesino*. We have thus been able to help draw the predicament of our neighbors to the attention of the government and press. But victory is not certain. We are proceeding with titling our land, but the process could take years and cost over $1,000. And even if we get our title, that offers no protection whatsoever to the rest of the community.

Should we and the community ultimately win this round against the timber contractors, we are faced with another threat in which, paradoxically, ITCO is involved. I say paradoxically because

ITCO (Instituto de Tierras y Colonización) was created to be the bureaucratic answer to *campesino* land titling problems. In theory, a *campesino* claiming a previously untitled piece of land can, by "improving" it and making payments to ITCO over a period of years, gain title to the land. In practice things have not worked so smoothly. In April 1979 hundreds of *campesinos* from all over Limón province demonstrated in front of the ITCO office in San José, demanding that something be done about titling their land.

The current problem in Coastal Talamanca stems from a lawsuit in another part of Costa Rica between ITCO and a speculator, in which the speculator won a judgment of something close to 20 million colones ($2.3 million). Now the fact is that ITCO doesn't have that kind of money. So the plan is to pay the speculator in timber rights.

Any clear day you can see a small plane flying over Gandoca surveying the "improved" and "unimproved" land. The latter is to be delivered to the speculator. After he and the timber contractors have gotten their satisfaction the land is to be turned over to others. Some 300 hectares along the Rio Gandoca are slated to become a cattle ranch, with the backing of the industrial livestock division of the Ministry of Agriculture. Most of this land appears on ITCO maps as a "national reserve." No one in Gandoca has ever heard of such a reserve, and several families believe they own this land. Other pieces are to be carved up into lots by ITCO to help solve another of their pressing problems—the constant demand for land by "landless peasants," some of them legitimate refugees from places like Guanacaste or El Salvador, others merely small-scale speculators themselves. From the Cocles Indian Reserve to the Rio Sixaola, *campesinos* are waking up to find new *trochas* dividing up the land they have held and protected for years—over fifty years in some cases.

What is at stake in Coastal Talamanca is the fate of land, soils, families, ecosystems—in a word, the future. Among the participants in the drama now being played out, it is the *campesinos* who behave as if there were a future here. They have never heard the word *ecology*, but in their concern for forests, soils, and waters, and in their daily lives as farmers, they live ecology.

At the other extreme, the fruit company, insofar as it is involved in what happens in the forested hills of Coastal Talamanca, and the timber contractors and speculators are denying the future of the zone. They know the consequences of their plans, but their job is to extract resources for sale and let the natives take care of themselves. If there is a future, for them it is somewhere else.

A friend at the University of Costa Rica, Dr. Alvaro Umaña, is giving a seminar on "ecology and world peace." He will find much of interest in Coastal Talamanca. To say that there is resentment by the *campesinos* who wish to live here in peace would be an understatement; there is already talk of violence. Whether or not violence comes to pass, and no matter its effect, the point is that the old colonial scenario is being re-enacted. By "colonial" I refer to extractive exploitation of resources for the benefit primarily of outsiders, without reference to nations or nationalities. If colonialism of resources is a form of aggression, then its opposite, which is ecological husbandry, is the pursuit of peace. In the light of recent events in the history of Central America, all concerned would do well to ponder this.

By the time this article appears in print, many critical events will have passed in Coastal Talamanca. The purpose of publication is not to rally support for our cause, but to point out something that has come to pass in Coastal Talamanca and will, if it has not already, in other Latin American rural zones. For lack of a better phrase, I will use the jargonesque term "consciousness raising." In my short time here, I have seen the ecological consciousness of the *campesino* rise greatly. The *campesino* has always lived close to nature, but he has suffered, along with the rest of us, from the notion that the only limitations on the degree to which nature can be manipulated are the limitations on our own power. But in the last few years, the *campesinos* have seen rainfall patterns altered by deforestation. They have seen soils depleted and ecosystems upset by chemical agriculture and cattle ranching. They have seen the frontier disappear before their eyes. They have watched creatures disappear that they took for granted and found they missed them. They have lived what you and I have gleaned from piles of data. In spite of the fact that *campesinos* have wielded little power compared to the affluent, mobile machine-wielding colonist, or perhaps because of it, they have seen their limitations sooner. The next step is to connect these observations with the political world; this is being done. So, even should we lose the battle of Coastal Talamanca, something will be gained for the future.

Energy

There are times when an editor's lot is not an easy one. I had developed something of an idée fixé for an article on energy for this issue. Wouldn't it be a good idea, I thought, to have someone write an assessment of the state of the art as of the early eighties. The author would discuss such things as the present or near-future applicability of wind generators and photovoltaics as well as small-scale hydropower and biofuels. It would help people begin to mull over various forms of renewable energy deciding which could be best adapted for their own use in the next few years.

Luckily, I have access to quite a few experts. I approached Ty Cashman, Joe Seale, J. Baldwin, and Gary Hirshberg, but for a variety of reasons none of them felt comfortable about complying with my request. I received instead Ty's article, which appears in the New Alchemy section that, based on his own experience, describes the kind of mind set that proceeds attitudinal and social change. From Joe came a profile, or geographic overview, of the country's renewable energy potential—somewhat closer, but still not what I had had in mind. J. presented me with "Autologic," which is included in this section and is about good and bad thinking about technology. Gary turned the assignment over to Greg Watson and Michael Greene, who described the forming of a local energy cooperative.

Once my editorial huff at having my directive sidestepped or ignored had subsided, it began to dawn on me that their response was suitable. The energy question is thorny and complex. (No single shot answers, remember, editor?) It is political and attitudinal and one that will force us to rethink what we really need and want and to do so clearly this time. Mollified, I find myself grateful to my recalcitrant writers. As Amory Lovins concludes his article in the Explorations section, "Using energy to worthy ends for right livelihood is profoundly difficult, and not a technical issue at all."

N.J.T.

Greasing the Windmill

It took Dad and me from afternoon on one day
Until sundown the next
to grease the windmill.

The first afternoon we went to town
for a six-pack of beer.
put the beers into a gunny sack
and hung the sack in the well on clothesline.
The mill above the well looked shorter than forty feet.

The next morning after milking and breakfast
we walked into the pasture.
Dad had an empty bucket to drain the old oil into
and I new oil in a new tin can.

Dad sighed
and started up the ladder,
each foot on a step for five steps,
then both feet on one step for three steps,
and then stood on the eighth step
complaining of dizziness.
He came back down.

It was my turn.
I made it twelve steps up,
one foot on a step but breathing hard,
when Dad called up that I had the new oil.
I had to go back for the empty bucket.

It was harder my second time
and slower with the bucket. The whole mill
shivered in sympathy. I managed only to peek
onto the platform, to lift the empty bucket above
my head with my free hand, and tip the bucket
onto the platform. Then I too was dizzy.
I came down, the old oil
still undrained.

Getting the better of ourselves
proved time-consuming. By now it was
coffee time. In the kitchen we admitted
to Mother that all we had achieved
was an empty bucket
on the platform.

Mother reminded us that my brother Klaas,
now, alas, in service,
used to grease the mill on his way to catch
the school bus,
starting out a half-hour early. And he never
even had a drop
of grease on him at school that day.

Mother reminded us that Gerrit Henry,
Klaas's friend around the corner,
not in service and available,
went up his dad's windmill
with the full can and
the empty can,
drained the old
oil, spread-eagled
himself flat against
the wheel, and had his dad
put the mill in gear. Afterwards
he said it had been better than a
ferris wheel. Running the mill
had got the last drop of oil
out, and he had added new oil
before coming down, all in one trip.
Why couldn't we be like that?
She might as well have said,
"Napoleon:
now there's a hero for you!"

In the pasture after coffee
Dad said, "We'll never make it
without the beer." He had hoped
he could bring the sixpack back to
Doc's Cafe, untouched. The trickle
and then the drip from the gunny sack,
the haul of the cold clothesline, and then
the beer itself, all would have restored us
if we had been thirsty and tired. We were
afraid, not thirsty and tired, and the
beer was our bitter anesthetic.
We needed a bottle apiece
for a full dose.

It was guilt
and not the beer
that got Dad to the top.
He had to prove to himself
that the beer had been necessary.
How explain the beer to God come Judgment
Day if he couldn't show that the beer had helped?
I cheered when he made it: Oranje boven! And I
    cheered
again when he opened the petcock and drained the old
    oil out
into the bucket I had delivered earlier at such pain.
    But his eyes
were bright as brimstone looking down, the guilt still
    there.
How could he ever know for sure he hadn't faked the
    fear
to justify the beer? He trembled all the way down,
step by step, rung by rung, the full bucket
tilting ominously as he changed it from
one hand to the other. The wind
whipped spatters over his bib-
overall and cast-off Sunday
tie. I remembered Klaas
greasing the mill,
clean.

After dinner
the windmill had doubled in size
in the full glow of an Iowa afternoon.
Dad and I began with a beer apiece on the ground.
Who knows? If I failed again, he would need to be
    ready.
Actually, I surprised us both. I scrambled up, poured
    the oil in,
closed the petcock, and threw the empty tin down. It
    bounced higher than Dad's
head! What a height, to make a can bounce higher
    than Dad's head.
Promptly I was paralyzed.

"You done real good," Dad called, "come down."
"Wait till I get a notion," I said, and didn't budge.
"I'll go home for tea without you."
I could no nothing.
"You got a piece of pie coming."
I could do nothing.
"There still are two beers in the well."
I still could do nothing.
"Must we get Gerrit Henry to fetch you down?"
Mention of Gerrit Henry
made me go prone on the platform,
clutch the edge, hunt for the spokes
and undertake my quavering descent.

Then it was tea-time.
Mother poured us tea
but gave us no hero's welcome.

After tea, we did chores,
after chores, we milked,
after milking, we ate supper,
and after supper, Dad remembered the beers.
You couldn't return two beers out of a six-pack to Doc's
    Cafe.

That beer—
    with Dad in twilight
    at the mill
    all fear gone,
    well, as gone as fear ever gets—
that beer is the only beer I have ever enjoyed.

But Mother's diary is too spare for June 11, 1944:
"Dad and Sietze greased the mill today."
If ever I did a day's work, I did it that day.

                Sietze Buning   June 11, 1944

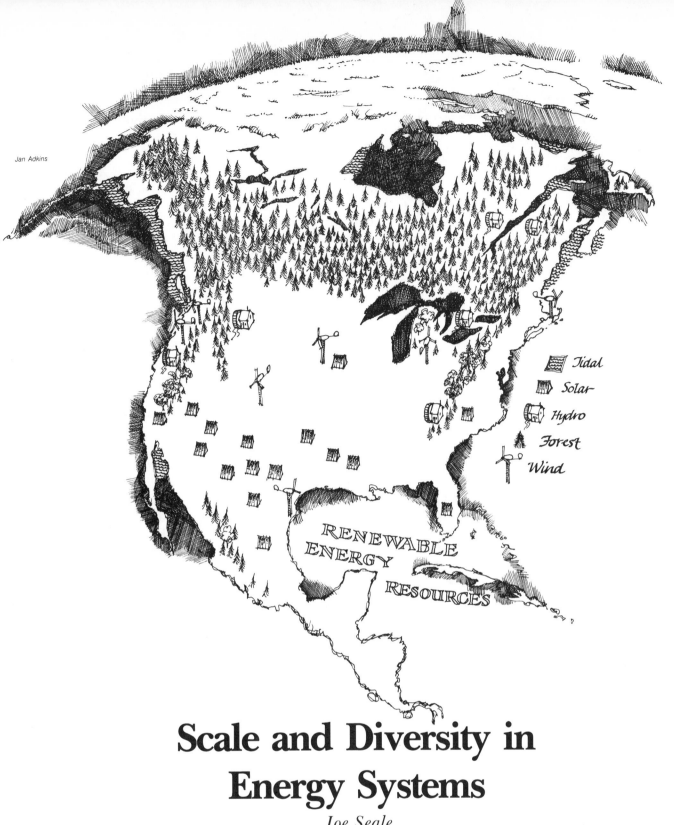

Jan Adkins

Tidal
Solar
Hydro
Forest
Wind

RENEWABLE ENERGY RESOURCES

Scale and Diversity in Energy Systems

Joe Seale

It is possible for the energy needs of this country to be supplied by applied solar technologies, if energy sources are matched to specifics of location and end use. The form of solar-derived energy must vary from place to place. Half of the United States lacks decent windpower sites. Both the wind and biofuel potentials of most of Nevada, Utah, Arizona, and New Mexico are poor. The Southeast and southern California have few good windpower sites. Solar energy prospects are poor for the Pa-

cific Northwest, especially near the Pacific coast, as well as for the eastern Great Lakes region extending into Pennsylvania and New York. But few regions lack the capacity for some form of solar-derived energy. The windpower-deficient Southeast and Southwest (in addition to the windy South Central region) have excellent solar potential. Biofuel prospects for the Southeast are favorable. The highest windpower-potential regions in the United States are the darkest corner of the Pacific Northwest, the cloudy eastern Great Lakes region, and the much sunnier coasts of southern New England. The less windy and not-so-sunny stretches of northern New England have forests that could, with good ecosystem management, provide indefinitely renewable biofuel energy for that region. The many hundreds of abandoned mill dams in New England could be outfitted to generate a total of many megawatts of hydropower. The Grand Coulee Dam, now rated at 6,000 megawatts and expandable to 10,000 megawatts within the capabilities of the watershed, could keep Washington state in the ranks of energy exporters.

Hydropower scale is limited by the flow and head available at a site. Because the cost of additional turbine-generators is small once the dam is there, the economics of rising energy costs will cause hydropower sites to be developed to their maximum potential. The scale and locations of good hydropower sites will play a large role in determining village scale and economic activity. The economics that caused mill towns to be built may well return with the depletion of nonrenewable energy resources.

Forest biofuel production per square mile is ultimately limited by the forest's capacity to replace biomass. The energy costs of wood shipment keep the practical radii from forest to generating plant down to a few tens of miles. An area with a 20 mile radius cannot renewably support a net electric power yield greater than approximately 100 megawatts. The income from that scale of operation would support no more than 1,000–2,000 workers engaged in plant upkeep, harvesting, forest management, business, and accounting, etc. Adding worker families and service industry workers and families gives a rough order of magnitude of the size of the community that might derive support from forest energy export: 10,000–20,000 at most. Space heating for the community ideally would come from waste heat. If some export took the form of manufactured goods that used the energy from the power plant and perhaps some of its heat (in a co-generation process), then the potential size of the community supported by forest energy would increase considerably. These figures indicate upper limits, not optimum size. They suggest a significant potential dispersion of population supported by biomass forest income.

In level windy regions, windpower potential can be fairly good at sufficient tower altitude, regardless of location. But the most economically attractive windpower sites will be determined by topographic features: ridges, coastlines, mountain gaps, and accessible mountain tops. These sites will generally not support large arrays of wind turbines, but more frequently a single row of turbines limited to the length of the ridge or the width of the wind gap. It turns out that the maximum power potential for such sites depends on the characteristic length or width of the topographic feature and on the vertical distance swept by rotors over that horizontal span. The implication is that large wind turbines extract more power at prime sites than small turbines when site saturation is achieved. There will be therefore pressure to install the largest practical wind turbines. The most economical scale for wind turbines is subject to debate, but it seems that a rated capacity of 1–3 megawatts is an upper bound beyond which complexity and sheer weight outweigh any further advantages of increased scale. Lest this scale cause some readers to flinch, it is worth recalling that the first megawatt-scale machine to operate (excepting the 1945 Smith-Putnam turbine on Grandpa's Knob, Vermont) was the 2 megawatt turbine that was designed, constructed, and financed almost entirely by students and faculty members of the Danish Technical High School/Junior College at Tvind in the mid seventies.

The examples so far have dealt with maximum scale for solar technologies and have assumed significant economic activity oriented around the energy supply. A more usual energy system for a village would serve the ordinary demands of residences, commercial establishments, and perhaps light industry, but not energy-intensive industries such as metal forging or glass production (from recycled materials or otherwise). The largest quantitative energy demands would be low-temperature thermal end-uses: space and hot water heating, refrigeration and freezing, and possibly air conditioning. Where solar potential was good, heat demands would best be met on a house-by-house basis using passive solar architecture, and trees should be the first defense against heat. If nights are cool, as at high altitudes and in the desert, passive storage of night coolness should be a function of housing design. But two factors may favor neighborhood (or larger) scale thermal systems. The first is existing housing that is difficult to retrofit. The other is regions of poor solar potential or air cooling needs. In these situations, large-scale insulated water tanks could store summer heat and winter cold on a seasonal basis. Hot water could be stored using year-round active solar collection or wind-driven heat pumps. Cold water could be stored using wintertime convective heat exchange to ambient or wind-driven mechanical refrigeration, perhaps with the same device whose other end is generating stored hot water. The advantage of the relatively large scale for seasonal thermal storage is declining cost per unit capacity and an improved surface-to-volume ratio that makes tank insulation relatively more efficient. Diseconomies of scale would arise in the distribution system, though the viable size range for seasonal thermal storage systems could be from 10 families up to a town.

Baseload electricity (electricity that is there when you want it) and energy-storing fuels will become increasingly costly, especially in places where hydropower and biofuels are not local resources. There will be ample incentive to conserve and convert organic wastes into methane or alcohol. Hydrogen from surplus electricity that cannot be stored will find a role in high-quality heat uses such as cooking; it will perhaps even be used in mantle gas lights. Refrigerators that can store ice during electricity surplus periods will find a market in a solar energy economy. But a few energy uses will continue to demand baseload electricity.

To meet baseload demands from local solar (photovoltaic) and wind energies will be difficult. The prospects for storage batteries and fuel cells are not very encouraging. The manufacturing energy costs of storage batteries averaged over their relatively short lifetimes are a discouragingly large fraction of the energy they handle. This makes them dubious prospects for a sustainable solar energy economy. Pumped-water energy storage for hydroelectric recovery is expensive and inefficient, and requires high places to locate storage ponds. Still, pumped-water storage has better prospects than batteries. Flywheel energy storage will mature to provide another alternative, but again a fairly expensive one.

The most likely prospects for baseload electricity in a solar economy are for decentralization of generation combined with interconnection through the existing electric distribution grid. Hydropower plants with sufficient stored-water volume could be fitted with more turbine-generators than average river flow would support and then used intermittently as premium backup energy stations. This would be an excellent complement to wind and solar electricity since no extra pumping equipment or energy conversion by pumping would be required. The energy of the river would simply be stored for short periods. Mathematical studies of windpower statistics are showing that as wind plants are interconnected over large regions, power fluctuations average out and the power source requires much less storage for "firm" power. The role of end-use thermal storage has been emphasized; this leaves a greatly reduced demand for hydropower, and possibly biofuel, backup. But the overall problem of energy supply seems economically soluble only by interconnection of villages, towns, and regions to take advantage of the diversity of their energy technologies. If the utility grid investment were yet to be made, there might be less incentive to create such a network from scratch. But there it is, bigger than we should ever need if we use energy as frugally as we must in order to get along with renewable resources. Only minor distribution branches need be added. Such an interconnected system would not be as vulnerable to disruption as our current system with centralized generation. With predictable hardships, the parts of such a dispersed system could survive without their interconnections.

The Forming of the Cape and Islands Self-Reliance Cooperative

Greg Watson and Michael Greene

Humanity is about to discover
That whatever it needs to do
And knows how to do
It can always afford to do
And that in fact is only
And all it can afford to do
      R. Buckminster Fuller

In the eleven years since the birth of New Alchemy, complex processes of societal evolution have triggered some profound shifts in the public consciousness of humanity's relationship with the natural world. Large numbers of individuals have come to realize the importance of confronting issues surrounding our personal, community, and regional patterns of food and energy production and consumption. This growing maturation of environmental awareness is honing some potential (perhaps even inevitable) new directions for New Alchemy as we enter the eighties.

For the past decade the New Alchemists have focused on designing and testing small-scale, ecologically sound food and energy-producing systems that are not dependent on fossil fuels. Early on we were primarily devoted to ascertaining the feasibility of this goal and, in turn, convincing a rather skeptical public of its practicability. Back then there was but a modicum of public interest in our work. Few people were concerned about society's ninety-five percent reliance on our "cap-ital" energy sources. Fewer still believed that an eclectic collection of scientists, artists, and philosophers growing vegetables and raising fish in geodesic domes on Cape Cod were doing much that was even remotely relevant to their lives. Consequently, as far as most people were concerned, there was ample reason to question both the need for and the practicality of our research.

As time passed many of the dangers inherent in energy-intensive strategies that had been adopted to meet our food and energy needs were becoming all too clear. Indeed, the latter part of the seventies seemed a harbinger of doom, with marathon gas lines, water shortages, acid rain, hazardous wastes, Love Canal, and Three Mile Island—to name just a frightening few. As the seventies drew to a close we found that we didn't have to work as hard to convince people that we had little choice but to develop and implement life-support systems that recognized not only the needs of the human community but those of *Gaia*, or the natural world, as well. A most welcome turn of events.

Change, of course, brings about more change. Mutual causality plays as important a role in social process as it does in biological, ecological, and physical interaction. It was only expected that the change in public attitude to meeting energy and food needs that New Alchemy had been instrumental in creating should in turn create a new niche for us in the social fabric.

Society's "back-door" discovery of the divine law of interrelatedness (bury enough chemical wastes in the earth, and sure enough, they'll come back to haunt you) which is the cornerstone of ecology, has inspired a growing interest in what is generally called appropriate technology. The demand for solar collectors, solar hot water systems, windmills, organically grown foods, and so forth, has increased dramatically within recent years, as has the demand for technical assistance and guidance in implementing these systems.

This is the niche that our environmental conscioiusness-raising has helped to create: there is a need for community appropriate technologists or in Byron Kunard's words, community-based innovation. To be sure, this is a role quite different from our former one as researchers/educators. It is nonetheless one that many of New Alchemy's supporters are now asking for and expecting us to assist in filling. The time has come, they seem to be saying, for us to put our reputation (and designs) on the line.

New Alchemy's education and outreach programs have accepted this challenge by committing more of the institute's resources to addressing the food and energy needs of the Cape Cod community. During the winter of 1979, along with three other local service agencies we were contacted by the Community Action Committee (CAC) of Cape Cod and asked to take part in planning and implementing a regional food and energy assistance agency for Cape Cod—the Cape and Islands Self-Reliance Cooperative.

The Community Action Committee is the Cape's antipoverty agency. Since its formation in 1965, it has been committed to the Cape's low-income residents. It has been successful in bringing about major changes in housing and health care for the Cape's poor. This work made CAC aware of the burden of rising fuel and food costs on the elderly, unemployed, and underemployed.

Cape Cod and the islands of Martha's Vineyard and Nantucket are at the top of the Massachusetts charts in both fuel and food costs. In many cases, families with annual incomes of less than $7,700 spend up to a quarter of that for heating. Thousands of Cape residents are forced to apply for fuel assistance. Having spent twenty-five percent of their income for fuel, Cape residents face the prospect of going to supermarkets where food prices are at least six percent above the national average.

While government programs such as fuel assistance and food stamps do help many families to meet fuel and food costs, they do next to nothing to lessen the recipients' dependence on fossil fuels, agribusiness, or future assistance. In contrast, the Self-Reliance Cooperative will offer individuals and families opportunities to achieve some measure of self-sufficiency in food and energy, and along with it, some promise of hope and increased dignity.

The goal of the Cape and Islands Self-Reliance Cooperative is to combine the technological expertise and the innovations of New Alchemy, the community organizing experience of the Community Action Committee of Cape Cod, the housing and energy financial counseling of the Housing Assistance Corporation (HAC), the energy auditing and weatherization skills of the Energy Resource Group (ERG) of Martha's Vineyard, and the fishing, farming, and aquaculture expertise of the Wampanog Tribal Councils of Mashpee and Gay Head. This collective organization will provide residents of the Cape and Islands with a vehicle through which they can achieve a measure of food and energy self-reliance and reduce overall regional dependence on fossil fuels. There is a kind of magic involved here called synergy—the increased capability resulting from combining and coordinating the actions of formerly separate individuals and groups with similar goals.

For many of us the Self-Reliance Cooperative offers a unique chance to be at once practical and idealistic. Philosophical ideas such as mutual aid, cooperation, synergy, self-reliance, and nonviolent social change that were in danger of being reduced to rhetoric or clichés have taken concrete meaning in the context of the co-op.

Conceptually the co-op is intended to foster cooperation on at least two levels: between organizations and between individuals and small groups. On an organizational level, each of the agencies brings a unique set of skills. Together they propose to provide a number of direct services to members, who will pay dues on a sliding scale depending on income. These services include:

1. Home energy and agricultural audits. This means a complete assessment of each member's house or apartment in terms of energy and water conservation, alternative energy potential, and food growing capabilities.

2. Financial counseling on federal, state, and local loan or grant programs available for weatherization and alternative energy efforts.

3. Discount and wholesale purchasing privileges for conservation, alternative energy, and food production materials and equipment, including insulation, tools, seeds, solar glazings, and so forth.

4. Access to services of home improvement and weatherization contractors at reduced rates.

5. A complete workshop/education program, including on-site courses in the member's house, special forums on subjects such as food production, pest control, energy conservation, and so forth.

The first and perhaps the most important part of the program is the home energy and food audit. Each member will be interviewed by a trained staff person to determine living pattern and financial status, evaluate space heating and domestic hot water, inspect and analyze the residence from basement to attic, and appraise general site conditions and potential for alternative energy production and intensive small-scale agriculture.

The audit will give detailed information on present energy use and the economics of energy and food-related home improvements. It will estimate the cost, first-year savings, payback, and rate of return for each applicable energy conservation, renewable resource, or food-production step. Each suggested strategy will be presented within the context of available financing.

The audit will provide the basis for a member's personal plan to improve the operating efficiency of his or her home and to begin to develop a home energy and food-production system.

The plan will identify a range of possibilities based upon cost-effectiveness and potential payback. Products and materials including solar glazings, wood stoves and stove pipe, solar water heaters, seeds, garden tools, compost starters, and so forth, will be available through the co-op at reduced prices. The co-op will offer training and instruction to members interested in their own home food and energy projects or will arrange for construction at preferential rates by contractors experienced in appropriate technologies.

The co-op expects to be of service to about two thousand Cape and Islands residents. Membership will be open, although special emphasis will be placed on recruiting low-income families. The membership will be encouraged to interact and cooperate in part through community networks that the co-op will assist in facilitating. Establishing a community network is critical to the success of the co-op, as we realize that many of the skills and resources needed to effect a shift to self-reliance exist already in our neighborhoods and communities.

Whereas the community network might appear the least tangible of the co-op's goals, it is critical in that it speaks to and demonstrates those values that must complement our technologies whether we are aware of it or not.

Initially, New Alchemy's role will be to train future co-op staff in specific technical areas. We are beginning an apprenticeship program for co-op trainees in which they will: (1) gain skills and knowledge in intensive agriculture, aquaculture, tree crops, solar, wind, and energy conservation by working with us for a full year; and (2) simultaneously assist local residents who require help in their particular interest areas. Thus, we shall be developing a professional staff who possess useful skills and are available to apply their knowledge to residential situations. New Alchemy will be conducting the initial food and fuel audits offering a comprehensive yearlong program of seminars.

We are very excited about the co-op. In our minds it is a logical outgrowth of nearly eleven years of work and the beginning of a valued and hoped for partnership. The new cooperative will enable us to continue our research efforts while providing technical assistance to those who need it now.

Ron Zweig

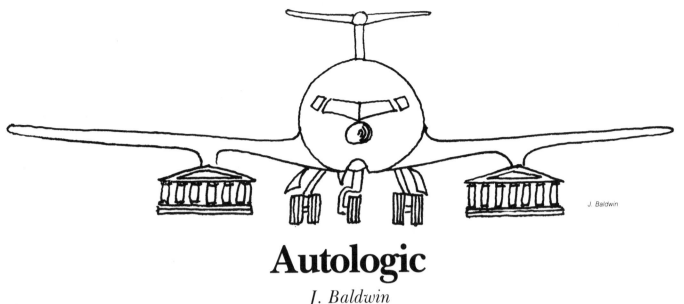

J. Baldwin

Autologic

J. Baldwin

Here comes the Parthenon! It's whizzing down the road on the nose of what is supposed to be the finest car built, a Rolls Royce. The finest automobile made today shoves a chrome-plated model of a Greek temple through the air and pays about ten miles per gallon to do so. "Built like a Rolls," we say. Countless manufactured items are compared to the Rolls. This hurtling place of worship is but one minor example of what I call *autologic*, a way of thinking that makes sense only if many realities are ignored and only if you are selling cars. The Greek facade calls up a "classic" image. Lesser cars call up an expensive image by resembling the Rolls or other expensive cars. Thus we see most cars sporting ludicrously unaerodynamic, gas-eating styling that now has implications as a threat to national security. Yet the shape of cars is not questioned in popular media, and government regulations ignore styling as well as other essentials of the automobile.

The way that cars are designed and integrated into our society seems to be the result of some irrefutable natural law. Cars are so convenient. They work. There's an irresistible magic in being able to go where you want when you want. It's all so easy that there doesn't seem to be any reason to question the phenomenon. Question-raisers are also greeted with less than enthusiasm politically. There's good reason for that too; about half of American paychecks come from some sort of involvement with the automobile. The economy of our nation rests largely on the auto and its "accessories" such as roads, bridges, parking lots, signs, fuel, repair, shelter, administration, the auto-caused damage industry (hospitals, body shops, and insurance), parking meters, meter maids and their scooters, unions, retirement plans, scooter

mechanics (and their unions, etc.) . . . if you carry things all the way back to the raw materials you can see how pervasive the car has become to our nation's smooth operation. Even car-haters have become so entangled in autologic that rational criticism becomes difficult and academic analysis subject to severe distortions arising mostly from unsystematic examination of one small facet of a very complex matter.

Distortions of reality should not be too surprising considering the character of the industry involved. Generally speaking, the auto industry isn't too much different from others; the idea is to make a profit. But to make that profit, Detroit has to sell cars in large numbers. In a good year three cars are made for each child born. Because cars have so many parts, and the parts come from so many sources, about a three-year lead time is necessary to get a new model into the showroom. A completely new model may require an entirely new factory. A recent front-wheel-drive compact was developed at a cost well over a billion dollars. Obviously, more profits can be made if the new model is not, in fact, new, but only seems that way.

Another ploy is to make the same car but with different nameplates at various levels of prestige. A cheap car gussied up to sell at a higher price brings in more profit. Prestige is mostly due to advertised image anyway. Remember the uproar when Olds owners discovered their cars had Chevy engines? That's nothing new! Anyway, to make a model seem new or more expensive, the selling points cannot be the parts that are not new, the expensive parts. Consequently, you see very little in advertising that refers to engines, axles, brakes, steering, and roadholding. What you do see is "features." These tend to be fluff such as speeding temples, dashboard change bins, hidden headlights, and black vinyl roofs that make it necessary to run the air conditioning on mild days. Features tend to be added on rather than part of a concept. (Mechanical concept, that is . . . they certainly are part of marketing concepts.)

To generate the needed mass market, the features are heavily advertised as if they were important. The vital parts are not mentioned and consequently the public is never usefully educated. The public doesn't know enough to demand better brakes, for instance. Thus there is no incentive to develop good brakes, and you can still buy cars that cannot be stopped fast in a straight line. People assume that such things as brakes are automatically taken care of by the engineers, much in the same way one expects a Winchester to refrain from exploding in one's face. Not so in the auto industry. Brakes could be extolled as a sales feature, of course, but market surveys have shown that such talk makes people think about safety and accidents, and that does not lead to a buying mood. In this way, essential issues are masked. About fifty thousand people are killed every year in cars in the U.S.A. and not much is done about it despite studies showing that each death costs society nearly two hundred thousand dollars in lost wages and work. (Grief isn't measured.) In the eyes of many designers, "safety features" as they are known, are optional or hated add-ons mandated by excessive government regulation.

Other issues are masked too. The whole pollution controversy is one, and I'll not belabor it here except to say that there is more than corporate malice involved in the industry's attempt to discourage improvement except under duress. Not only does the pollution issue require an admission of corporate social responsibility, it requires expensive tooling for parts that can't be featured on the sales floor.

There's a mask on the actual costs of running a car too. Hertz has come up with figures so high they are hard to believe—up to forty cents per mile. But even that price doesn't cover the less-obvious costs such as repairing the hole in your driveway, and doesn't admit social costs such as the physical damage and work-hours lost from accidents. "Life-cycle costs," the long-range total costs of owning a machine, are not available. I recently retired my trusty Citroen at three hundred thousand miles without an overhaul. At an extraordinarily low nine cents per mile overall, it still comes to about thirty thousand dollars! It's not exactly a conspiracy, but it is hard to come up with this sort of information. User costs could be cut by better fuel economy and easier repairability, but at the expense of the formidable oil industry and

the repair trade. Comparative costs of repair could be compiled from flat-rate repair rate books and parts price sheets, but even Consumer's Union doesn't attempt such a complex task. It'd be futile anyway; new cars are less and less repairable by owners with common tools.

Giving little thought to making cars easy to fix is typical of an industry that gives little thought to human beings except in their role as buyers. Most cars have poorly shaped seats designed to look good in the showroom. Those seats allegedly fit ninety-nine percent of the customers. That sounds fine until you figure that with an annual production of six million cars there are tens of thousands of cars with uncomfortable drivers. Sharp trunk-lid corners menace unsuspecting heads. Irritating reflections of the radio speaker mar the view through an often optically distorted windshield. More seriously, many cars become uncontrollable when they encounter a soft shoulder. The remedy for this has been known for decades, and being a matter of geometry, it doesn't cost anything. Yet millions of cars are made every year with this potential for disaster built in.

How can this happen?

One reason is that cars are designed by teams that may not have similar goals. The people designing steering systems don't talk to safety engineers. The result is steering mechanisms that can spear the driver in a crash. The autological answer to this problem has been to add on an expensive complex "feature"—the collapsing steering column—only after being forced to by legislation. By contrast, many European cars do not need a collapsing column because the steering engineers had safety in mind from the beginning and designed systems that didn't have parts that threatened the driver in the first place.

Even when Detroit designers are trying to do their best, years of autologic paralyzes clear thought. Consider the Jeep, a supposed all-terrain vehicle. In concept a Jeep is but a small conventional pickup with the front axle driven too. It clears the ground by the same distance as a Buick, although it appears to be up there out of harm's way. It sinks in mud and doesn't float in water. The belly is a tangled mess of parts that catch on things that mire the vehicle. Vital parts are exposed to damage from stones, and critical components are difficult to repair in the field. The Jeep's length is less than half loadspace, and it is inordinately heavy at no gain in strength. It is easily overturned. Not a very good show! It doesn't last long either. Similar ineptitude may be found in the design of tacked-on smog equipment and sadly (some say criminally) ineffective safety hardware.

The lifespan of a vehicle is another autological

fact of life that we have come to accept without much question. We've been trained to agree that a car lasts around one hundred thousand miles. This is not a law of nature, but is carefully engineered. The subject of planned obsolescence here rears its ugly head. The hundred-thousand-mile lifespan is arbitrary, and the manner in which the car deteriorates is purposefully chosen. On most cars such things as seats, door latches, and window mechanisms are designed to live just until the payments are finished. The engine and transmission are better because if they failed early, you'd never buy another of that brand. But a tacky interior is shameful when transporting friends, and is a considerable incentive to buy a new car. Many new cars have styling details made from plastic that is eaten by sunlight, resulting in a tacky exterior as well. Time for a new one! In this day of growing concern for resource depletion, such an attitude is no longer appropriate, but in an industry with a captive market (our country has been built in a way that requires a car in most circumstances) changing that attitude may mean even more legislation or other coercive action. A voluntary change seems unlikely.

Unfortunately, the problem goes far beyond the auto industry. It is my opinion as a designer that autologic has invaded all but a few enterprises, and is actually taught, by implication, in our universities. In times of cheap energy, the only recognized standard of performance is market performance. Catering to the demands of the consumer is what I call a political matter—that is, the constraints are largely a question of psychology. Market psychology is not "natural," as the buying public is manipulated by advertising aimed at maintaining the necessary mass demand for the product that must be mass produced in order to remain affordable to Mr. and Mrs. Front Porch. In effect, the public is told what it desires—mostly, as has already been pointed out, the unimportant sales features. Until recently such desires were easily satisfied. But when energy efficiency is a factor, there are different masters to satisfy: physical laws and the realities of resource supply. A primary concern with physical law does make a difference in the quality of design. Compare the auto and the airplane. As inventions they are about the same age, but look at the difference in the state of their development. The most modern Ford is conceptually only a Model T with a fatter body and detail improvements, while the latest Boeing is a far cry from the Wright brothers' Flyer. Airplanes must first and foremost fly reliably. If one fails, you can't get out and walk. Automobiles permit all manner of engineering carelessness as long as they go, stop, and within acceptable limits refrain from overturn-

ing—those limits being incestuously provided by the industry itself. However, the limits of resource management, the accumulative effects of pollution, and the political effects of inefficiency are not amenable to self-regulation. The auto makers and users are in trouble at last. They are not the only ones.

J. Baldwin

Regrettably some of the problem industries are ones close to our hearts—the soft technologies. Wind machines are an example. They must live outdoors without much maintenance under the worst possible conditions. Ice, lightning, hail, salt air, hurricanes, and inattention must all be accommodated in the design. Easy maintenance (or none) is essential to long life, and long life is not an arbitrary figure in this case. For if the machine doesn't last long enough to at least pay for itself, it isn't worth buying in the first place. And, more important, if the machine doesn't last long enough to make or save more energy than was used to make it, then it is in effect one more fossil fuel device. Yet I see all too many machines on the market with aluminum parts fastened with steel rivets, a practice sure to cause early failure from galvanic corrosion. I see machines that must be taken down from the pole for the most simple service. I talk to the president of a (still-respected) wind turbine company and he tells me that their machines must be completely dismantled every two years to replace the many swivel joints that are totally unprotected from weather and are undersized to begin with. I note with alarm the popular Windcharger with its governor mechanism built without bushings, so that the bolts soon wear egg-shaped holes and the speed regulation deteriorates to disaster. Bushings would have added at most twenty-five dollars to the retail cost of that six-hundred-dollar product.

In fairness, there are some well-designed wind turbines, but not many, and there is a deplorable tendency to design machines that have high output in high winds, a condition that is uncommon. The big numbers look well in a brochure though, especially to a public used to reading biggest-is-best in auto advertising. There is also very little research visible (and even fewer results) concerning the design of efficient devices that use windpower, despite the obvious benefits to be gained by systemic design. There are a lot of disillusioned wind machine purchasers out there if my mailbag is any indication. Apparently many wind machine manufacturers are using the public as a test program, another Detroit tactic. This practice is giving a fledgling industry a bad name that it can ill afford, for its market is not captive.

The same can be said for solar energy devices and architectural schemes. A shocking number of solar collectors are made in a way that is ignorantly and sometimes deliberately intended to require expensive repair or replacement before the device has paid for itself either in money or energy. Even reputable firms are shy about warranties extending into the payback period. And just as there has been little work done to reduce the need for electricity and consequently the need for electricity-making equipment, there has not been much done to reduce the need for solar collectors and the like. People seem to desire "things." A passive home that doesn't sport visible hardware on the roof somehow is not as appealing to an uneducated buyer. The principal passive work has thus been done by nonindustrial builders and experimenters whose "product" is an idea, rather than something that comes in a box. There has been some resistance to passive houses in many subtle forms, even overt disparagement from industry and from government as well, as a result of lobbying. I have attended government-sponsored "solar workshops" in which passive designs were derided openly as impractical when there were at least fifty successful passive houses operating within a half-hour drive of the lecture hall.

Though not the only guilty group, the auto industry has tended to be at the forefront of such shenanigans, and its enormous advertising budget spreads its attitude. (Witness the recent reduction in federal gas mileage standards in the same week as a supply-threatening Middle East war!) It's easy to see autologic in household appliances, but the house itself is harder to analyze. Regrettably, the expensive and tasteful houses many of us call "nice," are as much energy pigs as tract homes, apartments, and mobile homes. I call them Buick Houses, referring to Buick's long tradition of "giving you a lotta car for the money." It's hard to think about your house, isn't it? Have you ever thought that a separate bedroom might be silly for your needs? It sits there eating energy and mortgage payments but is used only one-third of the time—the rest of the day IT sleeps. There is a tendency to make your house a showplace of your belongings and mementos. The trend toward fake period furniture (molded from highly dangerous urethane foam) gives the illusion of expensive pieces, but it's not the real thing, just as autologic has photographs of wood glued to the dashboard in a Chevy. In a twenty-thousand-dollar Cadillac, you get more fake wood instead of the real thing, never mind the inappropriateness of wood in a car in the first place. In northern Europe there are many highly satisfactory houses—for our familes of four—of about six hundred square feet. That's practically a closet by our standards. Being big and showy is becoming expensive to run in a house just as it is in a car. Attempts to render a huge house acceptable environmentally by adding a solar hot water heater and insulation is rather like retro-fitting a Buick with a Briggs & Stratton—you may save some fuel, but the real problems are still there. It's time we rewarded designs that are less wasteful. More with less. I like Bucky Fuller's term *ephmeralization*.

A more insidious product of autologic may be seen in the bicycle business. Bicycles make a lot of sense as soft-tech. A person on a bike represents the most efficient means of transport known, exceeding even such a natural system as a running deer. The average auto trip is less than ten miles at an average speed of less than fifteen miles per hour, with a load statistically less than two people. That's bike talk. Then why are more bikes not used for commuting and other chores? Yes, there are questions of weather and safety. The weather we can't help, but safety questions arise from two sources. The first is that bikes are not accorded public funds to accommodate their needs. "Cars first" is another example of autologic. Second is that the bikes themselves are not very well designed for everyday use. The typical ten-speed, the most common type, is ill-suited to conditions met every day. It's fragile, easily stolen, difficult to store, park, and take on public transport. Its vital parts are heartlessly exposed to the elements, and many parts are made from materials that cannot withstand the assault of something as common as sunlight. Tires are easily popped by running over seeds and the inevitable glass crumbs. The lack of suspension is not only uncomfortable, but is unsafe on the rough edges of the road where bikes are most often used. Brakes don't work in the wet. All in all not a means of everyday transport for someone who might be dismissed for being late. The ten-speed is unsuitable largely because it is a weak imitation of a racing machine instead of being a strong statement of utility. The auto equivalents of the ten-speed, the pseudoracers like Camaro and Mustang, are among the least-useful cars. The thinking behind all these is the same. Sell dreams instead of elegant, useful, economical transport. Things need not be dowdy either. The idea that workday transportation has to be crude and ugly is also autologic intended to encourage the sales of luxury models. There was a time when selling illusions made good market sense even if it didn't mean a high degree of usefulness. But now that the energy and resource crunch is upon us, such frittermindedness is not only folly, it isn't even good business.

So what do we do about it? Well, it looks as if the American public is beginning to see what's going on, if only at a glimpse. Fat cars are not selling. Sale of insulation is booming. I think banks should give loans on solar houses only; in twenty years fossil-fueled housing may not be worth very much as collateral. Specification building codes should give way to performance codes. Five-dollar-per-gallon gasoline would do more for auto design than any number of government regulations. These are easily made changes—merely paperwork, but they could have a great impact.

Lastly, we have a responsibility to become increasingly critical. Those of us who know about net energy must be really tough when we propose another piece of hardware, regardless of the righteousness of the concept. We have to think in terms of whole systems instead of components. We must encourage people to look at life-cycle costs of technology, both economic and energetic, and we should pressure lending institutions to take this into account. But most of all we should look into our own minds to see how much of what we consider "reasonable" actually is so. The best antidote to autologic is to make everything you do a demonstration of clear thought.

J. Baldwin

Ron Zweig

Land
and Its Use

Thumbing through back issues of the journal, starting with the fifth, a trend becomes apparent. It was in the fifth journal that Earle Barnhart first wrote of his interest in tree crops in the article entitled "On the Feasibility of a Permanent Agricultural Landscape." Earle wrote it just before he became acquainted with the work of Bill Mollison of Australia. He had submitted it to me when, just prior to its publication, he appeared one day looking a bit disconcerted and announced that he had just discovered a book that he felt, in his words, "completely eclipsed" his own piece. We were both in something of a quandary. We finally decided that the best we could do at the eleventh hour was to have Earle write a book review of Mollison's Permaculture One that we would include as well. Since then Earle has published a second article, "Tree Crops," and Permaculture Two by Mollison has appeared. Bill Mollison is rapidly gaining a deserved reputation as a world leader in the field. Our own tree crops program under Earle and John Quinney also progresses satisfactorily.

The idea of tree crops is gaining strength rapidly these days. There are many reasons for this; the most obvious being the need to find forms of agriculture less dependent on fossil fuel than is the present norm. A more subtle reason is the slowly dawning realization that ecosystems might have something to teach us. In most of New England, for example, neglect a piece of cleared land for a while, it becomes evident that trees are what are intended to grow there. Gives one pause. At least it gave Earle sufficient pause to begin thinking about and then to begin planting trees. This has resulted in a recorded progression from theory to practice, from writing about the idea of tree culture to writing about our trees. The "Report From the Tree People" describes the work that each of the people involved in our tree research has done, reflecting the fact that permaculture has become an important part of New Alchemy's agriculture.

Our emphasis on gardening is by no means less for our newer interest in trees. Journal readers will have become familiar with Susan Ervin's report on her experiments with mulching, biological pest control, and irrigating with pond water. With this issue she is instituting a regular feature that she has called "Garden Notes." In it she still plans to record the results of scientific experiments and in addition some more casual observations based on her seven years of gardening experience.

N.J.T.

Henrike Kroeker

Garden Notes

Susan Ervin

Mulching

For five years we have been studying the effects of mulches on soil conditions and crop yields. Biodegradable mulches add organic material to the soil as they decompose at the same time they perform such functions generally attributed to mulch as water retention, temperature moderation, and weed control.

To summarize previous studies briefly: we have found that a mulch of azolla, a nitrogen-fixing aquatic fern, did not improve lettuce yields. Seaweed mulch tended to increase yields of beets, tomatoes, and Swiss chard, but resulted in decreasing yields of lettuce and peppers. Nitrate, potash, and soluble salt levels in the soil all increased under seaweed. Leaf mold was not as effective a mulch as seaweed. Supplemental watering did not significantly increase yields of either mulched or unmulched crops. Mulching reduces water runoff and the necessity of cultivation.[1]

Over the summer of 1979 we tested the effects of a straw mulch, as straw and spoiled hay are generally readily available. The plants on which the mulch was tested were Rutgers tomatoes, Salad Bowl let-tuce, Early Wonder beets, and Cubannelle peppers. We divided the test field into eight lengthwise plots, four of which we mulched with a 6 inch deep layer of straw. Four were not mulched. We did supplemental watering only at seeding and transplanting time.

We took soil moisture and temperature readings at a 5 inch depth daily at 4 P.M., when temperatures tend to be highest. Two sensors were installed at each of the sites at which data were collected. We decided to use two sensors although we have observed that two sensors frequently do not agree, a perversity I found frustrating. Despite differences of opinion among sensors, however, the trends of the effect of mulch on both moisture and temperature are consistent. The temperature variation between mulched and unmulched plots is as much as 11°F., a variation similar to that under seaweed mulch. These results are summarized in the accompanying graph.

Moisture readings were similar for plots with and without mulch until mid-July (see graph) when those without mulch rapidly became drier. The unmulched areas got a better soaking during several light rains; but the mulched areas tended to retain the moisture they received longer. However, in mid-August, a heavy all-night rain saturated all plots equally, and it was the mulched plots that dried out more quickly. The seaweed mulches we

[1]Susan Ervin. 1977. The effects of mulching with seaweed and azolla on lettuce productivity. *Journal of The New Alchemists* **4**: 58.

Susan Ervin. 1979. The effects of mulches. *Journal of The New Alchemists* **5**: 56–61.

Susan Ervin. 1980. Further experiments on the effects of mulches on crop yields and soil conditions. *Journal of The New Alchemists* **6**: 53–56.

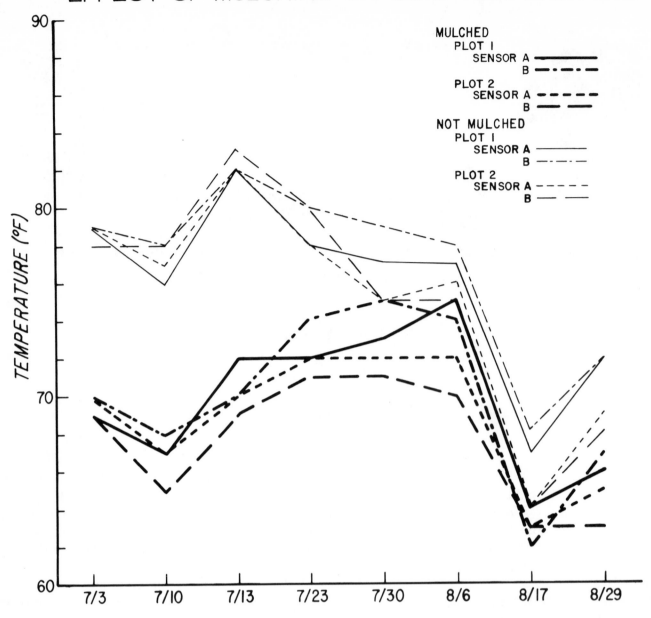

Total lettuce yields were 1.72% higher for plots without mulch.

Total beet yields were 49.92% higher for plots with mulch, the only yield difference likely to be statistically significant.

Total tomato yields were 29.4% higher for plots with mulch.

Total pepper yields were 37.1% higher in plots without mulch.

used in previous years seemed to absorb and retain moisture better than the straw mulch.

We found no mulch-related nutrient differences under straw mulch as we had under seaweed. The straw mulch did not increase the nitrogen, potash, or soluble salt levels of the soil. Whereas nitrogen and potash increases would be beneficial, the increase in salt caused by the seaweed could be damaging to some crops, although one winter's leaching subsequently returned all areas to equally low salt levels, whether or not they had been mulched with seaweed. Nitrate levels were quite low in all plots in mid-August, but rose again by fall.

In earlier trials beet yields were as much as 225% higher, and tomatoes, 7.3% higher under the seaweed mulch. Lettuce yields, however, were 33.9% greater without seaweed mulch. The straw-mulched crops of the most recent experiment followed the tendencies of earlier years; yields were higher under mulch for beets and tomatoes, but better without mulch for lettuce and peppers.

Whereas these experiments have increased our understanding of the effects of mulches, they have also pointed up the difficulty of isolating the effects of one particular aspect of soil management on "organically" managed soils. Early in the experiments we found that supplemental watering on a weekly basis did not significantly affect yields in either mulched or unmulched areas. Some irrigated areas were, in fact, drier at times than other unirrigated ones. This could possibly be caused by a very localized sand substrate. This countered our expectation that mulch would be especially beneficial when there was a lack of water. Subsequently, neither those experimental plots with nor those without mulch have been watered except to establish plants after transplanting or to facilitate germination. Although we have a four-to-six-week period without rain each summer, crops have done well, with no evidence of needing more water. We think the water retention capability of our soil has improved because of its increased content of organic material, which is now 8%. The effects of mulch would be more pronounced on soils low in organic material. Whether organic material is on top of the soil as a mulch or mixed into the soil, it will retain water. In the future we plan to compare moisture retention in both improved and unimproved sandy soils as well as crop response to different watering schedules on these soils. It is probable that the main advantage of mulching a soil already rich in humus is in weed control and further prevention of water runoff. In areas with extreme climates, temperature moderation would be an added benefit.

Some Tactical Maneuvers for Protecting Pumpkins and Squash

Squash vine borers and cucumber beetles are serious competitors for our squash and pumpkins. Early in the season the cucumber beetles eat the

Henrike Kroeker

leaves and can kill young plants, especially if the infestation is heavy when the plants have only their seed leaves. We plant most of the winter squash and pumpkins in peat pots in the Ark, and we have found that if we hold them there or in the cold frame until late May instead of setting them out as early as possible, there are fewer cucumber beetles and the larger plants can withstand what damage they do receive much better.

The vine borers bore into the base of the pumpkin and squash vines. We have tried slitting the stems, stabbing the ugly creatures, and rubbing rotenone in the slits. This kills the borers—and often the plants as well. We have also tried heaping dirt over the vines as they begin to run in an attempt to help them develop a second root system in case the primary stalk is destroyed. In some cases this helped. The most encouraging thing we have learned is that as our soil has improved, the loss to the borers has seemed to decline, especially in well-mulched, cool, moist areas. During the summer of 1979 the squash field, which was very fertile, had a deep mulch of leaf mold with a little straw and seaweed, and there was virtually no borer damage.

We did, however, acquire a new ailment, one we think we understand. Most of our apparently healthy pumpkins rotted from the inside and collapsed in the field. We had put a layer of fresh horsestable manure mixed with the inevitable woodchips on top of the thick leaf mulch, thinking the mulch would protect the plants from burning and allow the nutrients from the manure to leach through. The vines ran across the manure, and the fruits set on it. This probably caused some sort of bacterial disease. Perhaps after this rather disappointing experiment and the other rather more encouraging discoveries, we can look forward to a respectable harvest of squash and pumpkins with some degree of certainty.

Beans and Bean Beetles

Our bean beetle population has been much lower for several years. We don't know whether this fortunate development is due to the heavy parasitization by parasitic wasps as reported in the fifth journal, "Mexican Bean Battles," pp. 53–55, to hard winters that could kill overwintering adults, to improved soil conditions, or to a combination of events. In the summer of 1979 we put 100 parasitized beetle larvae in the bean field. Evidently the wasp hatch was low, because little subsequent parasitization occurred. Bean beetle damage was not severe. We grew two old New England varieties of beans for the first time this summer, Black Beauty and Brown Beauty. Both yielded quite well.

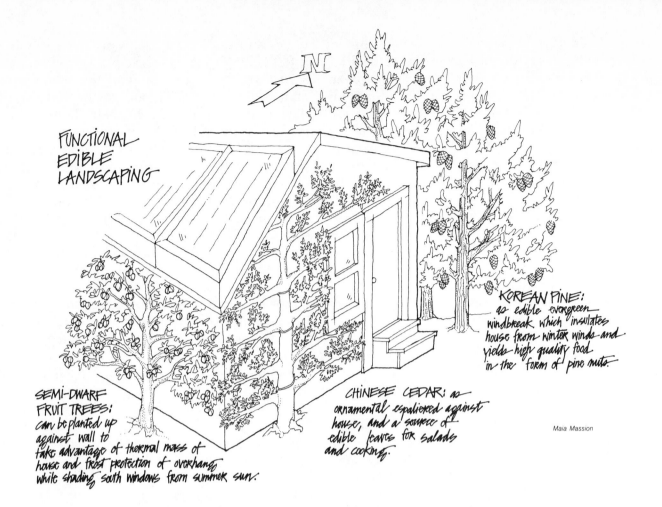

FUNCTIONAL EDIBLE LANDSCAPING

KOREAN PINE: as edible evergreen windbreak which insulates house from winter winds and yields high quality food in the form of pine nuts.

CHINESE CEDAR: as ornamental espaliered against house, and a source of edible leaves for salads and cooking.

SEMI-DWARF FRUIT TREES: can be planted up against wall to take advantage of thermal mass of house and frost protection of overhang while shading south windows from summer sun.

Maia Massion

A REPORT from the TREE PEOPLE

Introduction

John Quinney

In recent New Alchemy journals, Earle Barnhart has written on the nature of an ecologically inspired agricultural landscape. His article in the fifth journal begins with a critique of modern agricultural practices and then proceeds to abstract from ecological theory in order to arrive at a description of agriculture modeled on the patterns of native ecosystems. Earle's article in the sixth journal stresses the importance of perennial plants, especially trees, and describes various cultural techniques for propagation, transplanting, and food production in both urban and rural environments. Bill Mollison, a world authority on perennial agriculture working in Australia, has recently described perennial agricultural systems as *permacul-*

tures. In his 1978 book *Permaculture One*[1] he defines the term: "Permaculture is a word we have coined for an integrated, evolving system of perennial or self-perpetuating plant and animal species useful to man [*sic*]. It is, in essence, a complete agricultural ecosystem, modeled on existing but simpler examples."

Taken together, these publications have provided us with the theoretical basis for our agricultural forestry program at New Alchemy. The transition from theory to practice is now gaining expression in sections of the farm; subsequent contributions to this article diagram the process. Much of this work is experimental: we have access to considerations developed by ecologists and foresters, orchardists, and farmers but ultimately our Cape Cod landscape will speak to us more clearly than journals and books.

---

[1]See reference 3.

In addition to the work described herein, we have recently commenced several other projects.

Over the past three years, the number of Chinese weeding geese grazing a grass-alfalfa pasture beneath fruit, nut, and fodder trees has steadily increased. In their own unique and often loveable manner these creatures have impressed us. As biological lawnmowers, fertilizer spreaders, and herbicides they are effective replacements for machinery and fossil fuels. And they taste a lot better than oil!

In this same area a small ecological island has been planted to perennials used by our bees-in-residence. The lee of an evergreen windbreak contains staghorn sumacs (*Rhus typhina*) and a mature pussy willow (*Salix discolor*) interplanted with herbs and flowers.

Near the nurseries we have planted over fifty species of herbs. Over the next few years we will be watching this area closely to determine insect population levels. We will then be able to use particular herbs to provide habitats for specific insects. These predators will assist in establishing biological controls in our gardens and forest.

We continue to collect and propagate potentially valuable trees and shrubs. Among these are Oriental and American persimmons (*Diospyros kaki* and *D. virginiana*), Kiwi fruit (*Actinidia chinensis*), jujube (*Zizyphus jujuba*), blueberries (*Vaccinium* sp.), elderberries (*Sambucus* sp.), catalpa (*Catalpa* sp.), Buckeyes (*Aesculus* sp.), the Korean nut pine (*Pinus koraiensis*), and shagbark hickory (*Carya ovata*).

Future developments within the agricultural forestry program may include establishing fast-growing hardwoods for firewood, placing nutrient-retrieving plants near trees, working with mycorrhizal fungi, innoculating soils with active earthworm species, evaluating seaweed products for disease control in fruit trees, and establishing living mulches around fruit and nut trees.

REFERENCES

1. EARLE BARNHART. 1979. On the feasibility of a permanent agricultural landscape. *Journal of The New Alchemists* **5**: 73.

2. EARLE BARNHART. 1980. Tree crops: creating the foundation of a permanent agriculture. *Journal of The New Alchemists* **6**: 57.

3. BILL MOLLISON and DAVID HOLMGREN. 1978. *Permaculture One. A Perennial Agriculture for Human Settlements.* Melbourne: Transworld Publishers.

4. BILL MOLLISON. 1979. *Permaculture Two. Practical Design for Town and Country in Permanent Agriculture.* Tasmania: Tagari.

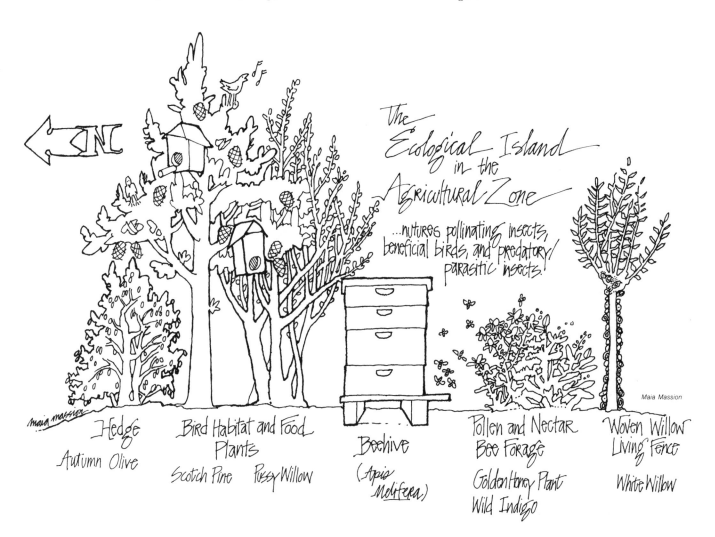

The Ecological Island in the Agricultural Zone ...nurtures pollinating insects, beneficial birds, and predatory/parasitic insects!

Maia Massion

Hedge
Autumn Olive

Bird Habitat and Food Plants
Scotch Pine   Pussy Willow

Beehive
(Apis Melifera)

Pollen and Nectar Bee Forage
Golden Honey Plant
Wild Indigo

Woven Willow Living Fence
White Willow

Surveying and Grafting Local and Antique Fruit Trees

Mavis Clark

We have undertaken the task of surveying the growth of fruit trees in the Upper Cape area in an effort to find varieties that are adapted to grow well under our local climatic conditions and to show resistance to diseases prevailing in the area. We aim to propagate such trees for further planting throughout the town of Falmouth.

Cape Cod has the reputation of being a very poor area for growing fruit, because its moist, foggy weather favors the rapid spread of fungal diseases, blights, and scabs. Commercial orchardists, now very few in number, spray their trees once every week during the growing season to combat these diseases and aphids, scale insects, borers, and caterpillars as well.

In 1977 and 1978, Earle Barnhart began the search for trees that seem well adapted to the Cape and are known for bearing consistently good crops. He enlisted the reliable food-foraging instincts of adolescents by asking Falmouth High School students to pinpoint such trees. This source of local lore produced a list of apple, pear, and peach trees that we started to check out in more detail. The 1977 research, which also included a survey of all the local history books in the Falmouth Public Library, revealed that the earliest settlers brought stock and seeds of fruit trees with them and established orchards that supplied them with plentiful fruit.

Once Earle had tracked down high-bearing trees, he encountered owners that were usually apologetic that their trees had been neglected. Everyone was very generous in allowing us to cut off young branches for scions in February 1978. After cold storage, these either were used for whip or wedge grafts in April, or budded in June. In 1977 Earle had planted the rootstock apple trees onto which these grafts were later made, using seeds from a commercial nursery. The seeds originated from wild trees in upstate New York. We have kept growth records of the rootstock trees, photographed them each year. They now stand about three feet tall. During the summer of 1979 we successfully grafted scions from several dozen grafts of local trees onto the rootstock. At that time we planted four antique trees and they were ready to have scions taken from them by the following spring. We shall check the local trees at harvest to try to identify varieties or at least to suggest possible parentage for them. As peach trees are better propagated by late spring budding, we shall graft local tree buds onto New Alchemy trees and onto some planted in a neighboring yard as well.

We were given much help and information by Howard Crowell, of Crow Farm, Sandwich, Massachusetts, who runs a fine commercial orchard. He retains some antique apple varieties along with many newer ones, numbering nineteen in all. He finds that although the russet apple does not bear as heavily as newer varieties, devotees of this fruit will come to buy russets and usually go off with other fruits and vegetables too. This old variety also shows a high natural resistance to diseases. We returned from Crow Farm with many scions, chiefly the antique and more naturally resistant varieties.

We are seeking out other resource people on the Cape knowledgeable of fruit orchardry. Their hard-earned experience could help point up to us early mistakes and lead us in turn to new investigations.

Recycling Leaf Nutrients

Ed Goodell

For a good many years now we have been asking area residents to bring us their leaves in the fall. People seem to like to do this, and our soil thereby receives a sizeable amount of nutrients.

The soil-conditioning properties of leaves are especially appreciated on our poor, sandy soils. Because of its capacity to absorb water and exchange nutrients, adequate humus is essential for a healthy soil. The humus formed from leaf decay has a long life because leaves contain relatively high proportions of lignin and hemicellulose, the most lasting constituents of humus.

At New Alchemy we have realized the value of leaves for quite a while. An early demonstration of the benefits they confer was provided when a young Chinese chestnut tree was planted on the site where a leaf pile had been the preceding year. Of 20 Chinese chestnuts planted at the same time, it rapidly outgrew the others.

We have used leaves regularly in moderate amounts for winter mulches, for trench composting between intensive garden beds, and for mulching trees. The leaf mold—the dark, crumbly humus formed by gradual fungal decay and weathering—from underneath the piles is in high

COMFREY CAGE
Quonset-type, woven cage
of split bamboo placed
over rows of comfrey, nibbled
by grazing poultry; dimensions are
approximately 3' high, 2' wide. (end section cut
away in illustration)

Maia Massion

demand for potting soil. We have turned leaves under the soil in the fall to decompose over the winter. We have also tried transforming sod into a growing medium by mulching it thickly. This was useful for growing potatoes and winter squashes. We are planning to use a large bin of leaves in the first stage of graywater treatment. Bags of leaves can be convenient and effective insulators around foundations, beehives, and tender young plants.

The amount of leaves at our disposal has increased dramatically since the fall of 1978, when we put up a sign at the Falmouth dump directing potential leaf donors to the farm. The leaf pile has advanced 100 yards from the original storage area. We remove leaves from the end opposite that to which they are added. As a result, the pile creeps slowly across the landscape, leaving a swath of nicely mulched, worm-worked soil. You may have heard of chicken tractors.[1] Apparently we have created a leaf tractor. Steering is easily accomplished with movable signs that indicate where the leaves should be deposited.

During the winter of 1979–1980 we estimate that we were given 750 cubic yards (575 cubic meters) of leaves weighing over 15 tons (13.6 metric tons). This amount of mixed leaves contains 230 lb, or 105 kilograms (kg), of nitrogen, 80 lb (36 kg) of phosphorus, and 130 lb (59 kg) of potash.[2] In terms of N-P-K (nitrogen-phosphorus-potassium), this is roughly equivalent to 1,000 lb (455 kg) of 20-10-10 fertilizer, or enough to apply more than 100 lb/acre (112 kg/hectare) annually to the entire farm. In addition to the other nutrients the leaves contain significant amounts of calcium, magnesium, and trace minerals.

Unlike the soluble nutrients in chemical fertilizers, those contained in leaves are released gradually as the leaves decay. Leaf decay can be thought of in terms of the half life of the leaves—the time it takes half of the material to decay. The half life of a leaf on the forest floor is 12–18 months. The decay process can be hastened by turning the leaves into the soil, shredding them, or piling them together.

Our current contributions of leaves far exceeds New Alchemy's capacity to use them. This enables us to accumulate large amounts of leaves for the two or three years required for them to decompose fully into leaf mold. A delight for worms and gardeners alike, leaf mold holds three to five times its weight in water, has no weed seeds, has a pH of 5.5–5.0, and is very enduring in the soil. We use it for potting soil, to top-dress individual plants, and, when available, for broad-scale mulching. Since New Alchemy has prospects of a generous supply of leaf mold, it will probably become our all-purpose soil amendment.

Ultimately, we would prefer that the leaves return to the soil from which they grew, to enrich that soil directly. We would like to see our leaf donors use their own leaves, and some of our educational efforts concern ways to encourage this. In the meantime, the productive capacity of our soil will continue to grow as we enrich it with a fertile mantle of leaf mold.

[1]Richard Merrill, ed. *Radical Agriculture*. N.Y.: Harper & Row.
[2]Bulletin No. 92, Clemson Agricultural College, Clemson University, South Carolina.

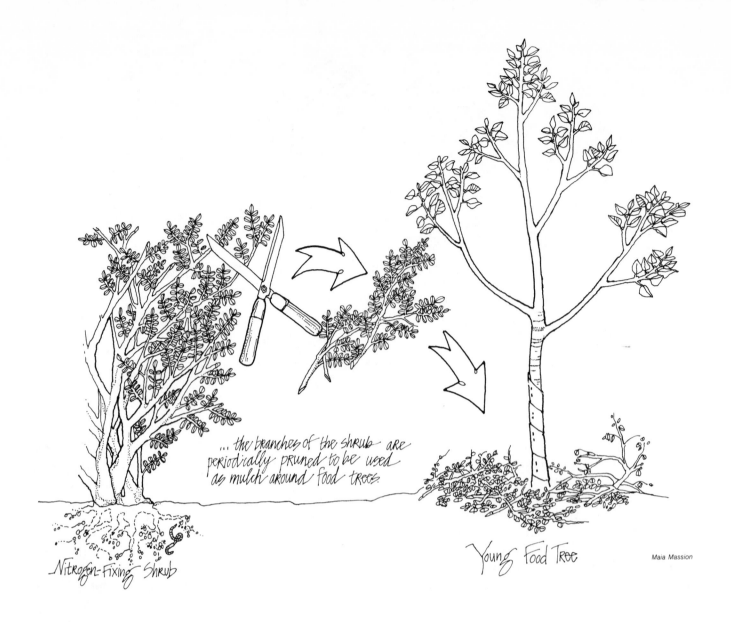

... the branches of the shrub are periodically pruned to be used as mulch around food trees.

Nitrogen-Fixing Shrub

Young Food Tree

Maia Massion

Nitrogen-Fixing Trees and Shrubs

John Quinney

Nitrogen is the most abundant element in the earth's atmosphere and is essential for plant growth and reproduction. However, atmospheric nitrogen can be utilized directly by plants only after it has been converted to either its nitrate or its ammonium forms. This process is known as fixation and can be achieved either chemically or biologically.

Chemical fixation involves the reaction of atmospheric nitrogen with hydrogen from natural gas at elevated temperatures and pressures in the presence of a catalyst—the Haber process. The ammonia thus produced can be applied directly to farmland or converted chemically to other nitrogenous fertilizers.

Biological fixation of nitrogen is carried out by a number of free-living organisms and also, most importantly, by virtue of two symbiotic associations between plants and bacteria—the rhizobium-legume association and the actinomycete–nonleguminous-angiosperm association (Table 1).

Chemical fixation is an energy-intensive process; it depends on diminishing supplies of fossil fuels. The chemical production of 150 kilograms (kg) of nitrogenous fertilizer (a typical per hectare application) requires 1.53 million kilocalories (kcal). For comparison, biological fixation of the same amount of nitrogen by the legume winter vetch (*Vicia villosa*) involves a seeding cost of only 90,000 kcal.[1]

Many farmers meet the nitrogen requirements of their land by planting legumes as green manure crops or as a part of crop rotations. Used in these

---

[1]Pimental et al., 1973. Reference 7.

Table 1. MAJOR PRESENT-DAY NITROGEN-FIXING PLANTS.[a]

1. *Free-Living Organisms:*
   a) Heterotrophic bacteria, e.g., *Azobacter, Clostridium, Spirillum, Beijerinckia, Klebsiella.*
   b) Autotrophic bacteria, e.g., *Rhodopseudomonas, Rhodospirillum, Thiobacillus.*
   c) Blue-green algae, e.g., *Anabaena, Calothrix, Nostoc, Plectonema,* etc.

2. *Root Nodule-Forming Symbioses:*
   a) Rhizobium-legume associations, e.g., *Glycine max* (soybean), *Phaseolus vulgaris, Vicia faba* (vetch), *Trifolium repens* (clover), etc.
   b) Actinomycete–nonleguminous-angiosperm associations, e.g., *Alnus glutinosa* (alder), *Robinia pseudoacacia* (black locust), *Hippophae rhamnoides* (sea buckthorn), etc.
   c) Cycad–blue-green-algae associations, e.g., *Bowenia, Cycas, Encephalartos,* etc.

[a]Source: W. P. D. Stewart, 1977. *Ambio* **6**:166.

ways alfalfa (*Medicago sativa*) and soybeans (*Glycine max*) can supply up to 450 and 100 kg nitrogen per hectare per year (N/ha/yr) respectively. However, not all legumes are capable of fixing nitrogen; for example, the legume Eastern redbud (*Cercis canadensis*) does not form root nodules and thus does not fix nitrogen.

The nonleguminous nitrogen-fixing plants, which are all trees and woody shrubs, have recently been recognized as an important source of fixed nitrogen. For example, alders (*Alnus* sp.) can fix up to 300 kg N/ha/yr and the sea buckthorn (*Hippophae rhamnoides*) up to 180 kg N/ha/yr. In temperate-region forested biomes the nitrogen-fixing trees and shrubs are usually pioneer species modifying the soil environment and establishing favorable conditions for succeeding trees. For example, in the Pacific Northwest the red alder (*Alnus rubra*) is succeeded by Douglas fir (*Pseudotsuga menziesii*); on Cape Cod, bayberry (*Myrica pensylvanica*), sweet fern (*Comptonia peregrina*), and black locust (*Robinia pseudoacacia*) are followed by pitch pine (*Pinus rigida*), and various oaks (*Quercus* sp.).

The nitrogen-fixing trees and shrubs make nitrate available to other species mainly through leaf fall; the nitrate enters the soil when the leaves are decomposed by soil microorganisms. Only when the bacterial root nodules are sloughed off or the host plant dies can nitrogen be made available more directly. As a forest matures and the nutrient cycles tighten because the forest has become increasingly efficient at processing organic matter, nitrogen usage is increasingly conservative, and the need for nitrogen fixation is correspondingly reduced. In these ecosystems the small nitrogen requirements needed for plant structural tissue and to replace losses by leaching are met mainly through fixation by various free-living organisms (see Table 1).

In the agricultural forestry work at New Alchemy, nitrogen-fixing trees and shrubs are important components of the overall ecology.

At New Alchemy the following nitrogen-fixing trees and shrubs are being studied:

Legumes: black locust, Scotch broom (*Cytisus scoparius*), Siberian pea shrub (*Caragana arborescens*), *Albizzia julibrissin,* and honey locust (*Gleditsia triacanthos*) (nitrogen-fixing ability not firmly established).

Nonlegumes: bayberry, sweet fern, autumn olive (*Elaeagnus umbellata*), Russian olive (*Elaeagnus angustifolia*), *Ceanothus* sp., alders (*Alnus rugosa, A. glutinosa*), and sea buckthorn.

A collection has been established that now consists of plantings of honey locust, *Albizzia,* black locust, Scotch broom, autumn olive, and bayberry. Additional species will be added over the years. This area will be used for education as well as for testing the growth of these trees and shrubs in the Cape Cod environment and providing propagation materials.

The honey locust and the alders are useful fodder trees. In New Zealand, cattle have been fed on honey locust pods; they fall from the trees over the three to four months of winter when other fodder is in short supply. Foliage from alders has been processed into silage and used to feed cattle, and at Hampshire College in western Massachusetts *A. rugosa* is being evaluated as a sheep feed. In due course these species will be tested at New Alchemy as livestock feeds, especially for geese and poultry.

We have begun various interplanting experiments in the polycultural forest area south of the Ark. Literature reports have documented the beneficial effects of black locust, alders, and autumn olive on the growth of interplanted lumber trees, apples, and black walnuts respectively. A stand of young black locust trees occurs naturally in a section of this area, and we shall manage these trees with some attendant controls on their propagation through vegetative spreading.

We have established experimental hedges of autumn olive and are propagating the tree by root and stem cuttings. The roots of these plants are well nodulated. We are planning hedgerow plantings of Siberian pea shrub, Russian olive, and *A. glutinosa.*

There is a named variety of the black locust (var. *"rectissima"*) that produces straight, durable lumber. Root cuttings of this variety, which is also known as the "ship-mast locust," are being sought. We hope to acquire and test additional species of nitrogen-fixing shrubs such as *Ceanothus* sp. and sea buckthorn.

We expect that careful integration of a variety of nitrogen-fixing species in our agricultural forests will make a substantial contribution to the productivity of the forests in a way that is both energetically conservative and environmentally gentle.

REFERENCES

1. W. E. NEWTON AND C. J. NYMA, eds. 1976. *Proceedings of the First International Symposium on Nitrogen Fixation.* Washington State University Press.

A detailed technical collection of papers concerned with all aspects of nitrogen fixation.

2. JOHN G. TORREY AND JOHN TJEPKEMA, eds. 1979. Symbiotic nitrogen fixation in actinomycete-nodulated plants. *Botanical Gazette* **140**, suppl.

The result of an informal conference held at the Harvard Forest in April 1978. The best introduction to the literature on these nitrogen-fixing species.

3. ROBERT H. BURRIS. 1978. Future of biological nitrogen fixation. *BioScience* **28**(9):563.

A special issue of *BioScience* covering crop legumes, energetic considerations, genetic modifications of N$_2$-fixing systems, algal associations, blue-green algae, and the actinomycete-nodulated angiosperms.

4. DONALD LARSON. 1976. Nitrogen-fixing shrubs: An answer to the world's firewood shortage? *The Futurist* **74**.

An analysis of the global potential of nitrogen-fixing shrubs for soil restoration and firewood. An excellent general introduction.

5. W. B. SILVESTER. 1977. Dinitrogen fixation by plant associations excluding legumes. In: *A Treatise of Dinitrogen Fixation,* ed. R. W. F. Hardy and A. H. Gibson, pp. 141–190. New York: John Wiley and Sons.

A detailed literature survey of all the actinomycete-nodulated species. Includes global distribution, economic value, historical studies, methods for assessing nitrogen increments, ecological significance of these species, etc.

6. EDWARD H. GRAHAM. 1941. *Legumes for Erosion Control and Wildlife.* USDA Miscellaneous Publication No. 412, U.S. Government Printing Office, Washington, D.C.

An exhaustive accumulation of pre-1940 information on the uses of legumes (all species). Includes detailed information on the legumes eaten by various animals.

7. DAVID PIMENTAL et al. 1973. Food production and the energy crisis. *Science* **182**:443–449.

Hedgerows and Living Fences

John Quinney

In any agricultural landscape the most obvious function of fences and hedgerows is to control the movement of animals—domestic and wild—so they will be excluded from food crops or selectively rotated through pastures. The advantage of hedge rows over fences is that they are multifunctional components of the landscape and as such can be integrated with the overall design strategy.

Perhaps one of the best-known examples occurs in the traditional English landscape. The English hawthorn (*Crataegus* sp.) was often originally planted to replace wooden post-and-rail fences, which are subject to inevitable decay. As well as providing an impenetrable barrier to the movement of sheep and cattle, such hedges have other important ecological functions. They provide a habitat for a wide variety of beneficial insects and birds. They facilitate the establishment of numerous volunteer herbs and "weeds." Cattle, sheep, and horses grazing on pastures thus enclosed have often been observed browsing these plants as well, presumably supplementing their diet with nutrients not available in the relatively simple pasture ecosystem. In windy areas of the country, especially East Anglia, the hedgerows reduced soil erosion, a function that has only become apparent since their removal for the sake of "efficient" large-scale agriculture.

At The New Alchemy Institute an experimental hedge of autumn olive (*Elaeagnus umbellata*) has been established and pruned to encourage dense bottom growth. An immediate goal of these plantings is to control the movement of domestic geese, restricting their access to the gardens and tree nursery.

We have also planted living fence posts of willows (*Salix* sp.). Eventually, prunings from the top of each fence post will be woven between them, providing an effective barrier. Ultimately, annual pruning will yield firewood.

These and other successive hedge plantings will be designed in order to create ecological landscape elements with diverse functions. They will be, in effect, ecological islands in which a variety of plants and animals may grow undisturbed by cultivation. They will be windbreaks and a source of food for a variety of birds and animals. For example, the Russian olive (*Elaeagnus angustifolia*), an important Midwest hedgerow species, is known to be used for food by at least forty birds, including chickens,

1st year (summer)   2nd year (spring)   (summer)   (late winter)   3rd year (summer)   4th year (spring)

... Pollarded Willows as Living Fence, the live posts woven with the trimmed shoots.

Maia Massion

ducks, and turkeys. Hedgerows planted in an east-west orientation can create local microenvironments with raised temperatures on the southern exposure. Such microenvironments allow the survival of plants and animals that might otherwise be absent from the landscape. Prunings from nitrogen-fixing hedgerows can be used as mulches around fruit and nut trees in order to supply some of their nutrient needs.

Although our work at New Alchemy is mainly with hedgerows, another kind of boundary is traditional here. In the years when our part of Cape Cod was extensively farmed, local stone was used for the construction of dry stone walls. Many of these walls still remain in areas of the Cape that have become forested. Their construction is admittedly labor intensive, but they have the advantages of being relatively permanent, made from a local resource, and largely maintenance free. Although these walls are obviously limited in their ecological functions, they offer a viable alternative to hedgerows and introduce a pleasant diversity to the landscape.

REFERENCES

1. A. E. BORELL. 1971. *Russian Olive for Wildlife and Other Conservation Uses.* USDA Leaflet No. 517, U.S. Government Printing Office, Washington, D.C.

A good general description of this plant, including planting and management details as well as alluding to its value to wildlife.

2. BILL MOLLISON AND DAVID HOLMGREN. 1978. *Permaculture One. A Perennial Agriculture for Human Settlements.* Melbourne: Transworld Publishers.

Includes a species listing for hedgerow plantings as well as general design considerations.

3. CYRIL L. MARSHALL. 1977. How to make a hedgerow English style. *Country Journal* **55**.

Establishment and maintenance of a hawthorn hedge.

4. FRED J. NISBET. 1977. Shelterbelts. *Country Journal* **48**.

A general introduction to the design, planting, and maintenance of windbreaks including a species listing.

5. E. POLLARD, M. D. HOOPER, AND N. W. MOORE. 1975. *Hedges.* N.Y.: Taplinger Publishing Co.

The best available text on English hedges—history, flora and fauna, farm hedges.

Birds and Biological Pest Control

Loie Urquhart

In observing the natural world, it is quite evident that birds help to regulate the numbers of insects and rodents. But since the advent of pesticides, comparatively little attention has been paid to encouraging birds as predators in the forest, orchard, field, and garden.

Birds can eat thousands of insects in a single day, especially in the spring, the season of highest consumption, when the birds are feeding their young. Owls and hawks prey upon mice, rabbits, and other small mammals that can damage fruit trees. In the winter, nonmigratory insect eaters such as woodpeckers, chickadees, and nuthatches search the bark of trees for hibernating insects.

By providing nesting sites, water, and winter shelter, we could encourage and foster populations of beneficial birds that would regulate insect and mammal pests.

Feeding Habits of Birds

Surveys of the feeding habits of birds conclude that the terms insectivorous and vegetivorous indicate predominance in a given diet, rather than restriction to one type of food. For instance, the most exclusive vegetarians—the finches, grouses, and pigeons—sometimes eat insects, while the most avid insect eaters—the swallows and flycatchers, will eat berries.

From the viewpoint of the farmer or orchard grower, insects can be classed as beneficial (which includes parasitic and predaceous varieties) injurious, and neutral. Birds do eat beneficial insects, but only, it seems, to the extent that keeps their numbers in proportion and maintains an equilibrium in the natural continuing flux.

Injurious insects are found in the air, on and within leaves, on and under the bark of trees (boring or hibernating insects), and on the ground. There are insects, such as the Mexican bean beetle, the monarch butterfly, and some insects of the suborder Heteroptera, that are protected from being eaten by birds by either a hard casing, a disagreeable odor and taste, or a camouflaging ability to meld into their surroundings. Birds that prey on insects can be grouped loosely, as the flying insect patrol, the foliage cleaners, the bark gleaners, and the ground eaters.

The Flying Insect Patrol

There are a number of birds who feed while in flight.

Daytime Patrol	*They Eat*
Swifts	Moths—gypsy moths
Swallows	Cabbage worm moths
Martins	Codling moths
Kingbirds	Cankerworm moths
Phoebes	Leaf-roller moths
Flycatchers	Locusts (short-horned
Vireos	grasshoppers)
Redstarts	Long-legged crane flies
Peewees	Leafhoppers
Mockingbirds	Aphids
Catbirds	Long-horned grasshoppers
Hawks	Hessian flies (wheat enemy)
	Horseflies
	Rose chafers
	Winged ants
	Butterflies
	Beetles

Nighttime Patrol	*They Eat*
Nighthawks	Night-flying or owlet moths
Whippoorwills	(*Noctuidae*)
	Moths—cotton boll worms
	Army worms
	Cutworms
	Mosquitoes
	Leafhoppers

Foliage Cleaners

Foliage cleaners concentrate on picking destructive insects off the leaves and branches of plants.

They Are	*They Eat*
Warblers	Leafhoppers (*Jassidae*)
Nuthatches	Plant lice or aphids (*Aphidiae*)
Chickadees	including common "green
Kinglets	fly"
Robins	Leaf-rollers (e.g., codling
Catbirds	moths)
Thrushes	Leaf-miners (e.g., apple leaf
Ruffed grouse	miners)
Baltimore orioles	Cankerworms
Blackbirds	Cutworms
Crows	Cotton boll worms
(many others)	Army worms
	Hairy caterpillars
	Tent caterpillars of apple and
	wild cherry trees
	Fall webworms
	Tussock caterpillars
	Gypsy moth larvae
	Leaf beetles—Colorado potato beetles
	Flea beetles

They Eat
Striped cucumber beetles
Asparagus beetles
Corn root worms
Rose beetle (larvae feed on roots)
Snout beetles—plum and apple curculios
Bean and pea weevils
Grain weevils
White pine borers
Spruce budworms

Bark Gleaners

Many birds dig under the bark of trees for boring and hibernating insects, as well as devouring those on the bark itself.

They Are	*They Eat*
Woodpeckers	Bark borers
Nuthatches	Hibernating insects (e.g., codling moths)
Creepers	
Chickadees	Trunk borers
Warblers	Timber ants
Kinglets	Plant lice
Wrens	Bark lice

Scraping the old, rough bark from the trunk and branches of orchard trees and covering the bare spots with an adhesive organic mixture will help to prevent these insects from nesting. Ringing tree trunks with a metal piece or sticky substance deters some insects from climbing into the tree.

Ground Eaters

A number of birds work on the ground.

They Are	*They Eat*
Robins	May beetles or June bugs
Bluebirds	Tiger beetles
Blackbirds	Rose beetles
Chipping sparrows	Strawberry slugs
	Root worms
Song sparrows	Leafhoppers
Wrens	Aphids
Warblers	Crane-fly maggots
Vireos	Cutworms
Phoebes	Cabbage worms
Meadowlarks	Root maggots
Crows	Grasshoppers
Bobolinks	Chinch bugs
Flickers	Army worms
Quails	Craneflies
Woodpeckers	White grubs
Catbirds	Root borers
Thrushes	Wireworms
Owls	Bollworms

They Are
Hawks

They Eat
Ants
Root lice
Larvae of plum and apple curculios
Bean and pea weevils
Grain weevils
White pine borers
Ants (Formicidae)
Thousand-legged worms (subclass Myriapoda; destructive to strawberries, but some predaceous.)
Frogs
Lizards
Snakes
Mice
Moles
Shrews
Groundhogs
Squirrels
Gophers

Predatory Birds

In winter, mice, moles, groundhogs, rabbits, and other mammals can cause considerable damage to the roots and trunks of orchard trees. Such rodents normally can be discouraged from chewing the bark of trees by wrapping burlap and/or wire mesh around the trunks of trees. Not all damage is inflicted at this level, however. The pine mouse burrows underground to chew the trunk and roots below ground level. Groundhogs will tunnel throughout the root systems of orchard trees and expose the roots to oxygen in the atmosphere; this can dehydrate them and eventually kill the tree.

Owls and hawks frequent areas where small mammals are plentiful and help to keep their numbers down. Owls can be attracted to houses of an appropriate size and can act as live-in rodent controls.

Bird Habitat

There are birds who can be persuaded to forsake their natural habitats and live in artificial structures. The destruction of forests and the thinning out of dead trees in orchards and woodlands has reduced the number of available nesting sites for many birds. If birdhouses are erected in late winter, before the birds are scouting for nesting locations, many birds will take up residence in them, some returning year after year. If a specific bird is required, it is best to put up a birdhouse specifically designed for that bird. For example, if you

Table 1. BIRDHOUSE SPECIFICATIONS FOR SELECTED BIRDS.

Species	Entrance Diameter (In.)	Entrance Above Floor (In.)	Floor Dimensions (In.)	House Depth (In.)	Box Above Ground (Ft.)	Comments
Bluebird	1½	6–7	5 × 5	8–9	5–10	Prefers on top of fence post.
Chickadee	1⅛	6–8	4 × 4	8–10	5–15	2–3 in. wood shavings on floor. Prefers hollow log homes.
Red-breasted nuthatch	1	6–8	4 × 4	8–10	5–20	Prefers hollow log-type home.
Robin & phoebe	Open front and sides		7 × 7	8	8–12	
Barn owl	6	4	10 × 18	15–18	12–18	
Tufted titmouse	1¼	6–8	4 × 4	8–10	4–5	
Downy woodpecker	1¼	6–8	4 × 4	8–10	6–20	Prefers hollow log. Wood shavings 2–3 in. deep.
Hairy woodpecker	1½	9–12	6 × 6	12–16	12–20	Prefers hollow log. Wood shavings 2–3 in. deep.
House & winter wren	1 × 2½	4–6	4 × 4	6–8	5–10	Especially likes gourds.
Yellow flicker	3	14–16	7 × 7	16–24	6–20	Prefers hollow log homes. Sawdust 2–3 in. deep.
Flycatcher (crested)	2	6–8	6 × 6	8–10	8–20	2–3 in. wood shavings.

Wood used best at ¾ in. thickness
Martins only ½ in.

are having trouble with the cranberry moth, a box suited to the tree swallow is wise as the tree swallow relishes the taste of the cranberry moth. Birdhouses can be made from hollowed-out gourds, logs, old bark nailed into the trunk of a tree, or three-quarter-inch pine boards (see Table 1). Houses should have drainage and ventilation holes and entrance holes. Size and other particulars for each bird have been outlined by the Audubon Society.

Natural Habitat

By providing an environment in which birds can thrive, injurious insects and rodents can be kept to a minimum. Because birds need food, shelter, and water it is important, when purposely attracting birds to an orchard or garden area, to provide enough food for them as an alternative to cultivated fruits and grains. They prefer the taste of wild fruits to cultivated ones. The more diverse the plantings, the better. The following are some suggested plantings:

Shelterbelt plantings: Russian olive (*Elaeagnus angustifolia*), eastern red cedar (*Juniperus virgiania*), European beech (*Sylvatica fagus*).

Hedgerows: autumn olive (*Elaeagnus umbellata*), white mulberry (*Morus alba*), Siberian pea shrub (*Caragana aborescens*).

Fruit-bearing trees: mountain ash (*Pyrus aucuparia*), honey locust (*Gleditsia triacanthos*), staghorn sumac (*Rhus typhina*).

Many varieties of flowers with their bright colors, fragrant smells, and nectar attract birds. An area left wild as an ecological island in a garden area can provide shelter, food, and beauty for birds and some beneficial insects. Brushpiles provide cover and nesting sites, and can be used as a support for plantings of wild grape or Virginia creeper.

Birdhouses

Forty-nine species of birds have been recorded to have nested in boxes:

Mountain bluebird
Western bluebird
Eastern bluebird
Robin
Chestnut-backed
  chickadee
Mountain chickadee
Carolina chickadee
Black-capped chickadee
Plain titmouse
Tufted titmouse
Red-breasted nuthatch
White-breasted nuthatch
Brown creeper
House wren
Winter wren
Bewick's wren
Carolina wren
Mockingbird
Brown thrasher
Violet-green swallow
Tree swallow
Barn swallow
Cliff swallow
Purple martin
Song sparrow

English sparrow
House finch
Purple grackle
Bullock's oriole
Orchard oriole
Starling
Eastern phoebe
Ash-throated flycatcher
Crested flycatcher
Arkansas kingbird
Red-shafted flicker
Yellow-shafted flicker
Golden-fronted
  woodpecker
Red-headed woodpecker
Downy woodpecker
Hairy woodpecker
Screech owl
Saw-whet owl
Barn owl
Sparrow hawk
Mourning dove
Wood duck
American goldeneye
Hooded merganser

Birds that will nest in gourds include the following: bluebirds, crested flycatcher, tree swallow (attracted to boxes also, in cranberry bogs, as they relish the cranberry moth), tufted titmouse, wrens (these like gourds the best), downy woodpecker, house sparrow, starling, white-breasted nuthatch, purple martin (the gourds should be placed in direct sunlight, fifteen feet above ground, and far enough apart so they won't knock together).

Winter Storm Shelters

In winter, when temperatures drop, roosting boxes in the garden can serve as warming houses for overwintering species.

Winter Supplementary Food

Severe winter temperatures can be fatal to birds, so it is essential to provide supplementary food for them when the pickings are slim, as a guarantee that they will remain in the vicinity. Placing beef suet, sunflower seeds, millet, and other grains in the orchard will provide birds with the fat and protein that they need.

REFERENCES

1. WALLACE BAILEY. 1968. *Birds of the Cape Cod National Seashore and Adjacent Areas.* National Park Service, U.S. Dept. of the Interior.

2. R. L. BEARD, et al. 1960. Handbook on biological control of plant pests. *Plants and Gardens* **16**(3), N.Y.: Brooklyn Botanic Garden, 97 pp.

3. M. M. BETTS. 1955. The food of titmice in oak woodlands. *Journal of Animal Ecology* **24**: 282.

4. CHARLES H. BUCKNER. 1965. The role of vertebrate predators in the biological control of forest insects. *Annual Review of Entomology* **11**: 449.

5. RICHARD DE GRAAF, and GRETCHEN M. WITMAN. 1979. *Trees, Shrubs and Vines for Attracting Birds.* Amherst: U. Mass. Press.

6. EDWARD H. FORBUSH. 1905. *Useful Birds and Their Protection.* Massachusetts State Board of Agriculture. Boston: Wright and Potter Printing Co., State Printers.

7. CATHERINE OSGOOD FOSTER. 1972. *The Organic Gardener.* N.Y.: Vintage Books.

8. RICHARD T. HOLMES, JOHN C. SCHULZ, and PHILIP NOTHNAGLE. 1979. Bird predation on forest insects: an enclosure experiment. *Science* **206**: 462

9. DAVID LACK. 1954. *The Natural Regulation of Animal Numbers.* London: Oxford Univ. Press.

10. GEORGE A. PETRIDES. 1972. *A Field Guide to Trees and Shrubs.* 2nd ed. Boston: Houghton Mifflin Co.

11. O. S. PETTINGILL. 1970. *Ornithology in Laboratory and Field.* Minneapolis: Burgess Publ. Co., 524 pp.

12. CHANDLER S. ROBBINS, et al.1966. *Birds of North America.* N.Y.: Western Publ. Co. Inc., Golden Press.

13. J. I. RODALE and staff. 1973 . *The Encyclopedia of Organic Gardening.* Emmaus, Pennsylvania: Rodale Books, Inc., 1,007 pp.

14. P. H. SCHWARTZ, JR. 1975. *Control of Insects on Deciduous Fruits and Tree Nuts in the Home Orchard—Without Insecticides.* USDA, Home and Garden Bulletin No. 211.

15. VIRGIL E. SCOTT, et al. 1977. *Cavity Nesting Birds of North American Forests.* Forest Service. USDA Agricultural Handbook 511, 112 pp.

16. M. E. SOLOMON. 1976. Predation of overwintering larvae of codling moth (*Cydia pomonella* L.) by birds. *Journal of Applied Ecology.* **13**: 341.

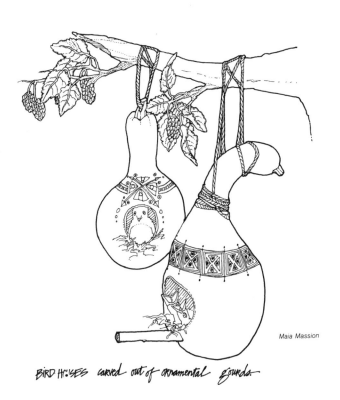

Maia Massion

BIRD HOUSES carved out of ornamental gourds

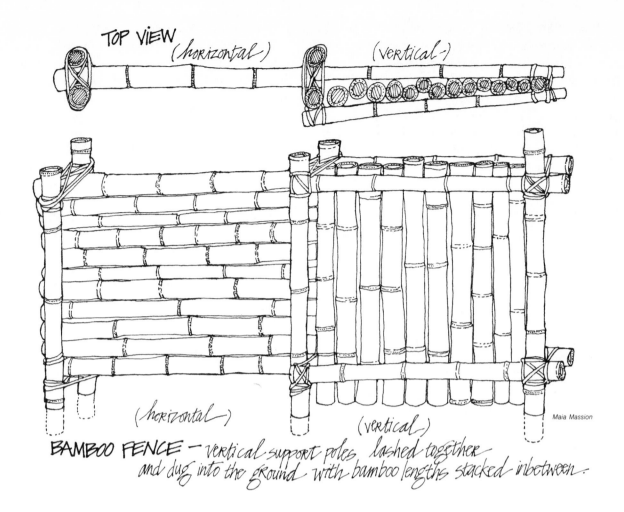

TOP VIEW (horizontal) (vertical)

(horizontal) (vertical)

Maia Massion

BAMBOO FENCE — vertical support poles, lashed together and dug into the ground, with bamboo lengths stacked inbetween.

Tree Crops for Structural Materials

Scott Stokoe

The cultivation of plants for structural materials is an important element of forest farming. Part of our research at New Alchemy is devoted to investigating and propagating perennial plants that yield construction materials. Throughout the long history of cultural development, indigenous wood products have been an important part of technical and material development. Wood and wood products were primary construction materials for many preindustrial civilizations. Wood for home construction, agricultural fencing, tools and equipment, plumbing, clothing, containers, fuel, artwork, manufacturing, and as a source of chemicals was utilized by virtually all societies, both in the East and the West. It was only with the advent of economically cheap (however, ecologically expensive) industrial materials that the reliance on wood waned. Abundant metal goods and fencing, ubiquitous plastic containers, connectors, and fibers, and a myriad of industrial byproducts all contributed to the decreased use of wood products. Yet wood is still used in many traditional ways. Part of our tree crops program is involved in collecting tree species with structural uses. By collecting and propagating such trees in our tree crops program, we expect to gain insight into their adaptability to the Cape Cod environment and their productivity and potential uses.

Bamboo

For centuries, throughout the tropical and subtropical areas of the East, bamboo has provided an abundant, naturally renewable source of building material, fabricating material, and food. It has been used in every aspect of shelter construction and furnishing, and serves as a durable, multi-purpose material. Bamboo has a vast number of uses in the home, from framing members, sheathing, and roofing to plumbing, furniture, and kitchen utensils. Further processing of bamboo stalks, known as culms, results in materials for baskets, screens, and fences. Bamboo is also a source of paper pulp. Bamboo culms for construction are generally the strongest when cut at the age of three years. In central China, bamboo is raised in agricultural forestry programs for both food and structural materials. When cut at the sprouting stage, bamboo stalks are edible. They generally require peeling and steaming. With fertilization and thinning, a mature stand of bamboo can produce one ton of food on a hectare of land (2.47 acres) in one year. This planting also provides 800 mature culms for structural use. Thus today as in the past, bamboo offers a dual crop from a single planting.

Such attractive characteristics have prompted us to incorporate bamboo into our tree crops research. In early 1980 we made an expedition to a USDA research station near Savannah, Georgia, and came home with a fine collection of 22 hardy species of oriental bamboo. We are observing their growth and development at the farm, and are beginning to investigate their uses. We plan a spring harvest of sprouts for eating and processing of mature culms for weaving into baskets and to use as structural members for hangings and supports. We are presently designing a bamboo condensation-gutter system for the Ark taking advantage of some of the larger stalks we retrieved from Georgia. We split some of the large-diameter culms and removed the internodal membranes to form long troughs to catch and direct condensation to collecting basins. Stakes can be cut from culms and used to support tomatoes, beans, or other vining plants. For larger supports, such as trellises, sections of bamboo can be lashed or nailed together. Baskets are made from split bamboo frames and weavers. A sharp knife, machete, or fixed blade can be used to split bamboo lengths into pliable weaving materials.

It is important to stress here that we are taking a necessary precaution with the bamboo. We realize that care must be taken when introducing a new or foreign plant into a bioregion. As completely as possible, the ecological ramifications must be considered. The scope of such considerations should span more than a single human generation. The ideal projected cultivating regime should remain ecologically benign if left unattended. Bamboo that survives in colder climates generally will spread rapidly, a characteristic that merits concern. Running bamboo is a self-propagating plant that expands its domain by sending out shoots horizontally underneath the ground. These shoots are capable of traveling long distances and are able to penetrate the smallest crevices or openings. Its strength can be witnessed by noting its ability to sprout up through asphalt driveways and through cracks in foundations and into buildings. Because of this, a part of our bamboo research is a search for an effective, simple root wall to contain the bamboo plantings. We are testing a standard three foot deep, poured concrete retaining wall and a buried vertical fiberglass sheet for containing the roots.

Traditional Coppicing Trees

There has been a comparable coevolution of civilization and an annual cropping of woody plants in Western as well as Eastern cultures. Of particular interest to us is the coppicing tradition of Western Europe. Coppicing is a form of perennial harvesting of wood. The word *coppice* comes from the Norman French word *couper*, "to cut," and denotes a form of selectively cropping from trees without taking the life of the tree as occurs in timbering. Coppicing is generally done by the ground-level cutting of certain trees capable of producing a new growth of shoots from the original root system the following year. In Western European cultures traditional coppice trees included alder (*Alnus* sp.), hazel (*Corylus* sp.), oak (*Quarcus* sp.), poplar, (*Populus* sp.) beech (*Fagus* sp.), and willows (*Salix* sp.). Each wood derived from these trees had a specific use. Hazel trees were cropped for hoops for baskets, twine for tying, and poles and stakes for agricultural structures and fences. A seven-year harvesting cycle offered optimally sized wood for bending and staking. Alder trees, which were harvested every nine years, produced a continual supply of rafter poles for roofs and other constructions and a durable water-resilient sole for clogs. Willow is one of the most diverse and versatile producers. It is a flexible, fast-growing wood, and particular varieties were grown for certain products. Some species were coppiced for weaving materials for baskets after one or two years growth. Others were grown larger for carving and for making household items; yet others were grown for firewood. A unique system evolved for natural, growing fences. A series of willow trees was planted in a row, in a suitable position for fence posts. After the trees matured, smaller upper branches were cut and laid in and out, weaving fashion, between the trunk posts. These branches formed the fencing material, and were used to build up and maintain the proper fence height. The living fence posts would sprout and grow new branches, which would be later used in turn for fencing. This practice of cutting trees off at some height above the ground is known as *pollarding* and in European cultures was generally used on trees in pastures. The wood was taken at a height above the reach of the cattle to allow the foliage to regenerate. Pollarding beech trees provided firewood on a 10–16 year cycle and oak trees on a 24 year cycle. Oak bark was a commercial source of tannin, a chemical used in the tanning of leather.

We have begun to culture some of these traditional coppicing trees. We have created a willow nursery to propagate large numbers of young wil-

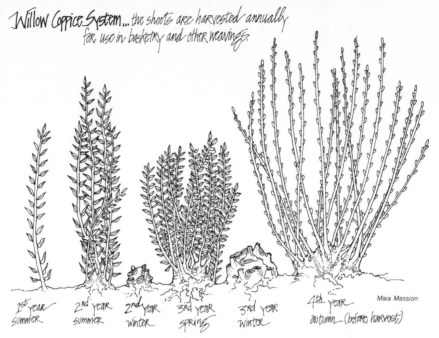

Willow Coppice System... the shoots are harvested annually for use in basketry and other weavings.

1st year summer   2nd year summer   2nd year winter   3rd year spring   3rd year winter   4th year autumn (before harvest)

Maia Massion

low trees. These are mainly European varieties that we selected for specific functions like weaving, growing natural fences, and firewood. So far these trees have demonstrated their adaptability and hardiness. From the basket-weaving variety come long, thin one-year-old cuttings that we can peel or store for later use. When the branches are soaked, the wood becomes very pliable, best for weaving baskets, boxes, and pots. We can use some of the early growth of branches for twine and tying. And we are also planning to establish a living fence with one of the willow varieties. Another project is a coppicing program for our eight-year-old hazel trees. We will be coppicing a few trees each year and using the wood for a poultry forage system in the form of a woven protective structure that allows poultry to feed on living plants without overharvesting. The hazel poles will also be used as stakes in the gardens for tomato and bean plants.

REFERENCES

1. Robert Austin, Dana Levy, and Koichiro Ueda. 1980. *Bamboo*. New York: John Weatherhill, Inc., 210 pp.

Inspirational photographic account of the beauty and functional elegance of bamboo. Information on cultivation and uses are covered, drawing from the tradition and craftsmanship of the East.

2. Herbert L. Edlin. 1973. *Woodland Crafts in Britain*. London: Country and Gardeners Book Society, 177 pp.

A fascinating compilation of the traditional British woodcrafting. Details and photographs explain skills, tools, techniques, and trees.

3. James L. Jones. 1979. Bamboo for northern gardens. *Horticulture*. LVII, 7: 24.

A basic back-yard explanation of the nature and use of bamboo in temperate climates.

Weaving With Willow

Maryann Fameli and Earle Barnhart

Basketry is one of the oldest arts. It has been practiced by nearly all cultures and can be traced back over six thousand years. Baskets remain integral to many cultures and they have many uses in agriculture and commerce. Baskets are strong, durable, and functional; their construction and use is an important example of human-scale technology. Though the skills of basketry have been nearly forgotten by Americans, there are still a few artisans who practice this craft.

Many pliable materials are used for weaving baskets. Before easy transportation overtook us, the basketmaker made use of such natural materials as sweet grass, rye straw, grapevines, bramble briars, willow rods, and bamboo. In the United States today, weaving materials are largely imported.

At New Alchemy we have begun to grow our own weaving materials. We have been able to obtain cuttings from the varieties of willows grown for the basketry trade in Europe. These "basket willows" include several species and varieties (*Salix purpurea, Salix viminalis*, and others). We are aware of no commercial sources of willow rods in the United States, yet experiments indicate that they can be grown easily. By propagating them we shall soon have our own willow crop and be able to supply ourselves and others.

Willow has characteristics that allow it to be used for many agricultural purposes, the most common being garden baskets for harvesting and storing vegetables. Sifting sieves, trays, and drying racks are other common willow implements. Our plan is to use willow for potting shrubs and small trees because it is long lasting and relatively weather resistant.

Aquaculture

As some of the aquaculture research at New Alchemy becomes ever more intricate and recondite, at least to a layperson (like me), it is well to keep in mind that its underlying rationale is quite simple and easily grasped—beyond the obvious fact that we like fish. What we are attempting to do in a hungry world is to develop ways of producing protein that are both economical and ecological. The first of the articles that follow illustrates this point most clearly. In growing and testing alternative fish foods, Bill McLarney and Jeff Parkin are trying both to reduce the costs of raising fish and to discover food sources for fish, such as earthworms, that produce adequate growth yet could not as readily be fed directly to people, as could soybeans or grains for example.

The articles on closed-system aquaculture, describing our research with solar-algae ponds, may seem more obscure, but the goals and ethics of the research are the same as those that prompt Bill's and Jeff's work. For readers who find themselves struggling with some of it, Donella Meadows, the brilliant systems analyst, best known for the "Limits to Growth" study, has written:

You already appreciate the innovative design of the NAI programs and the valuable scientific and practical lessons that are being learned. What I'd like to point out is the unique and useful process they have evolved for direct interaction between a simulation model of their aquaculture systems and management of those systems.

As you probably know, I teach modeling and policy design, and I've been involved with or an advisor to projects using computer simulation in many fields and for many purposes. I often lecture to my students about the ideal process of give-and-take between the model builder and the model user. But I have never seen that ideal achieved—except at New Alchemy. There John Wolfe has managed to keep his models transparent, directed to the actual problems of the group, and flexible to the changing knowledge and concerns of the group. He has transmitted a growing understanding of feedback structure and system dynamics to the others at NAI, while they were transmitting to him their knowledge, ideas, and hunches about aquaculture systems. The staff has been open to this new method of integrating their insights, constructively critical as the model evolved, and alert to discrepancies or consistencies between model predictions and real events. The result is a model that is an effective communication tool with which chemists, zoologists, and engineers can point out the connections among light penetration, ammonia concentration, and fish growth. New experiments can be designed and tested both in the model and in the solar ponds. And there is a tighter link between theory and practice than I have ever seen elsewhere; a fast cycling between the deductive and inductive phases of the scientific method. It really warms the heart of an old modeling proponent like me to see just once this powerful tool used with just the right mixture of skepticism and enthusiasm and with frequent checks back and forth between the model and the real world.

I'd also suggest that they document fully the experiments, not only the model, but also the process by which they have integrated the two. And I would hope that this description would be published in the scientific literature, to reach the vast audience that unfortunately has not caught on to New Alchemy's excellent self-produced publications.

Those of us who find ourselves a bit out of our depth in some of the details that Ron Zweig, David Engstrom, and John Wolfe write about and who lack Donella Meadows' expertise to analyze it, perhaps will be pleased to learn that much of the conclusion is hopeful, in the sense of providing food within the given paradigm and using computer simulation to test and improve ecological design.

N.J.T.

Ron Zweig

Alternatives to Commercial Feeds in the Diets of Cultured Fish

William O. McLarney and Jeffrey Parkin

One of the major impediments to the further development of aquaculture in North America is the cost of conventional fish feeds. A partial solution to the problem is to grow fish less dependent on high-quality animal protein than the channel catfish (*Ictalurus punctatus*) and rainbow trout (*Salmo gairdneri*) that dominate commercial aquaculture on this continent. At New Alchemy this approach is best exemplified by the cultivation of blue tilapia (*Sarotherodon aureus*) in algal "soups" where these filter feeders derive much of their nourishment from the phytoplankton (algae) that surround them. However, if satisfactory yields are to be obtained, we find it necessary to supplement the diets of even these fish with animal protein.

We also must acknowledge that for many potential fish culturists tilapia are not the best fish. In some places they are illegal. In the deep South, where they might survive the winter in the wild, we discourage their use for ecological reasons. In some places it may be impractical to provide water warm enough for tilapia culture. And some people simply prefer other types of fish.

Yet in attempting to identify North American counterparts of the tilapia, one comes up against a quirk of evolutionary fate. With very few exceptions (notably the buffalofishes, *Ictiobus* spp.), the North American filter feeding fishes are small or otherwise unsuited for cultivation as food animals. Some of our native panfishes, for example the bullheads and sunfishes, have less-exacting dietary requirements than channel cats or trout, but they are carnivores nonetheless. In fact, it is our experience that the term *herbivore*, as applied to fish, lacks precision. Most "herbivorous" fish, including tilapia, are opportunistic feeders, and benefit from

Table 1. APPROXIMATE COSTS ASSOCIATED WITH A 4 FT × 3 FT × 8 IN.
EARTHWORM BED.[a]

Initial stock (at maximum density) ....30 lbs @ $4/lb =	$120
Concrete block bed	35
50 lbs lime (powdered limestone)[b]	2
50 strips of litmus paper[b]	4
2 cubic ft peat moss (bedding additive)	3

[a]This cost can be reduced by half for each 3 months you allow the initial stock of worms to reproduce and grow under optimum conditions without harvesting. In fact, this is recommended not only for financial reasons but also to gain some working experience prior to relying on the worms.

[b]These qualities are sufficient for a minimum of 1 year.

inclusion of a certain amount of animal protein in their diets.

Faced with these facts, many beginning fish culturists give up searching for an alternative to commercial processed feeds. Others simply give up. There is no gainsaying the effectiveness of processed feeds in most situations. They offer a balanced diet and, when used properly, usually result in good growth, particularly of the species for which they are formulated. Of equal importance in their popularity is the convenience factor. It is just plain handy to feed a dry, packaged product that can be stored until needed, weighed precisely, and used without fuss or mess.

Over half of the production budget of a commercial catfish farmer goes for feed, and this is the rule throughout American aquaculture. The principal ingredients of commercial feeds include fish meal derived from marine fisheries, grains, and synthetic vitamins. In view of the costs of obtaining these materials (including the petroleum-related costs of fishing, agriculture, and vitamin manufacture) plus the costs of processing, packaging, and shipping, the price of fish feed is sure to rise.

Ecological reasoning also suggests the need for an alternative. The conversion of inexpensive fish into fish meal in order to make a feed for expensive fish may be economically justifiable in certain situations, but it is not going to result in cheap food or solve any human nutritional problems. In fact, as Israeli aquaculturist Gerald Schroeder points out, conventional North American aquaculture, using fish-meal-based feeds, results in a net loss of fish. Although alternative sources of animal protein might now prove impractical on a large scale, earthworms and flying nocturnal insects are already available to the small-scale fish producer.

Earthworms

The earthworm is the archetypical fish bait. Though its status as a favored food of freshwater fish is firmly entrenched in folklore, to our amazement we have not been able to find one paper in the scientific literature dealing with earthworms as a

component of cultured fish diets, despite the ease with which they can be cultured. (Some of their other attractive features for the small-scale, diversified food grower as well as details of earthworm culture are discussed in the fifth *Journal*.[1] Common sense and access to a good resource book[2] should enable any interested person to raise earthworms successfully.

In brief, earthworm culture entails providing housing, routine feeding and watering, and maintaining an approximately neutral pH and suitable temperatures in the "bedding" where the worms live. Most cultured earthworms exhibit greatest vitality at 16°–27° C, or 60°–80° F. Inexpensive housing may be provided by scrounging an old sink, bathtub, or refrigerator liner, or by constructing a plywood or concrete block container. Feeding should be done every two to four days (depending upon the type of feed) with household garbage, paper products, animal manures—almost anything that is biodegradable. It is said that the average American family of four generates enough biodegradable "wastes" to feed a 4 ft × 3 ft × 8 in. earthworm bed generously. Maintaining a pH near neutral is easier than it may sound; buffering is accomplished simply by dusting the feed with lime at feeding time. Table 1 summarizes the costs associated with starting up a 4 ft × 3 ft × 8 in. bed.

We have assumed one of the more expensive types of housing; this cost can be substantially reduced by using one of the options mentioned in the preceding paragraph. No costs are assigned to feed, bedding, or water; most readers will be able to supply the first two free and will be ridding themselves of a potential nuisance in the process.

No monetary value has been assigned to labor, but during a two-week period with five feedings (including watering and buffering the pH) and one pH sample, a generous estimate of the time invested in our system was 1½ hours, or six minutes

---

[1]Jeffrey Parkin. Some other friends of the earth. *Journal of the New Alchemists.* **5**: 69–72.

[2]Gaddie and Douglas. *Earthworms for Ecology and Profit.* Vol. I. Bookworm Pub. Co. 254 pp.

a day. To this should be added the labor of setting up a bed, which will vary quite widely according to the type of housing and bedding selected.

While harvesting earthworms will never be as convenient as pulling a handful of pelleted feed out of a bag, it is greatly facilitated by restricting food distribution to certain areas of the bed (e.g., along either side), which serves to concentrate the worms.

This practice also reduces the amount of bedding harvested with the worms. In weighing worms used as fish feed, some allowance must be made for the percentage bedding, which will remain relatively constant as long as the composition of the bedding and the method of feeding are not radically altered. So, after one or two samples, one can weigh the worms as they come out of the bed.

Unlike most artificial and many natural fish feeds, earthworms sink in water. A floating feed is essential in cage culture and desirable in most forms of fish culture, as it permits the culturist to observe feeding and prevents loss of feed in bottom sediments. We get around the problem with worms by using a special feeder, which consists of no more than a piece of perforated styrofoam on which the worms are spread. As worms instinctively flee the light, they pass down through the holes into the water and are eaten one by one. In addition to floating the worms, this system tends to equalize the distribution of worms among the fish. It also cleans the worms, since much of the bedding drops off as they slither down through the holes.

Bedding-free worms may be obtained simply by rinsing with water, but some allowance must be made for water clinging to the worms when they are weighed. A method that we prefer involves spreading the earthworms and bedding thinly over a sheet of burlap or other loosely woven material located under a light source and waiting 10–15 minutes. Seeking to avoid the light, the worms will crawl through the burlap and in the process be stripped of any bedding.

Flying Insects

There are many other organisms that may be cultured as fish food, but an alternative strategy is the capture of creatures that occur naturally in abundance. Among the most apparent sources are nocturnal flying insects, which may be captured with an ultraviolet light trap. Two types of traps are commercially available. The first, originally developed for pest control, employs an electrified grid that, with a flash of light and a crackle, electrocutes insects that light on it. On a "busy" night, the racket is considerable. A second, quieter type was developed specifically as a source of fish food. An impeller fan sucks in the attracted insects and blows them down through a duct into a collector bag or directly onto the water. (See Figure 1.)

We have used both types of bug traps, but prefer the fan type because it is quieter and safer. We are also not sure what "frying" does to the nutritional value of insects. Of the available impeller fan feeders we can recommend the Will-o-the-Wisp, made by Hedlunds of Medford, Wisconsin. We have operated several of these feeders for up to three years, with no maintenance beyond replacement of a bulb. As of spring 1980, the Will-o-the-Wisp sells for $140. It draws one kilowatt hour of electricity per 12 hours of operation, which at our present rate costs less than three cents a night.

The "bug season" on Cape Cod extends roughly from June through September. Even during this period nightly yields can vary dramatically, from literally nothing on a windy, wet evening to as much as 115 grams (g), or ¼ lb, on a warm, calm, dry night. Over the past seasons the average nightly yield of our feeders, equipped with collecting bags,

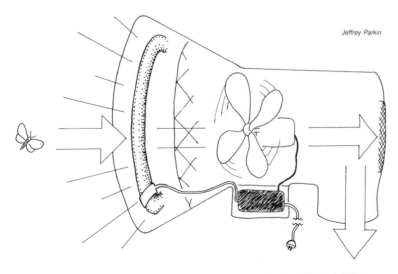

Jeffrey Parkin

Figure 1. Cross-sectional view of Hedlund-like bug light.

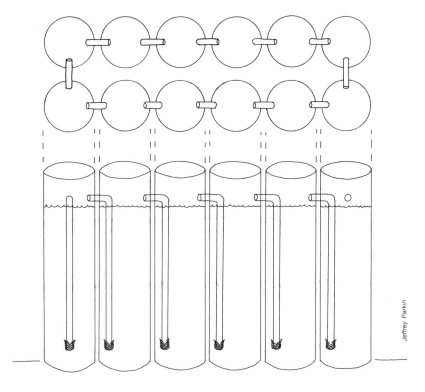

Figure 2. Recirculating aquaculture system. Tanks interconnected with airlift tubes.

Jeffrey Parkin

The Fish

The fish species used in this study were the mainstays of New Alchemy aquaculture, the blue tilapia and the yellow bullhead (*Ictalurus natalis*). Blue tilapia, an African cichlid, is the principal fish in New Alchemy's solar-algae pond research, and is described elsewhere in this as well as past *Journals*. Its natural adult diet consists mainly of plant proteins. When young, however, it tends to be a more opportunistic feeder. The yellow bullhead, a native North American catfish, is similarly predominant in our cage culture research. It is a bottom-feeding carnivore whose natural diet consists of small invertebrates. The hardiness of both these species makes them ideal experimental animals.

has been 16.2 g. It is our impression that, when feasible, the lights should be operated without bags, and catches will improve. Certainly better results will be obtained directly over water; not only is the field of the light less obstructed than in most terrestrial locations, but one can take advantage of insects emerging from the aquatic larval stage.

The kinds of insects captured do not vary nearly as much as their quantity. Apart from a very occasional lacewing, we do not get known beneficial insects as long as the lights are turned off at dawn. The bulk of our catches is composed of midges and moths; over water other types might predominate.

The Experimental Set-Up

The seven feeding trials described in this article were carried out in a recirculating system composed of twelve 60-gallon cylindrical tanks interconnected with airlift tubes (see Figure 2).

By recirculating the water we attempted to equalize any effects of water quality on growth. The siphon intakes were covered with nylon screens to eliminate the exchange of fish and/or food between tubes. Water flowed through the system at an average of 1.9 liters/minute (0.5 gallons/minute). As there was no purification system, 25% of the water was siphoned off from the bottom of each tube every month and replaced with tap water. Light was provided 14 hours/day by two overhead fluorescent fixtures. The bottom 18 inches of the tubes was wrapped with black plastic to give the bullheads a refuge with some semblance of "cover."

Diets Tested

The experimental diets were made up of three components in varying percentages: mixed nocturnal flying insects, as captured by a Will-o-the-Wisp bug light fish feeder; cultured earthworms (*Eisenia foetida*); and the commercial feed Purina Trout Chow® (henceforth referred to as PTC). The purpose was to determine what portion, if any, of a standard PTC diet could be replaced by either of the two fresh feeds without loss of growth, and if a small fresh dietary supplement added to a normal PTC feeding regime could result in increased growth. Because of the size of our fish and the pellet size of feed available, we ground the PTC and used that portion retained by a 1.0 millimeter (mm) sieve. The earthworms also had to be chopped, into 2–4 mm lengths, to make them acceptable to the fish and to ensure even distribution of this feed among the individual fish. Insects were weighed and fed fresh, as captured, except that some of the largest moths were removed.

All feeding was done while the lights were on. At least four hours separated feeding of one component of a mixed diet from another, so that neither feed was wasted as a result of preference by the fish for one or another.

In each of the trials, one of four diets was fed to three tanks of fish. In the tilapia trials there were eight individual fish per tank, fin clipped so that they could be individually weighed. Twenty unmarked bullheads were kept in each tank and weighed as a group. After weighing, all fish were returned to their tanks, except following Trial 6, when all the bullheads were randomly redistributed among the tanks. No group of three tanks received the same diet in two consecutive trials.

Results: Tilapia

Two replicate trials were conducted with tilapia. Water temperatures over Trials 1 and 2 ranged from 21.9°–23.3° C (71.5°–74.0° F), and 23.0°–24.4° C (73.5°–76.0° F), respectively.

Diurnal fluctuations in temperature never exceeded 0.3° C (1.0° F). Table 2 and Figure 3 summarize the results of these two trials.

Although the results obtained with diet B in Trial 1 are inconsistent with the rest of the data, Trials 1 and 2 suggest that with increased replacement of PTC by earthworms, the growth rate of

Table 2. FEEDING TRIALS 1 AND 2 WITH TILAPIA.

Trial No.		Diets %[a] PTC	%[a] Worms	%[a] Bugs	Mean Initial Wt. (g/fish)	Mean Gain (g/fish)	% Gain[b]	F[c]	Significance[c]
1	A	3.0	0	—	3.9	1.5	38.6		
	B	3.0	0.5	—	4.6	1.2	26.3	6.2	<97.5%
	C	2.5	0.5	—	4.1	1.5	36.6		
	D	1.5	1.5	—	4.5	1.1	23.7		
2	A	3.0	0	—	5.6	2.0	35.2		
	B	3.0	0.5	—	5.4	1.8	34.2	15.8	<99.5%
	C	2.5	0.5	—	5.8	1.7	29.2		
	D	1.5	1.5	—	5.6	1.2	21.9		

[a]Percent of total fishes' body weight fed daily (applies throughout tables).

[b]Based upon total weights, not the listed means (applies throughout tables).

[c]The two columns at the right in Tables 2–5 are the results of a statistical test called *analysis of variance*. This numerical manipulation basically takes into account variations (in growth rates) between the fish in individual tanks relative to variations between fish in tanks grouped by different diets; this is reflected in the F values. In so doing, one can get some measure of the probability that the overall observed results occurred as an outcome of the experiment and not by chance. The percentages in the Significance columns depict this probability. By statistical convention (and a conservative lot they are), any degree of significance less than 90% is considered chancy and of no statistical value.

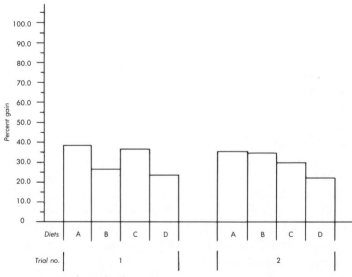

Figure 3. Results of tilapia feeding trials, nos. 1 and 2.

Table 3. FEEDING TRIALS 3 AND 4 WITH YELLOW BULLHEADS.

Trial No.		Diet % PTC	% Worms	% Bugs	Mean Initial Wt. (g/fish)	Mean Gain (g/fish)	% Gain	F	Significance
3	E	3.0	0	—	0.76	0.42	54.7		
	F	3.0	0.5	—	0.79	0.51	64.3		
	G	2.5	0.5	—	0.80	0.47	58.4	1.9	>90.0%
	H	1.5	1.5	—	0.76	0.40	52.5		
4	E	3.0	0	—	1.2	0.40	34.4		
	F	3.0	0.5	—	1.2	0.61	52.1		
	G	2.5	0.5	—	1.3	0.54	41.8	11.3	<99.5%
	H	1.5	1.5	—	1.3	0.44	34.8		

tilapia was reduced. Nor did the addition of a small percentage of worms to a 3% PTC diet improve the growth rate.

In a previous experiment at New Alchemy in which worms were fed to blue tilapia, similar amounts of earthworms were effective in increasing growth over that obtained with a base diet of roasted soy meal and rolled oats fed at the rate of percent of body weight per day.[3] Although the fish in this earlier experiment, unlike those in the current trials, were maintained in an algal "soup," their base diet contained no animal protein.

Results: Bullheads

Trials 3 through 7 were conducted with yellow bullheads and yielded more encouraging results than the tilapia trials. Trials 3 and 4 formed a pair of replicates, as did Trials 5 and 6. Trial 7 was not replicated.

During Trials 3 and 4 water temperatures ranged from 22.2°–23.3° C (72.0°–74.0° F) and 21.7°–25.6° C (71.0°–78.0° F) respectively. Diurnal fluctuations in temperature did not exceed 0.3° C (1.0° F). The experimental diets used in these trials were the same as those used with tilapia in Trials 1 and 2.

The fact that the growth rates are greater in Trial 3 than in Trial 4 can be attributed to better water quality in Trial 3, to the early effect of increased feed rations (these fish had been kept at subsistence levels prior to Trial 3), and to the slightly smaller size of the test fish in Trial 3.

Table 3 and Figure 4 summarize the data from these two trials.

Unlike tilapia, yellow bullheads do appear to derive significant nutritional benefits from earthworms either as a supplement to a normal PTC diet, or as a substitute for PTC at least up to 50%. Since in both Trials 3 and 4 the growth rate for diets E (PTC with no supplement) and H (half PTC and

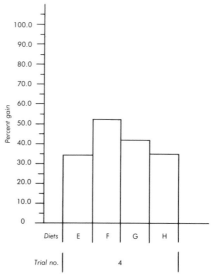

Figure 4. Results of yellow bullhead feeding trial no. 4. (Trial 3 not shown as the significance was less than 90%.)

half worms) were nearly identical, while supplementation with worms or substitution with a lower proportion of worms produced improved growth, it is possible that 50% represents the highest proportion of worms that can be substituted for PTC without adversely affecting growth. Higher proportions, or perhaps an all-earthworm diet, will be tested in future trials.

It is instructive to look at the feed conversion[4] in Trial 4. Commercial aquaculturists, using dry feeds, consider anything less than 2.0 respectable and aim to hit close to 1.0. In Trial 4, both diets E and H resulted in feed conversions of approximately 1.0. The small additions of earthworms in diets F and G produced conversions of 0.81 and 0.87 re-

---

[3]William O. McLarney and Jeffrey Parkin. Cage culture. *Journal of the New Alchemists.* **6**: 83–88.

---

[4]Feed conversion is the ratio of the amount of feed fed to the gain in weight of the animal. Theoretically, it is impossible to achieve a conversion less than 1.0, since that would indicate that output (growth) exceeded input (feed). However, when one is using an essentially dry feed, such as most commercial feeds, and measuring wet weight of fish, such figures are possible since the weight of fish includes the water in fish tissue. In almost all outdoor situations there is also some input of "natural" feed, which causes the conversion ratio of the feed supplied by the aquaculturist to appear lower than it really is. Input of "natural" feeds is virtually nil in indoor experiments.

Table 4. FEEDING TRIALS 5 AND 6 WITH YELLOW BULLHEADS.

Trial No.		Diet			Mean Initial Wt. (g/fish)	Mean Gain (g/fish)	% Gain	F	Significance
		% PTC	% Worms	% Bugs					
5	I	3.0	0	0	1.7	0.67	39.0		
	J	3.0	0	1.0	1.5	1.6	100.8	504.2	<99.5%
	K	2.0	0	1.0	1.8	1.6	84.7		
	L	2.0	1.0	0	1.8	0.89	49.8		
6	I	3.0	0	0	3.0	1.1	34.7		
	J	3.0	0	1.0	2.7	1.7	64.1	15.0	<99.5%
	K	2.0	0	1.0	2.9	1.5	50.4		
	L	2.0	1.0	0	2.9	1.2	42.1		

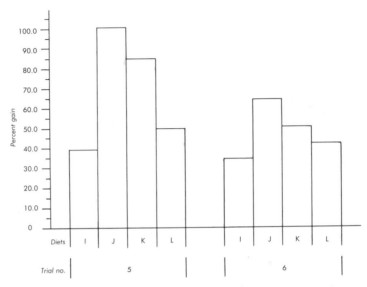

Figure 5. Results of yellow bullhead feeding trials, nos. 5 and 6.

spectively (based on dry weight of worms). It is evident that the effect of the earthworms cannot be accounted for in terms of their protein content alone. The addition of worms was, through some mechanism, improving the efficiency with which the fish were utilizing their feed. A similar synergistic effect was observed in feeding Chironomid midge larvae to tilapia.[5]

Replicate feeding Trials 5 and 6, incorporating flying insects as well as earthworms, were conducted with the same group of yellow bullheads. The water temperature ranges were 23.3°–25.6° C (74.0°–78.0° F) over Trial 5, and 21.1°–24.4° C (70.0°–76.0° F) over Trial 6. Diurnal temperature fluctuations did not exceed 0.5° C (2.0° F). Table 4 and Figure 5 summarize the information from these two trials.

There are a few published studies dealing with the use of ultraviolet bug lights in fish culture,[6] but to our knowledge these two feeding trials are

the first in which measured amounts of insects captured by this means were fed to fish and compared with other feeds. It may surprise some readers that bullheads, which are not surface feeders in nature, would feed on flying insects, which float. However, in these trials and in other situations at New Alchemy, captive yellow bullheads learned to accept this food the first time it was presented.

As is obvious from Table 4 and Figure 5, Trials 5 and 6 resulted in significant and parallel trends. The control diet plus a supplement of captured insects (diet J) yielded by far the greatest growth. The partial substitution of insects for the control diet resulted in the next highest growth (diet K). When earthworms were substituted in the same proportion as the insects, resultant growth was less, but it was still significantly greater than for the control diet. The control diet (I) of PTC again produced the lowest growth, albeit good in its own right. There was once more an overall reduction in the growth rates (percent gains) between these first and second replicate trials. Greater initial size at the start of Trial 6 and a 0.8° C (3° F) temperature drop may have contributed to this.

[5]William O. McLarney, Joseph S. Levine, and Marcus M. Sherman. Midge culture. *Journal of the New Alchemists.* **3:**80-84.

[6]Heidinger, 1971; Newton and Merkowsky, 1976.

Table 5. FEEDING TRIAL 7 WITH YELLOW BULLHEADS.

Trial No.		Diet			Mean Initial Wt. (g/fish)	Mean Gain (g/fish)	% Gain	F	Significance
		% PTC	% Worms	% Bugs					
7	M	4.0	0	—	4.0	1.9	47.4		
	Nª	4.0	0.5	—	4.1	2.2	54.8	13.8	<99.5%
	O	3.0	0.5	—	3.8	2.0	51.3		
	P	3.0	1.0	—	3.6	1.9	53.0		

ªThe three tanks receiving this diet ranked first, second, and twelfth (last) overall. The tank that ranked twelfth (35.4% weight gain) appeared to be an anomaly and we have thus omitted it from the data presented here.

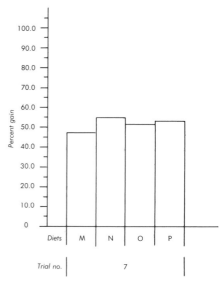

Figure 6. Results of yellow bullhead feeding trial no. 7.

Once again feed conversion was affected by supplementation or substitution of a portion of the PTC diet with fresh feeds. The conversion for diet I (all PTC) was 1.0; for the earthworm-substituted diet (L) it was 0.86, and the insect supplemented or substituted diets (J and K) produced conversions of 0.75 and 0.71 respectively.

Further trials with flying insects were not possible because of the end of our "bug season," but one more earthworm trial (Trial 7) was carried out. The purpose of this trial was to investigate the feasibility of further increasing the basic PTC ration to 4.0% of total body weight daily, with or without supplementation, and to compare such diets with supplemented diets based on the normal feeding rate of 3.0%. Table 5 and Figure 6 summarize the results of this trial.

The results indicate that even at higher rates of feeding, supplementation with worms increased the growth rate of yellow bullheads, and that diets O and P (3.0% PTC supplemented with 0.5% and 1.0% worms, respectively) were superior to a 4% daily feeding of PTC alone. Conversions for diets M through P were, respectively, 1.0, 0.98, 0.82, and 0.90, once again indicating that incorporation of earthworms in the diet increased the efficiency of utilization of other food.

Discussion

The ultimate goal of this sort of research is to enable aquaculturists to replace some or all of the costly and ecologically inappropriate fish-meal-based feeds with cheaper and more appropriate sources of protein. The studies reported here also suggest that the rate of growth and efficiency of feed utilization by fish receiving a full portion of a fish-meal-based commercial diet could be increased by supplementation with fresh feeds. This effect could be especially significant in the North, where getting a head start on the growing season can make the difference between a crop of "harvestable" or "subharvestable" fish in the fall.

Our work suggests that both earthworms and mixed flying insects could be used as substitutes or supplements for fish meal. Determining the economic feasibility of the two feeds and comparing them to other feeds in that respect is difficult. As consideration of Trials 1 and 2 reported here and the earlier work with blue tilapia and earthworms[7] shows, the appropriateness of a fresh feed supplement cannot be discussed apart from consideration of the base diet. Nor will the conclusions reached necessarily be the same for different species, size groups, or geographic regions. The most that can be done here is to discuss the economics of our operation.

Earthworms are the more complicated of the two feed sources to consider in economic terms. Although in our trials they were less valuable than insects as a supplement or substitute for commercial feed, they potentially confer three additional economic benefits. The first is the efficient disposal of biodegradable wastes, which leads directly to the second, provision of a superior potting soil and/or soil amendment. These benefits may be particularly significant in urban settings where space is limiting or in a highly diversified subsistence agriculture situation.

[7]William O. McLarney and Jeffrey Parkin. Cage culture. *Journal of the New Alchemists.* **6**: 83–88.

Ron Zweig

There is also the possibility of managing earthworms as a cash crop. (Earthworm casts or fecal matter are also incorporated into some of the best and most expensive commercial potting mixes.) Under optimal conditions, earthworm populations double every three to four months. In the case of the worm bed described earlier, this translates into 30 lb of worms every three to four months, or at least 90 lb of worms per year. With some luck in retailing, the costs listed in Table 1 could be covered within the first year, with worms to spare for the fish. From then on, the cost of worms would be minimal. Making back the costs solely through feeding the worms to fish and cutting back on commercial feed would require a long time.

At the present time, earthworm culture solely as a fish feed probably cannot be economically justified. (Much less can one justify the purchase of worms, at the current price of $4/lb, wet weight, compared to commercial fish feeds at 30 cents/lb, dry weight.) However, if worms are treated as a cash crop and/or if one quantifies the value of

biodegradable waste disposal and agricultural use of the resulting product, worm culture can often be justified. As the price of commercial fish feeds increases, the economic incentive to grow earthworms as a fish feed seems destined to increase, and eventually earthworm culture for that purpose alone may be justifiable.

The economics of "bug light" fish feeders are comparatively straightforward. Amortizing the total materials cost ($140 for a Will-o-the-Wisp plus $36 for two replacement bulbs) over a 10-year period yields an annual cost of $17.60. Added to this is a season's worth of electricity, amounting to about $3.40 at current rates, netting a total cost of $21 for a year. Our total catch averaged over the past two seasons was 1,820 g (4.01 lb) per season. Taking into account that these bugs are 75% water, the corresponding dry weight is 455 g (1.0 lb).

On that basis it would be difficult to justify economically the use of such a feeder under our conditions. However, Cape Cod is not prime "bug country," and even here we are sure we would do much better if our lights were placed directly over an outdoor fish culture system. More studies of the economic feasibility of bug-light feeders need to be made. The earliest such study indicated that they were economically feasible in rearing bluegills (*Lepomis macrochirus*) in cages in southern Illinois.[8] However, a later study did not indicate positive results in open pond culture of fingerling channel catfish in Arkansas.[9]

We attempted to find out what an average nightly catch might be in the Midwest or South, where hot, sultry summer nights are the rule, but the only other data we could obtain came from Vermont. Barry Pierce of Goddard College reports approximately twice our average nightly catch, though their bug season is a month shorter. Contributing to their catches are the bug light's focus on the college's compost pile and a one-week mayfly "bloom" (during which they get well in excess of 100 g, wet weight, per night).

The studies reported here, and earlier feeding trials at New Alchemy, represent only a tiny fraction of the possibilities that could be explored. We feel that the most important aspect of our work is to affirm that, at least for the small-scale grower, there are options to total dependence on fish-meal-based commercial feeds.

[8]Heidinger, 1971.
[9]Newton and Merkowsky, 1976.

Hilde Maingay

Defining and Defying Limits to Solar-Algae Pond Fish Culture

David Engstrom, John Wolfe, and Ron Zweig

After several years of careful experiments monitoring fish growth in solar-algae ponds, it began to seem as though we were coming up against a ceiling. We could grow fish rapidly for short periods of time, or slowly for long periods of time, but we could not achieve efficient fish growth past a surprisingly consistent limit of food introduced into the pond. Beyond this point, water-chemistry conditions made it too difficult to grow even the hardy tilapia very efficiently or rapidly. To regain good growth, we would have had to drain the pond, refill it with fresh water, reintroduce the fish.

The first section of this article delineates this limit to fish growth with our standard solar-algae pond methods. The second section describes a component we have added recently to some of our solar-algae ponds that circumvents the old limit.

This addition is a settling tank next to a series of connected solar-algae ponds. This modification doubles the amount of food we can introduce, and likewise the amount of fish growth we can expect.

Part 1: Growth Efficiencies Under Good Water Quality for All Experiments to Date

A summary of the feeding rates and growth relationships from selected solar-algae ponds from the summers of 1978 and 1979 illustrates our best tilapia fish growth (Table 1). In these experimental periods, during which water quality remained good, one gram of dry trout chow pellets led to approximately one gram of wet weight fish growth. Since the trout chow contains 8% nitrogen (by weight) and wet weight fish contains 4% nitrogen, the data indicates that the tilapia growth incor-

Table 1. FEEDING AND GROWTH DATA FOR SELECTED PONDS WITH GOOD WATER QUALITY.[1,2]

Ponds(s)	Year	NSF Report No. Experiment No.	Length of Good Water Quality (Weeks)	Total Food Fed (G)	Total Nitrogen Fed (G)	Feeding Rate, (G food/Day)	Growth Rate, (G/Day)	Growth Rate, (1b/Yr)	Total Growth, (G)	Nitrogen Assimilation Efficiency (%)	Unassimilated Food (G)
H	1978	3,2	3	2,210	172	105	75	60	1,575	44	1,238
L	1979	4,1	5	2,485	194	71	71	57	2,485	49	1,267
L	1978	3,2	6	2,562	200	61	68	50	2,856	48	1,485
J	1978	3,2	8	5,147[a]	196	92	44	35	2,464	49	2,514
GHIJ	1979	4,3c	8	2,520	197	45	45	35	2,520	53	1,184
K	1979	4,1	9	2,900	226	46	43	35	2,709	47	1,537
Selected averages					198				2,435	48	

[a]Rabbit feed (all others are trout chow).

porated roughly half of the nitrogen in the fish feed. Nitrogen is an interesting element to track because it is roughly proportional to protein content in feeds and fish biomass (though beware: different proteins contain different proportions of nitrogen, and different plants and animals contain different mixes of proteins) and because unassimilated nitrogen can be transformed into ammonia and nitrite, both toxic to fish. In all cases, a nitrogen input limit was reached, bringing an end to good water quality and rapid fish growth. We could stock a pond with between 20 and 400 fish, with an average size of 10–300 g per fish, at a density of 1–6 kilograms (kg) total per pond, and with good water quality could expect the same assimilation efficiency and growth. Once the limit of the pond to absorb the unassimilated feed was reached, growth declined. The trout feed data show the limit to be about 2½ kg of feed containing about 200 grams of nitrogen.

We also experimented with rabbit feed (see Table 1, Pond J, 1978). Rabbit feed contains half as much nitrogen and protein as trout chow, but costs one-third the price. The data suggest that the *nitrogen* input limit is nearly equal to trout chow. However, one must feed twice as much rabbit feed to put in the same amount of nitrogen. Since the fish are satiated by bulk of food (and not the nitrogen content), one cannot feed rabbit chow at twice the rate of trout chow. Even though the ultimate nitrogen input limits are nearly the same, the *rate* of nitrogen input must be lower with rabbit feed, and therefore the growth rates with rabbit feed must also be slower. Additionally, the ultimate nitrogen limit may also be lower for rabbit feed than with trout chow (Pond J had better long-term growth than two other replicate ponds with only beginning and end fish weights). This would be expected, since nitrogen in the feed is not the only contributor to declining water quality. The oxidation of carbonaceous materials also stresses the aquaculture system, lowering oxygen and pH levels and increasing carbon dioxide concentration.

Good water quality did not last long in Pond H in 1978 (three weeks) because the feeding rate quickly exceeded the ability of the ecosystem to absorb the excess nitrogen. At slower feeding rates, bacterial transformation and algal assimilation appeared to maintain acceptable water quality for extended growth periods. The dynamics are very complex, with the algae preventing nitrogen from appearing in soluble form while keeping only a two-to-three-day supply of excess nitrogen in the living algae biomass at one time. The great majority of nitrogen accumulates in floating and sedimented dead algal cells and fish feces, and the release of nitrogen back into solution (as toxic ammonia) depends heavily on bacterial activity.

For all ponds except Pond H (Table 1), breakdown in the ecosystem's ability to absorb unassimilated feed occurred when total nitrogen put into the system had reached about 200 g. At this point fish growth in all ponds was about 2.4 kg regardless of the total growing time.

Certain peculiarities of algal behavior from summer 1978, data now seem more understandable. All three closely monitored ponds exhibited strong declines in algal density from September 9 to 11, coinciding with a loss of water quality for Pond L but not for Pond J (Pond H had already experienced an influx of toxic nitrite two weeks earlier). Here Pond L had reached "critical" total nitrogen while Pond J reached that level two weeks later.

Within the limits of the 10%–20% weekly water replacement strategy practiced with all of these ponds, the recycling of nitrogen and suspended detritus may reach a "critical" level. Accumulated nitrogen load may combine with algae crashes to determine the time when water quality declines sharply. To overcome this over an entire year, one would have to transfer the fish to fresh water each time 200 g of feed nitrogen had entered the pond.

It is important to point out that although fish growth almost always drops off after a nitrogen input of 200 g, a period of recovery sometimes follows in which fish growth resumes at a fairly rapid rate. In 1978, Pond H demonstrated this phenomenon. The recovery is probably due to increased food availability: teeming bacteria populations foster a bloom of edible high-protein protozoans.[1] Nitrogen assimilation efficiencies of recovered ponds, however, never exceeded about 30%.

With the drain and restart strategy, feeding rate and growth time can be chosen, keeping in mind the labor of restarting a pond. One can choose a five-to-nine-week growth period and apportion the 2.5 kg of food (equivalent to 200 g nitrogen) accordingly to achieve the final 2.4 kg of fish. Obviously, shorter growth periods are desired for higher continual fish production.

These growth statistics are based on experiments during summer months. It now seems reasonable to project short-term growth periods over a six-month growing season. The ponds would yield 10 kg of fish growth over this time if restarted every six weeks. Since the fish are capable of growing faster, other methods of water purification to remove nitrogen and stimulate algal activity seem appropriate.

Part 2. Methods of Extending the Period of Good Water Quality

There exist many biologically-sound water purification methods that can propel solar-algae pond fish culture beyond the food input limit described here. Many of these methods can be combined in one solar aquaculture system. Six approaches that we are presently experimenting with are as follows:

1. Enhanced Algal Assimilation of Ammonia, Phosphate, and Carbon Dioxide

Rapid algal assimilation of fish toxins occurs with strong algae growth. The article in this journal, "Modeling Algal Growth and Decline in Solar-Algae Ponds" argues that increasing the settling rate of suspended midwater particulates enhances algal growth and nutrient assimilation.

2. Enhanced Detrital Removal by Incorporating Auxiliary Settling Tank Components

This method removes organic material before it can decompose. Otherwise, the decomposition process will release toxic ammonia and carbon dioxide, and will consume beneficial oxygen. One example of this approach is described in Part 2 of this article.

3. Hydroponic Vegetable Culture (Nitrogen and Phosphorus Removal)

Hydroponic filters attached to solar-algae ponds can simultaneously purify water and produce vegetables. The sole source of nitrogen and phosphorus for the plants is the ammonia, nitrate, and phosphate dissolved in the water column. This design directly incorporates the wastes of one process as a resource for another food-production unit, and may prove critical for high-yield winter greenhouse aquaculture.

4. Nitrifying Bacterial Filter (Transforms Toxic Ammonia and Nitrate to Relatively Benign Nitrate)

Nitrifying bacteria within the solar-algae ponds presently oxidize toxic ammonia into nitrite and finally into benign nitrate. However, the bacterial populations may be severely limited by the amount of stable surface area upon which to form colonies. An attached baterial filter with the correct flow-through rate may prove useful in avoiding high ammonia and nitrite concentrations by speeding up the nitrification process.[2]

5. Increased Exchange of Nutrient-Laden Water with Fresh Water

This approach "opens" the essentially closed solar-algae ponds researched to date. If the water is replaced in a slow continuous flow, the shock to the ecosystem of suddenly siphoning off and replacing a major fraction of the water column could be avoided. The removed water should be shunted to agriculture, since it is a fertile irrigant. Rapid water replacement should be avoided during winter operation unless the cold incoming water is pumped through a solar collector.

6. Bacterial Denitrification (Anaerobic Transformation of Nitrate into Nitrite and in Turn into Nitrogen Gas)

Denitrification has intentionally not been designed into solar aquaculture because it represents a direct loss of a nutrient source that could be further used in agriculture. However, recent analysis suggests that in the summer under heavy feeding rates, a significant portion of nitrogen in the solar-algae ponds appears to be unaccountably lost, and the most likely removal process is denitrification. Whether denitrification accounts for a predominant loss of nitrogen, and whether this should be

---

[1]Schroeder, 1979. Reference 3.

[2]For filter sizing and flow rate determination, see Wheaton, 1977. Reference 4.

FIGURE 1
SOLAR ALGAE POND RECIRCULATING RIVER

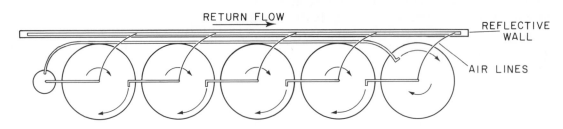

TOP VIEW

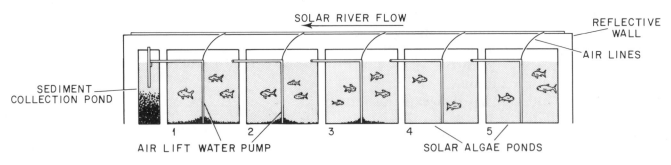

SIDE VIEW FROM SOUTH

├── 5' ──┤

enhanced for better water quality or discouraged on the basis of lost fertilizer value remains to be answered.

The next section reports the success of an early version of the second water purification approach (enhanced detrital removal) discussed above.

Part 3: A Recirculating Outdoor Solar River with a Settling Pond

Polyculture Feeding Trials in Linked Single-Skin Solar-Algae Ponds in Nonreflective Area (June 16 to October 28, 1979)

The solar river comprised five single-skin solar-algae ponds coupled to a settling tank roughly 5 ft tall, 18 in. in diameter, holding 66 gallons. (Ref. 5 describes another version of a solar river for trout culture). Figure 1 illustrates the arrangement. An airlift tube bubbled water up from the bottom center of each pond to an overflow at the edge of the next tank. The tube outlet faced clockwise to generate a mild circular flow in each tank, which tended to settle out the detritus at the centers of the ponds. After leaving Pond 1 and before re-entering Pond 5, water passed through the 66 gallon settling tank. The effluent from Pond 1 was piped to a point near the bottom of the settling tank to encourage the sedimentation of heavier detritus.

The total volume of the settling tank was drained once a day five times each week. This equals 10% of each pond's volume per week, much less than draining rates for the previous experiments. We hoped that this system would favor detrital removal while actually changing relatively low volumes of the water. This method required much less labor than siphon drain-down techniques.

We stocked the solar river ponds with high densities of tilapia (Sarotheradon aureus) and common carp (Cyprinus carpio). The carp were added 3½ weeks after the tilapia. Ponds 1 and 2 were each stocked with 600 tilapia, while Ponds 3, 4, and 5 were each stocked with 600 tilapia and 300 carp.

After shipping mortality of both species had subsided, heavy feeding was initiated with up to 150 g of trout food daily. Within two weeks, this high feeding rate led to substantial ammonia concentrations. Because the water had a high pH, much of this ammonia existed in its toxic unionized form. Feeding was then reduced until the ammonia disappeared. Water analysis showed that circulation was fast enough to create similar water quality conditions in all ponds.

Growth relationships for the solar river are summarized in Table 2. Final fish weights showed little growth for the carp species in all three polyculture ponds. The poor performance by the carp reinforces the results of earlier carp monoculture and

Table 2. SUMMARY OF GROWTH DATA FOR OUTDOOR SOLAR RIVER EXPERIMENT 4.

Total Food Input:	5,025 g trout food per pond.
Tilapia Growth Period:	6/16-9/28.
Carp Growth Period:	7/09-9/28.

Variable	Pond 1	Pond 2	Pond 3	Pond 4	Pond 5
Tilapia:					
Initial population	600	600	600	600	600
Initial average weight	2.4 g	2.4 g	2.4 g	2.4 g	2.4 g
Final population[a]	361	416	382	399	366
Final average weight	10.9 g	11.3 g	11.9 g	11.3 g	10.9 g
Common Carp:					
Initial population	0	0	300	300	300
Initial average weight			3.0 g	3.0 g	3.0 g
Final population[a]	0	0	95	74	110
Final average weight			7.0 g	5.0 g	5.0 g
Total Growth rate (g/day)	49.6	50.7	48.9	45.3	40.3
Total Growth rate (lb/yr)	39.9	40.9	39.4	36.5	32.0
Nitrogen assimilation Efficiency (%)	39	40	39	36	32

[a]The one-third mortality of tilapia and the two-thirds mortality of carp occurred soon after stocking and was probably due to stress during shipping.

carp/tilapia polyculture experiments in solar-algae ponds.[3] Nitrogen assimilation efficiencies represent primarily nitrogen assimilation by tilapia. The efficiencies of 32% and 40%, lower than the 44.50% efficiencies reported in Table 1, are expected on the basis of an early increase in ammonia concentration as well as the poor assimilation of food by the carp. Growth rates, however, gave a projected respectable yield of 14.7–18.5 kg per pond annually.

The method of draining small amounts of water from an auxiliary settling tank proved quite successful when the results were compared with the growth relationships found with 20% siphoning (Table 1). From Table 1, a decline in fish assimilation efficiency because of accrual of excess nitrogen would have been predicted at about six weeks. Instead, good water chemistry conditions and rapid growth continued for 20 weeks. Total food input to each pond was 5,025 g trout food, twice the feeding limit found in the ponds siphoned 20% weekly.

In conclusion, the settling tank system appears capable of selectively removing substantial quantities of detrital material containing nitrogen. Since the design is relatively easy to construct and its function is very effective, it holds great promise as one approach to enhancing solar-algae pond productivity.

[3]Reference 1.

ACKNOWLEDGMENTS

We are indebted to Carl Baum, Barbara Chase, Chris Copeland, Al Doolittle, Laurie Fulton, Michael Greene, and Paul Silverstein for their assistance collecting data used in this article.

REFERENCES

1. ANGEVIRE, R., DOOLITTLE, A., ENGSTROM, D., TODD, J., WOLFE, J., ZWEIG, R. 1979. Assessment of a semiclosed, renewably resource-based aquaculture system. Progress Report 3 to the Office of Problem Analysis, Applied Science and Research Applications, National Science Foundation.

2. ———. Progress Report 4.

3. GERALD L. SCHROEDER. 1979. Fish farming in manure-loaded ponds. Available from the author: Agricultural Research Organization, Fish and Aquaculture Research Station, Dor, Israel.

4. FREDERICK WHEATON. 1977. Aquacultural Engineering. N.Y.: John Wiley and Sons.

5. KENNETH T. MacKAY AND WAYNE VAN TOEVER. 1979. An ecological approach to a water recirculating system for salmonids: Preliminary experience. Presented to the Biological Engineering Symposium, sponsored by the American Fisheries Society, October 1979. Paper available from the authors: The Ark Project, The Institute of Man and Resources, Rural Route No. 4, Souris, PEI, Canada COA 2BO.

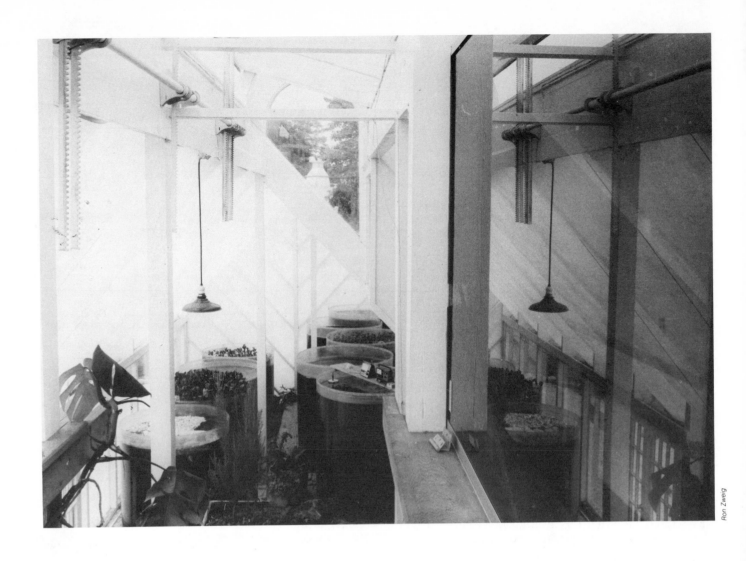

Ron Zweig

Modeling Algal Growth and Decline in Solar-Algae Ponds

John Wolfe, Ron Zweig, and David Engstrom

During the summer of 1978 the algae in the various solar courtyard ponds fluctuated in a remarkably similar pattern (see Figure 1; the darkest line indicates algal volume on each graph). All the algae peaked 24 to 30 days after the experiment's inception, then flocculated (clumped together) and declined rapidly to very low densities. The growth-and-collapse pattern occurred in all ponds, even though the dominant algal species differed: *Sphaerocystis schroeteri* and a large *Chlorella* species in Pond J; *Scenedesmus quadricauda* in Pond L; *Micractinium pusillum* in Pond H. After about 80 days the algae tended to cycle upward slightly again. Since algal growth and decomposition strongly affect water chemistry, it is critical to understand the cause of algal fluctuations.

Why did the algae crash suddenly? Several hy-

potheses have been offered by biologists in our group and elsewhere. They include the following:

1. A period of sunny weather was followed by a period of cloudy weather.

2. The algae grew to a point at which they shaded each other's incoming light.

3. Shading occurred not only from live algal cells, but also from dead algal cells still suspended in the water column.

4. The algae depleted a nonrenewable micronutrient (the macronutrients phosphorus and nitrogen were in soluble form in sufficient concentrations in all cases at the time of collapse).

5. The algae released a toxin that accumulated as their numbers increased.

6. The algae were attacked by predatory bacteria with an exponentially growing population.

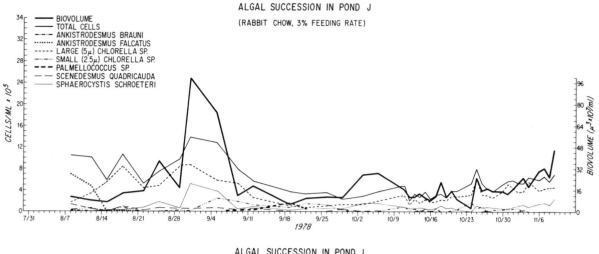

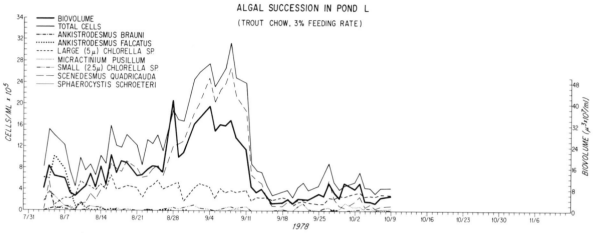

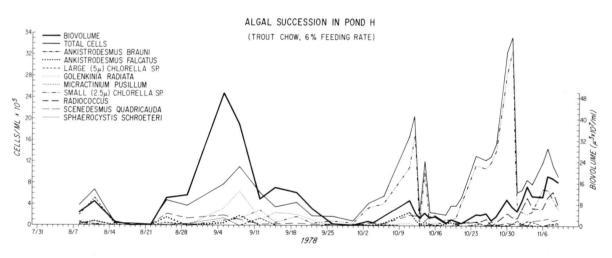

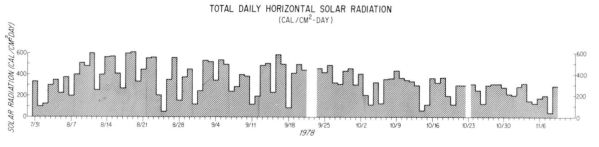

Figure 1. Modeling algal growth.

Most biologists would suspect that the last three hypotheses would be species-specific. We reject all three here because each pond displayed a different dominant species. An experiment has been devised to test Hypotheses 4, 5, and 6 (the experiment is scheduled to be carried out in the spring or summer of 1981).

The first three hypotheses all involve sunlight starvation. To compare these three hypotheses we expressed each hypothesis mathematically, and incorporated it into a computer simulation of solar-algae pond growth dynamics. To express the first hypothesis correctly, the solar radiation actually penetrating the walls and tops of the ponds, rather than the daily totals of horizontal solar radiation that we had recorded, had to be determined. A computer model, SOLAR6,[1] was devised to convert horizontal radiation measurements into the amounts of sunlight entering the solar-algae ponds.

Using SOLAR6, we put in horizontal solar mea-

---

[1]Wolfe, Engstrom, and Zweig, 1979. (Reference 5.) This article describes the principles and assumptions on which SOLAR6 is based.

surements in calories per square centimeter per day (cal/cm²/day) and got back the calculated solar energy entering the ponds (in cal/day).

These new data were the foundation of our first algal growth model. To express Hypothesis 1 mathematically, we can say the algae grew or declined according to Equation 1.

$$dA/dt = A(S - E)/T \qquad (1)$$

where

  A = algal density
  S = solar energy reaching the water column
  E = the level of sunlight at which
        the algae neither grow nor decline
  T = a constant (units: energy × time)

Equation 1 states that external light levels entirely control algal growth. A simple computer program, written in the system dynamics language DYNAMO, was constructed around the preceding equation and solar input data generated by SO-

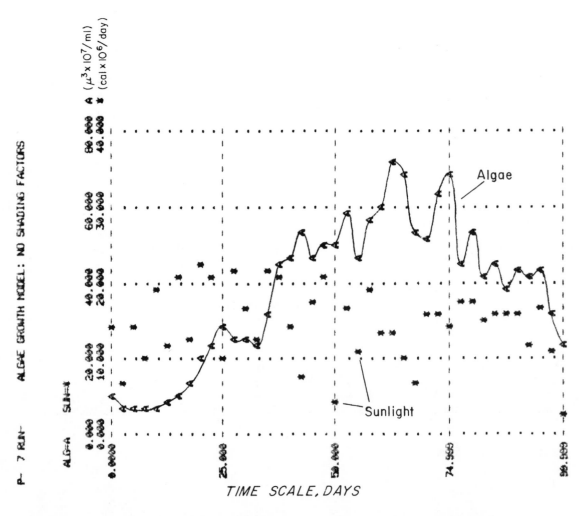

Figure 2. A run of the simple algae growth model based on solar energy fluctuations, with no shading factors. (Hypothesis no. 1)

LAR6. (For more information on system dynamics and DYNAMO, see the Bibliography.)

A run of the model is shown in Figure 2. The horizontal axis of the graph is time (in days). On the vertical axes, A represents algae volume and has the units ten million cubic microns per milliliter, and * stands for sunlight (measured in million calories per day). Unlike the algae curve, the points of sunlight on the plot remain unconnected because the time scale only shows a "snapshot" of light intensity every third day. Do not worry, though; the computer is using a complete daily sunlight data series and steps through time in tenth-of-a-day increments.

It is clear from inspecting Figure 2 that this model in no way approximates the early steep growth and decline of algae documented in Figure 1. No change in any of the model's parameters (excluding sunlight) created an output significantly closer to the real data than Figure 2. A more sophisticated model is needed.

Hypothesis 2, the self-shading of the algae, adds a limiting factor to the model's structure. Ex-

pressed mathematically, Hypothesis 2 might be written

$$dA/dt = A(b - bA/Sk_1) - Ad_1; \qquad Sk_1 \geqslant A \quad (2)$$

where (in addition to terms defined for Equation 1)

b = maximum algal growth rate (units: per day)
d_1 = death rate of the algae (units: per day)
k_1 = sunlight constant (units: algae volume/solar energy)

When solar inputs are very great, bA/Sk_1 approaches zero and $b - bA/sK_1$ approaches b, the maximum growth rate. When the sunlight factor Sk_1 is smallest it equals A, and the growth term $b - bA/Sk_1$ equals zero and falls out, leaving only the death rate.

Figure 3 depicts the output using Equation 2 to express Hypothesis 2. As shown, the model generates an overall pattern of sigmoidal growth to a maximum limit. Random fluctuations in sunlight causes the output to oscillate around the general

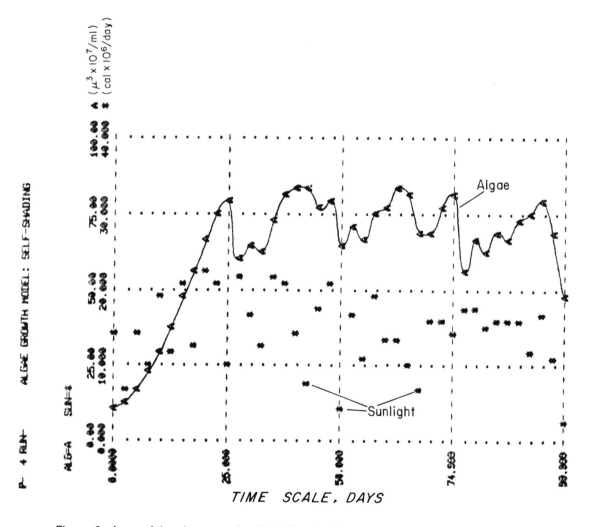

Figure 3. A run of the algae growth misel with solar fluctuations and self-shading factors. (Hypothesis no. 2)

growth-to-a-plateau curve. This too, is not the general behavior displayed by the algal populations in the summer of 1978.

A third factor, shading from dead algal cells (Hypothesis 3) was then added to the model. As any microscopic examination of the pond water after the first month of an experiment will show, midwater detritus (largely dead algae) is a common element in the ponds—often more prevalent than the algae themselves. Mathematically, their influence can be expressed as

$$dA/dt = A[b - b(A + OK_2)/Sk_1] - Ad_1 \qquad (3a)$$
$$dO/dt = Ad_1 - Od_2 \qquad (3b)$$

where (in addition to terms defined for Equations 1 and 2):

O = dead midwater organics
k_2 = shading impact of organics relative to algae
d_2 = disappearance rate (settling and decomposition) for midwater organics

A DYNAMO flow diagram of the resulting model is shown in Figure 4. Figure 5 shows a run of the model.

As illustrated in Figure 5, this model produces a growth and collapse curve quite similar to the real summer, 1978, data for Ponds J, L and H. In the mathematical simulation the algae do peak at about the twentieth day rather than the twenty-fifth to thirtieth day as in the real data. However, unique start-up conditions, if included in the model, would delay the peak for a more precise fit. These start-up conditions are: 1) the heavy successful predation of the algae when the tilapia are first introduced, before inedible algae species are selected for, and 2) moderate nutrient limitations, before feed inputs cycle through the fish and are transformed by the bacteria to generate the nutrients phosphate, ammonia and nitrate.

How can the algal crash, with its eventual negative impact on water quality, be avoided? The model can easily assess one approach: increasing the settling rate of the midwater particulates. Min-

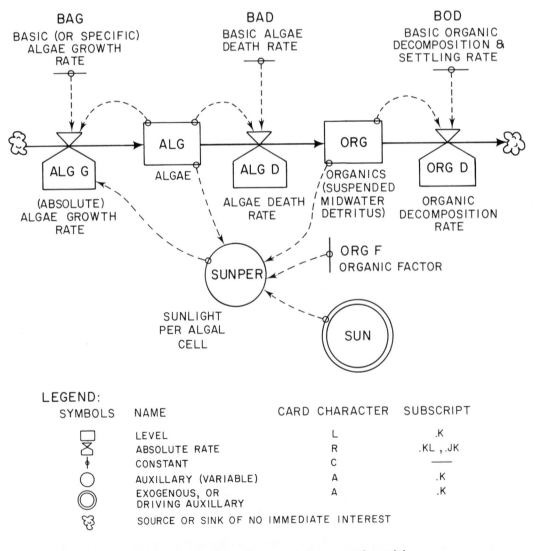

Figure 4. Dynamo flow diagram of algae growth model.

imizing water turbulence from aeration and installing separate settling ponds can both increase the settling rate. Figure 6 shows a run of the model where the settling rate is raised from 3% to 10% of the organics per day. The algae peak slightly higher and do not decline nearly as far—their final equilibrium level exceeds the baseline run of Figure 6 by roughly three times.

The higher resulting standing crop of algae does not necessarily mean better water quality, however. Good water quality derives from algal growth rates—not algal density directly. Algal growth removes toxic ammonia and carbon dioxide from the water and releases beneficial oxygen. To tell whether the algal growth rate, as well as the algal standing crop, had increased with faster particulate settling rates, the algal growth and death rates were plotted. The plots (not shown) proved that faster settling rates increased both growth and death rates. The increased algal growth rate would have an immediate beneficial impact on water quality. The increased death rate would eventually lead to decomposition and a loss of the gains made in water quality—unless the dead cells were removed in time.

This insight into the benefit of increasing the settling rate of particles suspended in the water column has inspired several new experimental designs. The new designs vary from adjacent settling or filtering units through which pond water cycles, to quiet zones within the pond created by vertical barriers across the bottom. Management solutions may include turning off water-churning aeration consistently during the day, or by relocating the air bubblers permanently from the pond bottom to halfway up the side of the pond, creating an undisturbed zone underneath. These methods should foster stronger, stabler algal growth, hence healthier water chemistry conditions and ultimately faster fish growth over longer periods.

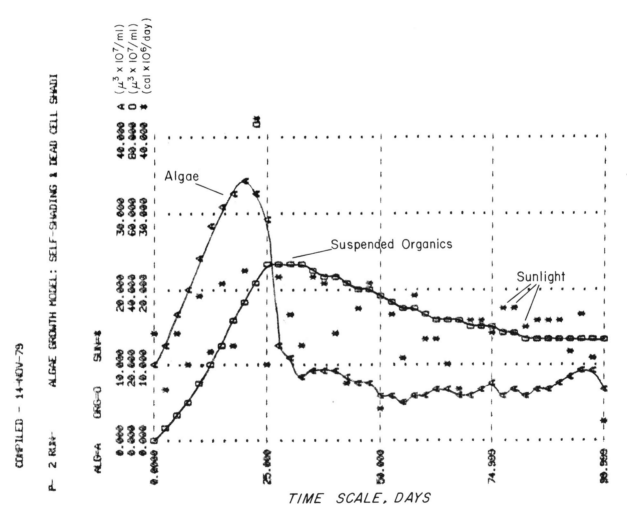

Figure 5. A run of the algae growth model with solar fluctuations, self-shading and mid-water particulate shading factors. (Hypothesis no. 3)

REFERENCES

1. MICHAEL R. GOODMAN. 1974. *Study Notes in System Dynamics*. Cambridge, Massachusetts: Wright-Allen Press, 388 pp.

2. DENNIS L. MEADOWS, W. W. BEHRENS, D. H. MEADOWS, R. F. NAILL, J. RANDERS AND E.K.O. ZAHN. 1974. *Dynamics of Growth in a Finite World*. Cambridge, Massachusetts: Wright-Allen Press, 637 pp.

3. ALEXANDER L. PUGH, III. 1977. *DYNAMO User's Manual*, 5th ed. Cambridge, Massachusetts: MIT Press, 131 pp.

4. WILLIAM A. SHAFFER. 1978. *Mini-DYNAMO User's Guide*. Cambridge, Massachusetts: Pugh-Roberts Associates, 67 pp.

5. JOHN WOLFE, DAVID ENGSTROM, AND RON ZWEIG. 1980. Sunlight patterns without, chemistry patterns within: the view from a solar-algae pond. *The Journal of The New Alchemists* **6**: Brattleboro: Stephen Greene Press.

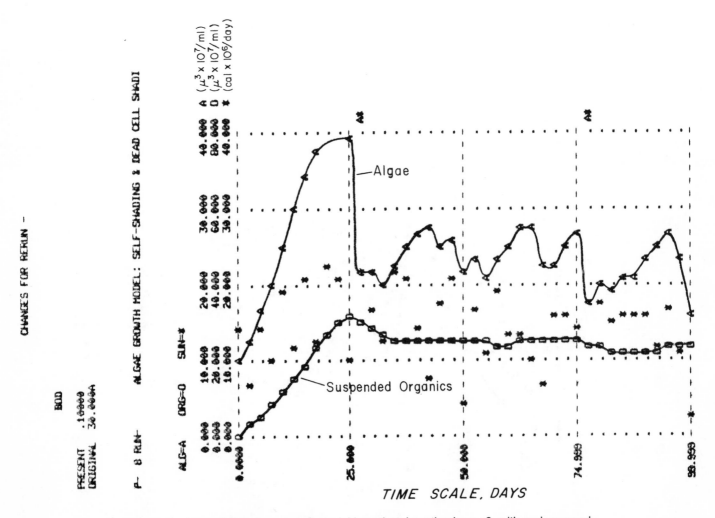

Figure 6. A run of the algae growth model based on hypothesis no. 3, with an increased midwater organics settling rate.

Bioshelters

This section on bioshelters is divided into two distinct parts, the one scientific and the other more or less domestic. The first, "Logging the Course of the Ark," reflects the range of our investigatory research in the Cape Cod Ark, which, at the age of five, has earned a venerable standing among solar greenhouses. Horticulture, pest control, modeling, toxic materials, and designing future bioshelters are discussed in the light of our current knowledge.

The second part, if less scholarly, is more broadly experiential. It is written by an assortment of people who having been exposed to the Ark have incorporated a bioshelter in some form or another into their lives. Any readers contemplating doing so themselves will be interested in the variety of approaches and costs represented.

N.J.T.

Hilde Maingay

LOGGING the COURSE of the ARK

Indoor Gardening

Colleen Armstrong

One of the goals underlying the design of the Ark was to point the way toward a solar-based, year-round, employment-creating agriculture for northern climates. Our goal was to devise a food-raising ecosystem that would require one-fifth to one-tenth the capital of an orthodox farm but use far less space. Our original target was for a bio-shelter-based microfarm costing $50,000, land included. The experimental prototype described on the following pages cost less.

Our strategy was to avoid mimicking and scaling down single-crop commercial farms. We adopted rather an ecological perspective, integrating into the design a blend of soft technologies, mixed crops (including greens, vegetables, flowers, fish, and other aquatic foods), and the mass propagation of trees. The microfarm was encapsulated in a solar building in which internal climate and the control of disease and pests were carried out by

ecological, structural, and data-processing subcomponents. This contained ecosystem with its interrelated and interdependent components of plants, earth, insects, fish, and people is a bioshelter, which we called the Cape Cod Ark.

Sterile soils and the use of toxic chemicals for intensive management are common elements of orthodox greenhouse food culture. We opted for deep, biologically diverse soils that we "seeded" from fields, meadow, and forest environments in alluvial, limestone, and glacial areas in southern New England. The process has become a continuing one. To the soils we added compost, seaweeds for trace elements and structure, and composted leaf litter. We wanted to create soils with the following characteristics:

1. High fertility.
2. High organic matter and water-holding ability.
3. Multiple nutrient-exchange pathways and storage capabilities.
4. Optimizes carbon dioxide production through dense bacterial activities.
5. Provides shelter for diverse animal population, including earthworms and pest predators.

Hilde Maingay

For agricultural purposes the most relevant indicator of soil fertility is the amount of produce a plant yields. In the Ark there are two important facts that should be considered when discussing soil fertility. First, the soil is the basic, essential source of plant nutrients; second, unlike the situation when seasonal cropping is practiced, the soil's nutrients are tapped 12 months of the year. We use crop rotation to balance nutrient demand. Two laboratories (Woods End Laboratory in Temple, Maine, and University of Massachusetts Suburban Experimental Station in Waltham, Massachusetts) have assisted us in evaluating our soil conditions by auditing Ark soil samples. Table 1 summarizes the basic composition and development of the Ark's soil over a two year period. A steady accumulation of organic matter and improved carbon: nitrogen ratio is attributed to cyclic introduction of properly composted material. Mineral levels fluctuate upon various demands of specific crops. Such reports are vital when selected crops are heavy feeders and possible nutrient deficiencies may arise.

Soil fertility is maintained through a process of annual innoculation. In September, after the summer season has come to a close, each bed is turned with well-decomposed organic matter. This rein-

Table 1.   SUMMARY OF ORGANIC MATTER AND MINERAL CONTENT OF CAPE COD BIOSHELTER'S SOIL, 1977–1979.[a]

		Date		
		11/77	*11/78*	*6/79*
Planned use		Leaf vegetables	Leaf vegetables	Tomatoes
Texture		Sandy loam	Sandy loam	Sandy loam
Organic matter		5.5%	8.1%	8.7%
Humus		3.8%	4.9%	5.7%
CEC (Meg/100 g)[b]		18.8	20.7	17.6
Soil pH		7.0	6.4	7.0
C:N balance		Good	Very good	Excellent
Available Nutrients		*11/77*	*11/78*	*6/79*
Nutrient Anions (1b/A)[c]				
Nitrogen (NO_3) annual releases	Desired level	100	100	200
	Level found	90–139 M	130–170 M	240 M
P_2O_5 reserve phosphorus	Desired level	350	250	130
	Level found	700 H	760 MH	660 MH
Exchangeable Cations (1b/A)				
Calcium	Desired level	4,900	5,800	4,900
	Level found	6,200	6,100	5,300
	Saturation	82% H	73% M	76% MH
Magnesium	Desired level	670	600	570
	Level found	580	1,000	830
	Saturation	13% M	20% H	20% MH
Potassium	Desired level	370	320	280
	Level found	570	590	590
	Saturation	4% M	4% MH	4% M

[a]Private circulation of Woods End Laboratory, RFD Box 65, Temple, Maine.

[b]Cation exchange capacity: a measure of the soil's capacity for holding available cations in reserve. Meg/100 g means milli-equivalent weights per 100 grams of soil; a milli-equivalent weight is the weight of a cation which exchanges with one equivalent weight or one gram of hydrogen.

[c]1b/A = pounds per Acre
H   = High
M   = Medium
MH   = Medium-High

states many microorganisms that break down organic matter with steady nutrient and mineral release. In addition, an irrigation program using the warm fish-pond water continually provides soluble nitrate-nitrogen, ammonium-nitrogen, and phosphate compounds.

Winter Crop Varieties

Over the past four winter seasons, from November through April, we have been evaluating many vegetable and flower varieties for their performance in the Ark. The Ark shares a number of characteristics with other passive solar greenhouses, but it it a bioshelter—a solar greenhouse with a difference. There are several qualities that distinguish it from other greenhouse environments. The primary difference lies in the concept of the Ark as an enclosed ecosystem, rich in diverse organisms. The practices of agriculture, aquaculture, and soil and insect ecology are all interdependent. When regulating the climate of the Ark, we must consider the living components. Fish can be more sensitive to thermal change than plants, and seasonal plants may require specific soil and air temperatures. The Ark may not provide optimal growing conditions for certain vegetable and flowers. Consequently, varieties must be chosen with these factors in mind.

In the Ark the average soil temperature at a 2 inch depth during the coldest months is as follows: November, 60° F; December, 59.5° F; January, 55° F; February, 59° F; March, 62° F. Average soil temperatures for two periods of November through April in 1977, 1978 and 1979 were 59° F at a depth of 2 inches, 54.1° F at 6 inches, and 53.2° F at 12 inches.

Although the soil beds provide more than sufficient temperatures for bountiful winter vegetable production, they are also considered a portion of the total thermal mass. The air temperatures fluctuate. Clear, sunny days will raise the daytime air temperature to 77° F, whereas on cloudy days it tends to drop to 55°–60° F. With an average minimum air temperature of 49.2° F and an average maximum air temperature of 70.8° F, the Ark's climate is similar to that of spring in a temperate zone. At this time, many foliage and root crops can be cultivated. The Ark provides an average of 25 portions of salad greens per day during the winter season. What better time to have access to fresh vegetables, rich in good nutrition?

Before we select which vegetables to grow, we give careful thought to each garden bed. These are a few of the questions we ask to make the most reasonable selections.

What is the size of the garden bed?

In the Ark, all of the beds are 5 feet or less in width and can be planted intensively. However, each bed borders a pathway and in our case must be able to take the abuse of reckless visitors and gardeners. Many dwarf flowering plants such as marigolds, alyssum, and lobelia make excellent borders, and we make use of them as such. A few hardy plants like beets, celery, parsley, and thyme can be employed as fences. Smaller areas should be planted with compact foliage crops that can be harvested by leaf. Loose-leaf lettuce, endive, celery, and chard can be planted close to one another and picked continuously for weeks. Larger beds offer freedom for all kinds of intercropping with broccoli, cauliflower, chard, kale, head lettuce, and herbs.

What is the quality of light striking the garden bed?

This is the most important question. Light can range from full through partly shaded, lightly shaded to deeply shaded. Full light exists when direct sunlight is present throughout the day. Moving down the scale, a partly shaded area has direct light for only a portion of the day. Light shade prevails when no direct sunlight reaches the bed, but a high light intensity is maintained. Deep shade is an extreme case in which there is low light intensity at all times.

Throughout the winter season, most vegetables require full light. Real sunworshippers are celery, head lettuce, leeks, broccoli, cauliflower, beets, dill, and thyme. Vegetables that will produce in partly or lightly shaded areas are endive, chard, parsley, kale, and Chinese greens. A few exceptional foliage crops continue to produce throught he dead of winter. They are endive, parsely, New Zealand spinach, beet greens, and both Swiss and red chard.

What is the condition of the soil?

A steady program to build and maintain soil fertility is an inherent part of our gardening practice. However, it's important to recognize that some crops are heavy feeders, and crop rotation should be employed.
Some vegetables may need additional compost dressing. If light conditions are stressing, a balanced rich soil and good air circulation will assist the plant to retain strength and will minimize pest problems.

Table 2. SUITABLE WINTER VEGETABLE VARIETIES FOR BIOSHELTERS IN NEW ENGLAND.

Vegetable	Name of Variety	Seed Co.	Transplant/ Seed	Fall/ Spring
Beet	Early Wonder Tall Top	Johnny's	Transplant	F
	Green Top Bunching	Stokes	Transplant	F
Broccoli	Cleopatra	Stokes	Transplant	F
	Ce Cicco	Johnny's	Transplant	S
Celery	Utah 52–70R Improved	Johnny's	Transplant	F & S
Chard, red	Burpee's Rhubarb®	Burpee	Transplant	F & S
Chard, Swiss	Fordhook Giant	Stokes	Transplant	F & S
Cauliflower	Opaal®	Rijk Zwaan	Transplant	F
Cabbage	Matsusitima	Johnny's	Transplant	F
Chinese	Chinese Pac Choi	Johnny's	Transplant	F & S
Endive	Full Heart Batavian	Johnny's	Transplant	F
	Green Curled	Stokes	Transplant	F
Kale	Harvester LD	Johnny's	Transplant	F & S
	Green Curled Scotch	Stokes	Transplant	F & S
Lettuce, Bibb type	Ravel RZ®	Rijk Zwaan	Transplant	F & S
	Rossini®	Rijk Zwaan	Transplant	F & S
	Ostinata	Stokes	Transplant	F & S
				F & S
Lettuce, head	Reskia RZ®	Rijk Zwaan	Transplant	S
	Zwaareese®	Rijk Zwaan	Transplant	F & S
Lettuce, loose-leaf	Grand Rapids Tip-burn Resistant	Stokes	Transplant	S
Parsley	Champion Moss Curled	Stokes	Transplant	F & S
	Plain Dark Green Italian	Stokes	Transplant	F & S
Spinach	New Zealand (perennial)	Stokes	Seed	F
	Malabar	Burpee	Seed Transplant	S

What vegetables should be given priority?

Criteria for choosing vegetables are that they please the intended consumer and are nutritionally complementary. A short story might be pertinent. A few years ago, we grew lots of New Zealand spinach. It was fabulous for re-enforcing the rock walls and was a nonstop producer. Unfortunately, only the most reckless of greens aficionados would chew it, sometimes with reluctance. Rumors developed that most of it was going to chickens and goats. Graffiti such as "Yuck" began to appear in the tally book. It seems sturdiness and nutritional value cannot stand alone. At least not with us.[1]

We have experimented with varieties of lettuce, endive, celery, chard, beet, brassicas, spinach, and parsley to ascertain which vegetables are most adapted to the thermal and light regimes inside the Ark. While a few crop varieties demand a specific season, most of the foliage crops can be cultivated throughout this cool period. See Table 2. Lettuce varieties from Holland have proved superior to domestic varieties. It is possible that Dutch greenhouse crop-breeding conditions may more closely approximate conditions in bioshelter

environments in northeastern United States. We set the following criteria for our varietal tests. Each variety of lettuce was rated for number of days until maturity, average ounces per plant, ounces per square foot, color, aphid resistance, disease and heat resistance, tip-burn and taste (see Table 3).

Undoubtedly, Ravel R2®, a bibb lettuce with outstanding qualities, is our favorite, most productive variety in the Ark. Grand Rapids Tip-Burn Tolerant is the preferred loose-leaf lettuce however; most of the bibb lettuces give higher yields per square foot.

Our vetetable production can be divided into two categories: overall production from the 517 square foot (ft²) growing area, and optimal production from testing areas (Tables 3 and 4). Over a three-year period, we have brought about several changes in the growing area. In fall 1978, we placed three solar-algae ponds in areas of low light, providing additional heat storage, accessible pond water, and warmer temperatures in the soil surrounding the ponds. At the same time, we designated a 35 ft² plot as a permanent area for tropical plants; this serves as an animal and insect sanctuary.

Figure 1 shows the six-month winter vegetable production from the 517 ft² area over a three-year period. The vegetables included lettuce, endive, tomatoes, celery, brassicas, chards, beets, and herbs.

---

[1]For readers uninitiated to New Zealand spinach, ruminating briefly on a rusty nail will provide a fair analogue of the taste, if not the texture, of sampling the real thing. *Ed.*

Valuable Crops

Celery

After a successful pretrial season, we cultivated celery as the main crop in the fall of 1979. Celery has a long maturing process from seed to harvest. Seed germination is approximately 21 days, an additional 45 days is required for developing as a transplant, and it is 76 more days until harvest. The advantages of growing celery in bioshelters include the long developing process, and the fact that it is a compact, verticle-axis crop. The crop occupies bedding space for 72–76 days, only about half of the total maturation time. Celery has the added advantage of being a relatively high priced, popular vegetable in American markets.

There are a few characteristics of celery that should be taken into consideration, however. It is one of the more difficult crops to grow. It is a rich feeder of nitrogen and requires an abundance of moisture from the soil. Blanching (preventing the development of color) and binding are required for a marketable crop. Offsetting such demands, celery can be spaced at one plant per square foot and weigh 1–2 pounds per plant. As of this writing it brings a retail price of 89 cents per bunch. Celery is a good storage vegetable and has a flexible harvest period. The first-year results have been encouraging, and crop evaluation will continue both in early spring and fall.

Tomatoes

During seasons that tomatoes are imported, retail prices on Cape Cod approach and often exceed $1 per pound. A review of the tomato culture literature indicates that greenhouse tomatoes have two seasons: spring and fall. Predictably, the spring season—with longer photoperiod and higher luminosity—is more profitable. With the rising cost

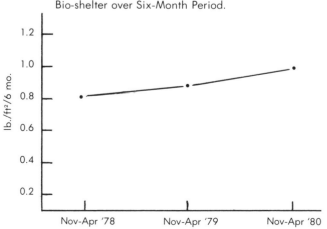

Figure 1. Average Winter Vegetable Production in Cape Cod Bio-shelter over Six-Month Period.

Table 3. VARIETAL TEST SHEET FOR LETTUCE IN CAPE COD BIOSHELTER.

Name of Variety	Time to Maturity (days)	Average weight (oz/plant)	Density (oz/ft²)	Equivalent 1b/ 1,000 ft²	Aphid Resistance	Bacterial Soft-Rot Resistance	Heat Resistance	Tip-Burn Resistance	Color	Taste
Deci-Minor (Holland)	75	5.4	10	625	Medium	Medium–high	High	High	Dark green	Very good
Grand Rapids[a] loose-leaf (US)	45	5.0	8.7	544	Medium	High	Medium–low	High	Light green	Very good
Ostinata (US)	60	4.9	9.3	581	Medium–high	Medium	Medium–high	High	Medium green	Good
Prizehead loose-leaf (US)	48	Failed	—	—	Low	High	Low	Low	Green/red	Failed
Ravel RZ® (Holland)	66	5.5	11	688	High	High	High	High	Dark green	Excellent
Reskia® (Holland)	74	8.0	8.2	512	Medium–high	Medium	Medium	High	Light green	Very good
Rossini® (Holland)	70	5.5	11	688	Medium	Medium	High	High	Dark green	Very good
Zwaareese (Holland)	74	8.0	8.2	512	Medium–high	Medium	Low	High	Light green	Good

[a]Grand Rapids Tip-Burn Tolerant Variety

Table 4. VARIETAL TEST SHEET FOR TOMATOES IN CAPE COD BIOSHELTER.

Name of Variety	Days Until Maturity (from Transplant)	Average Weight per Fruit (oz)	Yield (lb/ft²)	Equivalent lb/ 1,000 ft²	New England Production (lb/ft²)	Insect Resistance	Disease[a] Resistance
SPRING:							
Small Fry (US)	68	0.75	1.2	1,200	—	Medium–high	Medium
Lito® (Holland)	78	2.5	4.0	4,000 (double-pruned)	2.5	Medium	Medium–high
Tropic (US)	82	2.8	1.8	1,800	2.5	Medium–high	High
Type 127 (Holland)	72	2.3	3.6	3,600 (double-pruned)	2.5	Medium	Medium–high
FALL:							
Lito® (Holland)	78	2.5	1.2	1,200	—	Medium	Medium–high
Tiny Tim (US)	45	0.4	0.6	600	—	Low	Medium

[a]Diseases include verticillum wilt, fusarium wilt, leaf blight and anthracnose.

of fuel, many conventional tomato growers in New England have decreased production.

An evaluation of the first year of summer tomato production in the Ark showed an average of 2 lb/ft² for the 1978 season. This yield is probably low as we know part of the crop was snitched by visitors.

The following spring we evolved a more sophisticated program incorporating a valuable pruning technique. Double-pruning as it is called is a European method that incorporates a selected axial sucker or vegetative outgrowth into a second indeterminant stem. This pruning technique can double fruit yields while not affecting fruit size. It is an excellent method for maximum space utilization. We began our preliminary trials with Dutch seeds. To date, the favorite variety has been Lito® from the Rijk Zwaan Co. in Holland. This variety is slightly smaller than the average garden tomato although it tastes as sweet. Mid-March planting gave us fruit by early June and a production figure in July of an average of 5.5 lb/plant! Fruit production lasted 14 weeks with a final figure of 13 lb/plant, or 4 lb/ft², twice the yield of the first year. If the tomato area in the Ark were equivalent to 1,000 ft², Lito® could produce 4,000 lb of fruit in the spring season.

Fall tomato production also has merit in bioshelters. Again, timing is most important. Seeding begins on the first of June. Healthy plants are set in beds by the first week in August and the first tomatoes begin to ripen in mid-October. Fall fruit production is considerably less than spring production, measuring 1.2 lb/ft² compared to 4 lb/ft². However, top prices are paid at this time of year and further on into December. In the future, many additional factors such as light-reflection material, thermal curtains, and better glazing may contribute to boosting fall tomato production.

The results of our tests of several tomatoes are shown in Table 4.

Seedling Production

Besides the deep-dug, intensive beds in the Ark, there is approximately 75 ft² of bench space that we alot to young seedlings. The area is regarded as a nursery. A germination box provides the environment for optimal seed sprouting. Young plants are transplanted into containers that hold 3–10 of a particular variety. Although small, the bench space is essential to us and is most productive in late winter and in spring. In 1979 we produced over 6,000 transplants in the Ark for New Alchemy's gardens and experimental plots. A seedling schedule indicates what vegetable and flower seedlings to grow at the proper time of year. A cycle envolves; as mature transplants are moved to the cold frame, a second set of younger seedlings assumes their space. After a few weeks, the second set is taken out to be hardened off, and a third moves into the same space. Many growers find spring the most profitable season. On Cape Cod, three tomato plants can retail at $1. With adequate timing, spring transplant profits could exceed those of any other time of year.

Planting Regimes

Figure 2 displays three alternate vegetable-planting schedules. All can be made profitable ventures. Schedule A was the regime for the 1979/1980 season in the Ark. Table 5 lists the retail revenue per square foot using the three schedules. Schedule A

Table 5. REVENUE FROM ALTERNATE ANNUAL PLANTING REGIMES.

	Retail Price	Produce/ft²		Revenue ($/ft²/yr)
SCHEDULE A:				
Celery	89¢/bunch	1	bunch	$0.89
Tomato	avg. 69¢/lb	4	lb	2.76
Lettuce	69¢/head	(two) 1.9	head[a]	2.62
TOTAL				$6.27
SCHEDULE B:				
Celery	89¢/bunch	1	bunch	$0.89
Tomato[a]	99¢/lb	1.2	lb	1.18
Lettuce	69¢/head	1.9	head	1.31
Cauliflower	$1.89/head	0.4	head	0.76
TOTAL				$4.14
SCHEDULE C:				
Lettuce	69¢/head	(two) 1.9	head[a]	$2.62
Tomato	avg. 69¢/lb	4	lb	2.76
Cauliflower	$1.89/head	0.4	head	0.76
TOTAL				$6.14

[a]Two reasons

[b]Off-season price

offers the highest income at $6.27/per square foot per year; another plan may be selected to facilitate crop rotation and balance the nutrient requirements drawn from the soil. Comparing the three schedules, flexibility in crop selection is often narrowed by the premium price available at a particular season. We remind readers that with prices soaring, these prices shortly may be regarded as too conservative!

Biological Islands

Because crops are planted, removed, and altered from season to season, most agricultural environments are intrinsically unstable. Such instability can lead to pest outbreaks, since biological regulatory mechanisms are not usually well established. An example is the introduction of ladybird beetles (*Hippodamia convergens*) to control aphids. Once the crop is harvested, the number of aphids, which provide nourishment for the predator, is reduced. The ladybird beetle population will consequently drop or become nonexistent. In the Ark we increased ecological diversity and biological stability by creating aquatic and terrestrial microcontrol "islands" throughout the interior. These "islands" include such stable perennial plants as ginger, flowers, herbs, and grasses like bamboo that are not cropped. These in turn provide continuing habitats for pollinators, predators, and parasites of insect pests. The parasites include parasitic wasps, larvae of flies, predatory mites, spiders, frogs, and lizards. The entire island network, located in slightly suboptimal growing areas, also creates a pleasant surrounding.

Figure 2. Alternate Annual Planting Regimes.

[a]Lettuce grown under mature tomatoes.

Hilde Maingay

Controlling the Whitefly

Colleen Armstrong

At the time of my last chronicling of the greenhouse whitefly, *Trialeurodes vaporariorum* (Westwood), I felt secure that this harmful herbivore's existence would be relatively insignificant to the Ark's insect community.[1] Previous success stories of the use of *Encarsia formosa* (Gahan) in controlling greenhouse whitefly encouraged me to continue my investigation and I planned to devote more time to observing and monitoring interactions between host and parasite. Winter 1978/1979 was mild and cloudy, and the Ark was cool enough to limit the number of active whiteflies. The parasitic wasp *E. formosa* was undoubtedly present, though even quieter than its host. With a fall crop of tomatoes that lasted until mid-February, both insects were assured of one of their favorite food sources. The whitefly probed the tomato tissue, preferring apical leaves, while the *Encarsia* searched for immature whitefly in which to deposit their

eggs. It was a tranquil time of year for this particular host-parasite relationship.

When the tomatoes became diseased with a fungal growth, *Cladosporium* sp., we uprooted and composted the 12 ft plants. Realizing that the majority of the Ark's *E. formosa* population lived on the tomatoes, we scavenged each plant for black-coated, parasitized whitefly scales (sessile larval stages) and distributed leaves throughout the bioshelter. We pinned many leaves to the underside of young tomato plants above the rock storage bed. Little did I know we were about to enter a tumultuous season of whitefly.

You might say I've progressed to the trial-and-error stage of science, but my mistakes have taught me a great deal about insect control in bioshelter environments. The Ark is far from the conventional laboratory. Such variables as percise temperature and exact insect members are not controlled. Although we are practicing biological control in a contained environment, it can follow patterns of nature so closely that you often forget the feeling of walls.

Successful insect control can be a complicated process. To quote the *Source Book of Integrated Pest Management*, "A managed resource ecosystem is a component of the functioning ecosystem . . . actions are taken to restore, preserve or augment checks and balances in the system."[2] Over the growing season under discussion, various factors such as temperature, timing, and ratios of host to parasite contributed to the lack of stability in the Ark's gardens.

The average daily winter temperature in the Ark for the three coldest months, December, January, and February, was approximately 21° C (70° F). Its climate can be described as cool and moist. When the old tomato leaves were removed from the diseased mother plant and pinned to new plants, many of the leaves disintegrated in the dampness of the bioshelter.[3] Consequently, the parasitized scales were lost, and the *E. formosa* population took a drastic dip. At relatively low temperatures, 18–21° C (64–70° F), the whitefly's life span is longer and the female can lay many more eggs than the parasitic wasp can.[4] (See Figures 2 and 3.) In the spring, as the whitefly population began to gain momentum, the lack of *Encarsia* was most felt. I began to search for an outside source of *E. formosa*.

As routine practice, we made weekly counts of whitefly adults and scales, and took parasitized

---

[1]Armstrong, 1980. Reference 12.

[2]Reference 2.
[3]In summer, parasitized scales can be pinned to the underside of a fresh leaf surface with little disruption to *E. formosa's* life cycle.
[4]Helgesen and Tauber, 1974. Reference 4.

Figure 1. White Fly's and *E. formosa's* Life Cycles at 75°F (24°C).

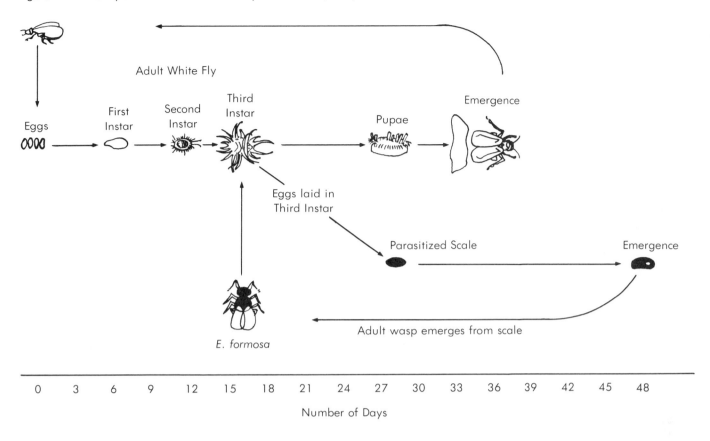

scales from the spring tomato crop. We tallied a random count from other plants in the Ark. In mid-May, I began to find parasitized scales on the oldest leaves of the tomatoes. The crop by then stood 6 ft tall, and was laden with clusters of fruit. By June, the plants approached 8 ft in height and the youngest leaves were well out of sight. Average daily temperatures reached 25° C (75.5° F), but the large whitefly scales outnumbered parasitized scales many times over. (See Figure 4.) At the end of the month, sooty mold began to grow on the tops of the leaves and the plants began to wilt.[5] This could only be attributed to an extreme infestation, with the whitefly multiplying to a high density. Then in the next two weeks, the number of parasitized scales skyrocketed, but too late. The tomato plants had sustained sufficient damage to curtail vigor and growth. Physically, they appeared beaten. We pulled the crop and I concluded that my management practices had failed.

[5]Black, sooty mold feeds on the whitefly's excretion, a sticky substance often called honeydew.

Figure 2. Lifetime Development for White Fly/*E. formosa.* *

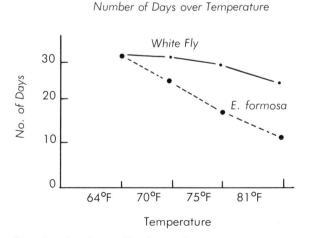

Number of Days over Temperature

*Data based on Burnett, T., reference 2.

Figure 3. White Fly/*E. formosa* Fecundity

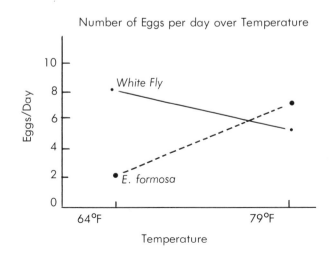

Number of Eggs per day over Temperature

Figure 4. White Fly and *E. formosa* Population Densities on Tomato Crop, Spring-Summer, 1979.

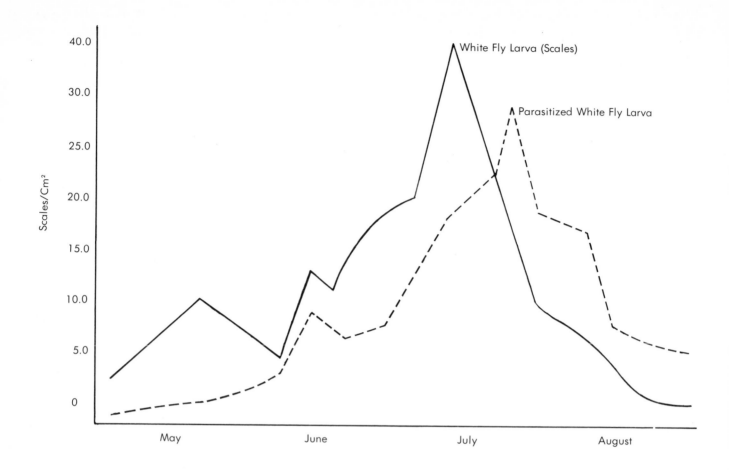

What were the mistakes? What was so different about that year compared to previous ones? The grower bows her head and sorrowfully states, "Optimism and ignorance; but for both our sakes let's recount them just the same."

Predictably, when the diseased tomato leaves decomposed, the mainstay in the diet of *E. formosa* was forfeited. We should have begun the search for a source of new parasites at that time. Waiting until the abundance of whiteflies became apparent made for too long a delay. Presently, only one commercial insectary on the North American continent, the Canadian firm Better Yields Insects, located in Tecumseh, Ontario, breeds *E. formosa*. A purchase from the United States requires an importation permit from the USDA Animal and Plant Protection Health Inspection Service. Permits take time, sometimes up to eight weeks.

The loss could have been otherwise prevented had more than one type of host plant been predominant in the Ark's breeding scheme. The whitefly is attracted to more than 200 vegetable and ornamental plants,[6] but *E. formosa* is not as extensive in the search for immature whitefly larvae. Tomato and tobacco cultivars are favored by both, though other cool-season plants can be utilized as breeding stations. Nasturtiums and scented geraniums are vigorous flowering plants that thrive in the winter season of the bioshelter. Long-lived or perennial host plants like these allow the *Encarsia* to develop without disturbing their life cycle. Yet another obstacle was a lack of information. It is hard to know when exactly the whitefly population density reaches a level injurious to fruit production.

When biological agents are depended on for insect control, it is necessary to have precise biological control recommendations for specific crops. One should know, for example, that vegetables can often take a higher pest population density than ornamental plants. Without this type of information, the grower cannot know when his/her crop is endangered. Luckmann and Metcalf state this in terms of a population density reaching an economic threshold level, or beyond, to an economic injury level.[7] (See Figure 5.) If the population density of the pest exceeds the economic threshold level for a particular crop, artificial controls are justified to prevent loss.

Tomatoes can tolerate a moderate number of

[6]Russell, 1963. Reference 10.

[7]Reference 8.

whiteflies, to 20 scales per square centimeter, until the pest adversely affects crop yields.[8] The survival of a certain age-class of whitefly such as eggs, first, second, third, and fourth instar, is variable, specifically with regard to temperature.[9] The ideal ratio of *E. formosa* to its host is 1:30; the wasp lays approximately 30 eggs in a lifetime.[10] The most effective control is reached when the parasite is introduced at a low whitefly population density, certainly below a level causing economic injury. For further coverage on how to establish *E. formosa* successfully, read R. G. Helgesen and Maurice J. Tauber's article on the biological control of the greenhouse whitefly.[11]

Are there other control methods compatible with *E. formosa* in checking whitefly populations? In the context of the bioshelter environment, it's an important question to ask. We hope other beneficial insects help control this pest. We have observed adult whitefly predation by damsel flies and spiders. Most likely, our quick-drawing frogs have lashed out at a naive few. Other interactions may have passed unnoticed. But evidently, the Ark's combination of food, temperature, and a lack of natural enemies favors the augmentation of a whitefly population, especially in the spring. If the managed resource ecosystem is to succeed, an integrated pest control scheme is necessary.

Trap plants like nasturtiums serve well. Repellent plants such as white geranium can be useful. Also helpful is learning what attracts both predators and prey. Many plant feeders are attracted to yellow and yellow-green colors.[12] A trapping scheme that uses boards painted yellow and coated with a sticky substance with a texture on the order of flypaper has snagged the adult whitefly successfully.[13] Among various trials, this method has proven effective in collaboration with *Encarsia formosa* for integrated control with established whitefly infestations.

Although biological control is the most desirable method for controlling pest populations in a bioshelter environment, effective mechanical controls may fill the void when beneficial insect activity is low. Overall the objective remains to minimize the existence of the pest by employing control strategies that will not disrupt the resource ecosystem. Source for *Encarsia formosa*:

Better Yields Insects
13310 Riverside Dr. E.
Tecumseh, Ontario N8N 1B2
Canada

Minimum Order: 2,000
Importation permit is required for U.S.

Address for Importation Permit:

Importation Permits
Technical Service Staff
Plant Protection and Quarantine, APHIS USDA
Federal Center Bldg.
Rm. 670
Hyattsville, Maryland 20782

Form 526

---

[8]Hussey et al, 1969. Reference 5.
[9]Helgesen and Tauber, 1974. Reference 4.
[10]Burnett, 1949. Reference 1.
[11]Reference 4.

Figure 5. Hypothetical Graph of a White Fly Population on Tomato Crop. Three Separate Cases Stating: (A) Low Population Density, No Additional Control Needed; (B) Population Density Approaching Economic Threshold Level; (C) Population Density Requires Additional Control Intervention to Prevent Crop Yield Damage.

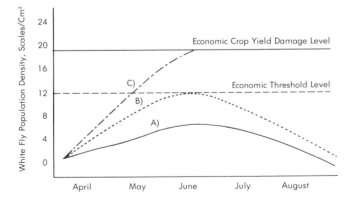

REFERENCES

1. THOMAS BURNETT. 1949. The effect of temperature on an insect host-parasite population. *Ecology* **30**:113.

2. M. L. FLINT and ROBERT VAN DEN BOSCH. 1977. *Source Book of Integrated Pest Management.* Unpublished.

3. A. G. GENTILLE and D. T. SCANLON. Floricultural insects and related pests—biology and control. *Florogram.* Cooperative Extension Service, Suburban Experiment Station, University of Massachusetts, USDA.

4. R. G. HELGESEN and M. J. TAUBER. 1974. Biological control of greenhouse whitefly, *Trialeurodes vaporariorum* (Aleyrodidae:Homoptera), on short-term crops by manipulating biotic and abiotic factors. *Canadian Entomology* **106**:1175.

5. N. W. HUSSEY, W. H. READ, and J. J. HESLING. 1969. *The Pests of Protected Cultivation.* London: Edward Arnold.

---

[12]Lloyd, 1921. Reference 7.
[13]Webb and Smith, 1979. Reference 11.

6. WILLIAM H. JORDAN, 1977. *Windowsill Ecology.* Emmaus, Pa: Rodale Press, pp 167–187.

7. L. LLOYD. 1921. Notes on colour tropism of *Asterochiton (aleurodes) vaporariorum* (Westwood). *Bulletin of Entomological Resources* **12**(3):355.

8. W. H. LUCKMANN and R. L. METCALF. 1975. *Introduction to Insect Pest Management.* N.Y.: JOHN WILEY, 587 pp.

9. J. R. NECHOLS and M. J. TAUBER. 1977. Age-specific interaction between the greenhouse whitefly and *Encarsia formosa*: Influence of host on the parasite's oviposition and development. *Environmental Entomology* **6**(1):143.

10. L. M. RUSSELL. 1963. Host and distribution of five species of *Trialeurodes* (Homoptera:Aleyrodiadae). *Annuals of Entomological Society of America* **56**:149.

11. R. E. WEBB and F. F. SMITH. 1979. Greenhouse whitefly control of an integrated regimen based on adult trapping and nymphal parasitism. Published for Fourth Conference for Biological Control of Glasshouses. OILB/SROP.

12. COLLEEN ARMSTRONG. 1980. Insects in the Ark. *The Journal of The New Alchemists* **6**:149. Battleboro: Stephen Greene Press.

Hilde Maingay

Toxic Materials in the Bioshelter Food Chains and Surrounding Ecosystems[1]

Dr. Han Tai,[2] Colleen Armstrong and John Todd

The following tables show the results of a preliminary screening of potentially toxic materials that might be found at the institute. DDT and chlordane, used some time before our tenancy on the New Alchemy farm, still persist in the soils—an unfortunate legacy from past farmers. The other toxin, heptachlor epoxide, is a pesticide used before World War II. Its occurrence in soil is a mystery.

The chlorinated hydrocarbons seemed to be locked into the soils, reaching their greatest concentrations in the field in front of the bioshelter, then diminishing in the Ark, and ultimately disappearing in the woods that ring the farm. A report on heavy metals is not yet complete. Perhaps the best news is that newer pesticides were not found in the samples.

Hilde Maingay

[1]The toxic substances study was financed jointly by Rockefeller Brothers Fund (sampling, shipping, and evaluation) and the Environmental Protection Agency.

[2]Toxicant Analysis Center NSTL/NASA Bay Saint Louis, MS 39529

Table 1. A COMPARISON: LEVELS OF TOXIC MATERIAL IN ASSORTED VEGETATION SURROUNDING NEW ALCHEMY INSTITUTE, OCTOBER 1979. RESULTS IN PARTS PER BILLION.

Sites	Technical Chlordane	pp DDE	op DDT	pp DDT	Heptachlor Epoxide	Dieldrin	Organo-Phosphates	Organo-Nitrogens	PCB's	Pathalates
Bioshelter I Kale (leaves)	ND[a]	ND	ND	ND	ND	ND	ND	ND	ND	ND
New Alchemy Inst. Garden plot Kale (leaves)	ND	ND	ND	ND	ND	ND	ND	ND	ND	ND
Non-organic Garden plot Kale (leaves)	ND	—[b]	—	—	—	—	—	—	—	—
Bioshelter I Tomato (fruit)	ND	—	—	—	—	—	—	—	—	—
New Alchemy Inst. Garden plots Tomato (fruit)	ND	—	—	—	—	—	—	—	—	—
Non-organic Garden plot Asparagus (leaves)	ND	—	—	—	—	—	—	—	—	—
New Alchemy Inst. Garden Plot Asparagus (leaves)	ND	—	—	—	—	—	—	—	—	—
New Alchemy Inst. Garden plot Carrot (root)	ND	—	—	—	—	—	—	—	—	—
N.A.I. Garden plot Adjacent road Carrot (root)	ND	—	—	—	—	—	—	—	—	—
Bioshelter I Celery (leaves)	ND	—	—	—	—	—	—	—	—	—
New Alchemy Inst. Garden Plot Celery (leaves)	ND	—	—	—	—	—	—	—	—	—
Woodlands adjacent New Alchemy Inst. Bishops laurel (leaves)	ND	—	—	—	—	—	—	—	—	—

[a]ND: Nondetectable, below detection limits.
[b]Dash means test failed, no data available.

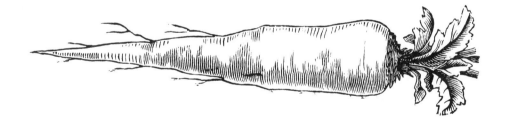

Table 2. A COMPARISON: LEVELS OF TOXIC MATERIAL IN WATER SOURES SURROUNDING NEW ALCHEMY INSTITUTE, DECEMBER 1979. RESULTS IN PARTS PER BILLION.

Sites	Technical Chlordane	pp DDE	op DDT	pp DDT	Heptachlor Epoxide	Dieldrin	Organo-Phosphates	Organo-Nitrogens	PCB's	Pathalates
Bioshelter I Solar-Algae Ponds	ND[a]	ND	ND	ND	ND	ND	ND	ND	ND	ND
Bioshelter I Cement Pond	ND	ND	ND	ND	ND	ND	ND	ND	ND	ND
New Alchemy Inst. Original water source	ND	ND	ND	ND	ND	ND	ND	ND	ND	ND
Natural Pond Adjacent New Alchemy Inst.	ND	ND	ND	ND	ND	ND	ND	ND	ND	ND
Spring Water Source	ND	ND	ND	ND	ND	ND	ND	ND	ND	ND

[a]ND: Nondetectable, below detection limits.

Table 3. LEVELS OF TOXIC MATERIAL IN SOILS SURROUNDING NEW ALCHEMY INSTITUTE, NOVEMBER 1979. RESULTS IN PARTS PER BILLION.

Sites	Technical Chlordane	pp DDE	op DDT	pp DDT	Heptachlor Epoxide	Dieldrin	Organo-Phosphates	Organo-Nitrogens	PCBs	Pathalates
Original farmer field	313.9	976.4	500.3	2794.7	8.8	8.5	ND[a]	ND	ND	ND
Field adjacent Bioshelter I	—[b]	320.6	80.2	506.2	ND	ND	ND	ND	ND	ND
Bioshelter I	249.7	160.0	64.8	300.8	9.8	ND	ND	ND	ND	ND
Nonorganic garden	67.2	51.8	29.8	120.8	ND	ND	ND	ND	ND	ND
NAI garden adjacent road	35.4	82.2	17.3	114.3	ND	ND	ND	ND	ND	ND
Household greenhouse	193.0	52.7	19.6	60.3	ND	ND	ND	ND	ND	ND
Experimental plot (bean field)	39.4	36.2	10.0	45.2	ND	ND	ND	ND	ND	ND
Leaf storage area	45.8	20.5	9.4	35.7	–	ND	ND	ND	ND	ND
Woodland adjacent to NAI	–	52.1	–	86.1	ND	ND	ND	ND	ND	ND

[a]ND: Nondetectable, below detection limits.
[b]Dash means test failed, no data available.

Table 4. EPA DETECTION LIMITS OF TOXIC MATERIAL ANALYSIS FOR SOIL AND VEGETATION SAMPLES.

Toxic Material	Detection Limits (ppb[a])
1. Early eluters: heptachlor epoxide	0.01
2. Late eluters: all DDTs, dieldrin	0.02
3. All multicomponent pesticides: technical chlordane, PCBs	0.05

[a]ppb: parts per billion.

Table 5. EPA DETECTION LIMITS OF TOXIC MATERIAL ANALYSIS FOR WATER SAMPLES.

Toxic Material	Detection Limits (ppb[a])
1. Early eluters: heptachlor epoxide	0.10
2. Late eluters: all DDTs, dieldrin	0.50
3. All multicomponent compounds: technical chlordane, PCBs	1.50
4. Organophosphates Early eluters	1.00
Mid eluters	2.50
Late eluters	5.00

[a]ppb: parts per billion.

Table 6. TIME COMPARISON OF TOXIC MATERIAL IN BIOSHELTER I SOILS 1979. RESULTS IN PARTS PER MILLION.

Toxic Material	January 1979	November 1979
Technical chlordane	0.51	0.25
p, p = DDE	0.14	0.16
o, p = DDT	0.09	0.06
P, P = DDT	0.34	0.30
Heptachlor epoxide	0.01	0.01

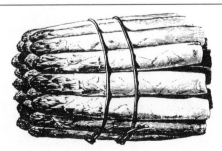

Reglazing
John Wolfe

The winter of 1978–1979 seemed unusually hard on Cape Cod Ark: plants grew slowly, the night air temperatures chilled almost to freezing, and the solar-algae ponds chilled to nearly the lethal limit for our tropical fish. Meanwhile, returning friends who last saw the Ark just after its completion kept commenting on how much whiter the fiberglass glazing appeared.

In late winter we made a computer prediction of light transmission through the fiberglass-reinforced plastic cover and into the Ark. We also measured light levels outside and in the Ark. Measured light transmission through the glazing into the Ark was only one-half to two-thirds of predicted levels. "Either a mistake in our computer program or the unpredicted effects of water condensation on the fiberglass," we surmised.

By midsummer we had second thoughts and contacted the manufacturer. Yes, they told us, it was possible for their oldest version of solar glazing to deteriorate in the Ark's three-year lifetime. No, painting new resin over the old probably wouldn't recover the original light transmissivity. According to the manufacturer, the old material degraded because glass fibers extended through the resin to the interior surface of the glazing. Moisture wicked through these fibers into the core of the glazing and under hot, sunny conditions turned into steam. This burst the fiberglass along a myriad of tiny cracks, crazing and whitening the glazing. Their new glazing, they assured us, had a protective coating on the interior side, and they donated enough new fiberglass to cover the south face of the Ark.

When the fiberglass arrived in September the work began. The old panels had been secured with hundreds of galvanized screws and sealed with an impressively durable and tenacious bead of silicone caulk. All the old work had to be undone, and new panels had to be assembled in the barn by pop-riveting the new fiberglass to both sides of aluminum channels that acted as spacers. The fiberglass sheets flex easily when not in place, and the most difficult task was moving the flexible panels without accidentally creasing or cracking the sheets. As a side project, we upgraded the Ark's weatherstripping and wall insulation.

Nearly every Alchemist and apprentice, skilled or inexperienced, helped in the mammoth undertaking, as well as volunteers from as near as Falmouth and as far away as Costa Rica. Proficiencies were cultivated in pop-riveting, caulking, drill-screwing, and teetering on ladders.

Would we repeat the same design next time? The panels, curving inward in the center to form concave troughs, have their advantages. The curve transmits light more evenly through the day than a flat surface, avoiding the sharp peak of heat input at noon characteristic of flat glazing surfaces. Comparing the curved surface with the flat, less light enters at noon, but more light enters near sunrise and sunset. New Alchemy computer simulations of light transmission suggest that over a day almost exactly the same total amount of light gets through the curved surface as a flat one. The more evenly distributed light of the curved panels probably increases plant photosynthesis by avoiding both leave overheating around noon and underlighting in the early morning and late afternoon. More constant light entry also prevents excessive air temperatures and allows storage components more time to soak up the heat.

The curves also give strength, allowing much less structural support. The bellies of the fiberglass draw water condensation away from the structural wood rafters and down to a drip edge that spills the condensation droplets into the gutter. Each panel collects as much as a gallon of condensate over a winter night.

On the negative side, the curves add 12 percent more surface area than a flat expanse on the south side, and the heat loss through the glazing is correspondingly higher. Curving the panels, hanging them in place, and sealing the edges consume enormous amounts of time.

If we did choose to keep the same shape, we might assemble the panels differently next time.

Rather than a sandwich of wood two-by-two inside, fiberglass sheet, aluinum channel, fiberglass sheet, wood 1x batten outside, we might use a sandwich of bevel-edged two-by-six support inside, fiberglass (0.025 in.), 1x wood spacer, fiberglass (0.04 in.), outside aluminum angle batten (see accompanying diagram).

The wooden spacers avoid the time-consuming procedure of pop-riveting the fiberglass to the aluminum channel. Wood spacers should also allow the fiberglass to be nailed directly to the support rafter. The thin outside aluminum batten avoids the early morning and late afternoon shading that occurs with thicker wooden battens that protrude above the glazing surfaces.

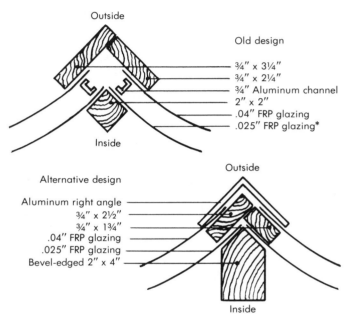

Old design
¾″ x 3¼″
¾″ x 2¼″
¾″ Aluminum channel
2″ x 2″
.04″ FRP glazing
.025″ FRP glazing*

Alternative design
Aluminum right angle
¾″ x 2½″
¾″ x 1¾″
.04″ FRP glazing
.025″ FRP glazing
Bevel-edged 2″ x 4″

*The original inner skin was 0.04 in. fiberglass reinforced polyester. The 0.025 in. skin was installed upon reglazing for better light transmission.

Time constraints limited the reglazing project to reassembling the old design. The project was completed in November 1979 and cost the institute $1,083 in professional carpentry help and $946 in materials beyond those contributed. In addition, the project required several person-months of New Alchemy staff labor. We trust that we will not have to repeat such a massive undertaking in the near future, that the manufacturer's claim of a 20 year lifetime for the new glazing is true. The longevity of solar glazings remains a critical question for materials science.

The initial results of installing the new glazing are encouraging. The panels appear more transparent than the old ones ever were. The vegetable crop in December 1979 outweighed production in December 1978 by 2.7 times. Though crops and weather differed slightly, the predominant change was the new glazing. The Ark once again sails through winter blizzards with a tropical climate within.

Paul Sun

Modeling and Design of Future Bioshelters

Joe Seale and John Wolfe

There are myriad design possibilities for the next generation of bioshelters. Questions that need to be answered concern such difficult design trade-offs as light vs. warmth and such elegant design synergies as aquaculture units doubling as heat storage. Building shape, glazing, thickness of insulation, insulated area, and internal components influence the interior solar climate. Creating computer models to test such design variables is considerably more economical than putting up separate buildings to do so. The computer model, called SUNAI1, explores domes with different types and numbers of solar membranes, with different aspects (height-to-diameter ratio) and with various interior configurations of soil, plants, and water.

Description of the Program

DOME 1 dynamically simulates solar dome temperatures based on hourly weather data measured at Boston's Logan Airport. The weather data consists of wind speed, temperature, total incidence of solar radiation, and a computed breakdown into direct and diffuse sunlight components. In comparison to Logan, New Alchemy on Cape Cod experiences lower wind speeds, slightly higher temperatures, and more sunlight.

The shape of the dome is approximated by 50 facets. Light penetration of each facet is based on the solar incidence angle with respect to the facet and a transmission function based on the glazing materials (five glazing configurations are tested). Structural framing reduces the effective glazing area. Light penetrating the dome and hitting the opposite glazing is partially transmitted and partially reflected back into the dome.

The absorption of entering light is divided three ways according to the solar elevation. The three absorptive surfaces are

1. Translucent aquaculture silos.
2. Soil.
3. Plant surfaces in thermal equilibrium with the air.

The heat storage elements are: air (includes plant mass), the water of the aquaculture units, and soil subdivided into three layers (0–3, 3–12, and 12–36 in. in depth).

Heat flow driven by temperature differences occurs between

1. The adjacent layers of soil.
2. The topsoil layer and interior air.
3. Water and interior air.
4. Interior air and exterior air.

Interior-to-exterior heat exchange includes a combined conduction/convection/radiation coefficient for the dome glazing and a comparable term for the structural members. Air infiltration comprises additional heat loss and depends on air humidity and wind speed.

Easily varied input parameters include the following:

1. Dome radius and height.
2. Shading from structural framing.
3. Thermal conductivity of structural framing.
4. Glazing configuration (number of layers and types of glazing, including Southwall Corporation's HEAT MIRROR.
5. Reference air infiltration rate and wind speed dependence.
6. Average dome humidity.
7. Plant cover as a fraction of total ground area.

8. Ground corrugation factor (corrects air/soil heat transfer area for raised growing beds).
9. Soil thermal conductivity and heat storage capacity.
10. Number of standard-size solar ponds (5 ft diameter and 5 ft high water-filled silos).
11. Overheating temperature above which heat is vented to the outside.
12. Time interval of the simulation.

The computer, directed by DOME 1, takes TMY weather data, combines it with the hypothetical building's characteristics, and predicts the resulting light and temperature levels within. The computer makes its predictions by moving through imaginary time in small increments (or steps), calculating temperatures within the building at each step. This is the process of computer simulation. For all simulation runs that follow, the interval was six minutes. For each time interval the program computes rates of heat flow according to present temperature differences and insulation rate (sunlight intensity) as thus rates of temperature change. These rates determine temperatures at the next time point and ultimately the temperature fluctuations through time.

The simulated temperatures may be slightly underestimated because

1. Air film thermal resistances on the inside and outside of the dome skin may be considerably higher than the standard ASHRAE (American Society of Heating, Refrigration, and Air Conditioning Engineers) coefficients used. The dome's shape may foster low turbulence air flow along its inner and outer surfaces, creating a thick insulating air film.
2. Reflection of light into the dome off the ground surrounding the dome is not considered.
3. Heat production from compost is not considered.

On the other hand, the simulated temperatures may be slightly overestimated because

1. Ground perimeter heat loss is not considered.
2. Reflection of light off interior surfaces and back out the dome is not considered.

Results

The results of the DOME1 simulation are summarized in Tables 1, 2, and 3. The program's weather data covers the period from January 15 to February 14, and encompasses the harshest combination of cold weather, cloudiness, and low sun angles. In all runs the dome diameter is set at 80 ft. The model assumes the dome contains no active fan-driven heat storage components, but does include 36 solar ponds (5ft diameter and 5ft high water-filled silos).

Table 1. CONDITIONS IN HYPOTHETICAL DOME BIOSHELTERS—JAN. 15 TO FEB. 14.

Glazings	Aspect[a]	Interior Light Level[b]	Temperatures (°F)		
			Avg. Midpoint	Avg. Daily Swings	Monthly Extremes
Three (heat mirror)	¼	277	55.3	13.9	42.4–74.3
	⅜	323	55.0	15.1	39.7–74.8
	½	378	53.0	16.4	36.3–73.6
Three (reg. film)	¼	345	53.6	16.5	37.8–74.7
	⅜	394	51.7	17.5	34.8–73.6
	½	453	49.6	18.5	31.7–72.3
Two reg. layers	¼	358	48.4	16.4	32.3–69.5
	⅜	408	46.7	17.4	29.7–68.5
	½	469	46.1	18.2	27.1–67.8

[a]Height/diameter; diameter is always 80 ft.
[b]Light has the units BTU ft^{-2} day^{-1} on the plant beds.

Although the computer calculates new light intensities every hour, and new heat flow rates and temperatures every six minutes, the information from a monthlong simulation can be summarized by the following five numbers.

1. Light intensity inside the dome striking the plant beds, averaged over the month (BTU ft^{-2} day^{-1}). Compare these figures to 550 BTU ft^{-2} day^{-1} day for average light levels striking the ground outside.

2. Average midpoint temperature of dome air: the *midpoint* between daily minimum and maximum temperatures, averaged for the month. This is near, and probably slightly higher than, the average temperature. The outside average midpoint temperature was 28.8° F for the simulation month.

3. Average daily temperature swing of dome air: the *difference* between daily minimum and maximum temperatures, averaged for the month. The average daily temperature swing for outside air was 12.4° F for the simulation.

4. & 5. Monthly temperature extremes for dome air: the coldest and hottest temperatures found inside the dome over the entire simulation month. The outside air temperature extremes were 6° and 55° F. The inside overheating temperature, at which venting occurs, is 80° F for all the following simulations.

All five variables affect plant productivity within the dome. Higher light levels enhance plant growth. All crop varieties have an optimum average tem-

perature and an optimum day/night temperature swing (cool night temperatures reduce plant respiration, encouraging more efficient growth). Extremely low and high temperatures can permanently damage crops. Temperatures that persist below freezing can destroy even cool-weather crops, and temperatures above 80°–85° F often cause bolting and bitter flavor.

Table 1 compares solar domes with different numbers and kinds of glazings, and with different height-to-diameter ratios (aspects). The glazings considered are the following:

1. Three layers of solar covers. The interior and exterior glazings are made of low-iron glass. Between them lies Suntek's Heat Mirror, a film that transmits some sunlight but reflects back into the dome most of the infrared radiation that would othewise represent a heat loss. Heat Mirror must be placed in a dessicated space between layers of vapor-impervious material (e.g., glass).
Maximum Light Transmission: 60%
Heat Loss Coefficient: 0.23 BTU ft^{-2} hr^{-1} °F^{-1}

2. Three layers of standard solar covers. Low-iron glass or a plastic equivalent make up the inner and outer skins. Between them lies a highly transparent solar film (e.g., one mil Teflon FEP film).
Maximum Light Transmission: 74%
Heat Loss Coefficient: 0.40 BTU ft^{-2} hr^{-1} °F^{-1}

3. Two layers of standard solar covers, consisting of low-iron glass or a plastic equivalent.
Maximum Light Transmission: 78%
Heat Loss Coefficient: 0.60 BTU ft^{-2} hr^{-1} °F^{-1}

These glazing alternatives represent a very important trade-off between light transmission and insulating value.

The height-to-diameter ratios, or aspects, considered are:

1. A shallow ¼ dome with a maximum height of 20 ft and a diameter of 80 ft.
2. A moderate ⅜ dome with a height of 30 ft.
3. A full hemisphere (½) dome with a height of 40 ft.

Table 2. INTERIOR LIGHT LEVELS AND MINIMUM TEMPERATURES FOR VARIOUS DOME GLAZINGS AND ASPECTS, INDEXED TO THE HEAT MIRROR SANDWICH AND TO THE SHALLOW ¼ DOME. BASED ON DATA FROM TABLE 1.

Light Index (Ratio):

Glazing Comparison		Aspect Comparison	
3 w/H.M. = 1.0		¼ = 1.0	
3 w/Film = 1.20 to 1.25		⅜ = 1.14 to 11.17	
2 Layers = 1.24 to 1.29		½ = 1.31 to 1.36	

Minimum Temperature Index (Degrees Fahrenheit):

Glazing Comparison		Aspect Comparison	
3 w/H.M. = 0.0		¼ = 0.0	
3 w/Film = −4.6 to −4.9		⅜ = −2.6 to −3.0	
2 Layers = −9.2 to −10.1		½ = −5.2 to −6.1	

Table 3. AIR AND WATER TEMPERATURE DATA FOR VARIOUS DESIGN CONFIGURATIONS AND MODEL COEFFICIENTS—
JAN. 15 TO FEB. 14.[a]

	Temperatures (°F)					
	Inside Air			Solar Ponds		
	Midpoint Avg.	Avg. Daily Swing	Monthly Extremes	Midpoint Avg.	Avg. Daily Swing	Monthly Extremes
STANDARD RUN						
3 w/H.M.	55.0	15.1	39.7–74.8	55.8	3.1	45.4–65.0
3 w/Film	51.7	17.5	34.8–73.6	52.7	3.6	42.2–62.9
2 Layers	46.7	17.4	29.,7–68.5	47.8	3.6	38.2–58.0
ALUMINUM STRUCTURE AS THERMAL BRIDGE						
3 w/H.M.	50.6	14.8	35.0–69.6	51.5	3.0	41.4–63.3
3 w/Film	48.8	17.2	31.9–70.0	49.9	3.5	39.7–61.7
2 Layers	44.9	17.1	27.9–66.7	46.1	3.5	36.9–57.1
LOWER AIR INFILTRATION RATE						
3 w/H.M.	57.5	15.5	43.1–78.9	57.7	3.2	48.7–67.8
3 w/Film	53.3	18.0	36.9–78.1	53.8	3.7	44.0–65.2
2 Layers	47.7	17.8	31.1–72.2	48.4	3.7	39.1–59.8
NO SOLAR PONDS						
3 w/H.M.	54.5	24.6	31.9–80.0	54.8	4.5	41.9–67.1
3 w/Film	51.6	27.8	27.3–80.0	51.8	5.0	39.1–65.0
2 Layers	47.4	27.6	23.4–80.0	47.3	4.8	35.0–60.5
NO PLANT COVER						
3 w/H.M.	53.9	11.3	40.1–70.4	55.9	2.7	45.9–64.4
3 w/Film	50.3	13.1	34.9–69.4	52.7	3.2	42.6–62.5
2 Layers	45.3	13.2	29.9–64.8	47.8	3.1	38.6–57.7
FLAT GROUND, NO RAISED BEDS						
3 w/H.M.	55.3	16.9	38.8–76.8	55.7	3.3	45.2–65.1
3 w/Film	52.0	19.5	33.8–75.7	52.6	3.7	42.0–62.6
2 Layers	47.0	19.2	28.9–70.5	47.7	3.7	38.1–58.2
WET, HEAVY SOIL						
3 w/H.M.	55.4	14.3	40.3–74.8	56.3	3.1	45.6–66.8
3 w/Film	51.8	16.7	35.2–72.8	52.8	3.6	42.3–64.3
2 Layers	46.7	16.6	30.1–67.6	47.9	3.6	38.3–59.5
DRY, LIGHT SOIL						
3 w/H.M.	55.0	15.9	39.1–75.5	55.5	3.2	45.3–64.5
3 w/Film	51.7	18.5	34.2–74.4	52.4	3.7	42.1–62.5
2 Layers	46.7	18.3	29.2–69.5	47.6	3.7	38.1–58.1
LOWER RELATIVE HUMIDITY (50%)						
3 w/H.M.	56.3	15.2	40.0–76.7	57.1	3.2	46.3–67.4
3 w/Film	52.4	17.7	35.3–74.6	53.3	3.7	42.7–64.5
2 Layers	47.2	17.5	30.1–69.5	48.1	3.6	38.5–58.8

[a]Height is always 30 ft, diameter 80 ft. Aspect is therefore ⅜.

Table 1 shows that during even the harshest month, the triple-glazed domes create an acceptable greenhouse environment. The table also reveals three very important trends:

1. The higher the aspect of the dome, the more light strikes the plant beds.
2. The higher the aspect of the dome, the wider the temperature swings and the lower the minimum monthly temperatures.
3. The heat mirror glazing sandwich creates the warmest temperatures but the lowest light levels, while the two layers of glazing create the highest light levels and the coolest temperatures.

The ⅜ aspect heat mirror dome and the ¼ aspect regular triple glazed dome represent the best compromise between light and warmth. Temperatures are a bit lower than the Cape Cod Ark, while light levels are slightly higher.

Table 3 evaluates the thermal impact of various design options (design testing), and examines changes in assumed model coefficients (sensitivity

testing). In all cases a ⅜ aspect 80 ft diameter dome is tested with the three glazing configurations listed above. All the results are compared to the "standard run," which matches the results listed in Table 1. Table 3 lists solar pond water temperatures as well as interior air temperatures.

In the standard run, the model assumes the aluminum framing for the geodesic structure has a thermal R-value of one (plus air film resistance). This insulating value could be provided by ¼ in. foam covering the inner or outer surface of the aluminum framing, or by a 1 in. wood spacer between inner and outer aluminum ribs.

The first design test in Table 3 looks at what happens if the aluminum structure is continuous from interior to exterior, creating a thermal "bridge" or "short circuit" for escaping heat. The change lowers minimum temperatures in all cases. It most drastically affects the best-insulated dome glazed with heat mirror (causing a 4.7° F drop in minimum temperature) and least affects the worst-insulated double glazed dome (causing only a 1.8°

F drop). Insulating the structural members is more critical in the well-insulated design because heat loss from uninsulated members is great relative to the small total heat loss.

The second design test, reducing the air infiltration rate, demonstrates the inverse of the same principle. Lowering the air infiltration rate makes a significant improvement in the well-insulated heat mirror dome (a 3.4° F gain) and a lesser improvement in the double glazed dome (a 1.4° F gain).

The third design test removes the aquaculture component from the building. With the removal of this major thermal mass, all the domes exhibit 10° F wider average daily temperature swings, and 6–8° F lower monthly minimum temperatures. This computer run demonstrates the critical role solar ponds play in storing heat.

The drop in minimum temperature is greatest in the heat mirror dome. Successive degradations in dome insulation or heat storage cause lessening decrements in temperature. In the extreme cases of no insulation or no storage, nighttime dome temperatures could drop no lower than ambient temperatures. Hence we find that the more poorly insulated dome configurations have less to lose by reductions in heat storage.

The inverse of the heat storage principle is demonstrated in the next case. Here the plant cover is removed (in the standard run, plants cover 70 percent of the available surface area). This allows sunlight to strike the soil directly, rather than striking plant leaves that in turn heat the air. Thus removing the plant cover increases the effectiveness of soil heat storage. As the heat-retention principle suggests, this leads to a 0.4° F improvement in minimum temperatures for the heat mirror dome, but only a 0.2° F increase for the double glazed dome. In absolute terms, plant cover is not a critical factor in either case.

In the standard run, soil surface exchange area is enhanced by taking into account the sides of walk-way trenches between raised plant beds (a 1.4 times greater surface area than flat was assumed). As shown in Table 3, a flat growing surface yields slightly wider temperature swings and slightly lower minimum temperatures. The drop is small, but perhaps significant (0.9° F for heat mirror, 0.8° F for double glazing).

The last three runs change assumed coefficients in the model, and provide what is known as a sensitivity test. The first two of these runs examine the assumed properties of the dome's soil. In the first run, a wetter and heavier soil than that in the standard run is assumed. In the second run, a drier and lighter (e.g., higher humus content) soil is assumed. The wetter and heavier the soil, the better it holds and conducts heat. The extremes between wet and dry soil properties account for only a 0.9° to 1.2° F change in minimum temperatures of the simulation runs. The model is therefore not very sensitive to the unknown properties of the particular soil in the dome.

The last run alters the assumed average relative humidity of the air. At typical indoor temperatures, small changes in relative humidity represent large changes in air heat content because of the heat content of the water vapor. Losing humid interior air means a much greater heat loss than losing dry air of the same temperature. The standard run assumes a relative humidity of 70% whereas the last run assumes 50 percent. A 0.4° to 1.1° F increase in minimum temperature results. The average relative humidity is a large unknown in the model; in the Cape Cod Ark relative humidity cycles as low as 30 percent during the day and as high as 100 percent at night. The relative humidity has more impact during the day, when temperatures are elevated, since warmer air holds more water vapor at a given relative humidity. In future models it may be worthwhile to model the humidity cycles directly, although the present model does not seem unduly sensitive to different assumed humidities.

In summary then, four conclusions can be drawn:

1. An acceptable winter greenhouse environment is created by a triple glazed dome (with or without the special heat mirror film) containing solar ponds and situated in coastal New England.

2. The shallower the dome, the darker and warmer the interior becomes.

3. Better insulation, more heat storage, and more heat-storage exchange surface all reduce temperature swings and raise temperatures.

4. Insulation and heat-storage improvements have a greater temperature effect on already well insulated domes.

The next step in modeling solar domes is to examine them with opaque, insulated walls having reflective inner surfaces. Examining light entry through separate facets of clear domes can suggest the best glazing/insulation boundary for domes partially clad with opaque insulation. The facets transmitting the least amount of light should be insulated first.

Figure 1 shows the average daily incoming light transmitted through 300 facets of a double-glazed hemispherical dome. Figure 2 depicts light entering each facet, *minus* light that enters from the opposite side, shoots through the dome, and exits out that facet. Negative numbers occur along the steep northern facets in Figure 2, indicating that more sunlight leaves through these facets than

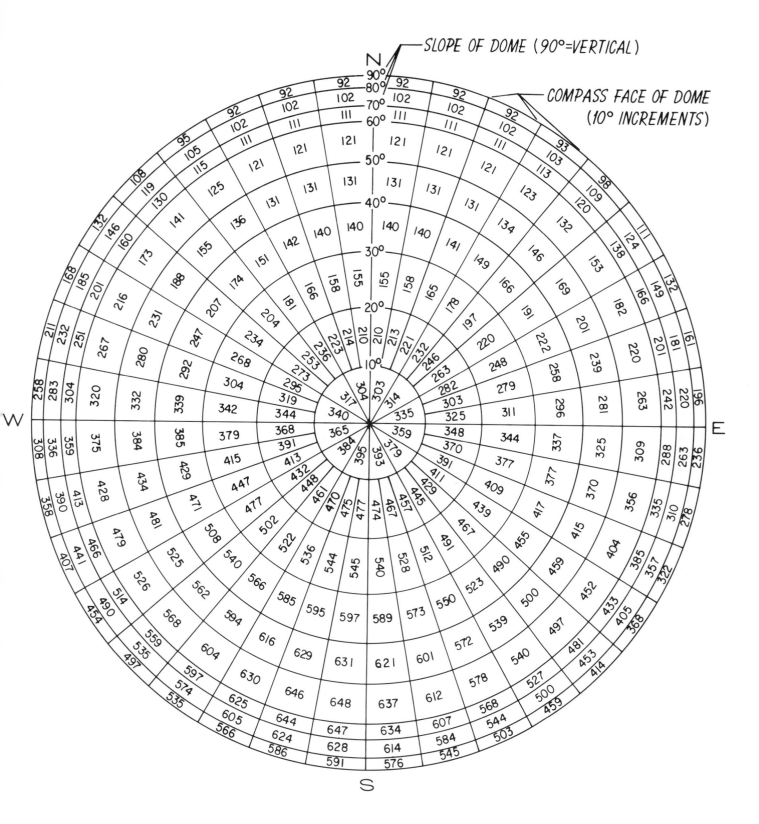

Figure 1. Incoming light gain transmitted through 300 facets of a double-glazed dome. Logan Airport, Boston, Massachusetts for a statistically typical January 15 to February 14 period.

enters. To maximize winter light levels on the growing beds, it is actually desirable to cover these facets with reflective foil to bounce outgoing light back into the building.

When using Figures 1 and 2, two caveats about the assumptions behind the model are in order:

1. No ground reflection is included in the model. This assumption underestimates light entry for steeper southerly surfaces.

2. Diffuse radiation is assumed evenly distributed across the sky. In fact, diffuse radiation clusters around the sun's position (see sky distribution patterns of dif-

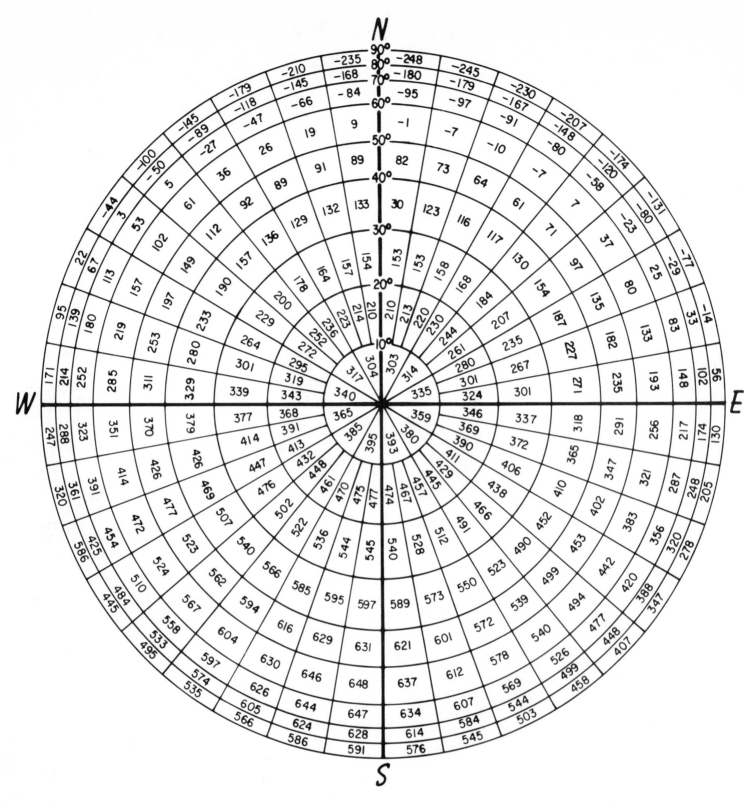

Figure 2. Net light gain (entering minus exiting light) through 300 facets of a double-glazed dome. Logan Airport, Boston, Massachusetts for a statistically typical January 15 to February 14 period.

fuse radiation diagrammed on p. 82 of Duffie and Beckman's *Solar Engineering of Thermal Processes*. The assumption tends to underestimate light entry on steeper south sides, overestimate it on the north.

Future versions of the computer model will examine north wall insulation, movable night insulation, and other shapes (such as Quonset and A-frame). With the climates of all these design options quantified by the computer model, we can then predict the crop productivity and capital cost of each design option. We will then know which design gives the maximum yield of organically grown off-season vegetables per dollar invested.

Ron Zweig

PUTTING OURSELVES
on the LINE

They say that there is often a certain simultaneity to new ideas. The experience of Alfred Wallace and Charles Darwin—who independently came up with similar theories of evolution—comes at once to mind. In a modest way, in early 1979 the same sort of thing occurred at New Alchemy. For years we had been shifting a bit uneasily when enthusiastic visitors to the farm would say something like, "It's wonderful! And I suppose you live like this at home too?"

Awkward. Because at the time, we didn't. But in the early winter of 1979, Denise—stationed in the main office, which functions rather like the central nervous system of the place—was the first to get wind of what was coming. She began to pick up scraps from various conversations, direct or over-heard. Piecing them together she came up with the news that six different New Alchemy households had decided to go solar. Predictably and charac-teristically, we were all intending to do so in six very different, highly individual ways. Just what the dynamics were that made this blossoming of solar structures close to simultaneous, we're still not sure. Perhaps sometimes ideas are contagious, like colds.

A year and more later our respective efforts at solarizing are complete. I asked the various people involved to tell their stories in their own ways. The pieces that follow are just that: why and how six different households incorporated solar green-houses into their lives and how it feels to have done so.

N.J.T.

The BAM[1] Greenhouse: Homemade Tapestry

Hilde Maingay

It is winter vacation 1980. Flowering geraniums, impatiens, and nasturtiums. A summer bouquet in the winter. Sitting at the table, I can stretch my arm to pick a big salad for dinner. I clip the lawn of the floor under the table—no sweeping here! The kids play a game of cards in T-shirts. Laughter and red, warm faces. A cool drink of grape juice,

---

[1]BAM = Barnhart–Atema–Maingay greenhouse.

just taken from the icehouse, in their hands. Not too much later and the grapevine just outside the greenhouse door wil be "watered" by the boys. Ate walks by the honey pot in the kitchen, sticks his finger in the pot and licks, then goes outside to get some logs of firewood.

The smells from the oven mix with those from the scented geraniums. A kale and chard soufflé is cooking. Sven takes the container with kitchen scraps and empty eggshells outside to the chickens, returns with a handful of beautiful eggs. Jurgen is in charge of making dinner. He loves custard pudding—the fresh eggs never make it to the cold storage in the icehouse. Layers of homemade applesauce alternate with layers of custard pudding and are topped with raspberry sauce! The raspberries last year were picked from the bushes in the chicken yard near by. The bushes give shade to the chickens and pollen to the bees, the chickens in turn keep the berry patch weeded and fertilized while the bees pollinate the berry flowers and give us honey to make the sauce.

While dinner is getting ready, I mix up some potting soil. As is the soil for the vegetable beds in the greenhouse, the potting soil is mainly made up from the soil and manure in the chicken yard (a bag of laying mash can go a long way—eggs, meat, compost), then mixed with the some peat moss and vermiculite. I seed a flat with birdhouse gourds, special seeds grown by a member of the American Gourd Society. The gourds last for several years and will attract many birds to the gardens where they will act as a natural pest control.

It is eighty degrees in the greenhouse, bright and light. The house is comfortable at seventy degrees, but the lights are already on. The kids' rooms in the basement are pretty constant at a cool sixty to sixty-five degrees. Little excess heat comes from the oil furnace—next to their rooms—these days, as it no longer needs to run except for domestic hot water. Ate starts the fire in the wood stove, puts the insulated shutters in the windows. The sun is low behind our neighbor's house. It will soon get chilly in the greenhouse. The kettles are filled with water and put on the stove. Drips of water sizzle as the stove is heating up—there will be hot water for dishes, coffee, and tea after dinner.

In the greenhouse the chameleon moves slowly behind the Spanish moss hanging in the bamboo. A spider drops down from the wooden beam. Ants crawl into their hideouts behind the stone walls, and O. J., our big white daddy goose, knocks on the glass door of the greenhouse asking for company and some fresh kale, chard, and grass shoots. Tomorrow I will sprinkle the wood stove ashes on the lawn so the grass will get rich and green in the spring when the goslings will hatch. Tomorrow I also will do some bench grafting onto the hardy apple rootstocks and pot the new bee plants that just arrived today through the mail. Let's see . . . and then I should also seed the tomatoes, eggplants, peppers, chard, marigolds, rosemary, thyme, parsley, and sage—and a few cucumbers to replace the winter greens in the greenhouse and provide shade in the summer—and I shouldn't forget to check on the nuts that are being stratified in the cold storage, and . . .

"Dinner is ready, Mom."

"Earle, dinner!"

Hilde Maingay

The BAM Greenhouse: It's Great

Ate Atema

It's great. The greenhouse adds a new feel to the house, a more unrestricted feel. At times, letting the temperature soar to 120 degrees and the humidity to saturation while reading or just simply relaxing can be undeniably therapeutic to mind and body.

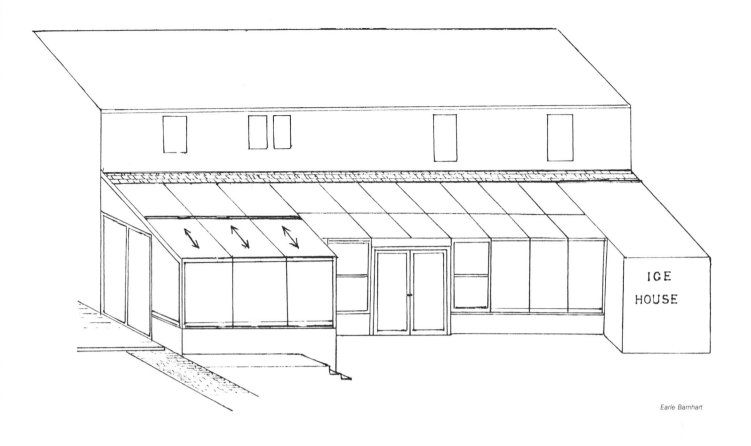

Earle Barnhart

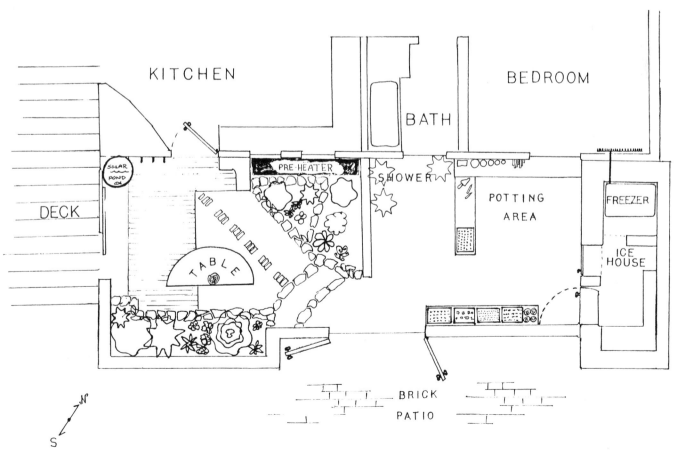

KITCHEN

BEDROOM

BATH

DECK

SOLAR POND

PRE-HEATER

SHOWER

POTTING AREA

FREEZER

ICE HOUSE

TABLE

N

S

BRICK PATIO

Earle Barnhart

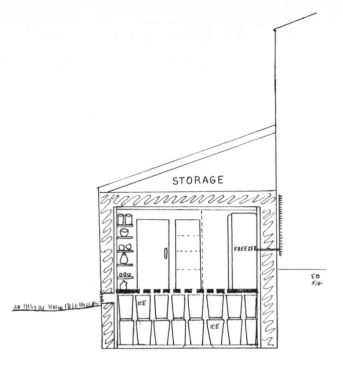

ICE HOUSE FOOD STORAGE

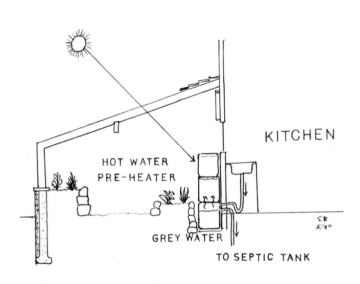

KITCHEN

HOT WATER
PRE-HEATER

GREY WATER

TO SEPTIC TANK

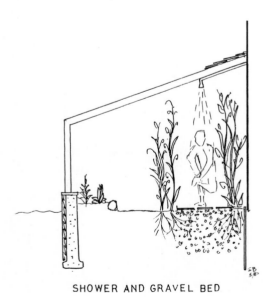

SHOWER AND GRAVEL BED

Earle Barnhart

An amazing fact of life with the greenhouse is its truly open warmth in the winter. If only we could tear down the wall separating it from our dining room; it would be quite an experience to have a formal meal by candlelight under the stars and surrounded by a crush of foliage in the midst of December.

Having the greenhouse is fantastic. As a matter of fact, it's so much fun, I don't think I could imagine having a house without at least something like this.

The BAM Greenhouse: Notes on Intent, Function, and Form

Earle Barnhart

In the lineage of bioshelters, the several attached home greenhouses built by New Alchemists this past year are not so much a second generation as they are stepchildren. Each is descended partly from New Alchemy's experimental/research bioshelters and partly from individual family style, and the resulting forms are surprisingly different. As an institute we will continue to evolve successive generations of experimental bioshelters to explore concepts, but as individuals we will find that these at-home systems will be the real test of practical viability.

Our greenhouse was designed to include several qualities either overlooked or lacking in the Ark. We wanted it to be architecturally durable, domestically comfortable, and relatively maintance-free. The clearest lesson we learned by planning and constructing the greenhouse is that there are great advantages to building carefully and slowly: carefully so that shortcuts are not forever-after regretted and slowly so that serendipitous changes can be considered and included. We did all of the construction ourselves, slowly, and in many instances suddenly saw that a variation from the original drawings would be much more convenient or aesthetic. These were invariably matters of perception, unpredictable from paper drawings, such as where was most pleasing to walk and what shapes of corners or heights of ceilings seemed comfortable. Often an array of strings or light poles at the proposed position would decide the matter.

Concepts and details of design that may be of interest include the following:

Durability—We wanted a structure that we would not have to worry about, replace, nor repair for a long time. The post-and-beam construction we chose will support every conceivable snow load and minimizes lapping lumber, which is prone to hold moisture. Thermopane glass inlaid into the beams minimizes maintenance. All connections are screwed for easier replacement.

Annual Function—There is a tendency for new greenhouse designers to think only of heat and only of midwinter. In reality the greenhouse is growing plants year-round, and for most of the year heat is not as important as enough light. We adopted the strategy of using the money normally put into several small vents toward large doors that open in summer and three glass roof panels that slide open. These changes reduce the distinction between inside and outside and let the greenhouse approach outdoor conditions.

Practical Matters—Our greenhouse has places to grow food, start seedlings, propagate perennial food plants, take a shower, eat lunch, and store food. Getting high and meditating through one means or another will not be treated in this section.

Innovation and Testing—There are a few ideas about bioshelters that can best be tested with the interactions of a household. We would like to test such integrations as: (1) Using heat from daily graywater to heat the greenhouse in the winter; (2) Using a wind-powered freezer to cool the icehouse adjacent to the greenhouse; (3) Gradually propagating the perennial food plants needed to landscape the property; (4)

Exploring the physical, psychic, and spiritual implications of someday living in a larger, community-scale bioshelter.

Architectural Aesthetics—Appearance and material beauty count as much as efficiency in a living space. We wanted to be able to see into our back yard, to have a table for greenhouse dining, and to be able to enter or travel through the area easily, enjoying the materials used. Our ideal is to have such a blend of plants, floors, glass, and terraces that one can't be certain whether one is inside or outside.

We Scrounged and Recycled

Denise and Dick Backus

Each winter afternoon at dusk the cry of "shade and curtain time" goes through the house as one of us reminds the rest to draw the shades and curtains against the night. We've also added insulation and used laminated reflective backing on curtains to seal up northern windows (unimportant in our house) in our attempts to keep in that precious heat we've paid so dearly for. What to do next?

Denise Backus

The main rooms of our house—the kitchen and the living room—face due south and invite the attachment of a solar greenhouse. Because we have a lot to learn, we have begun by putting up a small and inexpensive structure. The greenhouse is about 13 ft long, 6½ ft from front to back, and 10 ft high at its point of attachment to the house. It encloses two living room windows and two cellar windows. The living room windows open high up in the greenhouse and the cellar ones at ground level, offering a good arrangement for setting up a natural convection loop. When the sun shines and the windows between house and greenhouse are open, warm air flows into the living room and cool make-up air enters the greenhouse from the cellar.

The principal element in the construction of the greenhouse is 11 recycled window sashes, each about 50 in. on a side. Three sashes form the vertical front and two rows of three the sloping roof; there is one sash at the front of each of the end walls. The sashes are supported by a simple frame of two-by-fours that rests on a concrete footing. Inch-thick styrofoam extends 24 in. into the ground outside the footing. The end walls that are not glass are plywood with styrofoam insulation on the inside. Monsanto 602 stapled over the outside forms the second glazing. One end wall has a 4 ft high door, which is the only entrance. Two 55 gallon drums filled with water add to the thermal mass inside. Plastic stapled over the joint between house and greenhouse mostly eliminates the infiltration of cold air. Near the end of the greenhouse's first winter, we are still adding to it and altering it.

The make-up air entering the greenhouse through the cellar windows at first came directly from the cold cellar. Now we lead it from the coolest part of the living room through a floor register into a duct formed on the cellar overhead by boxing in two of the floor joists. The duct leads to one of the cellar windows and is connected to it by a plastic skirt. This way the make-up air entering the greenhouse is already somewhat warm.

If the windows between house and greenhouse are opened when the greenhouse is cool, the convection loop runs backward; warm air flows from the living room into the greenhouse and cold air from the greenhouse wells up into the living room via the cellar window, duct, and floor register. To prevent this from happening we installed valves in the windows between house and greenhouse. We tacked pieces of fishnet over the windows. Sheets of very light plastic, like the kind in which dry cleaning is returned, are fastened on the living room side of the net in the living room windows and on the greenhouse side of the net in the cellar

windows. When the greenhouse is hot, the plastic is easily wafted away from the fishnet in both windows by air flowing in the directions we want it to flow. When the greenhouse is cold and air wants to go the wrong way, the plastic is blown up against the fishnet, and the flow is stopped. This arrangement lets us open the windows between warm house and cold greenhouse early in the morning before we go to work with the assurance that the house will only gain heat from the greenhouse, not lose heat to it, no matter what the day's weather turns out to be.

Articles about solar greenhouse designs generally discuss a night-curtain last, if at all. If the greenhouse is a small one like ours, a night-curtain is absolutely necessary. (Large greenhouses can get by without one, because they have a large thermal mass in proportion to the area of the glazing through which heat comes and goes.) Designing and making a good night-curtain is not easy. An outside curtain is simple to fit, but it must withstand wind and weather and so is necessarily expensive. An inside curtain is hard to hold up into place.

We opted for an inside curtain. It is held up against the glazing by pieces of ½ in. electrical conduit at greenhouse ends and middle bent to follow the sloping roof and vertical front. The curtain itself is a so-called Roman curtain. It is made of two layers of Bubbl-pak®, a plastic material incorporating cells of air. Made for packing fragile articles for shipment, Bubbl-pak® is not bad insulation. Light strips of wood run across and are attached to the curtain at 1 ft intervals, and four sets of screw eyes are twisted into the strips. Four cords for accordioning the curtain run through the screw eyes and raise the curtain when pulled.

There are two main spaces for growing things in our greenhouse. Leafy vegetables can be grown in a ground bed along the front of the greenhouse. Plants in pots or flats sit on boards spanning the space between the two upright 55 gallon drums at the greenhouse rear. (There are also a few plants growing in the ground around the feet of the drums.)

Measuring greenhouse performance is a difficult thing. At present we can only say that on a sunny day we see and feel warm air coming from the greenhouse into our living room, raising the temperature there. And though it has mainly been a heater so far, we also have had things growing in the greenhouse when outside all was frozen. An alpine strawberry charmed us all winter with its glossy green leaves, flawless white blossoms, and red fruit.

So the greenhouse warms us a little and gives us a few plants to eat and to please the eye. It is

a serene and toasty place to sit for a few minutes on a winter noon. In all these ways it brings us into a direct contact with our physical surroundings and so, makes us feel more alive. The cost, because we scrounged and recycled, and don't reckon in our labor, is about $250.

We are weekend gardeners, so the weather is always an interesting topic at our house. And, as for most people who work all week, a good weather weekend is a treat and often indicates what work gets done. Now, however, we are more aware than ever of the kind of day it is. And what are we going to do about those nice old cedars that shade our greenhouse for part of the day? They are our trees but also supply some of the only shade our close neighbors have in their tiny backyard. We have also become thermometer buffs. How hot in the greenhouse? What soil temperature? How many degrees of heat did it add to the house? Today, in mid-April it is 50 degrees outside; our house is 70. No heat is on. We still have a long way to go in our efforts to get off the oil habit, but getting there is a lot of fun and a continuing challenge. And the first one out of bed still checks out the day. Aaaah . . . another sunny one.

From the Ground Up

Christina Rawley and Ron Zweig

On our land we have planted two apple trees, two mulberry trees, a black walnut, and a copper beach. These and other deciduous trees will replace the pitch pines we removed to create an opening in the forest for our new house. On the cleared ground we have seeded buckwheat as the first cover crop and have started a vegetable garden just to the east of the house. As the summer unfolds it will stand amidst a sea of buckwheat. From the south, it appears to be sailing easterly, where it is greeted by the sun over Deep Pond each morning. The design, a modified saltbox, sits unobtrusively in its Cape Cod setting, facing south on Lily Pond.

We had searched for a house within bicycling distance of New Alchemy for nearly two years, but were unable to find one that could be modified for passive solar heating without major and expensive changes. Finally we chose to build from scratch.

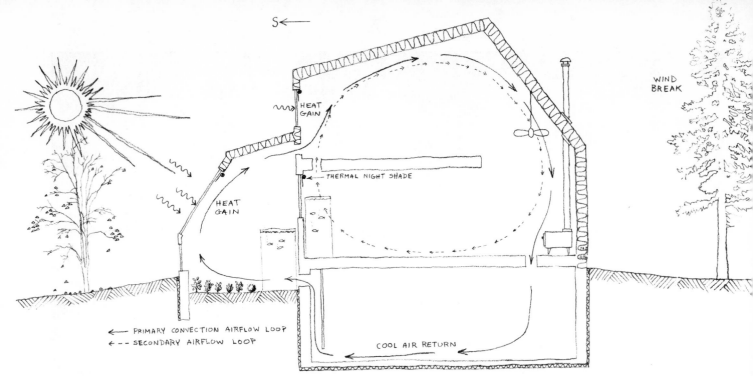

S ←

HEAT GAIN

THERMAL NIGHT SHADE

HEAT GAIN

WIND BREAK

← PRIMARY CONVECTION AIRFLOW LOOP
←-- SECONDARY AIRFLOW LOOP

COOL AIR RETURN

The house incorporates a synthesis of old and new concepts in both heating and cooling. Many are untested so far since we have just been living in it since early spring. The summer and winter months ahead will test it. The climate control lies in air convection through the house. There are vents in the floor and walls and a minimum of closed off areas.

The main convection heating loop incorporates the entire air volume including the greenhouse and basement. During the winter, air warmed in the greenhouse will rise into the second floor living area through air vents in the intervening wall. Cooler air will drop to the basement through floor vents on the north side of the first and second floors. A basement window in the lower level of the greenhouse provides a channel for the coolest air to circulate into the greenhouse for heating, thereby completing the convective loop. This should raise the temperature of the masonry, the cement foundation and basement walls and floor as the outside walls of the basement are fully insulated. At night the vents to the greenhouse will be closed. There will be solar-algae ponds in the greenhouse.

A wood stove back-up may be necessary on colder winter nights. When it is in use, south floor vents will be opened and the north ones closed. A ceiling fan in the stairwell will circulate heat through the house, minimizing stratification that would create a second air flow loop. the direction of the fan is reversible so that, during the summer, it can force cooler air upward and warmer air out upstairs open windows. So far the air flow pattern works quite well. We'll know how well by winter. It will depend largely on the effectiveness of the wall and ceiling insulation and the window shades we have yet to install.

We feel the house's real treasure is the green-house. We will be able to raise some of our food all year and apply many of the techniques we have developed and tested at New Alchemy. the agriculture/aquaculture will keep us in close contact with living plants and animals. Our work with New Alchemy's bioshelters has given us this more as vistors than co-inhabitants. We anticipate that the constant exposure to the micro-ecosystems in our greenhouse will give us an ongoing relationship with living things even in the starkest periods of New England winters. We shall be living as co-inhabitants in the processes and as co-cartakers of this dwelling and parcel of land.

Why Not a Solar Greenhouse on the Second Floor?

Barbara Chase

I first visited New Alchemy in the fall of 1978. At that time I was primarily interested in growing better food. I had decided to eat only organically grown food, having experienced six months of the ill effects of poisoning of some kind—possibly from grupper fish, which is high on the food chain, or from a cumulative effect from many poisons. Doctors could not determine the exact cause, since the poison had left my bloodstream quickly and settled in my nervous system. However, the helpless feeling and the ill effects were enough to make me determined to avoid all potentially harmful substances.

Ron Zweig

I was impressed with the accomplishments and the environment I found at New Alchemy. In January 1979 I became a volunteer. I worked with Earl Barnhart on experiments in tree propagation and with Hilde Maingay in the Six Pack solar greenhouse.

My time there, so close to nature, especially enjoying the sun in the greenhouse on long, cold winter days, was healing and inspiring, and gave me new hope.

I began to think a lot about whether I could incorporate such a greenhouse into my own house—and where. I have a steep hill at the back of my house on the south side. This slope of the land would make a first-floor greenhouse difficult, if not impossible. But why not on the second floor, where we have a walk-in closet off our bedroom on the south side of the house? I thought it could bear the weight because the house is framed in steel, and I've had a water bed on the second floor with no problem.

I called Solsearch, the architectural firm that helped design the Ark. Ole Hammarland drew some rough sketches for me with structural requirements and detail for materials. He gave me fair assurance that the second floor could carry the weight required.

I spoke to a neighbor in the business of remodeling houses who was interested in the uniqueness of the project. We agreed on a price, and much to my surprise, within a week construction was underway.

By mid to late April I was able to start seedlings for my outdoor summer gardens, a joyful experience that has increased with each new step toward completion of the greenhouse.

In the fall my husband built two garden beds for my vegetables and put up a shelf for potted plants. I began filling the beds with soil, compost, and peat moss. I moved plants from the outside garden to their new home for the winter.

To wake up in the morning to the sun shining on green growing vegetables, flowers, and aromatic herbs was a wonderful reward for the work almost completed. I put small stone for drainage into zinc pans, covering the wooden floor, and patio blocks the color of red bricks for walking between the garden beds. We put four solar-algae ponds in place and filled them with water for heat collection and storage.

In October 1979 I went to work for David Engstrom, assisting with the water chemistry and learning about aquaculture. I wanted an understanding of this in order to care for my fish.

By January I had twenty-two tilapia occupying two solar-algae ponds. I felt a sense of tranquillity watching the fish drift quietly or swim exhuberantly. The sunlight, especially the first morning rays, showed them off beautifully. The pond water was fertilizer for my plants. The system evolved into a balanced ecological cycle. My tranquillity comes from the search for an ecological balance and progress toward that end. All this life brought into a home gives me a feeling of rebirth. My happiest days are spent working in my solar greenhouse. I am recording information that will soon reveal how much food I'm growing. From what I've learned this year, I will be able to produce more next year.

Some of the energy I'm collecting is blown into the room below the bedroom with a half-horsepower fan. It is used to conserve other forms of energy-consuming heat, and is therefore turned on at opportune times, so as not to waste electricity.

Collecting heat from my solar greenhouse is an added benefit. I will soon tabulate statistics to show how much fuel this supplementary heat conserves.

My solar greenhouse symbolizes the ability to conserve nonrenewable energy resources. However, using the same energy to grow food and for heat is no symbol. My solar greenhouse is only my first step in the use of soft technology. The expanded use of solar greenhouses and other soft technology gives me hope in the larger scheme of world affairs. Our environment can become healthy without the need to use nuclear power and other polluting energy sources, and I hope the need for war over a limited supply of oil, or any essential life-sustaining resource can be eliminated.

Many people have the potential for growing some food all year round with the help of a passive solar addition to an existing house or a passive solar beginning for a new one. Once such a lifestyle is initiated, I believe the joy will be incentive for expansion.

The final benefit to me is a new opportunity for learning. I find the opportunity for exploration of nature intriguing and boundless, and the working toward an ecological balance equally so.

Rick Beck

Notes From a Professional

Rick Beck

Tanis Lane's greenhouse was designed and built to meet requirements she set forth. The main purpose of the greenhouse was to provide heat for the house, to allow plants to be grown year round, and yet to be roomy enough to feel comfortable and pleasant. Of course, it had to be as inexpensive as possible.

The design and construction of an attached bioshelter presents special problems not encountered in normal residential construction. The greenhouse designer must keep in mind that the design characteristics that yield maximum net heat gain are opposed to those that maximize biological production. Just as important is the careful consideration of details. As in most other activities, attention to detail makes the difference between adequacy and excellence. In the case of a bioshelter, it also determines the durability of the structure. Presumably any building addition beyond the most rudimentary should last as long as the house to which it is attached. I should like to relate these general problems to the design that evolved for Tanis's site.

The design emphasized the following:

1. Glazing all the way to the house wall to allow overhead light for plants.
2. Glazed end walls to allow maximum light in spring and fall. Removable insulation panels remain in place during winter to reduce heat loss.
3. Pit design to fit appropriate glazing angle to house and landscape, and to provide headroom inside.

4. A vent on the west wall, a door on the east wall, and a continous ridge vent to provide adequate ventilation.

The first and second design characteristics are somewhat opposed to those of the popular "sunspace" design, but from my experience with greenhouses, light penetration is very important if plant production is desired.

I researched the next set of problems, the construction details and choice of materials, carefully. The main enemy of a well-used greenhouse is rot. Clever construction copes with water and high humidity in two ways. Flowing and standing water from irrigation and condensation can be reduced by sloping all structural members and/or providing drainage holes. Water and humidity also require the use of corrosion and decay-resistant materials. I met these problems, and the problem of cost, by using salvaged materials from commerical greenhouses. These are materials designed and chosen to meet industrial durability standards. Redwood, cypress, galvanized iron, and glass are the main materials, and their worth is proven. They are milled to shed water, are of the finest grade, and can be reconstructed as energy efficient structures. Wood over fifty years old in excellent condition can still be found. With a little elbow grease, the wood and related hardware can be cleaned and repainted to be as serviceable as new materials in both appearance and structural integrity.

Such framing materials are easily adapted to many systems of double glazing, using combinations of glass, fiberglass, plastic, or insulated glass. In Tanis's greenhouse the outer glazing is recycled glass in the traditional lapped style (the upper pane of glass overlapping slightly the pane beneath it, like shingles). Inside we used a plastic film, which we are replacing with a second layer of glass, because the plastic has been destroyed several times by the household dog. Any of the inexpensive plastic films are subject to puncturing.

Commercial greenhouses are available for salvaging near most urban areas. They were designed for the age of cheap fossil fuels, and are not profitable in light of increased energy costs. When a commercial grower goes out of business, his greenhouse becomes a liability, and he will usually be very happy to relinquish it free, or at a very small price. Recycling then, seems sound, ethically and financially, particularly if redwood or cypress are wanted. From an ecological standpoint it is hardly justifiable to continue cutting redwoods, let alone cypress, for greenhouse construction, as they are being cut far faster than they are being replaced. Cypress management is not practiced because the trees grow so slowly as to be unprofitable.

We Threw Caution to the Sun

Nancy Jack Todd and John Todd

The house we have lived in for over ten years began its life as a late sixties ticky-tacky. It was heated by natural gas, and the insulation was close to nonexistent. It was definitely not the sort of house that lent credibility to our advocacy of the use of renewable sources of energy. Yet by some odds unlikely in so much of modern housing, our house was pretty. Its lines are good. It is on an acre and a half of land that slopes down to a pond. Some of the trees are quite large for the Cape. We have oaks and maples and locust and wild cherry, sumac, a poplar, and some willow. In the spring a dogwood hangs poetically over the pond. We love it here. It is where our children have grown and it is home.

Two years ago, however, we felt ourselves prompted by motivations for change more pressing than well-intentioned environmental ones. At that time the house had a deck on the east side. The door from the deck, which we always referred

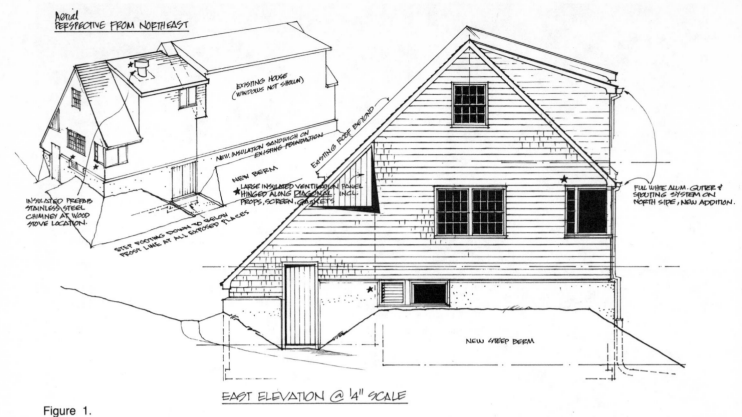

Aerial
PERSPECTIVE FROM NORTHEAST

EXISTING HOUSE (WINDOWS NOT SHOWN)

NEW. INSULATION SANDWICH ON EXISTING FOUNDATION

EXISTING ROOF BEYOND

NEW BERM

★ LARGE INSULATED VENTILATION PANEL HINGED ALONG DIAGONAL. INCL. PROPS, SCREEN, GASKETS

INSULATED PREFAB STAINLESS STEEL CHIMNEY AT WOOD STOVE LOCATION.

STEP FOOTING DOWN TO BELOW FROST LINE AT ALL EXPOSED PLACES

FULL WHITE ALUM. GUTTER & SPOUTING SYSTEM ON NORTH SIDE, NEW ADDITION.

NEW STEEP BERM

EAST ELEVATION @ ¼" SCALE

Figure 1.

DRAWN BY MALCOLM WELLS

★ REVISED 9.3
JUNE 1,

THE TODD HOUSE SHEET

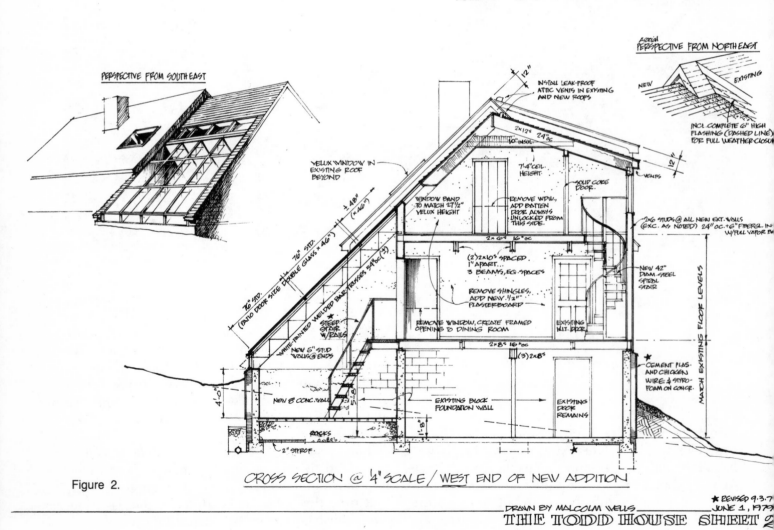

PERSPECTIVE FROM SOUTH EAST

Aerial
PERSPECTIVE FROM NORTHEAST

NEW   EXISTING

INSTALL LEAK-PROOF ATTIC VENTS IN EXISTING AND NEW ROOFS

INCL. COMPLETE 6" HIGH FLASHING (DASHED LINE) FOR FULL WEATHER CLOSUR

VENTS

VELUX WINDOW IN EXISTING ROOF BEYOND

2×12s 24" OC

30" INSUL.

7'-4" CEIL. HEIGHT.

SOLID CORE DOOR.

WINDOW BAND TO MATCH 27½" VELUX HEIGHT

REMOVE WDW., ADD BATTEN DOOR ALWAYS UNLOCKED FROM THIS SIDE.

2× 6"s   16" OC

2×6 STUDS @ ALL NEW EXT. WALLS (EXC. AS NOTED) 24" OC +6" FIBERGL IN W/FULL VAPOR B

(2) 2×10's SPACED. 1" APART... 3 BEAMS, EQ. SPACES

NEW 42" DIAM STEEL SPIRAL STAIR

REMOVE SHINGLES, ADD NEW. ½" PLASTERBOARD

REMOVE WINDOW, CREATE FRAMED OPENING TO DINING ROOM

EXISTING KIT. DOOR

STEEP STAIR W/RAILS

NEW 6" STUD WALLS @ ENDS

2×8s 16" OC

(3) 2×8's

★ CEMENT PLAS. AND CHICKEN WIRE. ¾ STYRO-FOAM ON CONCR.

NEW 6" CONC. WALL

EXISTING BLOCK FOUNDATION WALL

EXISTING DOOR REMAINS

MATCH EXISTING FLOOR LEVELS

ROCKS

2" STYROF.

Figure 2.

CROSS SECTION @ ¼" SCALE / WEST END OF NEW ADDITION

DRAWN BY MALCOLM WELLS

★ REVISED 9.3.7
JUNE 1, 1979

THE TODD HOUSE SHEET 2

to more familiarly as the porch, led into the kitchen and was the entrance to the house that everyone used. The porch was a wonderful place for early morning cups of coffee and sleepy conversations, and the railings made serviceable clotheslines. But slowly it was beginning to disintegrate. By Christmas of 1978 there were several planks loose or missing, and a shaky step. I was worried that my mother might trip during her Christmas visit.

The house posed another problem, this one a source of some friction. It was very small for a family of five, particularly when three of the five persisted in getting larger. One Sunday, as we were setting out on a late afternoon walk, while I was waiting for John to finish puttering with the goats, I paced about the porch. Then, as we headed toward the beach, I burst out . . . "What if we . . ." And the ideas tumbled out of both of us . . . "retrofit the whole house, then tear down the porch, replace it with a living room and a room above it for Jonathan. And in front of it . . . a greenhouse, solar heating, plants, vegetables, fish tanks, our own bioshelter."

We asked a lot of the project when we decided to retrofit our existing house to use less heating fuel and to add a new solar addition. We wanted the sun to do most of the work of heating not just the new addition, but the whole house as well. A wood stove was to provide the only backup except in extreme weather, when our old furnace would act as a standby. Another condition was that the electrical requirements for heat circulation and storage be minimal, say equivalent to two or three lightbulbs. We also wanted a fish farm as part of the deal, and last but not least, an interior that would be exciting for a lifetime. Architect Malcolm Wells came through with a solar design to match our heating and living goal and solar engineers Joe Seale and John Wolfe figured out how to keep electricity consumption to a minimum. We designed into the greenhouse area a household-scale solar fish farm for raising tilapia, catfish, trout, and eventually oysters in sea water.

The workings of the house are really quite simple. The fish farm, situated against the north wall of the partially submerged greenhouse, is made up of 10 "organ-pipe" translucent fiberglass tubes 8 ft high by 18 in. in diameter (see Figure 1), a variation in shape on the traditional New Alchemy solar-algae ponds. They serve double duty as fish-culture units and as primary heat-storage components. The tubes efficiently absorb solar energy during the day and release heat at night, warming the greenhouse and adding heat to the house as well. The other heat-storage component is the basement. Malcolm Wells recommended that it be clad on the outside with 4 in. of styrofoam and stuccoed. Now the interior basement walls and the contents of the basement, including furniture, boat, firewood, tools, and so forth, store heat blown in from the greenhouse.

The solar heating is primarily passive as the design called for a lot of thermopane tempered glass on the southern exposure (see Figure 2, Figure 3, and Figure 1). This effectively captures light and heat. Once trapped, the heat follows two basic routes: it is either stored in the fish tanks or is drawn by a 36 in. diameter fan powered by a ⅙ horsepower motor down from the apex of the greenhouse into the basement. Here it circulates the full length of the house before being recycled back into the base of the greenhouse. (See Figure 2 for air flow patterns through the house.)

Heat distribution to the living areas of the house is both active and passive. Air vents in each of the rooms and stairwells permit a passive upward flow of warm air from the basement. A more even and rapid distribution of air can be accomplished by activating the old blower system from the hot-air furnace. A ceiling fan in the living room allows us to circulate warmed air from the wood stove.

In the summer the glass on the southern side acts as an air accelerator, sucking cool outside air in, through the house, and up the stairs to exit via the north windows. The house is now much cooler in the summer. The solar heating cycles have worked well so far. We do not yet know if we will have to turn the old furnace on during extreme conditions in the dead of winter. Since the house was redesigned to be primarily, although not exclusively, heated by solar heat and a single wood stove, we would not see occasional use of the furnace in the future as a setback. A less-obvious reason why the house has performed as well as it has is the internal insulated shutter system created by Terry Eisen and Greg Wozena. The shutters placed on all of the vertical windows are elegant, easy to operate, and very saving in heating needs.

Malcolm Well's drawings (Figures 1 and 2) illustrate how we attempted to refine traditional Cape Cod architecture to solar needs. We think the synthesis and use of traditional roof angles works if one is lucky enough to live in a south-facing house as we are.

The project is by no means over. Future fantasies include a "zome-works"—a Steve Baer solar hot water collector installed in the upper part of the greenhouse interior. The collector would be connected to a hot tub in the greenhouse. The tub in turn would help keep a dancer's muscles (Nancy's) supple in winter, and the fish would like the warmed water pumped into their tanks after the people were through. It's a case of hedonistic closure of solar cycles. We contemplate more.

Now, as I write on the autumnal equinox, the first day of the fall of 1980, it is gusty and warm. It's hard to feel convinced that soon every evening we shall be closing the shutters that have stood open all summer. It seems very far away right now. But even I who crave warmth constantly can think even a bit smugly as I see the first traces of yellow leaves, that the green in our greenhouse will remain, that the geraniums and lettuce and parsley, the bamboo and fig and orange will last even as the green outside fades and is gone. The smell of moist earth too will stay as the ground freezes. And one day we'll look out at the first snowfall, but we'll see it through a screen of plants and flowers.

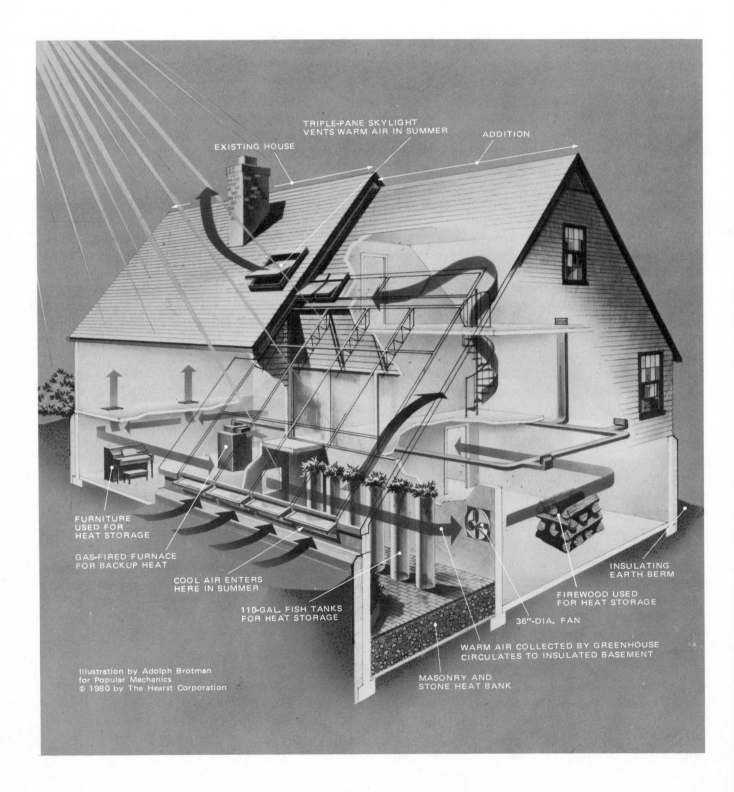

TRIPLE-PANE SKYLIGHT
VENTS WARM AIR IN SUMMER

EXISTING HOUSE

ADDITION

FURNITURE
USED FOR
HEAT STORAGE

GAS-FIRED FURNACE
FOR BACKUP HEAT

COOL AIR ENTERS
HERE IN SUMMER

110-GAL. FISH TANKS
FOR HEAT STORAGE

INSULATING
EARTH BERM

FIREWOOD USED
FOR HEAT STORAGE

36"-DIA. FAN

WARM AIR COLLECTED BY GREENHOUSE
CIRCULATES TO INSULATED BASEMENT

MASONRY AND
STONE HEAT BANK

Illustration by Adolph Brotman
for Popular Mechanics
© 1980 by The Hearst Corporation

Explorations

It is perhaps self-evident in this automobile- and petroleum-dominated age that energy sources and their uses shape culture and settlement patterns. What is less evident, but critical for the future, is the potential of renewable sources of energy to provide the foundation for new and more-equitable societies.

In the solar village, ecosystems will provide many of the bases for support. Climate will be modified and improved by them and market food economies will be integral to the overall design. Wastes will be treated in integrated heat-storage and nutrient-cycling systems. Even the landscapes will function to support the whole. Villages will be like earth ships.

The architecture of the future will be different in a number of fundamental ways. Bioshelters will be important. They will function as solar workhorses, heating and cooling, producing foods, and treating and recycling wastes. Unique new building materials will substitute for contemporary furnaces, air conditioners, fans, and motors. Energy needs will drop. Further, ecology will redefine solar and village architecture. It will become more indigenous and diverse. The very meaning of architecture will deepen. The following introduces this new architectural landscape.

The bioshelter is not a "monocrop" architecture. It is a state of mind and a way of rethinking how human communities can be sustained.

Bioshelters can be (1) alleys, (2) covered solar ditches, (3) wells with clear membranes, (4) greenhouses, (5) glassed roofs, (6) streets, (7) interconnected buildings, (8) domes, (9) glass-roofed barges, (10) ocean arks, (11) translucent tents, and (12) landscape microcosms. Bioshelters are the workhorses of a solar era.

N.J.T.

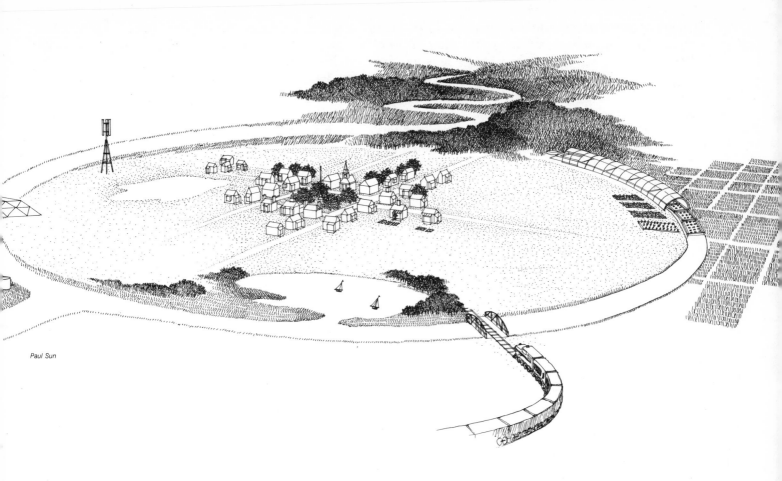

Paul Sun

The VILLAGE as SOLAR ECOLOGY

Prologue

Nancy Jack Todd

In early August of 1978, three months before her death, John Todd and I spent several days at a conference with Margaret Mead. She was a staunch supporter of the work of New Alchemy and was anxious to see its implications extended to touch the lives of greater numbers of people. What she said in effect was: You've created and developed the bioshelter. It's a good idea and it works. But most of the people in the world will never be able to afford private houses. You must start to think in terms of villages and neighborhoods, and of how the bioshelter fits there.

Such a legacy from a woman.

We could not, of course, nor would we have refused. And so in April the following year, we convened a conference entitled The Village As Solar Ecology: A Generic Design Conference.

Calling the conference, even funding it, proved to be straight-forward in comparison with our underlying assignment from Dr. Mead: defining and articulating a vision of the solar village, and subsequently evolving from the vision a communicable and tangible epistemology. That our task was a complex one was clear from the beginning, as we tried to decide who should attend. That we needed solar designers and architects was obvious, but we felt it equally important to hear from anthropologists and sociologists. To lengthen and deepen our perspective we included as well a cultural historian, social activists, and artists. As a group, New Alchemists brought biological, agricultural, aquacultural, and conceptual skills for ecological design. With this assemblage we felt that we had some of the pieces of the puzzle in hand, but as many more were missing. We knew that well beyond our reach, in the accumulated wealth of human experience, lay great repositories of wisdom that we could only intuit and try to recover. To be haunted by a dream of union, of Oneness, is not uncommon. One friend of mine once told me that she often had a feeling of almost remembering a time just beyond memory, when we understood better our destiny, our place in the cosmos. More recently I heard a woman of the Wampanoag tribe say to a group of women, talking to us as representatives of our culture, "We don't understand you. We don't understand what your instructions are, how you have been taught to live. A seed, a flower, unfolds according to the instructions it has been given. We don't understand yours."

I guess we have forgotten.

To help us to remember, to reinvent and recreate a sense of the human place in the cosmos, we realized that as important to the conference as physical design was a sense of the sacred. As one of the participants, Keith Critchow, put it, "The necessity of the sacred attitude is one of remembering: remembering the larger context of one's existence, one's duties to one's environment and to the invisible principles that regenerate life constantly. What is sacred?" As another one of the participants, Sim Van der Ryn, put it, "What isn't?"

Because the question is such a difficult one for us, formed as we have been by modern secular society, we have given it considerable space in the pages that follow. A sense of the sacred is the bedrock, however buried or amorphous, on which we build.

The pieces are arranged, somewhat arbitrarily, under the headings "Conceptualizing the Village," "Energy and Architecture," "Ecological Cycles," "Early Manifestations," and "A Farm in the Year 2030." We began with William Irwin Thompson because his essay is at once a definition of the problem and an overview from a much broader scanning of time and culture. The piece by Keith Critchlow is an attempt to convey his very rich understanding of how the sacred has been and can be the underlying and energizing force for a culture. In describing the tradition of Feng-Shui in China, Paul Sun makes more tangible the principles that Keith discusses.

With Mary Catherine Bateson's observations of "A Single Shared World," contemplating the village as a place where people actually live, and Hunter Lovins's hard question, what life there will be like, the difficult journey from the abstract to the hypothetical to the concrete is begun. John

Todd, looking at a specific area of land in southern Colorado, formulates guidelines for the questions that must be asked, questions of land ownership and tenure, energy, water rights and management, land and ecosystems, agriculture and forestry, and the incorporation of villages into the landscape as a whole. J. Baldwin describes a hypothetical dome, a kind of second-generation bioshelter. From Colleen Armstrong, Susan Ervin, Hunter Sheldon, and Ron Zweig come considerations for the sustenance, in the broadest sense, of the village. Then Steve Serfling, using the example of his own research with Solar Aquafarms, suggests an ecological method for village waste treatment. To all of the above Malcolm Wells adds comments, not exclusively from underground.

Toward the end of the conference, partly for relief after so much talk and partly to exercise our evolving principles, we set to work on creating the designs for three projects that are and were then in various stages of being actualized. Some sketches and designs are included.

The series of accumulated fantasies, rules, cautions, and designs concludes with an article by Wes Jackson from the imaginary vantage point of the year 2030. It seems comforting because it implies that we have—we must have—avoided nuclear holocaust, ecological disaster, and World War III to be living there among the prairie grasses of Kansas commenting and occasionally laughing at the follies of the present, long past.

Does such a conference, and the many like it, have meaning beyond that gleaned by the various participants? Perhaps through the slow integration of knowledge that is engendered and with subsequent further synthesis from fields as disparate as ecology, quantum physics, astronomy, religion, holography, anthropology, the contemplation of sacred art, architecture, geometry, and the study of *Gaia*, certain harmonies are being heard. Perhaps our sense of the world, rather than being cacophonous and diffuse with the claims of scientists and fundamentalists, economists and environmentalists, communists and capitalists, begins, at least intuitively, to make sense, to ring true. Perhaps a cosmology that is somewhere in Dream Time at once beyond memory and just out of reach of present knowledge yet still somehow alive within us is unfolding. Morphogenesis.

Paul Sun

The Village as Solar Ecology

John Todd

This series of articles is an early attempt to prepare for a transition to renewable-energy-based societies. The reader is cautioned that the articles are not so much technical documents as introductions to some of the areas of knowledge that will permit a shift to a genuine solar age. What follows is not engineering detailing but a new and potentially significant way of approaching the age-old need to sustain human cultures in their diverse forms.

The first cities were built a long time ago. Jericho, begun in 8350 BC was walled and occupied ten acres. Catal Hüyük in Anatolia (Turkey) was constructed in 6250 BC and spanned thirty-two unfortified acres. Both had many attributes we could associate with a contemporary town. The cities would feel familiar. Now for perhaps the first time since the appearance of cities almost ten thousand years ago, human knowledge has reached a point where it is possible and timely to rethink the nature of human settlements.

Based on a current revolution in science we have a newly acquired freedom to redesign the way in which communities are sustained. A unified body of knowledge is being formed that will allow modern societies to move from a petroleum era to a solar age. The nature of living systems is the unifying principle of this knowledge. Ecology is providing an intellectual framework that can link the polymer physics of the materials scientist to the electronic information of the computer specialist, to structural forms of the architect, to the knowledge of experts in diverse energy systems, food culture, and waste recycling, and ultimately to the special information of the sociologist, anthropologist, and artist, who speak for the human condition.

This new science is bound less to the metaphor of the machine than to the image of the forest or the meadow. We are shifting from an age dominated by mechanics to one concerned with biology. It is my contention that the shift in perception will allow us to undertake a beautiful and, as yet scarcely dreamed of, turn in the course of human history.

The practical as well as the good news implicit in the revolution in science is that it can truly create a solar age. Through humanly derived ecological and technical pathways the energy of the sun can be directed to sustain human settlements as magnificent as the world has known. Sun and solar derivatives, the wind and biofuels exclusively can power, heat, and cool all manner of villages and towns if structured according to an ecological blueprint of the kind that underlies a forest or a pond. Within a village or town designed to an ecological blueprint, wastes generated by people and by microindustry are channeled into nutrient cycles that in turn trigger such biological cycles as diverse food production, including aquaculture and food forestry. Gas for fuels can be produced as a by-product. Further connections are possible. Solar-algae ponds at New Alchemy, for example, have several functions: trapping solar heat, producing fish, and irrigating and fertilizing adjacent gardens. And that is not all. We are currently finding out if they can become methane-producing gas plants as well.

I make this point to illustrate how ecology can be a model for designers and to show that materials, ecosystems, and electronics together have a major role to play. Old divisions and specializations will break down in the process. Housing, manufacturing, educational facilities, market and government buildings may one day be connected to living elements and with each other in ways we are beginning to perceive for the first time.

It is rapidly becoming apparent that enough is already known to build solar-based settlements. It is further becoming clear in a period of increasing uncertainty about the costs and availability of petroleum, that solar economics, especially within the ecological framework, makes good sense.

These essays span a range of disciplines from the ancient siting techniques of the Chinese to advanced concepts in architecture and biology. A synthesis of this collective wisdom begins to come together in concrete forms, in the Cathedral, bioshelter, in a hypothetical village on the coast of Maine, in an agricultural village in the southwest, and in a California village of the sun.

As a document that is only a starting point. The "Village As Solar Ecology" will take many conceptual forms. Some will be retrofits of existing settlements and others will be new towns. If they combine practicality and self-reliance with powerful new notions of earth stewardship, they cannot fail to capture the popular imagination.

By the year 2000, sooner perhaps, our settlements will have begun to reflect the beginnings of a true solar age.

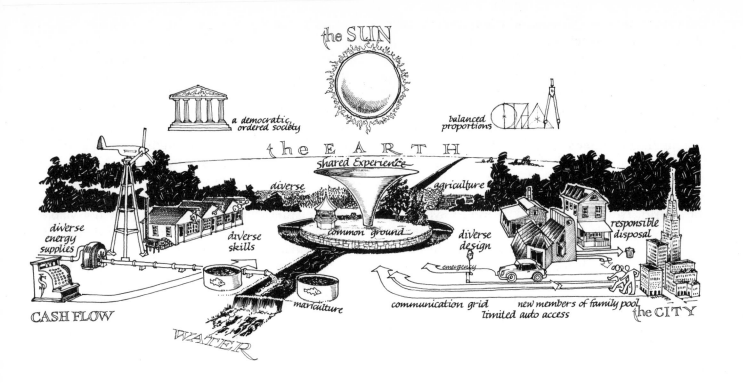

CONCEPTUALIZING the VILLAGE

The Need for Villages

William Irwin Thompson

I grew up in Los Angeles. Recently I had the misfortune to have to return there. As it turned out, the day of my visit was richly endowed with the worst smog in a quarter of a century. In addition, the foothills and mountains encircling the city were ablaze with forest fires. The first fires were natural, but they soon inspired arsonists to work in harmony with nature. As I flew over the city toward the airport, I remembered Nathaniel West's apocalyptic novel *The Day of the Locust*, in which the hero is obsessed with creating a painting called "The Burning of Los Angeles."

The ride on the freeway from the airport was equally unsettling. I sat in a five-mile-long traffic jam of cars, each with a single driver and each with its motor idling gently into the receptive air, and as I gazed out across the valley through the grayish-brown, thick flannel sky, I listened to the reports on the car radio of the sick and the elderly being rushed to the hospitals for oxygen. Looking at the freeway and wondering how anybody could be rushed anywhere, I remembered the excellent Pacific Electric mass transit system that Los Angeles had in the forties and early fifties, but, through the conniving of General Motors with the city fathers, had torn down to replace it with the more "modern" freeway system. Now there is talk of trying to rebuild the railway, but talk is cheap and capital is scarce. The dollar is declining, the international monetary system is disintegrating, and all our social systems are coming due for reconstruction at the same time: highways, railroads, hospitals, and ACBMs. People talk of rebuilding, but it is clear that we are entering a period of social and economic stagnation. The boom mentality that enabled the L.A. boosters to tear down the Pacific Electric railway system and build the freeways in the fifties cannot be conjured up again in the eighties.

People have been complaining about the smog in L.A. for thirty years, but when it comes down to a choice between the industrial values of development and high employment and the ecological values of conservation and public health, people in our society choose to buy more cars and build more freeways with their suburban appendages. As I sat in the car going nowhere on a freeway in L.A., I thought to myself: "And people think that Lindisfarne is a utopian community! This is the real utopian fantasy of freedom in an imagined consumer's paradise. Los Angeles is a historical mistake."

But if Los Angeles is the true nowhere city, where do we go from here, when the entire postwar world, from Long Island to Rio to Sydney to Tehran to Jeddah, has tried to imitate Los Angeles.

The answer is that we must turn on the historical spiral and approach the preindustrial village from the higher cultural level of postindustrial cybernetics and ecology.[1] But to tell a city planner that he should start thinking about villages is like telling a naval architect of supertankers that he should start thinking about sailboats.[2] It is a common cry among social activists that since so many people live in cities, all of our thinking and planning should be devoted to cities. Even to think about the village is for them an exercise in romanticism and escapism. The imperialism of this mentality is part of the problem, not the solution. But even beyond its arrogance, it is also ignorant. Two billion people, or roughly half the earth's population, live in villages.[3]

Even if one thinks that cities are the only cultural forms that matter, one needs to remember that historically cities, as Jane Jacobs has shown,[4] have often spun off their innovations to the countryside, where the landscape was more open to novel creations. The engineers may have gathered in eighteenth-century London, but they spun off their Industrial Revolution to Manchester and Birmingham. It is, therefore, part of the process of civilization for an urban intelligentsia to come together from New York, Boston, or San Francisco, but to spin off their metaindustrial villages from Manhattan to Crestone, Colorado, or coastal Maine.

Urbanization, nationalism, and industrialization have been the major forces that have shaped the modern world, but now that industrial world-system of warring nation-states is changing. Thermonuclear warfare in its mental form as an informational construct is eroding the traditional structure of the nineteenth-century railroad-consolidated nation-state. Industrialization is altering the global atmosphere and generating climatic changes that threaten the agricultural base of a postindustrial society like ours in which two percent feed the ninety-eight percent involved in the production of goods and service. And urbanization is straining the infrastructures of the vast megalopoloi that sprang up in the era of cheap fossil fuel. Cheap oil and gas allowed us to turn farmland into shopping malls and parking lots, and replace small nucleated towns with highway strips of gas stations and fast-food take-out joints. Now as the fuel crisis fuels the food crisis and both stimulate the currency crisis, we face a situation in which the postwar American way of life is simply not viable.

In 1800, more than ninety percent of the American population lived in rural areas; even as late as 1890, two-thirds of the American population lived in the countryside. By 1950, two-thirds of the population lived in cities.[5] Well, if a social movement can go that fast in one direction in an age of printed communication, it can move even faster in the other direction in an age of electronic communication. In point of fact, there is already evidence that the movement has begun to reverse and that people are moving out of the cities, not to the suburbs, but to rural areas.[6] But if we are not careful, this dispersal of the population could simply become the spreading of an oil slick of thin urban scum from Miami to Los Angeles. The trailer camps of Orlando, Florida, and El Monte, California, will move across the country to meet one another in the Ozarks. Clearly, we have to spend some time intuiting and thinking, not simply about cities and planned suburbs like Columbia, Maryland, but about villages.

Expressed in the move from an international, postindustrial city to a planetary, metaindustrial village is a shift from one world-system to another. It is a shift from consumer to contemplative values, a shift from an industrial mentality of the domination of nature and the mass production of culture to an ecological mentality of symbiosis, integration of the intuitive with the intellectual, and unique regional approaches to global processes. It is a shift from the coal-and-oil supported capital-intensive economies of the scale of the old factory systems of Detroit and Manchester to ecologically sound workshop-production for regional markets. Such an approach is already being pioneered by the multinational Phillips Company and its Utrecht Pilot Plant.

Nineteenth-century physics and technology created a way of seeing nature that influenced the way of organizing society, but now ecology is changing the way we see natural processes, and

---

[1]See William Irwin Thompson. 1978. The meta-industrial village. In *Darkness and Scattered Light*. N.Y.: Doubleday-Anchor, pp. 57–103.

[2]See John Todd, 1979. Ocean arks. *Co-Evolution Quarterly* 23:46.

[3]1979. Village economics. *The Economist*. p. 117.

[4]Jane Jacobs, 1970. *The Economy of Cities*. N.Y.: Vintage.

[5]See George Cabot Lodge. 1976. *The New American Ideology*. N.Y.: Knopf, p. 125.

[6]1979. Back to the Land. *The Economist*:49.

therefore it will influence the way we will organize society in the transition from one world-system to another. In the union of ecology and microelectronics we are beginning to re-*vision* the relationship of culture to nature. As the world restructures itself into a planetary culture, the nation-state will destructure itself into more viable areas of regional identity; concomitant with this process is a destructuring of the megalopolis. In the rise of the ecological and electronic village, we will not see the disappearance of the city; rather we will see an intensification and miniaturization of the city. The highly civilized city, like Ficino's Florence or Goethe's Weimar, does not have to be a megalopolis. In the relation of village to city, America could follow the pattern of Switzerland, where rural areas, villages, and highly cultured cities like Zurich or Basel coexist.

The example of Switzerland is instructive for America in other ways. The valleys in Switzerland have been cultivated for thousands of years. Closed in by the mountains, the Swiss could not develop the pioneer mentality to exploit nature and then move on. We, however, created the Dust Bowl and then moved on to California, and now that California is fast becoming destroyed, the leaders of the aerospace companies of the West are saying that we are meant to exhaust the earth's resources and then move on to artificial colonies in space. In the hucksterism of this industrial mentality the earth is simply another piece of Kleenex: use once and throw away. The proponents of unlimited industrialization cannot accept the limits of the biosphere as the Swiss accepted the limits of the mountains. But as we move into the eighties, it seems clear that the boom mentality of the sixties is not in touch with our historical condition.

America is being forced to change and to think in new ways. We are like a succession-forest culture that is changing into a climax-forest culture. The waves of rapid development are over, and a new, richly diversified ecology is being called forth. Once again, Switzerland can teach America a great deal about how a country can be a federation of decentralized cantons, how a nation can have many languages side by side, and how a rich agricultural tradition can coexist with highly complex precision industries. Perhaps now that Quebec is moving in an independent direction and Spanish is becoming the language of tens of millions in the United States, we are already well into a new and rich cultural transformation.

As the monolithic mentality disappears from nationalism, the monocrop mentality will disappear from agriculture, and the monolithic Los Angeles will disappear from urbanization. The Los Angelization of the planet cannot take the place, for in the greenhouse effect nature has her own negative feedback mechanisms for shutting down the furnace of industrial civilization. If we do not re-vision the relationship of culture to nature through a new alchemy, then the villages of the future will not be planetary, metaindustrial, and electronic; they will be provincial, preindustrial, and sputtering with the dwindling light of a growing Dark Age.

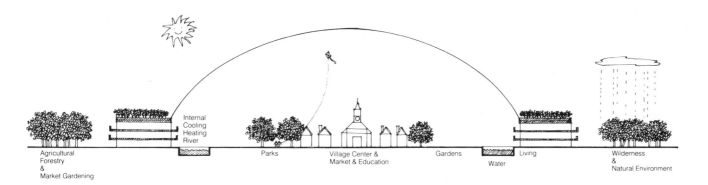

Agricultural Forestry & Market Gardening — Internal Cooling Heating River — Parks — Village Center & Market & Education — Gardens — Water — Living — Wilderness & Natural Environment

Ourkind[1]

Keith Critchlow

What is the sacred? The simple answer is, What isn't? But we can define it if we wish. The sacred is that which is essential to our existence.

[1] A word that emerged during the conference. It means the totality of the human family: ideal and actual.

Essential to our existence means not only the physical supports of our existence but the things that are simultaneously essential to our intelligence and being, in brief: right-livelihood. Ghandi expresses it succinctly: "There is always enough for our needs and never enough for our greeds." This is the very definition of greed—more energy out than the system can stand. Ultimately the only possible "profit" is one *of attitude—a metaphysical profit* of well-being and understanding. All else is vanity, as some would say. The universal law seems to be that a workman be worth his hire; there are correct returns for effort. But "profit" is the spiritual reward of attentiveness, acknowledgment, and the wisdom of knowing that everything is a *rite de passage*. Each step is a footfall of the way.

Our feet "handle" the earth as our hands "handle" the air, water, green life, and animals. Our "contact" is our awareness and sensitivity—our intrinsic choice. Caring is the basis of all good relationships.

The desecrated could now be defined as that taken which was not correctly available—more energy out than the system could stand. Thus it is the breakdown of the system, eutrophy, the diabolism of greed that is based on the part feeding itself in rejection of the whole, the part refusing to acknowledge the whole of which it is not only inevitably a part but without which it cannot exist. As Philip Deere said at the conference, "You cannot destroy ourkind without destroying nature, and you cannot destroy nature without destroying the Creator." The conclusion is crystal clear; it is only a form of madness when a part even contemplates doing without the whole of which it is a part.

So what is our first move back from the periphery to the heart of the matter? The first move back from the desecrated to a sacred space?

The first move is the demarcation of our intention for that space. The crossing of the threshold in our intentions is in our hearts and minds and in our bodily contact when we set first foot on any intended site. Paul Sun reminded us so often of the door or entrance that was a well proportioned and crafted symbol. We enter a new space, both physically, socially, intellectually, and spiritually when we pass through the doorway. Our attention to that passage is our responsibility.

Our solar villages express our intention to move from the "energy greed" context of "modern industrial culture" into a new relationship between ourselves and our planetary homes. This new order will be based on a mutual dependence or reciprocal maintance in accordance with cosmic rather than merely human justice.

Within our intended space we aim to express a sanity of wholeness that is the mark of the natural world. Interdependent domains based on a dynamic balance will be our wisdom, our cosmology. Because what else is wisdom or cosmology but a balanced whole, just as a balanced mind is sanity, and a balanced body is health. The sacrifice of the part to the whole will be in the original sense of the offering of the part to the whole—from within. There will have to be an unfolding of significance between the domains and parts that is perpetually regenerative, both symbolizing the ultimate regenerative principle of the sun and the regenerative principle of the solar village as a solution to post (massive) industrial Western culture.

We must replace the attention on energy with attention on light (the sun) and matter, or better, what matters—Mother Earth. After all we can only see by the light of the sun, directly or indirectly, in every sense of the meaning of the word. And when all matters are put together we must arrive at the profound significance of the immanence of our planetary condition and our mother, the Earth.

To leave a place in the center of our village as *temnos* or a sacred common ground, would be an ideal symbol and practical way of insuring a central remembrance or recollectivity.

A communal sacrifice in the offering sense, a giving thanks for the bounty of nature and our being, this central "village green" would function in the same sense as common land in the English tradition, which ensures that land is set aside for any contingencies in the community. Should, for instance, economic difficulties befall any member, the common green was a refuge, a resource, a sanctuary in all senses. This central space would also be a refuge for the whole community, as it would represent a way in which we could raise ourselves from the mechanistic model of eating, sleeping, procreating, and working; it would be a place set aside for contemplating the mystery of existence and for being thankful for one's fortunes—whatever. The keeping of the green would be a communal responsibility and would express communal joy.

All conditions of existence have to become sacred:

Space: giving existence location, inner and outer.

Time: giving it duration and timelessness.

Form: giving it recognizability, a whereness, and orientation.

Number: giving it accountability of people, things, and relationships.

Substance: giving it measurability, concretely and understandably.

Sacredness can be found at the center of all the conditions of existence, as sacredness is the invisible heart of any matter.

Feng-Shui: An Ancient Theory of Village Siting

Paul Sun (Sun Peng-Cheng)

Feng-shui, literally "winds and waters," is also known known by the more poetic name of *kanyu*, "the canopy of heaven and the chariot of earth." It evolved over centuries, in China as a set of seemingly superstitious principles governing the location and orientation of the residences of people both living and dead. In its broader sense, it is the art of cooperating and harmonizing with nature so that nature will shower wealth, health, and happiness on the inhabitants and their descendants in a given dwelling. The violation of these principles, it was believed, would bring ill fortune to individuals and families. As we will see, there is a rational scientific basis to the principles of *feng-shui*.

To understand why an early form of environmental science should be called *feng-shui*, winds and waters, one has only to ponder the overwhelming importance of these elemental forces in early China, or indeed in any ancient culture. The winds and waters had unlimited power to affect human life, and people felt helpless before such apparently capricious manifestations of nature's might. As a result, the ancient saying was true: "He who controls the water governs the empire." The cold northerly winds were a lethal threat to the people of North China, while southerly winds accompanied by rain could cause disastrous flooding in South China. Protection from winds, water management, and flood control were the very key to a better life for the people of China. Hence, the first priority in providing a comfortable dwelling and a happy homelife was to choose a house site that would be relatively free from natural disasters. According to *feng-shui*, therefore, the basic auspicious home site was a place surrounded by a horsehoe-shaped barrier of mountains to the north, with fresh water easily accessible, but no raging river near. In this and other practical examples, we see *feng-shui* as a conceptual system for understanding the physical environment and a method for selecting sites that will be harmonious with it.

In Western literature, we sometimes find the practice of *feng-shui* translated as "geomancy," a term that is quite misleading. According to the *Oxford English Dictionary*, geomancy means the "art of divination by means of signs derived from the earth, as by the figure assumed by a handful of earth thrown down some surface . . . Hence, usually, divination by means of lines or figures

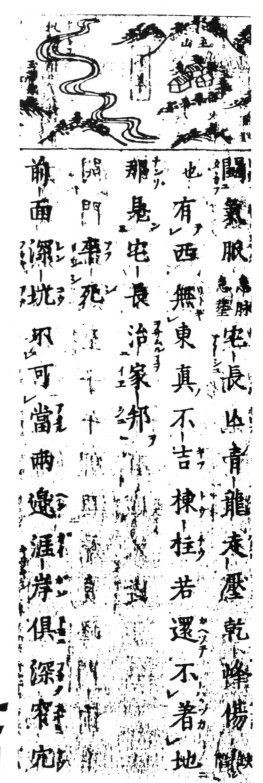

AUSPICIOUS — The northern mountain blocks the house from cold north winds. The winding river makes the water run smoothly so it can be used as resource without being dangerous. In addition it provides a nice view.

Figure 1.

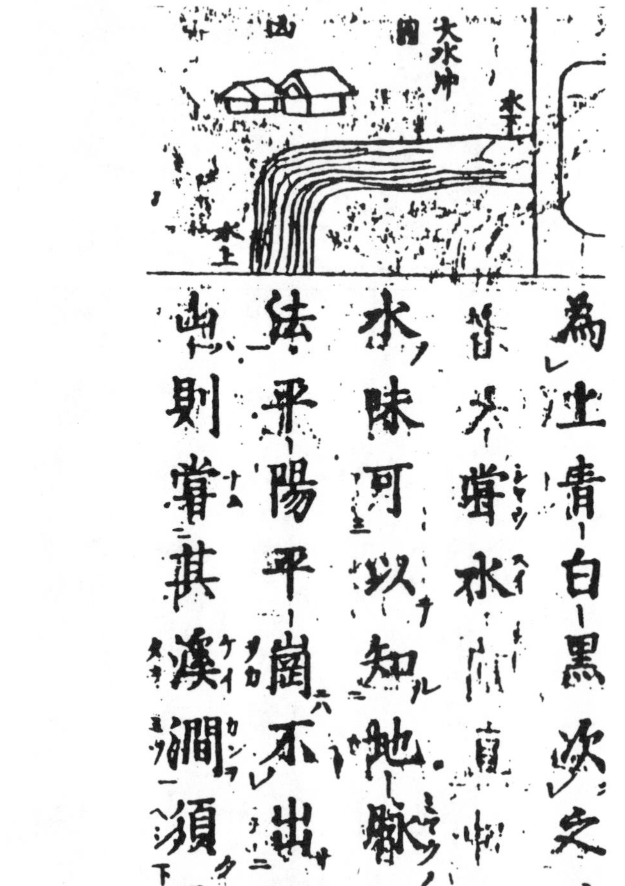

EVIL — The house situated at the turning point of a river is in jeopardy when the water erodes the bank.

Figure 2.

formed by jotting down on paper a number of dots at random." Clearly, the Chinese practice of *feng-shui* has nothing to do with geomancy as defined by this dictionary. Steven J. Bennett wrote in his article "Chinese Topographical Thinking," that he considered *feng-shui* to be a systematic theory. A case in point is the topographical science of "siting," used to discover the flow of energy through the earth so that residences of the living and the dead can be placed in areas that have favorable energy conditions. A conceptual analysis of classical Chinese siting texts reveals that siting always was a rational activity, attempting to structure reality through a theoretical quasi-religious framework. In short, *feng-shui* was a nascent science, explaining hitherto phenomena on a level that could be understood by even the most superstitious country dweller. To gain popular acceptance and respect, it cloaked common sense and scientific truth with the awesome authority of mystic revelation.

Feng-shui originated from the *Dzang Jing*, the *Burial Book*, which concerns itself with the selection of burial sites and the orientation of graves. According to one source, the *Dzang Jing* dated back to the ancient Zhou Dynasty (722–480 BC), but became most popular during the Sung Dynasty (960–1126 AD). Because of traditional emphasis on filial piety (honoring one's parents), proper burial was an important concern of heirs and descendants. During the Yuan (1260–1368 AD) and Ming Dynasties (1368–1644 AD), *feng-shui* florished in architecture, and its influence is especially discernible in the design of the palaces and temples of Beijing. During the Qing Dynasty (1644–1911 AD), *feng-shui* was widely used, both to establish orientation and to select propitious dates for such activities as moving into a new house. At present, *feng-shui* is still being practiced, though it has become an honored tradition rather than an entranched superstition. What may once have been followed in fear is now respected in reverence to a rich and ancient culture.

The principles of *feng-shui* provide a scheme for understanding land forms, as in the theory of the five basic elements, *wu-xing*. According to this theory, the rough shape of everything in nature falls into the category of metal, wood, water, fire, or earth. For example, in Figure 1, we see the classification of shapes of mountains and waters. When objects in nature are classified and placed in combination they present evil or good fortune. From this juxtaposition, good sites for building are found, because according to the theory of five elements, the five interacting forces either produce one another or destroy one another. For example, earth produces metal—literally metal is deposited in the earth. Thus, they complement each other and are good. In scientific terms, flat terrain (earth) is suitable for farming and building; the tall mountains (metal) benefit the land by sheltering it from the wind and providing water resources. Similarly, water nourished wood; wood produces fire; fire produces earth. All these combinations are good. Using the same logic, water destroys fire—literally water can extinguish fire; they conflict with each other and are thus evil. In scientific terms, hilly terrain is not suitable for agriculture or building. It is also not difficult to find a reason for fire destroying metal—fire can melt metal. Fire destroys wood—wood burns in fire.

Hence, gradually sloped mountains and ribbon-like, winding rivers are thought to be auspicious because "earth" mountains could be cultivated and "earth" rivers controlled. Sharp and irregular shapes are considered evil because the "fire" or "metal" mountains often have rocky foundations, unsuitable for farming.

The drawings (Figures 1 and 2) indicate the auspicious or evil placement of dwellings on a site is from one of the many books of *feng-shui*. The diagrams are explained in poems as superstitious predictions. However, one can see the scientific basis to them. These drawings represent the dwellings in their physical relationship to water, mountains, and roadways, and their orientation to sun or shade.

In some cases, the *feng-shui* principles reflect the social situation of the time. For example, a house is defenseless if placed at a crossroad.

Feng-shui also encourages auspicious planting of particular types of trees. For example, it is beneficial to plant plum or date trees to the south, apricot trees to the north, willows to the east, and pine trees to the west. Plum trees love sun, apricot trees prefer cool shade, willows wave in the morning sun creating lacy shadows, and the low westerly sun is shaded by dense pines.

The application of *feng-shui* to building location and design was based on a belief that whenever possible the house should face a southerly direction, toward the warmth of the sun, and sit with its back to a large hill that would protect the dwelling from the wind. There also should be two smaller hills flanking the sides to form a special enclosure that would provide a sense of unity and security. The fron view should be clear and open for defense. Hills should not block the light. Water was necessary; however, it should be located in front and parallel to the house. These considerations have led to a particularly refined appreciation of the topographical features of any locality, and the efforts to achieve a favorable balance of forces have brought about a uniquely sensitive environment with dwelling places quietly nestled in the contours of the landscape.

A Single Shared World

Mary Catherine Bateson

Traditionally, the village is characterized by a certain minimum level of diversity and a size that makes motion within it convenient. Although in complex societies villages live in awareness of urban centers, and villagers travel to the city to meet special needs, for pilgrimages or to petition authority, most of the day-to-day activity is carried on within the village. If the land is very fertile, the population may be large—say ten thousand. This is true in such places as Egypt, where small tracts of the Nile-fed land support large numbers of people. That number of people might live in a dense, compact cluster and be able to get up and walk to the farthest fields, carry on the necessary cultivation, and walk home, all between dawn and dusk. Alternatively, if the land is dry and hard, limitations of time and human and animal walking may mean that a village has only a few families, a hundred people or even fewer. A small village can support very few specialists, but it must have a few, usually a midwife, someone with some necessary healing or ritual skills, some pattern of leadership if only an elder who is habitually consulted, and one or more craftsmen such as a carpenter or metal worker who help in constructing housing and repairing tools. A large village can support a considerable number of specialists and can also have considerable diversity within its population, but even if village life is rich enough so that many inhabitants only participate in a part of it, a village is not a conglomeration of separate worlds but a single shared world.

This is all very different to think oneself back into today, and it is difficult even to find the appropriate characteristics of a preindustrial village to provide a model for the metaindustrial village. How much self-sufficiency are we concerned with, in food and energy and expertise? How tightly is the metaindustrial village integrated into a national power grid for its electricity, a national economic system that converts its crops into cash for buying merchandise produced elsewhere, and a national information system that subjects the opinions of the villagers and the music they can produce for their own festivals to the comparisons of the big time? In our discussions, we tended to assume a walking community with at least the capacity for self-sufficiency in an emergency, a bias toward producing its own foodstuffs, and at least one significant cash-producing activity.

Most difficult to think through are the social limitations. Every stable village society must solve

Jan Adkins

the problem of creating new households, and Americans are used to having a very large pool from which to select mates, even though the girl or boy next door is still a favored choice. In many cultures, however, villages are exogamous, and the importation of wives or, less frequently, husbands is one of the principal links to the wider society. This is true on the whole in Israeli *kibbutzim*, where the children grow up almost as members of the same family. Urban Americans are also used to living in a large-enough community to absorb severe perturbations and provide considerable privacy, so that when marriages split, estranged spouses do not keep running into each other at the same parties, and one is not marked forever by a notable piece of folly in the seventh grade. In most communes today, when a marriage breaks up, one partner leaves the community, which is too small to absorb the strain; this is one example of a general pattern of exporting individuals when they are discontented or their lives are disrupted, a common flaw of utopia.

Does village life inevitably have to be monotonous, so that regardless of who goes to start the village the next generations will become peasants? Unless this question is addressed, there seems to be little use in trying to swim against the tide that has made people through history anxious to *get away* from their villages, from the tedium of agriculture and from neighbors who know them all too well, and go to the city, where the range of choice of all kinds is so much greater, using old villages as, at the most, bedroom communities. It seems important that even if a village is able to be largely self-sufficient in food and energy production, it should not try for cultural self-sufficiency and it should have some specialties that are wanted by surrounding communities. Through history such exchanges as rotating rural markets have provided the moments of excitement. Most of us want to reduce the movement of people and objects in vehicles sharply, but not the movement of ideas and the stimulation of communication, perhaps through local and regional decentralized video.

It seems unlikely that small communities will be able to strike a balance between cultural openness and local generativity and to maintain the sense of common purpose and identity needed to balance the reduction in apparent choice that goes with leaving the city and reducing mobility without a shared sense of the sacred and common rituals. Over and over in our discussions, the sacred grove or meadow has seemed to be essential as a center to the community, bringing into focus a pattern of participation. Common rituals would have to address the ecological values that undergird the community and justify its basic choices. They would also have to address the transitions and steps in the life cycle that in America are so often dealt with by moving on. Closely linking to the centrality of a common sense of the sacred would be a provision for the very young and the very old, both groups a focus of common care, and neither segregated from the work and production of the community.

It is really only the automobile that makes us think of villages in primarily spatial rather than social terms. A village is not so much a place where a given house is located as the locus of a family, a festival, a garden, or a fish pool, a focus of the lives of many individuals, closely interlocked. In effect, we are talking about breathing new life into what we mean when we say that we *live* in a given place.

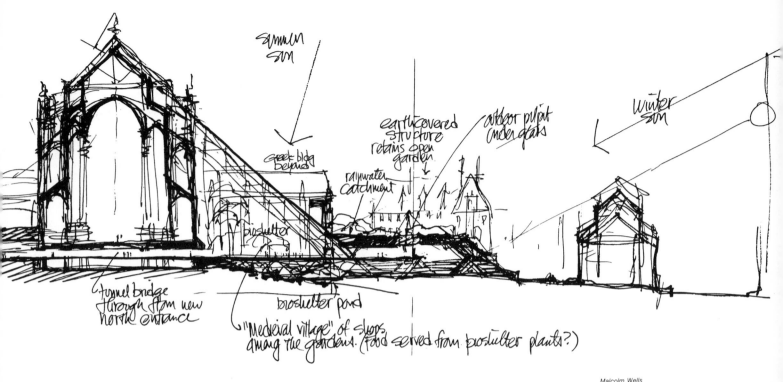

Malcolm Wells

ENERGY and ARCHITECTURE

Solar Village Principles and Construction Ideas

Malcolm Wells

Approaching self-sufficient living through reverence for life, using systems tested by America's experts in soft technology. Food. Land Husbandry. Shelter. Networks. Appropriate Scale. Wastes. Aquaculture. Sharing. Solar and Wind Energy. Privacy. Limits. Conservation. Fun. And Elephants.

Expressive

It must not need explanation. It must say "reverence for life." It must exhibit its dependence on rain, wind, sunlight, earth, and oxygen.

Identifiable

It must say "here we are" without recourse to the use of signs, lights, or arrogance of architecture.

Beautiful

(Unattainable, but always the goal.)

Wild

Over and over, we stumble on the obvious: if the habitat is provided, the wildlife will reappear. Can we afford to set aside ten percent of the land around the village as forever wild? Can we afford not to?

Secure

There may be no refuge from terrorism, but the village must offer shelter from storm and noise, and perhaps from vibration as well.

Consistent

Each village will inevitably develop a direction, an emphasis, at least slightly different from that of all the others. The more clearly the village expresses itself the better the design.

Contoured

Nothing says "husbandry" more directly than does contouring, following the design of the land, not fighting it.

Permanent

If trees and topsoil grow at a hundred-year pace, we can't be tearing up and rebuilding and tearing up again every ten or twenty years. Interiors, occupancies, these can change at will, but let the earth-platforms and the encircling land be at peace, untouched again for generations.

Flexible

Organic, growing and shrinking, responsive to new knowledge, new needs—not locked into whole, perfect forms.

Inevitable

Appropriate, local, right for its time and place. As if it grew there.

Earth-Related

Stable, horizontal, sheltered, permanent.

Continuous

No more dot-dot-dot architecture! No more parts instead of wholes. The village must flow out of the land and through time as well. As if it is growing there.

Linear

The wheeled vehicle, whether it be a pushcart or a self-propelled device, seems to dictate flow-through, as opposed cellular, circular, or stepped-floor spaces. Nonvehicular areas (living units, for instance) can line the linear parts and be delightfully stepped, sloped, and interrupted, but since the village, in order to be successful, must first of all *work*, the ease-of-work aspect, especially when combined with the need for contoured forms, seems to dictate linearness.

Diverse

From Jane Jacobs to the speakers at our conference, all seem to agree that diversity at all levels (occupancy, crops, life support, human insterests) is the key to long-range success.

Simple

Understandable, consistent, geometric.

Exciting

Filled with the unexpected, not with pitfalls and booby traps, but with changes of pace and scale; architecture without all the fun extracted.

World-Linked

Part of the growing information network.

Accessible

Accessible not only to visitors but to the kinds of work crews, machinery, and vehicles we hope will never be needed: emergency equipment, rescue teams, major structural replacement machinery, and so forth.

Educational

Of course. Life processes (and the processes of learning about life) always on display.

Democratic

With a few Republicans thrown in for balance, perhaps.

And what about these? Limits to growth? The use of chemicals and poisons? Private ownership? Private belongings? Inheritance? Existing structures (demolish, salvage, restore, retrofit, preserve?)? Evil? Imports (how much fuel, food, containers and wrappings; how many experts, specialists?)? Village characteristics and rules (how much should be *imposed* in the way of aesthetic controls, diversity, design; and who should do the imposing?)? Domestication vs. wildness of animals? What's the best way to hide the village dump?

More and more, I think a tools/models-book will generate a vast first-generation village-activity all around the world, and from *that* experience, from its successes and failures, will spring the really worthwhile villages we're all talking about. We can't begin to lay down all the rules at this time.

The labels in the illustration read:
The RENEWING FOREST
Hydro
Syn fuel plant
Wind Power
Local solar heat
Local bio fuel
Bio-fuel power plant
Coal train
Oil Imports
Electric Grid
Lessening Nuclear

Jan Adkins

Soft-Energy Paths From Here to the Village

Amory Lovins

In any sustainable human settlement the renewable energies of sun, wind, water, and biofuels suffice to meet all reasonable human needs for energy—provided the energy is used very efficiently. Energy would be harnessed via various commercial technologies from the renewable energies that impinge on the area, and in the case of a city, on its environs. Economic efficiency, engineering elegance, and ecological benignity all seem to lead to the same combination of very efficient use with soft technologies or appropriate renewable sources. Supplying energy at a scale and quality appropriate to the task tends to minimize the economic and social costs of distribution and conversion respectively.[1]

Just what energy technologies make sense is a use-and a site-specific question. What tasks do we want energy for? What forms or qualities of energy will do these tasks most simply and effectively, with the best opportunities for integration and for cascading energy through successively lower-grade tasks? How little energy can we get away with, at what scale of unit use, with what distribution and variation in time and space? How low-tech, reliable, convenient, durable, and resilient do we want our supplies to be? How might these things change in the future or with different people? How precisely do we know these things?

These are the main things we need to know before we start asking what renewable energy flows are available to us and how to harness them. For each site, some forms of energy, or degrees of reliability, or scales of supply are much more easily achieved then others; no site is average or routine. Each needs ideas. Knowing the quirks, we can re-examine how hard we want to work to get the right kinds of energy to do the tasks we started with; maybe we don't really need a steel mill after all.

Important types of energy needed may include heat at low temperatures (say, below the boiling point of water), at medium temperatures (cooking and most other chemistry), and at high temperatures (metallurgy and ceramics); mechanical energy at fixed sites (to run machines) or in vehicles; electricity for the tasks that require this special, costly form of energy (electronics, electrochemistry, arc-welding) and for substitutable tasks (motors that can run instead on compressed air, lights that can run instead on methane, and so forth). Road and air vehicles can generally do with solid fuels (external-combustion engines or gasifiers), electricity stored chemically or in flywheels, the coolness of liquid air, or possibly other methods. The array of energy carriers and conversion devices available to marry a renewable energy form with a task is as rich as your imagination. Most of the things that look as though they ought to work do work, and many of the brightest ideas have come from ordinary people without special technical backgrounds.

[1] Soft technology is the friendliest name for what has also been called alternative and, by E. F. Shumacher, appropriate technology. Stewart Brand, the editor of *The Next Whole Earth Catalogue* and the *CoEvolution Quarterly*, has written, " 'soft' signifies something that is alive, resilient, adaptive, maybe even lovable." My own favorite description for the kind of technology we're talking about is that it is forgiving. Scale and locale are implied. It is not endlessly consuming of non-renewable resources. A bioshelter, a windmill, small scale farm machinery, a windbreak of trees, wind-driven commercial and passenger sailing ships could qualify as soft technology. Nuclear bombs and nuclear power, the wan Dam, the Four Corners Power Plant, and the private car are not. There are also intimations of sustainability, a possibility of a future in the term. And it is reversible. One can undo it.

N.J.T.

The most obvious soft technologies, each best suited to particular uses in very rough order or decreasing share of typical end-use needs include the following:

Passive solar heating, cooling, and crop drying.

Seasonal storage of ice or warmth from a solar pond.

Active solar heating and cooling (often integrated) at low temperatures (a need for active solar space cooling is a symptom of bad buildings, in any climate).

Active solar heating at medium temperatures, through mirrors (which can be aluminized plastic films), Fresnel lenses, or very selective collectors in a hard vaccum (these can yield 5,000 to 6,000 degrees Celsius under load on a cloudy winter day).

Active solar heating at high temperatures (over 1,000 degrees Celsius); this required high concentration ratios and direct (not diffuse) sunlight, though a low-tech, low-cost solar furnace on the Olympic Peninsula has given an impressive performance running a steam-engine generator.

Burning wood or farm or forestry wastes, taking great care to conserve soil fertility (and possibly adding steps like gasification or densification).

Converting such residues to liquid fuels (mainly alcohols or pyrolysis oils), using pyrolysis, acid or enzymatic hydrolysis, fermentation, and so forth.

Anaerobic digestion of some wet residues, expecially those rich in nitrogen.

Windpower to make electricity (with or without grid integration) or hydrogen, directly drive machinery (including water pumps), or compress storable air to run machines.

Existing, or low-head high-volume, or high-head low-volume, or run-of-the-river hydropower, or (in special cases) small-scale wavepower, again for electricity or direct mechanical drive.

Solar ponds operating tow-temperature heat engines (this appears to be the cheapest known source of baseload electricity in many climates).

Solar cells (photovoltaics), which may yield medium-temperature heat as a coproduct if they have concentrators—and cheap amorphous cells will almost certainly be here in the next few years before we know what to do with them.

Hybirds of these technologies, such as a photovoltaic coating on a flat-plate solar collector, a bioconversion system driven by solar process heat or stirred by windpower, a plastic-film solar still/greenhouse, an integrated microhydro/wind/photovoltaic/electrolysis/fuel-cell system, or a small wood-fired co-generation/pyrolysis/district-heating plant.

Hybrids of these technologies (and others, including those we haven't yet thought of) with other processes, including water and nutrient recycling, food production, shelter, and manufacturing. The possible combinations are too numerous for a computer to enumerate in the lifetime of the universe.

Most of these systems are several times cheaper than alternative long-run replacements for dwindling oil and gas, and some are cheaper than oil and gas today if one uses the best present art— which the government has probably never heard of—cleverly built, well run, at the right scale, used efficiently, and done right. It is just as possible, though not as dangerous, to screw up a solar panel as a nuclear reator.

The first, second, and third priority is efficient energy use, far beyond the levels of improvement conventionally discussed. No kind of heating system makes sense if you live in a sieve. No kind of liquid-fuel supply system makes sense if you drive a Brontomobile. The "supply curve" for most soft technologies—measuring the increase in cost, difficulty, or nastiness with increasing volume of supply—rises discontinuously and, toward the top, very steeply, leading into hard solar technologies such as monocultural biomass plantations, solar power towers, and solar space satellites (which work better if you lay them on the ground in Seattle).

It is far better to save before the supply runs low, to try to make supply superfluous, and to retrofit one's house—using leak-plugging, heavy insulation (say, R-40 and R-60 ceiling in a cold climate), an airtight vapor barrier, good ventilation through a heat exchanger so that it's heated largely or wholly by people, windows, lights, and appliances. In a new house in our worst climates the net space-heating load and the extra capital cost can both be about zero. Any residual need can be covered by slightly oversizing the solar water heater, or if heating with a greenhouse, putting the water-heating panels inside it to avoid the costs of frost-proofing them. Efficient energy use is synergistic with cheap, effective soft-tech design: a tight house can get better performance from a five-to-ten-times-smaller active solar system, and a simpler one to boot, than can a sieve, because the heating load is tiny and unpeaky, the thermal mass of the house is much amplified by its slow heat loss, and no heat

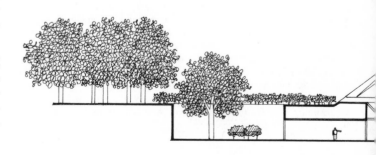

distribution system is needed. No official study counts this essential synergism. Integration with food, water, shelter, and materials systems is equally essential.

We must remember that we are seeking not energy for its own sake, but energy services. There are lots of ways to skin an alternator. The objects of transport may be achieved by living where one wants to be, telecommunications, walking, riding a horse or bicycle or scooter or driving a super-efficient car, hitchhiking, taking public transport, airships, or out-of-body trips.

Even on the most barren/dull/cloudy land, there's abundant renewable energy, even wind in the High Arctic winter. The problem is the amount of trouble to get it. One can live better (materially) than the U.S. average on a total energy budget of two kilowatts (thermal), and in the U.S. that's the average rate of insolation on only twelve square meters; so even with collection, conversion, and storage losses, the areas needed aren't unreasonable. Urban densities improve solar economics. But that doesn't mean all forms of energy are equally easy to get at any given site.

For an existing settlement, we need to figure out present and long-term future (post-conservation) structures of end-use needs, to devise a matching soft supply system, then work backward to now to see what has to be built when and what policy instruments will be needed to do it.[1] The only important questions have to do with implementation—what happens in people's heads and how to help it happen from the bottom up by helping people see the energy problem as their problem.

In the long run, energy probably isn't a terribly interesting problem, because we already know conceptually how to solve it, and are starting to do so in practice. If we get out in one piece, then we can get on with some of the really interesting problems: water, soil fertility, food/population, climatic change,

[1]For methods, see *Soft Energy Notes*, May 1979. Available from IPSEP, 124 Spear, San Francisco, CA 94105.

ecological resilience, social justice, and peace. In energy, technique is in a sense trivial: full or delights and traps for the techno-twit, but no longer full of deep, scary conceptual gulfs. But using energy to worthy ends, for right livelihood, is profoundly difficult, and is not a technical issue at all.

A Dome Bioshelter as a Village Component

J. Baldwin

Serious concern with energy efficiency in buildings requires a standard of performance and reliability rather better than the traditional norm. Many designers, including those aware of the need to conserve resources, do not have the regard for detail necessary to deliver long-term high net energy performance. If we are truly interested in saving energy and materials, we must analyze building design for energy savings in construction, use, and maintenance. Massive amounts of concrete, for instance, mean both a high energy cost in manufacturing the concrete and reinforcing steel, and energy-intensive transportation to the site. Structures that develop leaks due to warp, rot, caulk failure, and ultraviolet deterioration are not going to help society's energy difficulties in the long run. It seems clear that "life-cycle costing" demands a new attitude toward architecture. When the structure is sheltering biological systems, continuing mechanical reliability must be of a very high order lest a component failure result in loss of the cash crop or other function.

One strategy for achieving good performance and reliability is to develop a machine-made structure utilizing high-quality materials in precision components. Not only is quality control thus as-

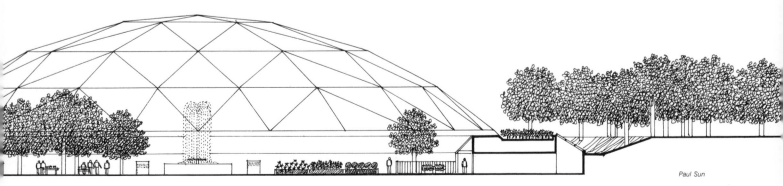

Paul Sun

sured, but the vagaries of construction crews are much less likely to result in poor assembly. Moreover, well-designed industrialized building systems are much faster to erect, thus reducing the critical time between cash outlay and cash return. Speedy installation also reduces the risk of work being interrupted by poor weather conditions, strikes, and inflation. Machine-made systems can also be designed to fit tightly into transport modules such as sea-land containers; parts can be nested and packed in a manner that minimizes transport energy and damage.

A likely candidate for such an architectural system is the geodesic dome. Domes lend themselves well to mass production techniques. Indeed, the reputation of domes for leaking and other weaknesses is almost entirely due to inaccurate preparation and assembly of handmade parts. Domes are also materials-efficient, typically using about 25 percent less material than a conventional structure of similar size. They are well known for easy, rapid erection by inexperienced crews. There are many instances on record of domes as large as 200 feet in diameter being put up in one day. Clever designs do not even require the assistance of an expensive crane.

Domes typically use many parts, but these tend to be of only a few different types. This means relatively low tooling costs and tends to maximize the economic advantages of mass producing a large number of similar items. It also means low inventory and storage costs both for domes awaiting utilization and for repair parts. This reduces both dollar and energy costs associated with stocking. In fact, many dome systems use materials that do not require covered storage, a further saving.

Perhaps the most interesting advantage of the dome is good thermal performance. This advantage arises from the geometry, rather than mechanical devices. Domes have superior surface-to-volume ratios when compared to most other configurations. A relatively low skin area means less skin to lose heat through as well as less skin to buy and maintain. This skin is smooth, offering little resistance to wind. A greatly reduced heat loss due to wind scrub is thus achieved effortlessly; it also imparts an unusually high resistance to weather damage. This, among other reasons, is why domes are used for radar enclosures, especially where weather is violent. The smooth shape has an advantage inside too; natural toroidal convection current patterns eliminate stratification, reducing differences in temperature between top and bottom and the consequent need for circulation fans and/or extra-high heating demands to insure acceptable temperatures at the floor. In the summer these air currents can be used to cool the structure, also without the need for fans. These naturally occurring air motions benefit plants by bringing needed carbon dioxide past them at no fossil fuel cost. Preliminary investigations suggest that control of the aerodynamics of boundary layers inside a dome may result in unusually good insulating effects.

Another benefit of the shape of the dome, which is essentially that of an inverted bowl, is that it can act to reflect radiation back into itself. This is especially important in a greenhouse, where the radiant heat losses can be very high. On the other hand, the dome's spherical section means that sun can penetrate the glazing at a 90 degree angle somewhere on the surface during the entire day. This reduces losses in the morning and evening, when the flat surface of a conventional structure reflects a significant percentage of the available sunlight. This holds true regardless of season. Domes tend to be self-snow-shedding too.

There are advantages to a circular floor plan in a greenhouse: a central mast can support a boom carrying irrigation nozzles and platforms from which the plants can be cared for and harvested without the necessity for space-wasting aisles (typically 20 percent of the floor area). Such a mast could also be used to speed erection of the dome's framework as well as aiding the pouring of the foundation. Circular concrete form-work is also much easier and cheaper, as it can be braced with tension bands instead of many stakes and woodwork. The boom could also ease window washing and other maintenance. Fish feeding could be accomplished from the boom as could tank filling and draining, harvesting, and cleaning. Such a boom could be very simple in concept and execution, in contrast to complex apparatus necessary in other floor plans.

Assuming that the advantages of the dome are now apparent, what other possibilities exist for these structures? One is the potential for very large domes. Buckminster Fuller has proposed domes up to three miles in diameter; his suggestion for covering downtown Manhattan is one such proposal. Bucky estimated this dome would quickly pay for itself in snow-removal savings alone, not to mention the greatly reduced heat and air-conditioning loads that result when the "fin area" of hundreds of buildings is effectively reduced by having the membrane buffer the ambient weather. Such large structures have not been built, though there may be no technical reason why they cannot be. However, smaller structures usually seem to be much less threatening to many people and would be a good way to test such ideas. The capital outlay for smaller domes would be within the capabilities of groups of people; neighborhoods, even small towns or villages might be protected by a dome shelter with the inhabitants living in the perimeter of the structure, perhaps in earth-tempered housing overlooking the central shared space. Such a scheme would be ideally suited to the community-sized seasonal heat storage suggested by Ted Taylor. Consider a sample dome 300 feet in diameter. That gives us about 1.6 acres of climate-controlled space. If housing were in a raised berm around the perimeter and the housing units had a 30 foot frontage inside and outside the dome, there would be space for 30 homes—perhaps 120 people. A 1.6 acre bioshelter could supply them with all their food—except perhaps Twinkies—with a substantial cash crop left over. Hydroponics is another possibility. The synergistic interactions of a tuned bioshelter/Ark would be visible to the occupants. The maintenance of it would be divided. Thirty families is getting near the critical mass necessary for efficient methane production and could be served by a wind generator in the 50–100 kilowatt range, a size that has in itself advantages of being suitable for mass production and distribution. Load management reducing peaks and waste could result in very high performance and excellent efficiency, assuming that the machinery is built to last. This could be rather easily accomplished in such a compact "neighborhood structure."

High-quality hardware would be capital intensive, but it is absolutely necessary for reliability and long-term energy economy. There are several ways that the initial outlay could be managed. First, a cash crop could be used to make much higher mortgage payments than is usual. Second, running costs of such a structure, including the dwellings, should be very low. And third, food costs for occupants would be much less than store-bought food, which carries high costs of transport, packaging (and disposal of packaging), middleman costs, and the expense of fertilizers and pesticides. It might also be feasible to rent such structures through an arrangement comparable to the telephone rental system. This would ensure that the quality of the structure would not need to be compromised in order to meet first-cost market price competition. Such a compromise would reduce system reliability, just as low-quality telephone handsets would reduce the reliability of the Bell System. (If you don't think that this can be a serious matter, you must not have lived where the phone system isn't by Bell.) Competition in hardware marketing always results in the lowest common denominator being adopted as industry standard. It might be realistic for banks to amend mortgage policies to accommodate bioshelters, since high-quality, high-performance domes would only appreciate in value while maintaining reliability over many more years than is "normal." The average commercial building, including downtown skyscrapers, in the United States is torn down after 37 years. A properly de-

signed dome/Ark could be dismantled and moved easily and without damage, except to the current crop. This could be yet another advantage, as the structures would then never wear out or have to be torn down and would make communities resistant to economic disaster arising from being located in increasingly undesirable locations, which is common. (One could conceive of a used-Ark market!)

Our proposed 300 foot dome community would be a true neighborhood. A good many bits of shared hardware besides the dome itself and the power system and sewage treatment would act as social cement. Shared workshops, recreation space, and laundry facilities would further reduce family expenditures and increase social interaction. Freezer space and facilities for repair and maintenance could be common. The 30 families could share a huge tape library, much larger than any single family could afford. Heavy transport such as Dodge vans could serve as mass transit at this scale with shared costs far less than those resulting from individual daily car use. Recent studies show typical cost of owning a Big American Car to be 38 cents per mile. Perhaps the families could support a modest fleet of identical economical cars to reduce maintenance costs.

The neighborhood dome idea offers the exciting potential of several such domes interacting with one another and the rest of the world in a way that would reduce transportation needs as well as strengthening a regional cooperation in larger enterprises including field farming and forest management. The domes could raise seed stocks, tree seedlings, cover crops for erosion control, and specialty crops such as herbs. They would permit an acceptable high-density housing without creeping "slurb." Properly spaced, a group could be serviced by electric vehicles using power generated by the domes. There is some evidence that domes greatly accelerate air movements in a way that is advantageous to wind generators.

It should be emphasized that the most desirable size for such proposed domes has not yet been determined. To do so would require an examination of economics including mortgage policy and payback periods, requirements of the housing systems, people's needs and demands, structural integrity, codes, fire safety, net energetics of specific systems, implications of materials supply with respect to pollution and other environmental degradation, politics, quality control, environmental effects of the Arks and of accretions thereof, transportation effects to avoid creating commuter communities, and various sociological aspects. What does seem clear is that a neighborhood-sized bioshelter/dome could be the basis for a community that really does tread lightly on the earth.

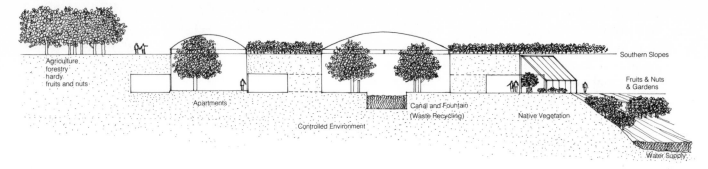

Paul Sun

Notes on An Agricultural/ Cultural Solar Village in the American Southwest

John Todd

Ownership

In an ideal community, land should not be bought or sold piecemeal. In an ideal village, all land would be held in trust. As a result, there could be no land speculation. Buildings, roads, ponds, mills, barns, trees, houses, housing complexes, bioshelters, and offices could be bought and sold privately between individuals and the land-holding trust or corporation.

A bioregional plan would provide a map for development and determine the limits and relative proportions of activities. The plan would provide building and zoning codes.

The holding corporation would earn its profits from long-term agricultural lease/trust agreements with farmers, through the building, financing, sale, and leasing of the many village components and facilities, and from the leasing of energy-producing rights to private groups within the village and community, or through the direct sale of electricity, water, and other key elements. Sheer diversity of activities would ensure that it would not become a dull or oppressive company town.

Energy

Indigenous energy sources would determine the first set of limits of the scale of activities and the population. Apart from direct solar heating and cooling, I see hydroelectric, solar-thermal-electric, and biofuels from waste recycling as the principal sources of energy. After a certain population had been reached based on per unit or per person energy consumption under this regime, then an increase in population or activity could occur, but only with a concomitant increase in the efficiency of energy use or through further conservation of energy. If per capita energy use were halved, for example, then, in theory at least, the population could double.

Water

In semiarid zones, water is the ultimate arbiter of human activity and density. I would propose that the volume of surface waters, pumped at indefinitely sustainable volumes through turbines and shallow wells, would determine the absolute limit on development. Water would not be imported.

Water use in agriculture and aquaculture as distinct from wasteful spray irrigation would be intensified and given top priority. Gray water and sewage would be purified and recycled within the village. The more times the water can be safely reused in village cycles, the better. Drinking water would be fresh.

Land and Ecosystems

The existing natural biological carrying capacity and ecosystem structure in this region is climate- and water-limited. The region is semiarid with a long, cold winter. As a consequence, the ecology is very fragile. Except for paths, the woods on the hills and valleys reaching into the mountains above the existing settlement should remain untouched for all time. They act as sponges absorbing the otherwise rapid flooding of rain and melting snow. They store moisture for the ground table and protect the area from destructive floods.

Other sacrosanct areas should be the outwashes and the streams lined with cottonwoods. They are the only areas where intensive agriculture can naturally flourish. The outwashes should be saved for agricultural forests, orchards, intensive aquaculture, and for market gardens. I can't overemphasize how precious these lands are. These cottonwood areas will be the ones most sought after for houses. Their use in this way would amount to a real tragedy.

Topographic features also need honoring, particularly the tops of ridges where the hills comprise vertical shallow valleys and ridges. Drought-tolerant trees, including the piñon, should be planted on some of the ridges.

Agriculture, Aquaculture, and Agricultural Forestry

The economy of the area would be at least half agricultural. The farmers would live with the other citizens within the villages, not segregated. The village, or perhaps two or three villages each linked to a watershed, would be the hub for all of the people.

Food production would take place in five distinct biological zones. Overall, each of these would help strengthen the others through integration. The zones are (1) bioshelters; (2) the village, which would house fish hatcheries as well; (3) stream outwashes for intensive agriculture; (4) semiarid hillsides for extensive agricultural forestry; and (5) the valley for a mixed agriculture of tree crops, grains, fodder crops, and livestock.

To optimize energy use, materials, machinery, and especially moisture and nutrients, broad planning would be done to see that agriculture was dealt with as a system of interconnected parts. The land would be protected from salting or monocrop abuse. In the extensive agriculture and planting of perennial grains and grasses, drought- and cold-resistant strains would be emphasized following the ideas of Wes Jackson. Livestock breeds better adapted to ecological conditions would be investigated. Livestock would not range freely but would be rotated in order to "tune" the various forage ecosystems.

The Village(s)

The village would borrow a leaf from the book of native American pueblos and cliff cities and from various European cities and towns. Separate and isolated family housing would be stringently avoided. Instead the village would comprise connected and shared structural elements. Housing, bioshelters, schools and institutes, civic and religious centers, commerce, and even manufacturing would be combined into an integrated solar framework. The sun, walls, and materials would be shared and do double or treble duty. The level of crafts of the village would be extremely high, and building would not be rushed. A medieval or sacred attitude toward architecture as an expression of divine powers would be intrinsic to the enterprise. Some of the builders would be artists. Local materials would be used whenever possible.

I believe that bioshelters are going to be the key connective element in the Village of the Sun and in future solar villages. Recently, J. Baldwin and I began designing a 300 foot diameter (1.6 acre) shallow-aspect glass-covered geodesic structure that has 30 partially bermed, protected apartments around its periphery; they open out into a solar courtyard and the land beyond. In this design the bioshelter elegantly provides heating, food, and recreation including swimming for a population of up to 120 people at a cost that may be competitive with standard multiple-family dwellings.

I mention this to point out that bioshelters should not be additions to architecture. They should be central elements in the architecture of villages, for they will help heat and cool the inhabited structures and provide a basis for household and community food production.

Transportation

Transportation will need careful thought. Agriculture will require special energy-efficient machinery matched to the type of agriculture and the distances traveled. Initially much of this machinery may have to be imported from Europe or the Orient or be manufactured on site. Unlike the people, the equipment would probably be dispersed around the agricultural zones and housed and maintained in energy-efficient underground facilities. On the hillside farms and in the agricultural forests, horses would be used as principal sources of power. Cooperative arrangements between farmers could help minimize amounts of machinery, time in transit, repair and fuel use.

Private cars within the village would be banned. Narrow "back alley" roads would be for service and repair vehicles. The main thoroughfares within the village would be narrow roads for bikes and walking. Old or infirm people could use some form of electric transportation. The village would be linked with the agricultural zones by bike roads and horse paths.

Another alternative, with the least environmental impact, would be a small, fast train that would service the whole ranch and allow agriculturalists, hikers and picnickers, shepherds and cowboys/girls to move back and forth from the village.

Attention to transportation efficiency and to the development of a viable bicycle and horse network would quickly pay for itself in lessened pollution, reduced costs and noise, more pleasurable transportation, and lessened dependency upon petroleum.

ECOLOGICAL CYCLES

Jan Adkins

Some Considerations for Agriculture in a Solar Village

Susan Ervin

Food production in a solar village would include both small home-scale production and larger-scale public production. Home-scale food growing would probably include winter vegetables in a solar greenhouse, fruit trees, and small vegetable and herb plots. Both cooperative groups and specialists would engage in larger-scale production. Cooperatives would include such groups as students and teachers, who would partially supply the food needs of their schools; neighborhoods or smaller groups primarily involved in other occupations, who would grow food as a part-time effort; and commercial cooperatives. Specialists would simplify overall food production by providing vegetable and tree seedlings, biological control agents, and locally adapted seeds. Certain crops like grains, beans, dairy products, meats, some greenhouse-grown fruits, and wool would in most cases be produced by the co-

operatives or specialists instead of on a home-scale. Foods requiring special preparation such as tofu, cheese, baked goods, sprouts, wine, smoked fish, and medicinal herbs would also be offered by co-ops or specialists.

Food preservation would be done on different levels. Some people might use a large freezer cooperatively, while others would take their food to a managed freezer locker, and still others might purchase frozen food from a small commerical operator. Such a small business could either grow and preserve food or purchase crops from local growers. A cannery would be available for individual use, but co-ops could have their own canning equipment. There would be new jobs, involving such necessary activities as the management of a large root cellar in which root crops would be stored for the winter. The manager would check for spoilage, bring the vegetables out for distribution, and make sure storage conditions were proper. Technologies for solar food drying would be perfected; they would use adequately sized solar dryers with backup systems of small wood fires or wind-generated electricity. Depending on community preference, either small conventional businesses or co-ops could fill the functions described above.

Effective small-scale farm machinery would be used. Individuals and small groups would have access to good tools and machinery through co-ops or rentals. There would be an adequate supply of machines and tools and idle ones would be rare.

Various patterns for land organization could be used. Public buildings could be in the center, with the homes and their gardens in the next ring, the larger fields and orchards and food-processing areas beyond these, and woodlands ringing the whole scheme. Or with public buildings still grouped in the center, homes could lie beyond the agricultural areas, next to the wild lands. A combination would be possible, depending on the size of the village. A small community might decide that dwellings should be clustered so some land could be left open and wild.

Whenever possible, biology would take precedence over technology; rather than installing an expensive irrigation system, the village would achieve maximum water retention through humus building. When possible, a fish or solar-algae pond would be placed uphill from a garden plot, eliminating the use of a pump for irrigation. Crops would be rotated, and fields left fallow periodically.

Living leguminous mulches would be interplanted among heavy-feeding crops.

Imported foods would be expensive and considered to be treats, like oranges for Christmas. There would be a few luxury items like coffee, tea, and exotic spices for which people would be willing to pay the price.

The Need for Trees

L. Hunter Lovins

Village as solar ecology. Not city nor wilderness, we seek a settlement to harmonize ourselves and earth. We seek a metadimension from the rural-urban axis. Among the tools we have lacked has been a measure by which we may sense the scale we seek. As city visionaries have turned to urban forestry, so we need a village forestry. Our measure is, of course, the tree.

Trees give the scale, psychically and architecturally, of the solar village. The presence of trees—and more important, our involvement with them, propagating and caring for them—gently imparts a sense of the appropriate human role. Our trees reach beyond us, to remind us that the fertility of our soils and the freshness of our skies are gifts from those who touched this land before. The trees they planted now give us shade. With each tree we plant we are reminded of their perhaps inadvertent generosity, and minded to pass on a bit of our own. Martin Luther spoke of this when he said, "If I knew the world would end tomorrow, I'd plant a tree today."

Plant a tree—a thought
in biologic time.
To see the city as a forest,
green instead of gray; bark
for concrete. Leaf
leads consciousness of cycles.

Today we plant a tree
into a century beyond:
vision village forest—
biome—and I am
bonded to today, this earth and you.

L. Hunter Lovins

The very architecture of a tree should guide our own. Monoliths erected in the clouds overreach the scale intuitive to living things, imposing their linearity on both those who dwell below and those within. We should seek to settle more softly within the landforms about us, our skylines an ornamentation of the treeline rather than a negation.

From the Druids to Gandhi, from the Buddha to E. F. Schumacher, trees have represented a spiritual and practical foundation for interaction with the earth. Because it makes a difference when you plant a tree. Perhaps it is the simple sense of giving something back—a joy our species little knows—perhaps the touch of soil and of life. Perhaps the bond is best left undefined: a mythic teaching, an essence of villageness and much more. In the words of the Southern spiritual, "Ain't you got a right to the tree of life?"

Walking through our village this right is everywhere embodied. We have reclaimed forestry, like the care of our bodies, from the technicians, and have invited the participation of all the villagers in creating and maintaining our woodlands. The bioshelters of the seedling nursery bubble about with children and excitement. The skills one needs to grow a seed into a young apple tree come mostly from the heart, and what's left is easily taught. The village forester is the steward of our efforts, and the hostess, but the trees are our own. Each day different villagers spend an hour or the day in the care of the seedbeds, orchards, woodlots, shelterbelts, and street trees.

The nurseries are part of our school, and particularly its responsibility. Older folk join the youngsters potting, pruning, and planting, both in the bioshelters and farther afield. Older classes are given the craft of logging, and learn the exhilarating arts of using saws, selecting trees for harvest, felling them, and skidding them out with care between the younger trees. Horses do this best, we've found, with less compaction. Our forest is diverse—young and old, hard and soft, old-snag habitat tree and ranks of heart-strong saplings—rather like the village; and a bulldozer can't discriminate.

In town, we've grown an edible village, richly endowed with fruit and nut trees. Rare and unique specimens abound where individuals have taken special interest. Many homes have arbors, crawling with fruiting and flowering vines. Village forestry is integrated with a general consciousness of green and growing things, and with the cycles, seasonal and nutritional, of which they are a part. Our celebrations follow the round of harvest and renewal. And because the lawyer has helped, the celebration is hers; because the shopkeepers, artists, plumbers, and bankers have each sprouted their seedlings, turned the compost, and taken a turn with the pruning shears, the festival belongs to us all.

In the same way there is no such thing here as

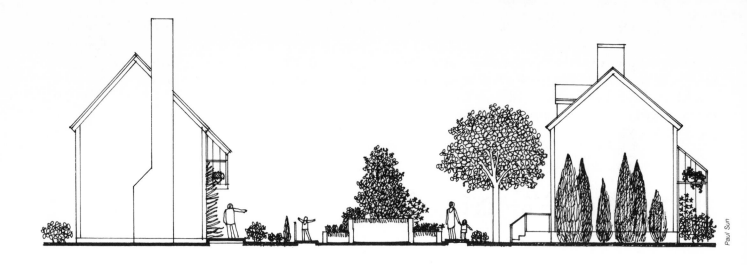

Paul Sun

a landfill: "refuse" rejigged to "re-use." Wastes that a city dweller would dispose of are our resources to be recycled. In Los Angeles County alone, between four and eight thousand tons of pure tree material—clippings, brush, downed limbs, and other such biodegradable "trash"—are daily dumped into increasingly costly landfills. In our village our somewhat more modest contribution is chipped by the student crews for easy use in our gasifiers. The urban biomass joins the woodlot slash as an essential energy feedstock. Much of our organic residues from the community farms and gardens, aquaculture, and even kitchen scraps are composted, but often they have spent an interim in a biogas plant, releasing their hydrogen and a bit of carbon as methane, before returning most of their carbon, their nitrogen, and all of their trace elements to the soil. The more cellulosic crop wastes are fermented into alcohols, and most of the wood wastes pyrolyzed. The paper is recycled separately, though, and returned to the little pulp mill with its hydropower rig by the river. Even the mill contributes to the town's energy, co-generating electricity off its process heat cycle, which is itself fired by its wood residues. As with all our systems, we have taken care to utilize what would otherwise be waste—cascading nutrient, fiber, and energy flows—and returning only clean residues to our village environment.

Some of the technology of this village forestry is modern: the integrated food and energy systems and the sophisticated microbial partnerships. But much is metamodern, concerned to nourish participation and satisfaction of the craft, not necessarily to expedite. The village forester and her interns teach the skills, but more, their role is to convey a larger curriculum of care: the poetry of trees, and the art. The efficiency of industrial forestry leaves shrubland and deserts, the desperation of primitive forestry denudes. We seek a greater balance of the earth's abilities and our own.

E. F. Schumacher said, "Tree planting is a very nonviolent technology and a very democratic one." I think we shall have to learn more and more to look out for and develop nonviolent, democratic technologies. By democratic I mean you don't have to have studied for years and years, you can do it yourself, you don't have to be rich, you don't have to have great equipment. It's something everybody can do, and something with which he can and she can enrich the country and for once do something for future generations, not only for themselves. My reading of the situation is that the technological development has become extremely antidemocratic. So I'm most interested in any technology, even to the humble and wonderful simple level of tree planting, that everybody can use.

Waste Water Reclamation Through Ecological Processes

Steve Serfling

Conventional sewage treatment processes that have proven adequate with no major design changes for over 50 years are now recognized as unable to meet the present Federal Water Pollution Control Act Amendments without extensive modification, additions, and extreme construction expense. They are also costly to operate, have high electrical demands, and consume precious natural resources including fossil fuels, chemicals, and water. Conventional treatment processes are incapable of removing or detoxifying the majority of the most harmful components of modern-day waste water, for example, pesticides, herbicides, phenols, heavy metals, and a host of complex domestic and industrial chemicals now recognized as potentially carcinogenic. In contrast, biological lagoon systems containing aquatic plants have proven capable of doing so. Furthermore, conventional technology was never intended or designed to fulfill the pressing need for water reclamation or resource recovery.

Most waste water treatment systems are essentially "biological," since even conventional, high-technology facilities such as trickling filters or activated sludge are entirely dependent on the growth, survival, productivity, and "harvesting" of bacteria to provide treatment. However, ecological theory and practice have clearly demonstrated that monoculture systems, for example, bacteria only, are inherently less stable and efficient than multispecies, polyculture systems containing a variety of bacteria, invertebrates, sludge grazers, algae, and plants.

Recent studies by the U.S. Environmental Protection Agency[1] evaluated 15 different aquaculture-type treatment systems utilizing polyculture lagoons containing a variety of algae, invertebrates, and fish. These were compared to four different conventional treatment methods (activated sludge and trickling filters), and in *all* cases where treatment objectives could be met, the aquaculture systems reduced projected treatment costs from 4% to as much as 94% of conventional technology methods.

The main advantages of the ecological system over conventional high-technology or lagoon treatment systems are as follows:

1. Reduction of Operating and Energy Costs. The system uses low-energy lagoon processes, including solar radiation for heating and oxygen production, inexpensive, air-inflated plastic films for insulation and control of the lagoon environment, efficient aeration systems, and water distribution methods using gravity to reduce electrical pumping requirements. Methane can be produced by anaerobically digesting the sludge, as well as aquatic plants raised in the system, to provide 50%–80% of the electrical energy requirements for the water treatment facility. The need for expensive chemicals is also eliminated.

2. Less Construction Expense. For achieving secondary-quality water, the system is approximately 50% less expensive to construct and operate than conventional secondary-treatment systems. For achieving advanced-quality or potable water, an ecological system can save up to 75% of the cost of average conventional tertiary systems. Furthermore, because a plant can be located in each community for treatment and direct recycling of reclaimed water, expensive sewerage transportation lines and pumping costs are greatly reduced.

3. Reliability, Process Stability, and Flexibility. The system can be designed as a multiple series of AquaCells® that can operate in any combination of parallel or series flow, thereby allowing shutdown, independent performance monitoring, variation of effluent quality, or adjustment of any component without interfering with overall waste treatment. The two-to-six-day retention time and use of hardy species is designed to allow a large elasticity factor to handle wide ranges in nutrient loads (in contrast, bacteria or phytoplankton systems must receive relatively constant nutrient input to operate at designed efficiency levels). Finally, because the system is modularized, expansion can be made easily as needed.

4. Economizing Land Use. In spite of longer retention periods of two to six days, an ecological lagoon system requires little or no more land area than most conventional, high-technology treatment plants with retention times of only four to six hours. This may seem surprising, but it is due to the large open space required by conventional systems for vehicle access to numerous individual tanks for grinding, grit removal, clarification, air compression, aeration and biofiltration, sludge digestion, sludge thickening, disinfection, chemical storage, and so forth, and all the associated piping, valves, and process control equipment. Only one acre of pond area, plus one acre of pretreatment and posttreatment area is required for secondary treatment of 0.5–1.0 million gallons per day flow by the AquaCell process.

5. Year-Round Efficiency. Insulated solar greenhouse covers and solar heat exchangers provide for retention of heat in both the water and the air during colder winter months, thereby maintaining operating efficiencies of highly productive tropical species year-round. This feature also eliminates the need for expensive, oversized facilities designed to meet treatment requirements during the least efficient period of colder winter months.

---

[1]Henderson and Wert, 1976; and Dufter and Moyer, 1978. References 1 and 4.

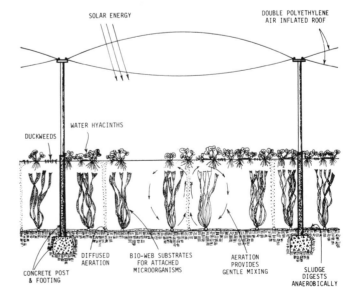

SECTION VIEW - SOLAR AQUACELL SYSTEM

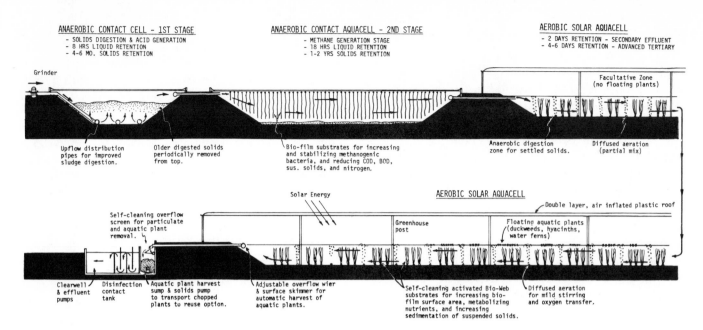

ANAEROBIC CONTACT CELL - 1ST STAGE
- SOLIDS DIGESTION & ACID GENERATION
- 8 HRS LIQUID RETENTION
- 4-6 MO. SOLIDS RETENTION

ANAEROBIC CONTACT AQUACELL - 2ND STAGE
- METHANE GENERATION STAGE
- 18 HRS LIQUID RETENTION
- 1-2 YRS SOLIDS RETENTION

AEROBIC SOLAR AQUACELL
- 2 DAYS RETENTION - SECONDARY EFFLUENT
- 4-6 DAYS RETENTION - ADVANCED TERTIARY

6. No Unpleasant Odors and Unsightly Ponds, Waste Lagoons, and Treatment Tanks. These are eliminated by the greenhouse covers and well-oxygenated, balanced ecosystem, thereby allowing location of the operation in urban areas.

7. Pathogenic Bacteria and Viruses are Eliminated Naturally. Natural biochemical processes of the polyculture system, including endogenous metabolism and food chain consumption, reduce the danger of disease and the amount of chemical treatment required for purification. Ozone, rather than chlorine, is recommended for disinfection after secondary treatment.

8. Byproduct Reuse. Aquatic plants high in protein and nitrogen are harvested on a regular basis, and can be used to provide a valuable, rich organic mulch or compost, used as supplemental livestock feed, or digested anaerobically to produce methane gas for process operation.

9. Reduction of Total Dissolved Salt (TDS) Content. Instead of a TDS increase such as occurs with conventional lagoon treatment, a TDS reduction can be achieved because of the greenhouse cover reducing evaporation and the cultured plants and invertebrate biomass removing minerals from the system.

10. Community Water Resource Planning and Recreation. The potential byproduct and reuse business and recreational-activity potentials can provide numerous opportunities for community benefits from an otherwise negatively viewed aspect of life. For example, in Santee, California, treated waste water is completely recycled for use in a beautiful series of recreational lakes and parks, now the major swimming, boating, fishing, picnicking, and golfing activity center for the community.

The Solar AquaCell System

The Solar AquaCell System consists of multicell, aerated lagoons covered by solar-heated green-houses that contain aquatic plants and biologically active substrates. It has been designed to combine the best features—low construction and operation costs—of aerated lagoons with the control, reliability, advanced-treatment capability, and reduced land requirements of conventional, high-technology treatment plants. By trading off expensive concrete, steel, chemicals, and electricity for natural ecological processes utilizing earthen ponds, greenhouses, hardy pollution-consuming plants, microorganisms and invertebrates, and solar energy, this process has demonstrated the ability to convert raw waste water into high-quality, reclaimed water at substantially lower cost than with conventional treatment methods.

The system has the following characteristics:

1. *Multicell, aerated, earthen lagoons* provide inexpensive holding capacity to allow two-to-six-day retention times (1–3 acres per 10,000 people).

2. *Floating aquatic macrophytic plants*, for example, water hyacinth, duckweeds, azolla, and other hardy species proven to have the ability to remove and metabolize waste water nutrients and toxic compounds are used. The floating plant cover also provides the important advantage of shading out any growth of undesirable suspended algae, which are difficult to harvest and contribute to high biological oxygen demand and suspended solids in conventional pond effluent.

3. *Submerged activated bio-web subtrates*, a form of fixed biofilm substrates whose function is promoting an attached biological film of aerobic bacteria and protozoa are well proven in conventional trickling filter and biodisc processes. The low-density, vertically suspended bio-webs increase the biologically active surface area up to 50 times that of a conventional pond.

4. *A greenhouse and solar pond cover* are used to entrap solar heat during the daytime, even during cloudy pe-

riods, and to reduce pond heat losses at night. Biological rates of reaction are well known to increase by a factor of 1.5–2.0 for every 10° F temperature rise. This means a treatment pond or tank system maintained at 65° F instead of 55° F during winter months can treat up to twice the flow, or be constructed to one-half the size, saving construction and land area costs.

5. *A dual-aeration solar-heat-exchange system*, consisting of a simple diffused, submerged aeration piping system to provide a partial mixing and oxygen exchange, and modified surface aerators (operated during the daytime), is used to provide transfer of both oxygen and solar-heated air to the pond.

REFERENCES

1. WILLIAM R. DUFFER AND JAMES E. MOYER. 1978. *Municipal Wastewater Aquaculture.* Environmental Protection Agency Report No. 600/2–78–110.

2. WILLIAM S. HILLMAN AND DUDLEY D. CULLEY JR. 1978. The uses of duckweed. *American Scientist,* July-August, pp. 442–451.

3. ERNEST S. DEL FOSSE. 1977. Waterhyacinth biomass yield potentials. In: *Symposium Papers, Clean Fuels from Biomass Wastes.* Chicago: Institute of Gas Technology.

4. UPTON B. HENDERSON, AND FRANK S. WERT. 1976. *Economic Assessment of Wastewater Aquaculture Treatment Systems.* Environmental Protection Agency Report No. 600/2–76–293.

SOLAR AQUACELL – PROCESS FLOW DIAGRAM

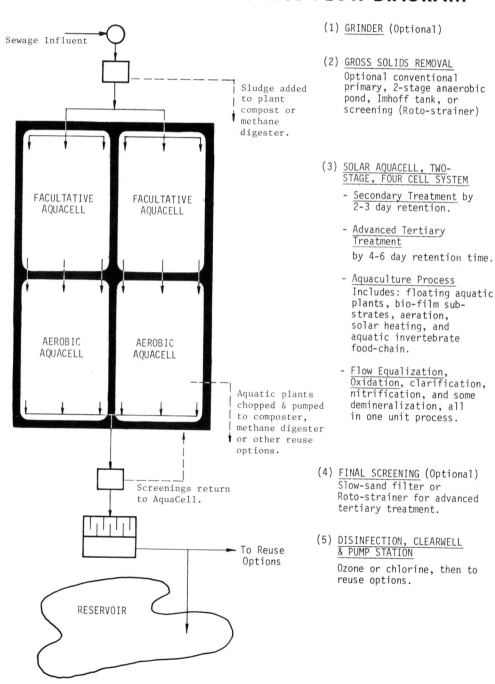

(1) GRINDER (Optional)

(2) GROSS SOLIDS REMOVAL
Optional conventional primary, 2-stage anaerobic pond, Imhoff tank, or screening (Roto-strainer)

(3) SOLAR AQUACELL, TWO-STAGE, FOUR CELL SYSTEM

- Secondary Treatment by 2-3 day retention.

- Advanced Tertiary Treatment
  by 4-6 day retention time.

- Aquaculture Process
  Includes: floating aquatic plants, bio-film substrates, aeration, solar heating, and aquatic invertebrate food-chain.

- Flow Equalization, Oxidation, clarification, nitrification, and some demineralization, all in one unit process.

(4) FINAL SCREENING (Optional)
Slow-sand filter or Roto-strainer for advanced tertiary treatment.

(5) DISINFECTION, CLEARWELL & PUMP STATION
Ozone or chlorine, then to reuse options.

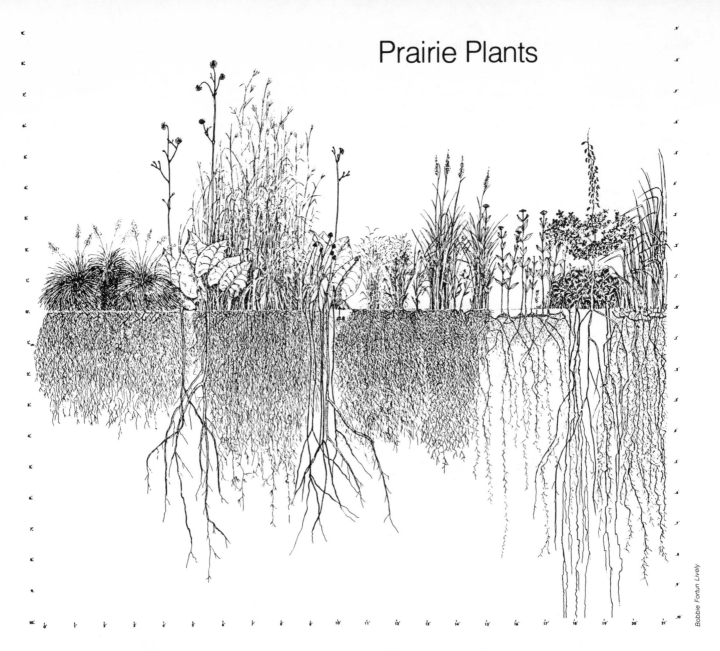

Bobbie Fortun Lively

The Sustainable Farm

Wes Jackson

Assumptions

General

1. A viable nearby village and a distant city are necessary supporting elements for a viable farm. *Supporting* is emphasized, for the farm does not exist for the village or the city but rather land is the foremost and most highly protected of any component in the entire support system.

2. Though the farm described here is characteristic of a region of highly specific needs, the principles employed by the New Age farmer would be the same throughout the land, from New England to Southern California.

Religious Considerations

3. For humans, as well as for all species on earth, our planet is the best of all possible worlds. There is no meaningful escape valve for most of us.

4. In the long run, land determines more of the possible patterns of activity on the planet than humans.

5. Land is a community that includes the living and nonliving and is not just dirt.

6. The highest calling of an individual is to participate with the land in the promotion of a healthy and productive biosphere in order to meet, in Thoreau's words, "the expectations of the land." Holistic land stewardship is a way of life.

7. We are to encroach upon wilderness only as "strangers and sojourners." Wilderness is the standard against which we judge our agricultural and cultural practices. Therefore all natural ecosystems are to be protected. Such systems are the most reliable source of information for a sustainable future.

Institutional Consideration

8. Land is too important to be an item for speculation. Therefore, some form of land-trust system will be necessary to regulate its use.

An Agricultural Shift

9. Because a safe, sustainable culture must rely on sunshine, almost exclusively, the land will be called upon to be a sustainable and net energy producer for food, clothing, shelter, and transportation.

10. Because seeds are now, and have historically been, a central item in our diets, most alternatives in agriculture must include them. The closest approximation to the former natural vegetation in vegetative structure is a high-seed-yielding perennial polyculture. Therefore, the majority of the acreage would be devoted to this form of agricultural ecosystem.

Technological and Institutional Change

11. Essentially all the technology on the land should be powered from a sustainable energy source near at hand. Direct solar power, windpower, and hydropower should be used when possible.

12. Though machinery may be manufactured in a distant place, most repair should occur at the village level if not on the farm.

Equipment and Support Buildings

Operator-Owned Equipment

One 45 horsepower tractor run on alcohol. One multiple reaper combine (pulled and powered by PTO from tractor). One side-delivery rake. One baler for 1,000–1,200 lb bales. Windmill for pumping water. (Water tank is the accumulator.) Wind-electric power for refrigeration to store food. Freezing condition "accumulates." Wind-electric power with induction motor to put power on line. Ordinary wrenches and small tools.

Village Rental

Easy Flow Fertilizer (phosphorus and calcium) distributor. Chisel (attached to tractor) for breaking sod-bound soils. Annual seedbed-preparation equipment. Miscellaneous small tools and power equipment.

Support Buildings

Machinery and solar-heated tool shed and workshop. One hundred percent solar (passive and active) partially underground house set into bank. Solar and mobile hog and chicken pens.

The 160 Acre Farm

"The Fuel 40"

A six-species polyculture: five grasses, one legume. These seeds are high in carbohydrates, low in protein. The field averages about 20 barrels of crude equivalent per year. Livestock are cycled onto this acreage for a few weeks to enhance crumb structure of soil.

"The Multiple Purpose 40"

A six-species polyculture: four grasses, two legumes. Beef stock turned in for "finishing" on seeds. Some years seeds harvested for cash crop. Early vegetation to methanol still in village with limit of 2–5 barrels of crude equivalent per year. This 40 is "cushion" acreage, often using the poorest land.

"The Cash Grain-Hay 40"

A six-species polyculture: four grasses, one legume, one composite. Fall harvest for cash grain. Livestock pasture June 1–August 15. Hay in windows and large bales after seed harvest. Winter area for hybrid derivative of buffalo-domestic cow.

Windmill

Carry-Over Native Pasture

Bottom Land Boundary

Creek bottom for garden and annual cereals (corn, wheat, soybeans, etc.). Managed mixed woodlot. Mixed orchard.

Bottom Land

Workshop, machine, and tool shed. House. Wind-electric machines for four families. Commons.

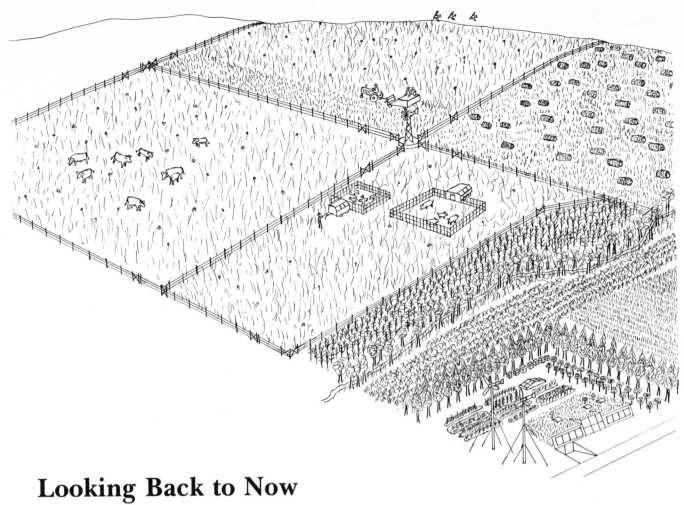

Looking Back to Now

Wes Jackson

The year is 2030 in a world with a heightened consciousness. People everywhere—on farms, in villages, and in cities—have sustainability as their central paradigm. They think globally and act locally. Regional semi-self-sufficiency is emphasized, but the principles of the New Age farmers are the same from New England to Southern California. Our utopian farm is in Kansas, below the 39th parallel and east of the 98th meridian. The area averages about 28 inches of rainfall each year, but the evaporation is in excess of rainfall. This is farming country that before being plowed more than a century ago was biotically rich. Stories handed down through the grandparents tell school-age children how the breaking of this virgin sod sounded like the opening of a zipper. A few miles east is the western edge of the vast Tallgrass Prairie, dominated by such species as big bluestem, Indian grass, and switchgrass. Scarcely 30 miles to the west are the mixed prairies dominated by bluestem and sideoats grama.

Because of the minimal landscape relief, the Great Plains is one of the few regions where it makes sense to divide the land into one-mile-square parcels. A road surrounds almost every square mile. This is a land that after the "Great Plowing" in the early 1900s supported such high-producing annual crops as wheat, sorghum, milo, and soybeans. Between then and 1990 only native pastureland and roadsides carried the principal grasses that were characteristic of the region before the Europeans arrived. Even so, this prairie, mostly because of forced grazing, had long since lost 20 or 25 native prairie species. What was left was not prairie but grassland. During most of the last century, wheat was an important export crop for the region; we are fortunate that even more grassland wasn't plowed. Church leaders, farmers, and grain men had said that we must sell grain to feed a hungry world. It was mostly a moral veneer over a basically economic consideration, but it was enough to discourage the initial development of mixed perennials. Traditional crops were proven producers regardless of their tremendous toll on finite energy resources, soil, and, for western corn growers, fossil ground water.

But now in 2030 the settlement pattern differs drastically from what it was in 1980. In this immediate area, each family lives on 160 acres, or four families per square mile (640 acres). The dwellings of all four families are near the middle of the square-mile section but on their own property. Therefore, within 200–300 yards of each other there are 16–20 people. Their small village and main trading center, which includes both school and churches, is 2½ miles away. No one in the rural service area of the village is ever any farther away. The village's service area covers 16 square miles (4 miles on each side), which includes 64 farm families totaling about 250 people. Westward, in the mixed prairie, one-half of a section (320 acres) is needed to support a single family, and nearly 200 miles west of the mixed-grass country, in the short-grass prairie, 2 square miles is usually necessary to support one family. Eastward and in some of the west, it is another story. Along the Missouri in Nebraska; the southwestern half of Minnesota, most of Iowa, in southeastern Wisconsin, northern Indiana, northwestern Ohio, east central Michigan, along the Mississippi, in western Tennessee and northwestern Mississippi, in much of the Sacramento Valley, as well as in numerous other localized areas throughout the country, often fewer than 10 acres but never more than 20 is enough to support a family. It is not that production is always higher than in our area, it is just that a combination of factors, including rainfall, makes a sustainable yield more assured. The carrying capacity of the land is so varied that when we say the average farm, nationwide, is 40 acres, we must immediately realize the limited meaning of that statistic.

Regardless of farm size, the village population seldom exceeds the farm population by more than a factor of two. An entire community in our region consists of around 750 people, including the 260 people on farms. Let us compare this to the distribution pattern nationwide. The population of the United States is around 300 million and is scheduled to stabilize completely in the next seven years, in spite of the fact that zero population growth procedures have been in effect since the early 1980s. The momentum of that past is still with us, though insignificantly so. But it is the distribution of the population that has been radically altered over the last 50 years. Most of the major cities have experienced drastic declines and the number of cities of 40,000 or less has greatly increased. Optimum city size was widely discussed in the last century. Many of the New Age pioneers concluded, though there was nothing like unanimous agreement, that much of the social pathology of our former urban areas could be attributed to the spiritual dangers that arise when people no longer know or feel their rootedness in the land. When heat comes from a furnace, food from a grocery store, building materials from the lumber yard, and the automobile from the showroom floor, the spiritual loss is devastating to the society. It doesn't necessarily take a city of a million, many concluded, to provide the "critical mass" necessary to help a large number of humans live up to a broad spectrum of their innate potentialities. A population of 40,000 seems to have a special associated energy. When the cathedral of Notre Dame on the Île de France was begun, the population of Paris was 35,000. Renaissance Florence had a population of 35,000–40,000. Regional cities now seldom exceed 40,000, and there are somewhat fewer than 4,000 such cities totaling fewer than 160 million people. Of course, some of the major cities still contain a few million people, but they are mostly emptied and much of the area now produces food, clothing, and shelter where concrete and stone formerly dominated the environment. The civilization was a long time learning that, by and large, the only people who really liked big-city life were merchants and intellectuals.

Of the 300 million people in the United States, some 20 million, or about one-fifteenth of the population, work in the rural areas not associated with rangeland and forestry. Nearly 10 million families, totaling about 40 million people, are living on 400 million acres of cropland. This amounts to a little over 13 percent of the total population, well over twice the percentage of 50 years ago and nearly three times the total rural population of that time. The rural villages, however, contain twice as many people as the countryside they support. I mentioned earlier that the land holdings vary drastically in size. For example, in much of northeastern Illinois, a family of four can live on 5 acres. This amounts to 128 small farms or 512 people per square mile. This is a very high density, but the productivity of the land is the determining factor. Over 8,000 people live within the 16 square mile rural service area. Its supporting village has over 16,000 people.

Our solar village of 500 or so is necessarily different from the northeastern Illinois village of 16,000. Aside from the differing political dynamics associated with different sizes and densities, there is a commonness of purpose best reflected in the numerous bioshelters that grow what might be described as a healthful diet, though not an abundance of calories. The fields provide most of the protein and carbohydrates for this society, and it is up to the people in the villages and cities to provide vegetables and fruits and a certain amount of protein, mostly from fish, in the passive bioshelters pioneered by the New Alchemists in the last century. The major differences among these villages have to do with the regional responses of village people in their work with farmers to meet the expectations of the land. A pluralistic society does not preclude the possibility of holding a common allegiance.

Neither does pluralism mean that certain patterns of both young and old cannot be similar everywhere. Throughout the country, older people have the option of living in the village, but their presence is cherished on the farm. Nearly all have chosen to live in the village, but most return to the farm daily to assist their families and neighbors in various chores. These are the people who play the most important part in the children's education.

Most communities now emphasize the value of history, and history becomes more real when adults tell personal stories that link the past to the present. The stories are about heroes, the prophets of the solar age, and the pioneers in the era of decentralization and land resettlement, and villains who were responsible for chemical contamination of the land and its people. The older people tell of a past in which nuclear power was tried, discovered to be filled with unresolvable uncertainties, and abandoned. Many of these older people lived during what is now called the "Age of the Recognition of Limits." These former doom-watching pioneers were like the children of Israel who had escaped the grasp of the Egyptians and then wandered in the wilderness for 40 years, saddled with their own slave mentality, waiting for a new generation of free minds to develop and be fit for life in the "promised land." Many of the pioneers have readily admitted their earlier addiction to all the consumer products of affluence, and work hard at teaching their young the true source of sustenance and health—the land. They are living reminders that this sun-powered civilization has arrived as the result of nothing less than a religious reformation.

The strong new land ethic has resulted in a different concept of land ownership. Under the land-trust system, land is not owned by individuals in the same sense that it was 50 years ago. Nevertheless, it can be passed on from one generation to the next, and people have a strong sense of ownership. They cannot do exactly as they please with the property. They cannot willfully pollute it with toxic chemicals, sell it off for housing developments, or in any way speculate with it. Such wasteful exploitation discounts too much of the future. Activity that is potentially destructive is prohibited by a board of nonfarming elders from the village and two from the regional city. Both sexes are equally represented.

On our farm, the well-insulated house is partially underground and is equipped with both passive and active solar installations for hot water and space heating. Though it is 100 percent solar, a backup system consisting of a wood-burning stove is in place. A water-pumping windmill and two wind-electric systems provide power for the farmstead. A combination of technologies from the past are appropriate for the farm's water system. A water-pumping windmill pumps water, which is stored in tanks for the livestock and household use. Trenching machines and plastic pipe are used to deliver the water wherever needed for human convenience. One wind generator takes care of all refrigeration needs and simply cools the freezer and refrigerator when the wind is blowing. Since the refrigerator itself is the "accumulator," no batteries are needed. The other wind-electric system consists of an induction motor that kicks in when the output of the wind-powered generator is greater than the load on the service line. The induction motor, which is similar to that found on washing machines in the 1930s, is plugged into the wall receptacle and runs the kilowatt-hour meter backward, giving the farmstead an electrical energy credit. A special meter records the numbers of hours generated. If this household wishes to break even on the utility bill, its unit must provide four kilowatts of electricity to a privately owned utility for each one it receives. There is just enough electricity generated in the area from both wind and low-head hydroelectric turbines to supply the needs of the countryside, village, and regional city. This is because in the last 50 years, solar power for space and hot water heating has become so widespread. In combination with the appropriate design and construction of new shelters, heating needs have been met with a modest amount of wood, grown for the specific purpose of backing up the solar systems.

In the 20 acres of creek bottom land, people grow such annual monocultures as wheat, corn, rye, barley, and oats. Orchards and vegetable gardens are near the houses. Canning of garden products takes place outside, using energy derived from concentrating collectors. Dried foods take precedence over canned foods, and root crops are very important.

A single solar hog house on wheels is large enough to accommodate no more than 2 sows and 20 feeder pigs. A similar solar chicken house, surrounded by a 25 square foot fence accommodates from 25 to 50 chickens. About half are frying chickens, which are eaten during the summer months. Unlike the chickens grown in closed confinement 50 years ago, these animals experience far fewer tumors, and the yolks of their eggs are a brilliant gold.

Pigs and chickens "graze" on fresh pasture during the growing season. Their mobile pens are easily advanced a few feet each day with hand levers operated by schoolchildren or grandparents from the village. The mobile pens allow for an economy of fencing materials. This managed migration simulates the migration of large animals in presettlement times. Only the breeding stock for pigs, the laying hens, and two roosters are maintained throughout the winter.

The one large outbuilding is devoted to covering the small amount of machinery. The expensive equipment consists of a small, multiple-harvesting combine, a 45 horsepower tractor, and a hay baler. The combine with a 7 foot cutter bar runs off the tractor's power take-off.

The traction and transportation fuel needs are met with alcohol, derived from crops grown on the farm. The "Fuel 40" is the principal energy producer. This is a six-species polyculture consisting of five grasses and one legume. These species are selected for their high carbohydrate content and relatively low protein yield. This 40 acre field averages about 20 barrels of crude oil equivalent per year.[1] Livestock are cycled onto this acreage for a few weeks each year to enhance the crumb structure of the soil

One hundred years ago, approximately 25 percent of the total acreage was devoted to horses and mules for traction purposes. Now, about eight barrels of crude equivalent, or only 10 percent of the total acreage on the farm, is devoted to farm traction. This is because horses and mules would burn energy just standing around being horses and mules, but the tractor can be turned off. However, the tractor cannot become pregnant and build a replacement on solar energy. A pregnant mare at rest is not really resting. Furthermore, parts wear out on the tractor and cannot be replaced by ordinary cell division as with the traction animal. Nevertheless, from the point of view of total energy expenditure, the tractor is used rather than the beast of burden, so long as other livestock are around to enhance the crumb structure of the soil. The other 12 barrel equivalents from the Fuel 40, representing about 15 percent of the total acreage, are sent to the village and city for their portable liquid fuel needs.

The alcohol fuel "refinery" requires some elaboration. Organic material produced at the farm is delivered to a privately owned or co-op still in the village. The production of portable liquid fuels is part of a fine-grained approach to our overall en-

ergy needs. It has become economically feasible as farming methods have become less energy-intensive and less capital-intensive. It wasn't economically feasible in the 1980s and produced a very low net energy yield, but the agricultural sector was enthusiastic about producing alcohol fuel from farm crops. Hundreds of on-farm stills were built and closed down in 18 months, after federal and state subsidies were withdrawn. Major stills costing $20 million and more were built, and many closed within three years, after losing the subsidies. In those years, each automobile would consume in calories what nearly two dozen people would consume in the same period. American farmers learned a valuable and painful lesson about the potential of alcohol fuel production to meet the enormous energy demands of that time. Soil loss accelerated during this period, and farmers gradually learned to curtail their alcohol-production programs to a very moderate level.

Another source of energy comes from the "Multiple Purpose 40." Leaf and stem material are harvested from a herbacious polyculture after the early summer seed harvest and are converted into methanol, equivalent to two to five barrels of crude oil each year. In the fall, some of the net wood production of the woodlot and orchard is also converted. Upon arrival at the still, all organic matter is weighed, moisture is determined, and nutrients are calculated. The farmer may sell some or all of his alcohol into the public sector, but the nutrients left over after distillation are returned to the farm and are usually spread on the field or woodlot from which they were taken. This is to prevent soil mining and reduce the amount of chemical fertilizer applied.

One concern that is constantly discussed and fine tuned has to do with what tools and equipment should be owned and operated by the farm and which ones made available through the rental place in the village. At this time the rental place provides an Easy Flo fertilizer distributor (for phosphorus and nitrogen), a chisel that is attached to the tractor to break sod-bound soils, seedbed-preparation equipment for the annual crops, and numerous other pieces of equipment that are used infrequently.

People on this land have a deep distrust of commercially produced chemicals being introduced on their land. It is amazing that this distrust began to develop some 40 years ago in the churches. In many seminaries during the 1980s, cadres of students began to debate the possibility that the Genesis version of the Creation had contributed to much of the environmental problem. During the 1970s, the question of *dominion* had been much discussed. Since most defenders of the Genesis

---

[1]Nationwide, roughly 25%, or approximately 100 million acres of cropland, is devoted to growing alcohol fuels. The yield amounts to about 50 million barrels of oil equivalent. An additional seven million barrels equivalent is gained in the form of methanol from the farm. In 1979, this would have amounted to only a three-day supply of oil, or less than 1% of the annual consumption.

story had insisted that *dominion* was not the current word, but that *stewardship* was implied, church people began to relax. That turned out to be a rather unimportant consideration. During the 1980s another discussion began, much more quietly. The emphasis this time was on the cultural impact of a subtlety in our religious heritage. The culture had fostered, however unwittingly, the belief that humans are a separate creation. After all, the biblical creation story held that the earth and the living world were created, and then there was a pause. Following the pause, in a special effort, came human beings. But our biologists in the last century demonstrated that the same 20 amino acids are in the redwood, the snail, the human, and the elm tree, as well as in the lowly microbe. Furthermore, the nucleotides that make up the code are mostly the same throughout. Native Americans had talked about Brother Wolf and Sister Tree long before these discoveries. Now in our churches it is frequently mentioned that our cells have had no evolutionary experience with such and such a pesticide, or that the concentration of a "natural" chemical much greater than our tissues have ever experienced is to be avoided. A toxic level is defined as a quantity beyond the evolutionary standards of our cells.

Because a sustainable agriculture is more important than one that is highly productive, upland crops consist of recently developed herbaceous perennial polycultures. The polycultures are ensembles of species developed by the land grant universities through the experimental stations. Perennials were selected because of their soil-holding capability. High-yielding, nutritious seed-producing perennials were first inventoried in numerous experimental gardens. Next, an intense selection program was initiated to increase the yields of individual species. Later, thousands of species combinations were tried. From then on, plant breeders sought to improve performances of individual species within the polyculture environment.

These perennial polycultures have several distinct advantages over the former annual monocultures.

First, soil loss has been reduced to replacement levels. We had expected this, for the reduction of soil loss was a major motivation behind the extensive research. Second, spring water has returned to the area. Many springs are now trickling all year, and the microhydroelectric capacity has increased, along with a rise in the water table. Land with perennial vegetation has become a huge battery for stored "electricity." A third advantage is that the energy required for maintenance and harvest after the initial planting is just 5 percent of that required by the former high-yielding monocultures of annuals. And finally, although the usual pathogens and insects are still around, they do not reach epidemic proportions.

Our particular farm has fields consisting mostly of grasses, a few legumes, and even members of the sunflower family. Some of the fields are harvested in early summer, some in the fall. The early summer or July harvest in one field includes descendants of intermediate wheatgrass, Canada wild rye, sideoats grama, tall wheatgrass, and Stueve's lespedeza. The fall harvest consists of four grasses, a legume and a member of the sunflower family. The grasses include descendants of switchgrass, lovegrass, Indian grass, and weeping lovegrass. The legume, wild senna, and a perennial soybean provide the nitrogen plus some seed, and a high-yielding descendant of the gray-headed coneflower produces seeds with two important oils.

Some of the early objections to harvest and separation of seeds from the polycultures were quickly dampened when agricultural engineers began to invent machinery. In fact, it is ironic, but the return to polycultures became possible only in our age of mechanization. Some have since made the argument that monoculture arose because of the need to harvest small seeds efficiently when all we had was hand labor. The age of mechanization, then, has allowed us to develop an agriculture with a vegetative structure that closely mimics that of preagricultural times. Much of the machinery has allowed our psyches to resemble those of hunters and gatherers again, but of course in a modern context.

The fossil fuels used during the transition era, 1985–2025, as we moved from mining and destruction of land as a way of life to the solar age, afforded us opportunities not only in plant breeding, but in animal improvement as well. This period gave us the chance to develop crops that were less dependent on humans. The same was true with the livestock. For example, the American bison was crossed with domestic cattle, and the thicker hides made the critters more resistant to severe winters.[2] In a way, we are now using solar energy (stored in grass) to maintain barns—the hides of animals. Protective shelter made of lumber for large animals is not necessary.

Livestock are moved from one polyculture to

---

[2]Grandparents amuse the children with stories about square tomatoes and featherless chickens. The featherless chicken was developed in the 1970s by reductionistic technologists who thought they would help corporate chicken growers and processors cut costs in cleaning chickens. The consequence was a funny-looking chicken that required such a warm environment that the energy costs were in excess of the cleaning costs. The moral of the story is that big money is a sure license for big foolishness.

another in a rhythm that does not jeopardize flowering and seed set. Most grazing does occur in areas that produce seed for human consumption, but certain polycultures are grown for the livestock exclusively. A few weeks before slaughter buffalo/beef graze on mixed perennials that are setting seed. This is a weak simulation of the feedlot of former times. No hay is hauled to the barn for winter feeding, for there is no barn. Some of the hay is windrowed with a side-delivery rake and is left, but most raked hay is rolled into 1,000–1,200 pound bales and remains in the field. This system reduces the need to spend time and energy moving hay and manure, and the nutrients are left where they are most useful.

The movement of livestock on the farm turns out to be critical. In natural ecosystems there were no fences. Even though we are forced to use fences for all our livestock, our management program recognizes that animal wastes on the farm contribute to the crumb structure of the soil as mentioned earlier, which allows the soil to release nutrients slowly while holding moisture.

Many of the problems caused by farming techniques of the 1960s and 1970s have been solved in this new era. Seedbed preparation occurs mostly where the few acres of annuals are grown, and since tillage has been dramatically reduced, soil loss is almost nonexistent. Silting of streams is minimal, and more species and larger populations of fish thrive in the waterways. Energy-expensive terracing is no longer as necessary, and where check dams and small farm ponds exist, they serve the farmer mostly as pools for catfish culture. Irrigation is reduced, for the perennial polycultures slow the water so thoroughly that hundreds of thousands of springs throughout the country have been reborn. Fertilizer application is minimal because the diversity of crops has maintained a better nutrient balance with less nutrient runoff. The recordbreaking fish kills of the last century due to fertilizer and feedlot runoff are now only part of the legends about our unenlightened grandparents. Weeding is essentially a thing of the past,

except in gardens and where annual monocultures are grown. Pesticide application is almost nonexistent because of both polyculture and a broader genetic base in our crops. A broader genetic base in livestock and the demise of high-density feedlots have made the use of antibiotics for livestock seldom necessary. The life of farm machinery has increased by a factor of 16 in the last 50 years. All of these changes have resulted in a drastic cut in energy consumption for farm production.

The major changes began to surface during the 1980s, when a few young agricultural professionals, having adopted a sustainable agriculture as their paradigm, looked for the sustainable alternatives rather than placing their bets on corporately controlled agriculture. In many respects, they were the true heroes of the era. Some took the theory of the quantitative gene developed during the 1960s and, using it along with the known virtues of hybrid vigor, made repeated breakthroughs in new crop development.

There was a unifying theme from Massachusetts to Kansas to California. People recognized that in the long run, and often in the short run, land is the determining factor. Citizens sought to meet the expectations of the land and to look at the natural ecosystems of different regions as the standards against which to judge their agricultural practices. Suddenly, as is so often the case with profound statements, there was a new meaning to the words that Thoreau had uttered from the Concord Lyceum in the mid-1800s: "In wilderness is the preservation of the world." The policy-makers began to take seriously the prediction of Charles Lindberg: "The human future depends on our ability to combine the knowledge of science with the wisdom of wildness." When this concept was applied to our farms, they became waterproof, diversified family hearths. Our fields are no longer vulnerable, oil-hungry monocultures, although they are not wilderness either. But without wilderness, we would not have developed a sustainable agriculture and culture.

EARLY MANIFESTATIONS

Project 1: The Cathedral Church of St. John the Divine

John Todd

In most of its teachings, Christianity ignores ecology. However, within it are profound notions of stewardship for all living things that have been all but ignored in our secular age. The teachings of Christ may be given new meaning in a union of Christianity and ecology. For the Very Reverend James Parks Morton of The Cathedral of St. John The Divine in New York, this union is essential to the reinspiration of Christianity.

Cathedrals in medieval times were seats of culture as well as religious practice. They had their schools, hospitals, artisans, and crafts as well as music and theater. They were like whole towns woven into a religious economy.

This earlier vision of the cathedral inspired the bioshelter and school projects that follow. At the conference the bioshelter Ark and eco-school were conceived. Afterwards, with support from the Threshold Foundation, several architects were asked to continue bioshelter proposals on their own. Some of their ideas follow.

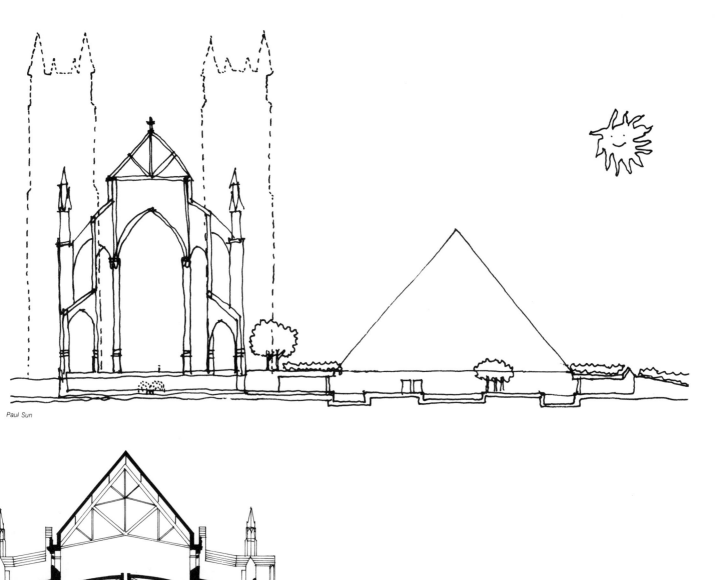

Paul Sun

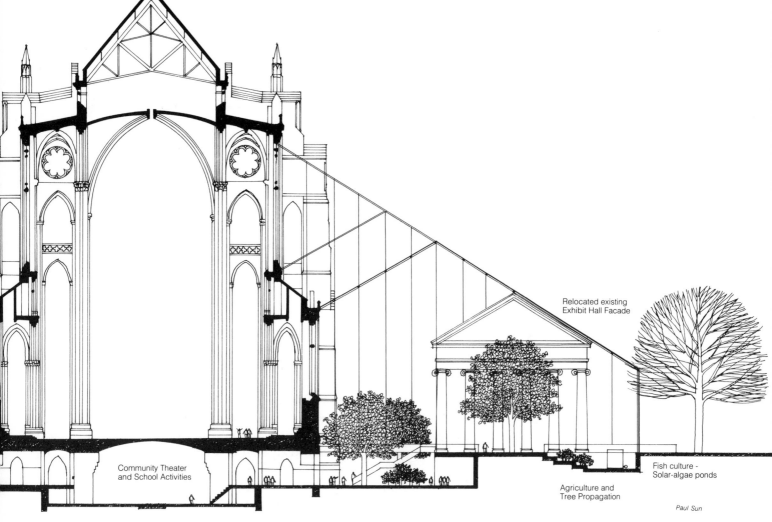

Community Theater
and School Activities

Relocated existing
Exhibit Hall Facade

Agriculture and
Tree Propagation

Fish culture -
Solar-algae ponds

Paul Sun

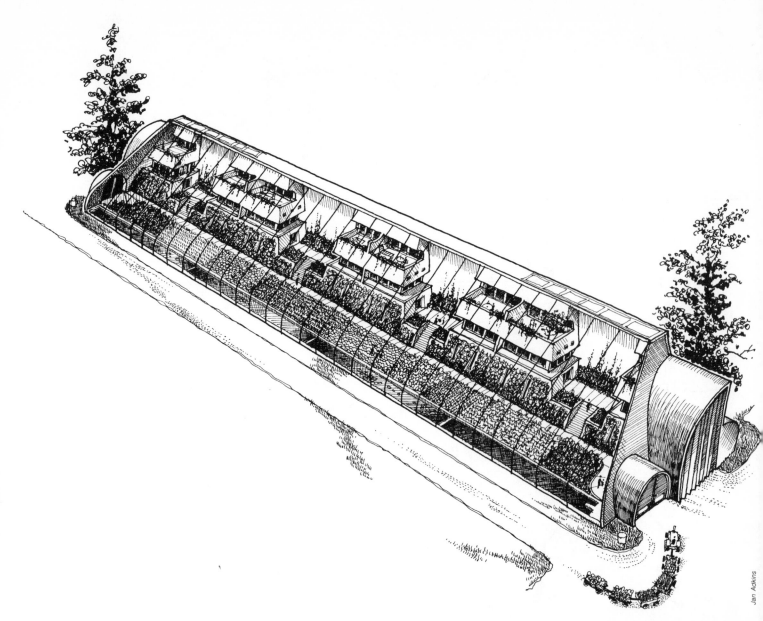

Jan Adkins

Project 2: A Maine Coastal Village

John Todd

Acquaintances of ours owned a farm on the coast of Maine that they were considering turning into a community land trust. The community was to be based on the traditional economics of agriculture, fishing, and boat building but within a thoroughly modern context. It was to strive to create a symbiotic relationship with the nearest existing town.

This project created a lot of excitement at the conference as the dream seemed close at hand and would be most attainable by individuals cooperating in groups.

The community would be powered by traditional and modern renewable technologies. Hydropower and windpower would provide the electricity. The forest would be the source of biofuels. Ice would be cut in winter for the fishery. Bioshelters would be used for growing all-season produce. The main biological economy of the village would most likely be mariculture and sea products. Bioshelters would serve as hatcheries and as food-rearing facilities.

Inshore fishing vessels might be built by the community, combining traditional methods and advanced propulsion technologies including windpower.

The architecture was to be solar using a combination of traditional and modern ideas. A Maine village architecture—which we called arkipelagos—emerged from the conference.

Arkipelagos would be apartments within a solar bioshelter. Individual and community gardens would be part of the interior architecture. It was felt that arkipelagos might take some of the sting out of harsh Maine winters.

The Maine solar village would look to the sea, but like intertidal dwellers it would also be firmly rooted to the land of which it is a part.

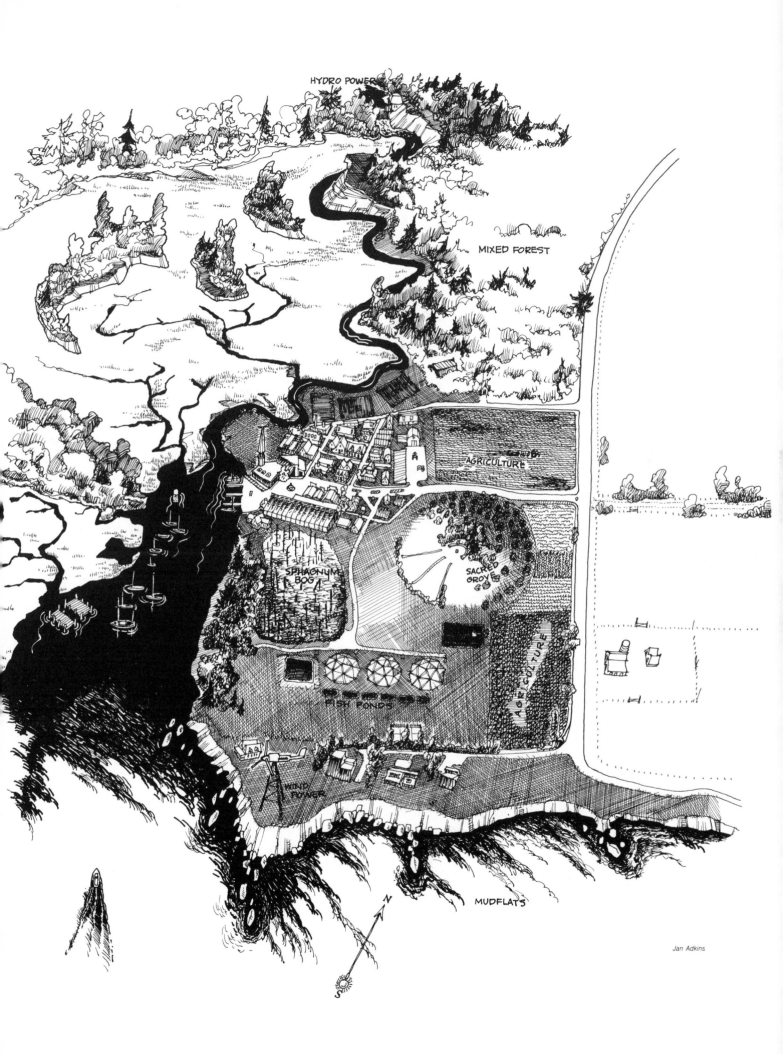

HYDRO POWER

MIXED FOREST

AGRICULTURE

SPHAGNUM BOG

SACRED GROVE

AGRICULTURE

FISH PONDS

WIND POWER

MUDFLATS

Jan Adkins

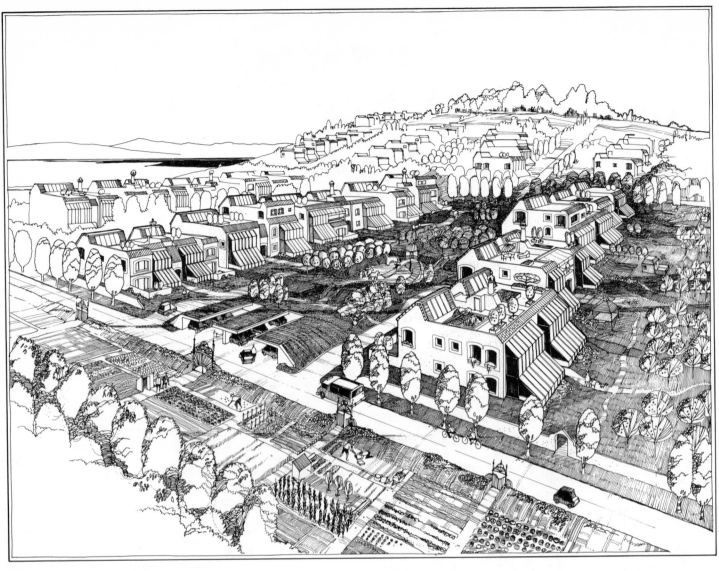

NEW SOLAR HOUSING

Project 3: Marin Solar Village

John Todd

Marin Solar Village, adjacent to San Francisco, is the brainchild of Sim Van der Ryn and his associates. It is a bold attempt to create from an Air Force base a village of the sun with wide public acceptance.

As of this writing, many of the political hurdles have been overcome. Underway now are the intensive design and cost-projection phases. The following text and drawings provide an overview of what may become the first village of the sun. It is also the beginning of a village as a solar ecology. It could well become an important milestone for us all.

The reuse of Hamilton Air Force Base is an opportunity to build the most modern community on the planet designed to sustain a high-quality life based on ecological balance and the efficient use of energy. It will provide 800 new solar dwellings, 1,500 new jobs in a corporate center and light industry, a transit center to ease freeway congestion, on-site food and energy production, and an open space for wildlife and recreation. Solar Village will be privately financed with no cost to the county, making Marin first in the nation with practical approaches to our problems of energy, economics, and environment.

INDEX

Commercial Banks and Economic Development

The Experience of Eastern Africa

Ali Issa Abdi

PRAEGER SPECIAL STUDIES IN INTERNATIONAL BUSINESS, FINANCE, AND TRADE

Praeger Publishers   New York   London

Library of Congress Cataloging in Publication Data

Abdi, Ali Issa.
    Commercial banks and economic development.

    (Praeger special studies in international business, finance, and trade)
    Bibliography: p.
    Includes index.
    1. Banks and banking—Africa, East.
2. Underdeveloped areas—Banks and banking.
I. Title.
HG3392.A6A2   1977   332.1'2'0967   77-12813
ISBN 0-03-023031-4

PRAEGER SPECIAL STUDIES
200 Park Avenue, New York, N.Y., 10017, U.S.A.

Published in the United States of America in 1977
by Praeger Publishers,
A Division of Holt, Rinehart and Winston, CBS, Inc.

789   038   987654321

To My Father
Haji Issa Abdi
and to
"Sayed" Mohamed

PREFACE

Theoretical analysis of economic development issues in the developing countries has traditionally emphasized real resource limitations and labor skill constraints. It is only recently that a few economists have emphasized the foreign exchange and domestic savings gaps. This study focuses on the mobilization of domestic savings via commercial banks and other financial institutions. Unlike the academicians, the policy makers of the developing countries are aware of the significance of domestic savings mobilization, particularly in countries where foreign aid is unavailable or unwelcome and where external foreign debts have become truly burdensome.

This study is primarily concerned with the role of the banking systems of Eastern Africa, 1950–73, in the real economic development of the respective economies. In evaluating the larger role of the commercial banks, I have particularly emphasized their contribution to the development of indigenous enterprises during the postindependence years. The performances of the different banking systems of Eastern Africa, which include completely government-owned as well as private, predominantly foreign-owned systems, are also examined and compared. In appraising each system's performance, the experiences of some high-financial-growth economies such as those of Korea, Germany, and Japan are reviewed.

In examining the determinants of the recent performances of the Eastern African banking systems, and the poor performances associated with the financial systems of developing countries, two hypotheses are considered: the financial repression hypothesis, which views government intervention in bank operations as the determining factor, and the structuralist hypothesis that holds the relative development level of an economy as the determining factor. In the Eastern African case, I have shown that deposit and interest rate ceilings were maintained since independence. However, I have indicated that, although the imposed deposit ceilings might have reduced the level of financial and other savings, the effect of the interest rate ceilings and other government controls on the allocation of bank assets were small. The study attributes the recent poor performances of the Eastern African banking systems primarily to deficiencies in the effective demand for bank services and to imperfections in the financial markets.

ACKNOWLEDGMENTS

The idea for this study originated with Somalia's nationalization of the foreign branch banks operating in that country in 1970. This book would not have been possible, however, without the guidance and wise counsel of Professors David Felix and Hyman Minsky of Washington University, St. Louis. I am deeply grateful to them for helping me from the proposal stage to the completion of this study. To the other professors at Washington University whom I have been privileged to know I am also thankful.

I wish to acknowledge as well the assistance and support that I received from my colleagues at the International Monetary Fund. I am especially thankful to Omutunde Johnson and Festus Osunsade, who reviewed some chapters. Finally, I would like to express my appreciation to Hudon Issa, Mohamed Ali Issa, and the rest of my family for their support and patience. Of course, none of the above individuals or institutions with which I have been associated is responsible for the views expressed here, or for any errors that may remain.

CONTENTS

LIST OF TABLES AND FIGURES

Figure

1

The role of financial institutions in the economic growth of the developing economies has come under increasing scrutiny by economic planners and other policy makers in these countries. Mobilization of domestic financial resources, either to supplant or to supplement external financial assistance where it is available, has assumed a central role in development programming. Financial institutions are also being increasingly utilized to channel such resources to economic sectors considered essential for growth and social equity. The attention focused on the financial intermediaries has induced the governments of a wide range of developing countries to assume direct control of financial institutions. Other governments have elected to participate in the management and ownership of the financial institutions with private interests, while still others are satisfied to direct and regulate institutions that are exclusively in private hands. In all cases, however, financial intermediation has taken on added importance in the search for ways to improve the growth prospects of these economies. Furthermore, the selective credit controls imposed in most developing economies, and the proposed regulation of bank credit distribution in some industrial countries (the United Kingdom and the United States), are examples of the importance attached to the intermediary function of the commercial banks.

However, problems associated with the development of financial institutions in the developing countries, and particularly in Africa, have not figured prominently in theoretical economic analysis. Analyses of economic development issues have concentrated on real factors and have only recently concerned themselves with some obvious financial constraints (primarily related to the external sector of these economies). This book is, therefore, one of the few case studies exploring the role of the development of financial institutions in the growth process of the developing economies. It is further distinguished from the few recent case studies exploring the interaction of financial and real development in that within the selected countries a sizeable portion of transactions are made outside the monetized sphere. Mindful of these basic differences in the experiences of the selected countries and those of other developing countries at higher levels of financial and real development, this book explores both the impact of financial development on the growth process and the implications of relative levels of real development for the performance of financial institutions.

The main objectives of this book are to explore in detail the structure and operations of the commercial banking systems of Kenya, Somalia, and Tanzania (that is, Eastern Africa), to investigate how well the banks' operations have coincided with the development objectives of these countries, to analyze the determinants of the performance of the banking systems, and to prescribe policies to improve the banks' operations and their contribution to the realization of development objectives. The study concentrates on the operations of the commercial banking systems of Eastern Africa with a view to resolving a few key questions about their development and performance. Among these questions is to what extent the banks have contributed to the savings-investment process of these economies. Other questions include how well the banks have met some requirements, indispensable for economic development, such as monetization of the subsistence sectors and innovations in the services provided to both the monetary and nonmonetary sectors.

This detailed investigation of the role of the Eastern African commercial banking systems should contribute to resolving whether the structure and ownership of commercial banks matter for economic development. In this respect the Eastern African experiences are well chosen, as they cover different institutional structures as well as different types of ownership. Although the banking systems of the three countries are rooted in colonial branch banking traditions, throughout most of the period Kenya has maintained a predominantly foreign branch banking system with minimum interference from the government. Somalia as well continued the foreign branch banking system during the initial ten years of independence. However, Somalia also maintained strong publicly owned commercial banking facilities and finally opted for complete nationalization of the banking system. Tanzania also opted for a unitary state banking system, but at a much earlier date.

In addition, the analysis of the role of the commercial banks in the real development of the Eastern African economies should also contribute to an understanding of the interaction of financial and real development in other countries at the same levels of development. Since a banking system may reflect the characteristics of the real sector of an economy, generalizations across all developing economies are unwarranted. Where the financial and real characteristics are similar, the experiences of Eastern Africa are significant. In sum, therefore, the study is about the economics of financial intermediation in the developing countries, with special emphasis on the role of commercial banks in the mobilization and allocation of savings.

THE SAVINGS-INVESTMENT PROCESS: SOME THEORETICAL CONSIDERATIONS

The adequacy of the transfer of resources, through financial institutions, from savers to investors, reflects for the most part the effect of financial structure and development on economic growth. This process of financial intermediation is thus emphasized while other effects, such as the direct contribution of financial institutions to gross domestic product and the monetary effects of bank operation, are not stressed. Depending on the success of the intermediation function, increased financial savings and aggregate savings in general may result. Improved financial intermediation may also bring forth higher levels of capital formation in the productive sectors and in sectors considered essential for development and social equity.

Even in the least developed economies some form of transfer of financial resources occurs, mostly through the activities of merchants and eventually money lenders. Once the earnings and expenditures of individuals cease to be synchronized, some form of transfer of financial resources evolves. Direct placement of financial liabilities with surplus units (that is, units with excess income over expenditures), often dependent on family and other ties, may precede the development of money lenders and curb markets. At this stage of financial resources transfer, mobilized savings are limited, and the external finance of investment is almost nonexistent. Investors depend on their own finances or retained earnings, which in turn limit the size of feasible investments. However, as the pattern of development becomes more complex, alternative methods of transferring financial resources become essential. The primary alternatives include direct external finance via the issuance of the liabilities of the deficit units to surplus units, irrespective of prior relationship; government transfer of resources through the fiscal mechanism; and transfers by financial institutions.

Financial institutions transfer resources by issuing their debts to surplus units and relending the funds to deficit units. By eliminating this coincidence of wants between lenders and borrowers (or even direct contact between them, as would be necessary in direct external finance), the financial intermediaries reduce the basic conflicts that limit the transfer of resources. The financial institution provides savers highly liquid, divisible assets at a lower risk, while investors receive a larger pool of resources, often at a lower cost. How well the financial institution satisfies the preferences of both lenders and borrowers determines the success of this intermediation function in any economy. Accordingly, the effect of the financial institution on economic growth is investigated here from the point of view of the mobilization and allocation of savings.

A fundamental question concerning the impact of the development of financial institutions on the savings-investment process is whether it brings forth higher savings than would be available otherwise. Those calling for the expansion of financial intermediaries implicitly assume that they augment the available savings. There are also strong theoretical considerations of why, indeed, financial intermediation may stimulate savings. The empirical verification of increased savings through financial intermediaries as institutions develop is well established. This could be due to a shift of savings from other sources; it has, in fact, been shown that such shifts take place even among the different types of financial intermediaries. The reasons financial development may instigate an increase in the aggregate volume of real savings are basically three: the opportunity to save via the introduction of new assets that dominate all previously available assets, the improved yield of the available variety of assets, and finally the direct institutional effect.

The improved-opportunity-to-save effect is based on the assumption that the rudimentary nature of financial development in the Eastern African and other developing economies retards the desire to save. The portfolio choice of domestic surplus units is limited to holding either currency or physical assets (including inventory changes). The introduction of other financial assets (such as savings certificates, savings and loan shares, and in this case bank deposits) increases the variety of assets available. The new assets introduced by the development of financial institutions dominate the initially available assets in terms of earnings, safety, and liquidity, since the risks attached to them are small compared to the physical capital assets, and since currency is a barren asset at best. The response of the rate of savings to new opportunities to save would depend on the prior stage of development of the money and capital markets.[1]

A related effect is the interest-elasticity of savings. Irrespective of the low economic surplus in developing economies, the scarcity of savings may be partially attributed to the low rewards and occasional sacrifices associated with savings. In the majority of developing countries the demand deposits of private savers do not earn any interest, and the median rates offered for one-year time deposits are in the range of 3 to 4 percent. In numerous cases, time and savings deposits actually earn negative returns, despite moderate rates of inflation.

In the few cases where interest on bank deposits has been increased substantially, from negative to high positive rates, financial institutions' holdings have also increased sharply. This, however, may be explained by a shift of the same volume of savings from one channel to another. The less obvious and theoretically more onerous question is the direction and magnitude of the interest-elasticity of aggregate domestic savings. Empirical estimates of the relationship of real interest rates and private savings (or any component thereof) are not available for the Eastern African economies, to my knowledge. However, even where such figures are available for other developing countries, the empirical evidence is inconclusive.[2]

In all cases a positive substitution effect is hypothesized, that is, as interest rates increase so does the rate of savings. How significant the income effects of the increment in interest payments are depends on a number of factors. The savers' expectations and planning horizons, not to mention whether they are target-savers or not, may determine the magnitude of the income effect. A conclusive statement of the general magnitude of the interest-elasticity of private domestic savings could only be achieved by actual case studies of the Eastern African economies.

Finally, the existence of financial institutions may promote higher marginal propensities to save. This may best be described as a direct effect of institutional development on the aggregate volume of savings. The institution-elasticity of private aggregate domestic savings would obviously depend on the existence of alternative channels. In postulating this effect, W. Arthur Lewis claims, "There is a whole range of savings institutions that can be developed. . . . Experience shows that the amount of saving depends partly on how widespread these facilities are; if they are pushed right under the individual's nose, to the extent of having street savings groups, or factory groups, or even deductions from earnings at source, people save more than if the nearest savings institution is some distance away."[3] In a more recent study, U Tun Wai, after estimating the relationship between financial savings and retained earnings, concludes that "the statistical evidence seems to support the hypothesis that the greater the financial intermediaries, the larger will be the amount of national savings."[4]

The efficient allocation of savings is based on a premise that the more developed the financial institutional system, the higher the proportion of domestic, private savings channeled through it. It is primarily this ability of financial institutions to offer assets preferable to internal savings and primary securities ownership that justifies their existence. Furthermore, a shift of savings from other channels, in particular from currency hoards, precious metal hoards, or inventory accumulation, and in favor of financial intermediation, improves the efficient allocation of savings. In each of the alternative assets (currency or inventory accumulation), the individual decides on his portfolio with little or no evaluation of the opportunity cost of that investment.

The major allocative efficiencies introduced via financial savings (savings through the financial intermediaries) are attributable to their ability to reduce or eliminate the constraints of investment indivisibilities. Without financial intermediaries, the only available sources of capital finance are retained earnings and direct finance. In the extreme, each individual can invest only up to his savings. Allowing for limited direct finance or issue of primary securities, there is still no guarantee that the investments with the highest net social return, or even private return, will be funded. This type of market fragmentation, which results in the finance of projects with low social returns while those with higher returns are rejected, is prevalent in developing economies and may exist in advanced economies. A developed financial institutional system, operating efficiently, should eliminate such market disparities. By synchronizing the needs of the deficit and surplus units across an economy, financial institutions may allocate savings more efficiently than internal finance and external direct finance.

Besides the allocation of savings through banks, which may result in higher returns on investments, development of financial institutions may increase the amount of capital available from any given amount of gross savings. Again, where capital and money markets are deficient, financial institutions offer the only means of financing large investments. There are obviously some investments which, because of indivisibilities in optimum plant size, require financing far in excess of the savings of most economic units. The advantage of financial institutions in pooling the savings of many economic units, and lending them in larger sums (and often to riskier investments) has long been recognized.

Another channel through which the impact of financial institutions is felt in the savings-investment process and economic growth is the elimination of financial dualism. Financial dualism is distinct from, though parallel to, social and technological dualism, and exists in most developing economies. Among the characteristics of financial dualism is the coexistence of organized and nonorganized money markets within the same economy. These markets are often distinct in terms of credit, general availability of funds, and even geographical location. There is hardly any systematic arbitrage between these markets, one controlled by modern financial institutions and the other by traditional merchants and money lenders. In the extreme case, financial dualism indicates the existence of a highly monetized market serviced by modern financial institutions and nonmonetized barter markets, side by side.

The benefits resulting from the elimination of financial dualism are reflected in further improvements in the mobilization and allocation of savings. First, the introduction of financial institutions into the normally stagnant barter economy is expected to increase the desire for and aggregate level of saving in that sector. Unlike perishable commodities, the liquidity and relative predictability of currency (if not the return on deposits) should stimulate savings. Owing to the shifts in assets held and to an assumed increase in the level of savings in the initially nonmonetized sectors, the level of financial savings is augmented. In like manner, the allocational efficiency of existing savings is improved through financial integration of both sectors of the economy. Where initially the efficiency gains result from proper allocation of finance between two like projects, we now reduce the distortion in the allocation of funds between two economic sectors. It is conventionally assumed that the modern sector, with modern financial and technological applications, has higher productivity on the average; if such is the case, then the savings mobilized in the "traditional" sector will be available to the more productive "modern" sector. Where the opposite is true, as indeed may be the case in the Eastern African economies, savings mobilized in the modern sector will be utilized for investment in traditional enterprise. Regardless of the direction of flow of the increased savings, the most severe case of fragmentation in an economy will be eliminated.

A PREVIEW

The book is divided into seven chapters. Following this introduction, Chapter 2 reviews the literature on the interaction of financial and real development. Theoretical arguments that pertain to the contribution of financial institutions to growth and empirical investigations of this interaction are summarized. The summary includes the views of both those who consider financial development a necessary factor in economic development and those who consider it neither a necessary nor a sufficient factor. Another major issue raised is the direction of the causality between financial and real development. Whether financial development lags behind real growth, and thus merely adjusts to the demand on its services, or whether it leads real growth, is one of the continuing controversies in the field. In this chapter, it is first noted that only if financial development precedes real development would it be growth-inducing. It is also indicated, however, that financial underdevelopment acts as a constraint whether it leads or merely adjusts to real growth.

Also in Chapter 2, the two major hypotheses that explain the role of financial institutions in developing economies are presented. In one case the contribution of the financial institutions is hypothesized to be determined by the amount of government intervention, while the other hypothesis holds that the structure of the economy and its level of development determine the contribution of the financial institutions to capital formation and real growth.

Chapter 3 turns to the recent history of the Eastern African economies. Beginning with 1950 and the last decade of colonial occupation, the economic setting of each country and particularly the issues pertaining to the levels and composition of capital formation are highlighted. The nature of economic dependency and of the associated dualistic development is explored. The first part of the chapter is intended to give the reader an overview of the position of subsistence production in those economies and the minimal transformations that have occurred in this sector. Next the origins of the modern financial institutions and their operations in the last decade before independence are discussed. Finally, the main features of these economies in the first decade of independence are examined with a view to comparing them with their preindependence economic setting. Changes in real growth rates, and in the level and composition of capital formation and structural transformation, where such have occurred, are noted.

In Chapter 4, the development strategy of each country is reviewed. Within these strategies the development objectives and the role allotted to financial institutions in their attainment are presented. How the respective authorities view their development priorities and the implications of these priorities for financial development are examined. Alternative sources of financial development are briefly reviewed.

Chapters 5 and 6 analyze the performances of the Eastern African banking systems and the determinants of these performances. Developments in the banking systems for the decade ending in 1973 are detailed. How well they have mobilized savings, whether they have allocated these savings according to development priorities, and whether they have reduced financial dualism in these economies are dealt with in Chapter 5. Within this chapter, the performances of the various countries' banking system are compared, and each is in turn compared with its preindependence performance. Chapter 6 compares the performance of the Eastern African banking systems with those of some selected high-financial-growth economies. In reviewing the determinants of the banking systems' performance, the effects of deposit and interest-rate ceilings imposed by the authorities are investigated. I have also indicated the effects of deficient demand for bank services on the performance of the banking system. Thus, in this chapter the relevance of the two hypotheses to the post-independence banking experiences of Eastern Africa is reviewed.

In Chapter 7, the material in the book is summarized, the main conclusions are stated, and a program for financial development in Eastern Africa is prescribed. It shows that the characterization of colonial banking systems as not contributing to the indigenous economic development of the dependent countries is justified in the case of Eastern Africa. Also it leaves no doubt that operation of the postindependence banking system has not, for the most part, departed significantly from preindependence performance. It concludes that for the banking systems to be development-oriented, direct government intervention would be essential, at least in the initial stages of the development process.

NOTES

1. U Tun Wai, *Financial Intermediaries and National Savings in Developing Countries* (New York: Praeger, 1972), pp. 31, 85–98. His simple model hypothesizes that
$$S = f (A, W, O)$$
where S=savings, A=ability, W=willingness, and O=opportunity, such that
$$A = A (Y, N, K \ldots)$$

where Y=income, N=dependency rates, K=wealth

$$W = W (i, L, C \ldots)$$

where i=interest, L=stage of life cycle, C=social classification

$$O = O (F, 1_r \ldots)$$

where F=financial intermediation, 1_r=available internal funds

2. Raymond Mikesell and James Zinser, "The Nature of the Savings Function in Developing Countries: A Survey of the Theoretical and Empirical Literature," *Journal of Economic Literature* 11, no. 1 (March 1973): 17, 18.

3. W. Arthur Lewis, *The Theory of Economic Growth* (New York: Harper & Row, 1970), p. 229.

4. U Tun Wai, op. cit., p. 111.

2

FINANCIAL INSTITUTIONS
AND GROWTH IN
DEVELOPING COUNTRIES

This chapter reviews the literature on the role of financial institutions in the real growth of developing economies. The theories and historical interpretations that have been offered are surveyed in detail. The role of financial institutions in mature capitalist economies and advanced socialist economies is explored only insofar as it illuminates the focus of the book. The major concern of this introductory survey is to lay the foundations for exploring the relations between financial and economic development in a group of developing countries.

Numerous characteristics distinguish the typical economy under study. A prominent feature is that such economies are the least developed, in both financial and real terms, and regardless of the process by which development is measured. Low per capita incomes and traditional production technologies prevail. Low levels of industrial production and extensive dependence of the labor force on subsistence agriculture are also associated with such economies. A more pertinent criterion, however, is the existence of rudimentary capital markets, or none at all. Furthermore, in such economies the commercial banks are the dominant, if not the only, type of modern financial institution.

FINANCIAL STRUCTURE AND ECONOMIC DEVELOPMENT

"One of the most important problems in the field of finance, if not the single most important one, almost everyone would agree, is the effect that financial structure and development have on economic growth."[1] The question of whether financial structure and development have any impact on the real sectors of the economy, and if so how much, has elicited a wide range of answers from economists. A major point of the resulting controversy is whether the development of financial institutions matters at all for real growth. The diversity of opinions varies from considering the development of financial institutions (banks in particular and occasionally including nonmonetary financial institutions) as a necessary factor for the real growth of developing economies, to holding that it is neither necessary nor sufficient for growth.

The more positive view of the role of financial development is held by a substantial proportion of the students of financial and real development. Abstracting initially from the differences of opinion within this school, some of which are explored later, they all attribute a positive effect to financial institutions in the development process. This view is traditionally associated with Schumpeter's analysis of the theory of economic development, more aptly termed the theory of capitalist economic development.[2]

Other proponents of the positive view of the role of financial institutions include Adelman and Morris, Cameron et al., Gerschenkron, Goldsmith, McKinnon, Minsky, Patrick, and Shaw to name but a few.[3] The relative magnitudes of the impact attributed to banks and other financial institutions in developing economies differ among these authors. In the following paragraphs I present only the earliest and some of the more recent advocates of the positive view.

In the Schumpeterian analysis of capitalist economic development, banks, financial institutions, or new credit creation per se is considered one of the two primary and essential factors for development. The other factor is the availability of entrepreneurs. The important position of entrepreneurship and innovation finance is evident from Schumpeter's definition of economic development as a spontaneous, discontinuous, and internally generated change, distinct from ordinary economic growth, through which an economy's resources are channeled into more productive uses. He points out that "the fundamental notion that the essence of economic development consists in a *different* employment of *existing* resources of labor and land leads us to the statement that the carrying out of new combinations takes place through the withdrawal of services of labor and land from their previous employment."[4]

According to Schumpeter these two factors are absolutely essential for the new combinations and the process of reemployment to be realized. He thus states: "Now two things are essential for the phenomena incident to the carrying out of such new combinations. In the first place, it is not essential to the matter—though it may happen—that the new combinations should be carried out by the same people who control the productive or commercial process which is to be replaced by the new process." On the contrary, he argues that these new combinations are invariably initiated by a new class of entrepreneurs. In the second place, and more significantly, he holds that "in carrying out new combinations, 'financing' as a special act is fundamentally necessary in practice as in theory."[5]

This view is corroborated in some current studies, not restricted to the early history of capitalist development. Among them is the Adelman and Morris view of the contribution of banks and other financial institutions in economic development, which is especially relevant to the contemporary developing countries. Their conclusions are based on a quantitative model that focuses on the measurable determinants of a country's potential for economic development. The data used in their studies come from 74 developing countries for the years 1950–63. They have evaluated the relative impact of 39 socioeconomic and political variables on the capacity of these nations to develop. Out of 14 purely economic variables explored, they found the level of financial institutions' development to be the best indicator of a country's development potential. They used discriminant analysis to classify the total sample according to a country's capacity for successful growth; among all the variables, the degree of improvement in financial institutions was said to be statistically most significant.[6]

In their estimates of the relative impact of all the variables tested, economic and noneconomic, on the capacity to grow, they have computed composite multipliers via a simultaneous solution of all the equations in the model. The composite multipliers include both the direct impact of a variable on the index of the capacity to grow and all indirect impacts through other variables affecting the index. In the case of the impact of improvements in financial institutions, both its direct effect on the indicator and its indirect effect through the levels of industrial and agricultural development are considered. According to the evaluation of the magnitudes of the total impact of each variable on the potential of a country to develop, they have concluded that the degree of improvement in financial institutions has the largest multiplier. They have estimated this multiplier at 2.309, followed by the impact of the decrease in the degree of social dualism, at 2.133. The rest of the 39 variables have been found to have multipliers of less than 2. Furthermore, Adelman and Morris have found that the only economic variables with a high impact on increasing development potential, among all those they have identified and tested, were improvements of financial institutions, increases in physical capital overhead, more rapid expansion of industry, and (to a lesser extent) technical modernization of agriculture.

Despite the limited scope of their analysis, which was not solely concerned with the role of financial institutions in economic development, their studies have attributed a positive and significant role to financial development. In their representation of the role of financial institutions' effectiveness, they were mainly concerned with the increase in savings through the banking system and the volume of lending by banks to agriculture and industry. Thus they state:

To measure changes in institutional effectiveness in attracting savings, we computed the percentage point change in the ratio of the volume of time and demand deposits to GNP for the period 1950–51—1962–63. As a rough measure of the extent of institutional lending to private persons and businesses, we calculated the approximate increase in the real value of private domestic liabilities to the banking system during the same period.[7]

As is indicated by alternative attempts to quantify the role and effectiveness of financial institutions later in this study, they have defined improvements in financial institutions quite narrowly. However, even with this limited scope they have offered the development of financial institutions as one of the most relevant variables for the growth of developing countries.

The negative view of the contribution of banks and financial institutions to developing economies is based on the recent experiences of the socialist economies and developing countries. This negative view is particularly associated with the studies of J. Gurley.[8] He explicitly states his skepticism about the prominence attached to financial development as separate from the other institutional choices a country makes to advance growth. The main reason he considers a developed system of financial institutions expendable is that the other possible methods through which countries have in the past realized, and can still accomplish, the same results. However, he does not question the efficacy of the development of financial institutions per se, but insists on the existence of alternative techniques that may prove more feasible in a country's comprehensive aggregate planning approach. Gurley allows that "This technique of finance [development of financial institutions] flourishes when there is a decentralization of decision-making, specialization of savings and investment, and heavy emphasis on external rather than internal financing of investment."[9]

Among the close substitutes for the technique of finance (which according to him all lead to greater centralization of the savings-investment process and reduction of external finance of investment by the economic units) are central planning and the fiscal or tax-subsidy technique. Besides these domestically available alternatives, he also considers transfers of foreign savings. As to rating these alternatives, he points out that the actual choice among them depends on the social costs and benefits of each. He adds, though, that economic costing may prove secondary, and the overriding criterion may be whether the chosen technique is generally compatible with the ideology of the country.

Gurley readily admits that he has not performed any systematic analysis of the costs and benefits of these alternatives for a country over time or for a group of countries. More pertinent for the purposes of this book, he does not consider any technique as best for all countries, or for any one country over its entire development path. He contends that such choices are subject to change as the balance of benefits and costs is altered over time, and that some countries may find it profitable to use tight central planning through many stages of development, until it finally becomes more profitable to decentralize decision making to some extent. In this case, some real resources would be moved from planning bureaus to financial institutions and markets.

With limited exploratory steps toward what he calls the inherent weaknesses of finance as a vehicle of economic development, and with obtuse references to the experiences of developing countries, he contends that the development of financial institutions is not necessary for growth. In fact, after reviewing the historical evidence assembled by Cameron et al., he concludes that "recent experiences strongly suggest that banking systems as intermediaries are not highly essential to the growth process."[10]

Relationship Between Financial and Real Development

The central issue of the controversy over the role of financial institutions in economic development is whether the development of financial institutions precedes, and therefore plays an active role in, economic development, or whether it passively adjusts to the growth of the real sector. The direction of this causal relationship between financial and real development is not conclusively established. However, that these two phenomena are interrelated is beyond dispute. With a few possible qualifications, prominent among which is Gurley's alternative set of relationships instead of a fixed association, most would agree with Porter's statement that "the visible correlations in the world [between financial and real development] are indeed commanding. Whether one relates the development of the nation's financial system (however measured) to its per capita income across countries at a moment of time or across time for a particular country, the relationship between real and monetary variables is undeniable."[11] Furthermore, this interdependence has been recognized by economists since Adam Smith.[12]

More recently, the monumental study of Goldsmith has demonstrated this relationship—without, however, resolving the causality controversy. In a study of financial structure and development for 35 countries, developed as well as developing, he quantified the association between the financial superstructure and real infrastructure. In this study, Goldsmith concludes that, with the exception of centrally planned economies, there is one path of financial development associated with economic growth:

> The evidence now available is more in favor of the hypothesis that there exists only one major path of financial development, a path marked by certain regularities in the course of the financial interrelations ratio, in the

share of the financial institutions in the total financial assets, and in the position of the banking system ... a path from which [countries] have deviated only to a minor extent.[13]

According to Goldsmith, the participation of the government in the means of production and control of the management of financial institutions introduces some minor differences for the developing countries, yet reasonably accurate projections of their future financial position could be made. Among the inevitable developments are a more diversified financial structure, with expanded equity securities and relatively lower debt claims outstanding. Also, a relative decline in the prominence of deposit banks and expansion in the assets of nonmonetary financial institutions is considered inevitable as the real economy grows, and as developing countries reach the same level of financial sophistication as the industrial countries.

Goldsmith's conclusions are based on the statistical evidence compiled for each country as far back as data allow and for this limited sample. The statistical measures compared for all countries, and for each country over time, include the financial interrelations ratio and the ratio of financial institutions' assets to gross national product (GNP). The financial interrelations ratio, described as the ratio of the aggregate market value of all the financial instruments in a country to the value of its tangible net wealth, indicates a direct (though nonproportional) relationship between financial and real development. This ratio is found to be in the range of 1 to 1 1/2 in developed markets or mixed economies, and generally within the range of 2/3 to 1 for developing economies.[14] The values of the financial interrelations ratio of the developing economies correspond to those reached and surpassed in the United States and Western European industrial nations during the second half of the nineteenth century.

The relation of the assets of financial institutions to GNP also shows this direct association between financial and real development. The statistical evidence gathered in Goldsmith's study again shows a wide spread in the values of this ratio comparable to the disparity in real development among these nations. He found a high of 272 percent for Switzerland and a low of 20 percent for Nigeria in 1963, with the rest of the 35 countries in his sample having values withing this range. This is not to suggest that real growth alone explains the accumulation of financial assets; for instance, the United States was found to have the seventh largest ratio of financial institution assets to GNP in the same year. Nevertheless, the gap between the unweighted average ratios of financial institution assets to GNP of developed and developing countries is unmistakable. Indeed, as Table 2.1 shows, the financial development disparity resembles the ever widening, better known, real development gap between developed and developing countries.

TABLE 2.1

Financial Institutions' Assets as a Percentage of GNP
(unweighted country averages)

Year	1880	1900	1913	1929	1938	1948	1963
Developed countries	72.9	102.5	122.8	133.1	159.5	132.5	155.9
All developing countries	—	24.2	39.6	41.9	49.5	51.3	65.4
European	—	—	45.8	64.7	75.2	62.7	108.5
Latin American	—	35.1	54.5	44.8	48.3	59.2	56.3
Afro-Asian	—	7.0	20.5	21.1	35.4	36.6	54.5

Source: Summarized from Raymond Goldsmith, *Financial Structure and Development* (New Haven and London: Yale University Press, 1969).

The relationship of financial and real development is considered direct and visible, as the above empirical evidence shows. However, because this study is limited to commercial banks, we tested for whether there is as visible and commanding an association between the growth of commercial bank assets and real development, as measured by GNP per capita.

In testing for this association, a sample of 30 countries was arbitrarily selected. The selected countries include 14 developed countries and 16 less developed countries, equally divided between developing and least developed economies. (These classifications are based on GNP per capita, with countries at or below US$300 classified as least developed.) The 8 countries in this category are former British colonies in Africa. The rest were chosen from as wide a geographical base as possible. For the countries in the sample, the GNP per capita in 1973 ranged from US$6,200 for the United States to US$110 for Malawi.

A comparison of commercial bank assets as a percentage of GNP shows a wide gap not unlike the per capita income differentials. The banking ratios (bank assets as a percentage of GNP) ranged from Switzerland's 107.9 to Nigeria's 14.8. As the unweighted country averages of the categories are compared, there is an unmistakable difference between the developed countries and the less developed countries, and also between the developing and least developed. In 1973, the unweighted average commercial bank assets as a percentage of GNP amounted to 83.3 for developed countries, 41.2 for developing countries, and 26.1 for the least developed countries.

The association between commercial bank assets and real growth was measured using rank correlation analysis. By relating the independent ordinal rankings of the 30 countries according to GNP per capita and according to the banking ratio, a measure of the association was obtained. When all 30 countries in the sample were included, the correlation between the two rankings was found to equal 0.80, which indicates a large positive association. For the separate subclassifications of the 14 developed countries and the 16 developing countries, different results were obtained. The correlation between bank assets and real growth in the developed countries was –0.18, while for the developing countries it was 0.54. For the sample countries and the data, see Table 2.2.

These results indicate that, although there is a large association between bank assets and real growth across the spectrum of the levels of development, the significance of the association declines within close ranges of development. It further indicates that as economies advance there is no evidence of a direct association between banking and real growth. This is to be expected, however, since the competition for financial intermediation becomes more pronounced as economies develop. In developed economies, specialized financial institutions and capital markets become more sophisticated, and the prominence of the banks as financial intermediaries declines.

Demand-Following and Supply-Leading Finance

Statistical evidence aside, the controversy over the relationship between financial and real development is most thoroughly discussed in Patrick's analysis of finance in developing economies, in which he delineates the two opposing viewpoints sharply.[15] The type of financial development that is viewed as somehow accommodating or reacting passively to the growth of the real economy, he terms demand-following finance. As the economy moves from traditional subsistence production, grows more complex, and generally becomes monetized, certain demands are generated for the services of financial institutions. Such demands are created by the growing needs of firms for external finance, as their retained profits fall short of their investment expansion needs. In this demand-following type of financial development, emphasis is placed on the demand for financial assets, and the responsiveness of existing or new financial institutions is taken for granted—a case of demand creating its own supply. A further distinction of the demand-following type of financial development is that its contribution to economic development is minimal, though it could be of critical importance as an obstacle to economic development.

Such demand-following financial development phenomena are often associated with the English banking system of the late eighteenth and early nine-

TABLE 2.2

Association between GNP Per Capita and Commercial Bank Assets as Percentage of GNP, 1973

	GNP Per Capita (U.S. dollars)	Commercial (Deposit) Bank Assets (billions of currency units)	GNP (billions of currency units)	Bank Assets as Percentage of GNP	Bank Development Ranking
Developed economies					
United States	6,200	1,101.8	1,306.3	84.4	8
Switzerland	6,100	145.2	134.5	107.9	1
Canada	5,450	87.4	120.4	72.6	11
West Germany	5,320	863.5	926.9	93.2	4
Denmark	5,210	83.3	164.6	52.4	16
Norway	4,660	65.2	110.1	59.2	14
Belgium	4,560	1,273.0	1,796.0	70.9	12
France	4,540	992.1	1,144.0	86.7	6
Netherlands	4,330	129.0	166.5	77.5	9
Japan	3,630	116,652.0	111,061.0	105.0	2
Austria	3,510	424.7	533.3	74.6	10
United Kingdom	3,060	72.0	72.9	98.8	3
Italy	2,450	74,997.0	80,963.0	92.6	5
Ireland*	2,150	2,300.0	2,683.0	85.7	7
Simple average				83.3	
Developing economies					
Brazil	760	115.6	473.2	32.9	22
Chile*	720	416.1	1,235.7	33.7	21
Taiwan	660	254.3	388.6	65.4	13
Malaysia*	570	9,589.0	16,434.0	58.3	15
Colombia*	440	49.7	238.0	20.9	26
Syria*	400	3,086.0	9,413.0	32.8	23
Korea	340	2,449.9	4,928.7	49.7	17
Jordan*	340	101.6	286.6	35.5	20
Simple average				41.2	
Least developed economies					
Ghana*	300	635.1	317.4	20.0	27
Egypt*	250	1,688.1	3,634.0	46.5	18
Nigeria*	210	1,315.1	8,900.0	14.8	30
Kenya*	170	334.2	770.9	43.4	19
Uganda*	150	2,479.0	11,109.0	22.3	25
Sudan*	130	144.7	787.0	18.4	28
Tanzania*	130	3,556.0	13,107.0	27.1	24
Malawi*	110	71.5	430.8	16.6	29
Simple average				26.1	
Simple average, developing and least developed				33.6	

*Millions of currency units.

Sources: International Monetary Fund (IMF), *International Financial Statistics*, various issues; and International Bank for Reconstruction and Development (IBRD), *World Bank Atlas*, 1975.

teenth centuries, and those modeled after it. Though economic historians differ in their assessments of the contributions of these banking systems to their respective economies, the bank operations are all characterized by caution and lack of innovation. The traditional short-term, commercial loan specialization of these English banks is considered to be one of the main properties of demand-following banking systems. Whether the English banking system contributed only minimally to the early industrialization and economic growth of the country is disputed. For example, Mathias, in a study of credit in the Industrial Revolution, has concluded that "the older generalization that English banks lent 'short' rather than 'long,' that they financed trade rather than supplied the long-term capital for financing the fixed assets of industry misleads as much as it illuminates."[16]

There is more of a consensus in distinguishing the English banking system from those which are known to have played a more active role in the industrialization and overall economic development of their economies. The latter systems are classified as taking the supply-leading financial development approach. Prominent historical examples often cited for the supply-leading phenomenon include the financial development experiences of Germany since 1830 and Japan since 1870. In this type of development the financial institutions act as a leading sector; that is, the banking institutions are created before the demand for their assets and liabilities is evident.

The properties of supply-leading finance are in many ways the exact opposite of those of passive, demand-following financial development. In addition to the few historical instances in which financial institutions have contributed to industrial expansion and economic development, there are theoretical justifications for supply-leading finance. The positive growth-inducing aspects of supply-leading financial development are attributed to its allocative efficiency and to its encouragement of enterprise. Supply-leading finance transfers resources from the traditional non-growth-producing sectors to the modern sectors of an economy with higher growth potential. Such a transfer of resources may be achieved by collecting the savings of the traditional sectors, or through forced savings via new bank credits. In either case, if the traditional-sector savings are transferred to more efficient and more productive sectors, the growth of the economy is enhanced. This growth-inducing tendency is often compared to the Schumpeterian concept of "innovation finance," where innovative producers gain control of the factor resources through bank intermediation only. The success of the resource transfer depends on the assumption that there is a class of entrepreneurs ready to invest in new production techniques, more efficient than the traditional methods of production replaced.

Another reason offered to explain the growth-inducing nature of supply-leading finance is the promotion of entrepreneurship. Where the entrepreneurship response is not developed, the banks can stimulate it. The availability of finance alone could affect the operations of the small farmers, merchants, and traders with which most developing economies are abundantly endowed. Patrick thus points out:

> The new access to such supply-leading funds may in itself have substantial, favorable expectation and psychological effects on entrepreneurs. It opens new horizons as to the possible alternative enabling the entrepreneur to "think big." This may be the most significant effect of all, particularly in countries where entrepreneurship is a major constraint on development.[17]

Supply-leading finance, however, may play a more direct role in the development of the entrepreneurial impulse by extending nonfinancial services to economic units. In some instances banks have directly participated in the promotion and control of industrial and other nonfinancial enterprises. The German banks, the epitome of mixed banking, offered industrial concerns both short-term operating funds and medium- to long-term capital, as well as nonfinancial assistance. The bank managers were said to have participated in the major financial decisions as well as the daily operations of industry. In the German system of mixed banking, "there was scarcely a joint-stock company, founded in 'the Rhineland' between 1830–1870, that did not have one or more bankers in a key managerial position—either on the direction which handled day-to-day decisions or on the administrative council, which handled less frequent and more important decisions such as the awarding of large contracts." In some instances the bankers initially perceived new opportunities for investment and suggested methods of exploiting them.[18] This participation of banks in industrial enterprises in German development is considered unique in some ways, but in other ways it has been duplicated elsewhere.

The debate on the interpretation of the role of banks in early industrialization aside, it would seem that there have been cases where banks preceded real growth and others where they followed. Such supply-leading, demand-following classifications, however, do not conclusively explain the direction of the causality. In fact, the differing interpretations of economic historians may be a product of the fact that the two phenomena interact for each economy at any moment and over time. The true classification of the relationship may indeed change as the country's economy develops.

Even if there is no fixed causal relationship between financial and real development, there are some indications that the supply-leading phenomenon is more applicable in the early stages of development. First, for developed economies the dependence on financial institutions for finance and entrepreneurship is less severe. Second, innovation finance removes other major obstacles to economic development that are absent from mature economies. In any case, this classification of the relationship between financial and real development, though not central, does provide a useful frame of reference for this book. If the financial institutions were to be a major contributory factor in economic development, the characteristics associated with the supply-leading system would have to be manifested.

FINANCIAL INSTITUTIONS IN THE SAVINGS-INVESTMENT PROCESS

This book departs from the majority of studies reviewed up to now in a fundamental way; because the question of the causal relationship between financial and real development is not central to it. This is not to suggest that this question is unimportant or, as some economists do, to liken it to a chicken-or-egg controversy and dismiss it as of secondary importance at the present state of knowledge. Whatever difficulties may be encountered in resolving the causality controversy are, however, matched by the vagueness and generality of the question posed, that is, how to encourage the development of the "banking habit." Thus, a major purpose of this book is to identify more precisely the relationship between financial and real development and to examine closely the connection between them. After the channels of interaction are identified, a more meaningful exposition of the casual relationship can be suggested.

At the outset we can eliminate any significant direct contribution of financial development to economic growth. Indeed it is obvious that the direct contribution of financial institutions to growth is minute. It has been estimated elsewhere as between 0.5 and 1.0 percent of gross national product for financially mature market economies. In the case of developing economies, where the services offered by financial institutions are often fewer and far less sophisticated, the contribution of financial institutions is estimated to be less than 0.1 percent.

Therefore, if the financial institutions were to play a meaningful role in economic development, it would necessarily be through their indirect contribution. Thus, the only channels of interaction explored here are in this general category. Moreover, not all the indirect channels are treated in equal detail. Prominent among the indirect impacts of financial institutions not explored in any detail is the encouragement or development of entrepreneurship. Nor is the role of financial institutions in the stabilization process of developing economies seriously considered.

In general, this book focuses on the indirect contribution of financial institutions to growth, and within this scope will stress the more tractable (and, I expect, more productive) approach of exploring the role of banks in the savings-investment process of developing economies. This approach is based on the generally accepted assumption that a permanent increase in physical capital formation is essential for real growth. The proponents of the supremacy of capital formation (the savings-investment dilemma) among the prerequisites for economic development are found in every major school of economic thought. However, as seen below, a number of reservations held by eminent economists merit consideration.

Capital Formation and Growth

The most fundamental question here is the conceptualization and definition of capital formation. The exceptions taken to capital formation as a prime instigator of economic development grow geometrically with the restrictiveness of the definition applied. Throughout this study, and unless otherwise qualified, capital formation refers to current additions to the stock of physical assets. In utilizing this narrow definition of current gross investments, we are obviously excluding all forms of human capital investment, such as expenditures on education, training, health, and mininum nutritional intake. This exclusion may be hard to justify to those who believe that human capital scarcity is the strategic variable in the development potential of the Eastern African economies. Yet it can be justified in that one can estimate the impact of financial institutions on human capital formation as negligible at best. Bank household finance, where it exists in developing countries, is primarily for current consumption and occasionally for consumer durables.

That physical capital formation exerts a strategic influence on the path and pace of economic expansion is well founded in economic thought. The vital role of physical capital accumulation in growing economies has indeed been a point of agreement of all major schools of economics. This emphasis on capital formation is obvious, to varying degrees, in classical, Marxist, Keynesian, and neoclassical analysis of the growth process. The current literature concerned with the economic development problems of developing countries also stresses, in varying degrees, the role of capital formation.

In classical doctrine, the growth of an economy was thought to be determined by the availability of the factors of production alone. As the supply side of the economy was dominant, the more abundant these factors of production, the fewer the limitations on the capacity to grow. Moreover, since land was assumed to be fixed, and labor was considered a surplus input, capital accumulation was allotted center stage. In commenting on the consideration of capital accumulation as the mainspring of economic progress, Mathias summarizes:

A long intellectual tradition emphasized that capital was the critical factor of production and that shortage of savings, and hence capital, was a critical constraint upon the growth of an economy. This certainly was the main emphasis of classical economists, led by Adam Smith, who emphasized that expansion was limited by the powers of "accumulation"; and that capital was created by parsimony sparing resources from consumption.[19]

Marx, in the manner of the classical tradition before him that gave prominence to the supply side, placed capital accumulation at the center of his analysis. Marx's views on capital form an integral—indeed the critical—part of his general theory. Marx's capital accumulation model is in fact equally essential for his propositions pertaining to the secular growth and decline of a capitalist economy. Both the development and the final destruction of the system are explained by the historical mission of capitalists to accumulate, accumulate, save, save. The positive growth is attributed to the reinvestment of the surplus, and the crisis to the eventual centralization and accumulation of capital in progressively fewer hands. This emphasis on capital accumulation is still evident in the current Marxian tradition of scholarship and actual economic applications.

Keynes, in his *General Theory of Employment, Interest, and Money* and more specifically in responding to the reviews of this work in the *Quarterly Journal of Economics,*[20] offers capital investments as an essential explanatory variable of economic expansion, decline, and stagnation. In Keynesian analysis of the path of economic growth, the rate of investment is a definite indicator of the turning points, be they booms or crises. In Keynesian theory, not only did capital investment play a central role in the capacity of production expansion and labor productivity, as in the classical doctrine before it, but it was also found to be the most volatile component of aggregate effective demand of the economy.

In a fundamental difference with his predecessors, Keynes concluded that production and employment were primarily determined by the effective aggregate demand of an economy. Furthermore, Keynesian aggregate (private) demand is made up of the investment and consumption components, the latter of which was considered as a stable function of income. Thus, in Keynesian theory the rate of investment or capital formation determines not only the levels of employment and production but also the feasible level of consumption goods demand.

In one interpretation of Keynesian theory—"Keynesian theory as an investment theory of the cycle"[21]—the essential factors that determine investment fluctuations are held responsible for economic booms, deflations, and crises. The Keynesian view of investment as a strategic variable in economic expansion or decline is indicated by this conclusion:

The theory can be summed up by saying that, given the psychology of the public, the level of output and employment as a whole depends on the amount of investment. I put it in this way, not because this is the only factor on which aggregate output depends, but because it is usual in a complex system to regard as the *causa causans* that factor which is most prone to sudden and wide fluctuations.[22]

Post-Keynesian capitalist growth theory for the mature economy generally has insisted on placing capital accumulation at center stage and focusing on the resultant secular increases in labor productivity. It has consistently emphasized the twin conditions governing such increases: the willingness of a society to refrain from consumption and the fact that the investment into which savings may be channeled will result in increased productive capacity along with increased flow of income. The current growth literature, in both its neoclassical and neo-Keynesian forms, is based on extensions and improvements on the basic Harrod-Domar model.[23] In its simplest form, which is substantially removed from the complexity of succeeding models, the Harrod-Domar formulation holds that the rate of (warranted) growth is determined by the marginal propensity to save and the marginal capital-output ratio. Like the Harrod-Domar analysis, which they extend and modify, the more recent models are also wedded to the primacy of capital in the growth process.

The emphasis on capital formation in the contemporary growth models is based on the fact that investment increases income as well as productive capacity. "This *dual* character of the investment process makes the approach to the equilibrium rate of growth from the investment (capital) point of view more promising: if investment both increases productive capacity and generates incomes, it provides us with *both* sides of the equation, the solution of which may yield the required rate of growth." In summary, the Harrod-Domar equilibrium rate of growth (G), which equals the rate of growth of investments ($\Delta I/I$), is determined by the net investment and the average social productivity of investment on the supply side, and the multiplied net investment change on the demand side.[24]

The current economic literature pertaining to the economic problems of developing countries has also stressed the shortage of savings and low levels of investments. In its most popular presentations, the emphasis on the savings-investment process in the limited growth of developing countries is indicated by the vicious-circle-of-poverty arguments. The same emphasis is evident in Lewis's contention:

> The central problem in the theory of economic development is to understand the process by which a community, which was previously saving and investing 4 or 5 percent of its national income or less, converts itself into an economy where voluntary saving is running at about 12 to 15 percent of national income or more. This is the central problem because the central fact of economic development is rapid capital accumulation (including knowledge and skills with capital)."[25]

This view has been adopted by Rostow in his *Stages of Economic Growth* and has since received wider circulation. According to Rostow, the increase of capital investments from 5 percent to 10 percent or more of net national product is a necessary requirement for the take-off of any economy.[26]

The emphasis on capital formation has been dominant among modern development economists to the extent that a reaction has set in; reservations are held about the strategic role assigned to capital formation to the neglect of all other factors. The major qualification to the traditional primacy of capital investments in economic growth is based on whether capital formation is a necessary or sufficient factor for growth. The classic counterexample of an economy saving and investing more than 15 percent of its national income with no measurable development invalidates the sufficiency condition. Whether it is a necessary condition is of limited relevance to this book since, unlike the Rostovian prerequisite, the weaker assumption that physical capital formation is one of the strategic variables that determine real growth is sufficient for my purposes. In the case of Eastern Africa there are obviously other essential factors for the region's development; however, there are hardly any reservations necessary to the contention that physical capital formation is one of the major determinants (if not the most serious bottleneck) in the development of these economies.[27]

In policy pronouncements, Eastern African authorities have consistently indicated the need for domestic savings and investment. In each government report on the state of the economy or development plan, there is a stipulation to increase the level of domestic saving and investment. In particular, since all the countries of the region profess to practice some form of socialism—African socialism in the cases of Kenya and Tanzania, and scientific socialism in Somalia—they emphasize the central role of domestic capital formation. Thus, in one of his policy speeches, Dr. Julius K. Nyerere, the president of Tanzania, stated: "The nation has decided . . . that it will spend as much as possible of the current wealth on things which will in the long run produce wealth."[28]

ALTERNATIVE HYPOTHESES WITH RESPECT TO THE ROLE OF BANKS IN ECONOMIC DEVELOPMENT

The effectiveness of commercial banks and other financial institutions in the economic growth of developing countries can only be evaluated with a specific objective function in mind. Considering the general scarcity of capital postulated in most developing economies, a maximization of "productive investment" finance subject to bank liquidity and earning constraints will indicate effectiveness. In fact, the impact of banks has traditionally been evaluated in terms of their contribution to industrial capital formation alone.

The literature on the role of commercial banks in the savings-investment process, and in particular comprehensive studies of the contribution of banks to capital formation, may be classified under two distinct hypotheses: the financial repression hypothesis and the structuralist hypothesis. Before analyzing either hypothesis, we should clarify that their respective conclusions are based primarily on historical interpretation of early European industrialization, and only rarely on the experiences of contemporary developing superior explanation of this early evidence; rather, our interest is limited to evaluating which hypothesis better explains the Eastern African experience.

Financial Repression Hypothesis

The financial repression hypothesis is associated with the recent works of Cameron, McKinnon, and Shaw.[29] All three authors are strong advocates of the efficacy of financial development in contributing significantly to the real growth of developing economies. They contend that the banking system (financial institutions system in the case of McKinnon and Shaw) is invariably growth-inducing and that only when it is repressed, which in their view is often the case, would it fail to make a positive contribution or act as an obstacle to real growth. Thus, Shaw emphasizes that "the financial sector of an economy does matter in economic development . . . if it is repressed and distorted it can intercept and destroy impulses to development."[30] In like manner, Cameron concludes that "if the banking system is 'tilted' by the unwise legislation and policy, it can distort and even thwart the growth of the economy."[31] According to them, without these distortions and deviations from the free-market system, the banks will have the largest impact on developing economies.

The financial repression hypothesis explains the traditionally "poor" performances of organized banks in developing countries as being related to the regulated interest rates and other forms of intervention in bank lending policies or in the operation of a market economy. In these countries a first priority in financial intervention is a stipulation of loan and deposit rates at banks as well as other institutions of the organized capital market. These stipulations are always in nominal terms and may take the form of ceilings on the loan and deposit rates or else specified percentages. Moreover, given a variable, high inflation rate, the original nominal ceiling in effect may result in negative real deposit rates and limited or nonexistent charges on loans. Before examining the implications of these controls on the supply and demand for banks' loanable funds and financial assets in general, we will explore the causes suggested for this type of "repression."

Financial Repression and Savings Investment Propensities in Developing Economies

The reasons leading to financial repression are said to be so numerous that liberalization is an exception in developing economies. The proponents of the theory, however, contend that the central cause of financial repression is misguided theory. A prime target of the financial repression hypothesis is the basic assumption of simple portfolio theory that all assets are cross-substitutes. Assuming no change in wealth, it is generally accepted that if the rate of return of asset k among n assets increases, the demand for k increases while the amount held of all other assets either decreases or stays constant. Thus, considering the choice between real balances and physical capital assets in private portfolios, both neoclassical and Keynesian theories hold that an increase in the rate of return on real balances will result in substitution against physical capital assets.

In neoclassical doctrine it is assumed that the only need for money is to avoid the costs of synchronizing expenditures and earnings, since it is not necessary to hold money as a store of value in a truly perfect capital market with perfect foresight assumed. In both their stationary and growth models, the returns on all physical capital assets and financial assets (other than money) are equated to the market interest rate.

The substitution effect is deduced from all neoclassical growth models irrespective of how money is introduced. Whether it is introduced as a consumer or producer good, the substitution effect can be derived as shown below. Considering money as a producer good, the aggregate production function of the economy is

$$Y = f(k, L, M/P)$$

where Y = output; k = capital; L = labor units; and M/P = real balances. If Yd = income and S = savings,

$$Yd = Y + d\,(M/P)/dt \qquad (1)$$

and investment
$$\frac{dk}{dt} = Y - (1 - S)\,Yd \qquad (2)$$

Substituting equation (2) into equation (1),

$$\frac{dk}{dt} = Y - (1-S)\,(Y + d\,(M/P)/dt)$$
$$= SY + (S - 1)\,(d(M/P)/dt)$$

Assuming $0 < S < 1$ and $d(M/P)/dt > 0$, then dk/dt decreases as $d(M/P)/dt$ increases; that is, real balances held compete with capital investments.

In similar fashion, Keynesian theory holds to this basic substitution effect between money and physical capital assets, even though it allows for the possibility of risks and uncertainty. In fact it is on the grounds of this risk aversion, and the inherent variance of returns on physical assets and financial assets, that the substitution effect is explained. Also, the Keynesian liquidity preference theory is one manifestation of this substitution. The Keynesian doctrine is said to adhere to this substitution more strongly to the extent that Keynes considered the Gessellian stamp tax on money as a means of counteracting the desire of wealth holders to substitute money for physical assets in their portfolios.

Given the characteristics of sophisticated capital markets with which the neoclassical and Keynesian doctrines are concerned, McKinnon and Shaw emphasize that such a substitution effect is plausible. However, they add that once the realities of the developing economies are considered, such a position is indefensible. Furthermore, it leads to inappropriate policy decisions in such economies, foremost among which is the repression of the financial system.

The assumption of perfect capital markets in the neoclassical theory is replaced by a rudimentary or completely imperfect capital market in the case of developing economies. A major implication of this replacement is that real balances are the only financial instruments available that can be accumulated or exchanged freely. It also implies that there is no uniform rate of return even within physical capital assets, but an array of rates due to the fragmented nature of the imperfect markets.

The market fragmentation and indivisibilities of investments inherent in the imperfect capital markets create a complementarity effect between money and physical capital holdings. Assuming the prevalence of self-finance, which indeed is the case for most private investors in developing economies, a rise in the desired rate of capital formation at any given level of income is tantamount to an augmentation of the level of private savings and the amount of real cash balances held.[32]

In summary, the McKinnon-Shaw thesis proposes that a complementarity effect of money and physical assets is more appropriate in the analysis of private portfolios in developing economies. Real balances in private portfolios are viewed as a conduit through which accumulation of capital takes place rather than as a competing asset. A rise in the productivity of physical capital assets will therefore increase the demand for real balances because of this conduit effect, which is more powerful than the competing asset effect in such economies. They allow that with extremely high real rates of return on real balances the competing asset effect may predominate even in developing economies.

Implications of the Modified Neoclassical Model

Abstracting from the theoretical foundations of this reformulated neoclassical model, we will evaluate the validity of its conclusions that low deposit rates and the low ceiling on loan rates restrict financial development and subsequently real development. Parallel to the earlier taxonomy developed in this study, these conclusions and the following discussion of their applicability to the Eastern African economies are grouped under three major subtitles: the impact of financial repression on bank intermediation and savings mobilization in developing economies, its effect on the efficient allocation of bank loanable funds, and its impact on financial dualism. This simple compartmentalization of the implications of the financial repression hypothesis is purely a matter of convenience. It should be stressed that the essential features of this hypothesis are comprehensively treated within the adopted framework, even though it is a much wider-ranging thesis.

Financial Repression and the Market for Loanable Funds in Developing Economies

This hypothesis suggests that interest rate ceilings create a repressed level of private savings in general, and through financial institutions in particular. The proponents of the financial repression hypothesis assume private savings to be quite sensitive to the real returns on physical and financial assets and their stability. Thus, Shaw argues on a priori grounds that savers do respond through self-finance, direct finance, and indirect finance as yields to wealth fluctuate between negative and positive levels. "Savers may ignore a possibly transitory increase from, say 4 to 6 percent in rates of return, but they are less likely to maintain consumption-saving patterns when rates of return change, in a context of economic reform, from negative levels to positive 10 to 15 percent and more."[33] Inversely, private savings through financial institutions and the availability of loanable funds through all channels are thus repressed by the low or negative real deposit rates which actually prevail under financial repression. The demand for claims against banks in particular is doubly depressed by the low levels of private savings and the low or negative returns on bank deposits. On the other hand, the demand for loanable funds is considered both interest-sensitive and extremely high in developing economies. Again, Shaw states, with little evidence offered, that "the typical lagging economy, short of physical and human wealth, is long on investment opportunities at high real rates of return. . . . There is no shortage of investment opportunities, there is a shortage of savings for their finance, especially for the best ones among them."[34] The pressures on the loanable funds market are further aggravated by a sizable demand for consumption loans. The combination of this high investment opportunity and the controls over loan rates in the organized money markets results in a chronic excess demand for loanable funds. Furthermore, the low regulated bank rates do not show the true scarcity of capital and are insufficient to discriminate between bids for loans. In such markets, credit rationing is believed to be inevitable, and it is only a matter of taste whether it is administered according to the dictates of the monetary authorities or the bankers.

Financial Repression and the Allocation of Savings

According to the financial repression thesis, the total outlays of the organized credit markets are offered to a small group of favored economic sectors. In the extreme, "even ordinary government deficits on current accounts frequently preempt the limited lending resources of the deposit banks. Financing of the rest of the economy must be met from the meagre resources of money lenders, pawn brokers and cooperatives."[35] If not the government itself, such a favored group could be public corporations, private export-import firms, and occasionally a few established manufacturing companies.

Financial repression is held responsible for both the small amount of the original loanable funds and the subsequent inefficient allocation. Effective low ceilings on real loan rates intensify risk aversion and liquidity preferences on the part of bank portfolio managers. Because of such low ceilings, Shaw emphasizes, "banks and others keep a privileged place in their portfolios for established borrowers, especially trading firms with a long record of stability. They have little incentive to explore new and less certain lending opportunities."[36] Elsewhere, McKinnon echoes the same sentiments: "In addition to restricting the overall volume of bank lending, the interest rate ceiling ensures that the trickle of available finance flows to completely safe borrowers whose reputation is known or whose collateral is riskless. Or worse, the great excess demand for loans allows allocation to be contingent on political or establishment connections."[37]

According to the financial repression hypothesis, the apparent excessive risk aversion of bankers in developing economies is in actuality a product of financial market interventions by the authorities. The involvement of bankers with the established import-export sector in developing economies is in response to the interest-rate ceilings on other loans with high default risks and high costs of administration. In this view, the banks could be expected to lend to emerging industries and small-scale borrowers of all types only if the returns compensated for the risks involved. More significantly, the proponents of this view argue that the flow of organized bank credit to the established and stable lines of business need not mean most efficient allocation. On the contrary, these interventions guarantee a distorted flow of credits, which are determined by the minimization of risks. It need not be emphasized that in their view, once such repression is eliminated, the market forces would guarantee maximum financial deepening and most efficient credit allocation.

Banking Restraint and Financial Integration

According to the financial repression theorists, the lack of organized bank penetration of the "economic hinterland" is partially attributed to interventions in market operations. They point to the extreme interest-rate differential on loans issued by the organized banks and unorganized money lenders, respectively. The rates of the latter are often anywhere from two to ten times higher than the bank lending rates. Furthermore, they assume that the interest rates at unorganized money markets are better measures of the scarcity of capital and the objective risks associated with small loans in developing economies. In any case, the mere existence of the organized and unorganized markets simultaneously in the same economy implies financial repression. An extension of bank lending to new enterprises is essential to eliminate such dualism and, as explained above, that depends on market liberalization.

The financial repression hypothesis essentially preaches the virtues of reliance on market forces. Central to their criticism of financial repression is that it sidesteps market allocation. The financial system—primarily the banking system in these economies— is most conducive to economic growth once it is allowed to operate under free-market direction. In summary, this hypothesis explains most if not all the factors contributing to the "poor" performances of the lagging economies in terms of internal policy-induced distortions. The low ratios of bank deposits to total domestic savings, where such is indicated, is traced to the low ceilings on deposit rates. The record of organized bank loan issues being biased against small industrial and agricultural producers is explained as a direct manifestation of the low ceilings on loan rates. Therefore, the more pervasive the government's intervention in the terms of deposit and loan rates, in direct portfolio control, and so on, the less responsive will the banking system be to economic development.

The Structuralist Hypothesis

The structuralist hypothesis, better known as the Gerschenkron hypothesis,[38] is derived from historical interpretations of the role of banks in the capital formation processes of early European industrialization. The Gerschenkron hypothesis is a comprehensive analysis of early European industrialization and allows banks a considerable role in differentiating among the patterns of development. In considering different banking systems in earlier industrialization, Gerschenkron attributes to them a greater influence in the period and process of industrialization of some countries than any other economic institution. According to him, the pattern of industrialization in an economy, and the contribution of institutions such as the state and the banks, is determined by its "relative backwardness."

Gerschenkron utilizes this relative degree of backwardness not only as an indicator of the potential of a country's industrialization, but also as a determinant of the behavior of its economic institutions. In his analysis, a country's relative backwardness is judged in terms of its spatial and temporal distance from the industrial revolution in England. Within such a scale of relative backwardness, the more removed a country down the scale, or the less developed relative to others on the scale, the more its industrialization will differ from the others. The deviation of the latecomers from the early patterns of industrial development are thus summarized by Gerschenkron. Depending on a given country's degree of economic backwardness on the eve of its industrialization, the course and character of the latter tended to vary in a number of important respects. Among those variations are that:

> 1. The more backward a country's economy, the more pronounced was the stress in its industrialization of bigness of both plant and enterprise.
>
> 2. The more backward a country's economy, the greater was the part played by special institutional factors designed to increase supply of capital to the nascent industries and, in addition, to provide them with less decentralized and better informed entrepreneurial guidance; the more backward the country, the more pronounced was the coerciveness and comprehensiveness of those factors.[39]

In generalizing from the industrial capital needs and financial sources of early European industrializations, and in particular the English, German, and Russian experiences, he concludes that the role of banking in industrial capital formation is determined by the relative backwardness of an economy and its structural peculiarities.

Following the chronological order of European industrialization, he contends that the more advanced economy of England required only minimum capital investments to launch the Industrial Revolution. According to him, household earnings and internal business or agricultural savings were sufficient to finance the small plants necessary for manufacturing. Thus, for advanced (developed) economies, the capital needs of industrialization are met outside the banking system. Furthermore, the more gradual character of industrialization obviates the pressures for developing any special institutions to provide long-term capital to industry.

In contrast, the relatively backward economy (moderately backward) does require some special institutions to supply long-term funds for industrial capital. First, there are no substantial prior retained earnings, and second, the average plant size is hypothesized to be much larger. The experiences of Germany and other continental European nations are said to denote this pattern of industrial development. The banks in essence were the prime source of capital and entrepreneurship for this type of industrialization. In emphasizing this point, Gerschenkron states:

> A German bank, as the saying went, accompanied an industrial enterprise from cradle to grave, from establishment to liquidation throughout all the vicissitudes of its existence. Through the device of formally short-term but in reality long-term current account credits . . . the banks acquired a formidable degree of ascendancy over industrial enterprises, which extended far beyond the sphere of financial control into that of entrepreneurial and managerial decisions.[40]

Finally, in the case of extremely backward economies (developing countries), the structure is such that not even the banks could supply the necessary capital and entrepreneurship for industrialization. To the large investments necessary, and the drastic shortage of private savings, Gerschenkron adds the extreme lack of enterprise. Within his survey, the Russian "late-coming" industrialization approached this extreme form of backwardness. He therefore concludes:

> The scarcity of capital in Russia was such that no banking system could conceivably succeed in attracting sufficient funds to finance a large-scale industrialization; the standards of honesty in business were so disastrously low, the general distrust of the public so great, that no bank could have hoped to attract even such small capital funds as were available, and no bank could have successfully engaged in long-term credit policies in an economy where fraudulent bankruptcy had been almost elevated to the rank of a general business practice.[41]

The Structuralist Hypothesis and Bank Effectiveness

The contribution of the banks to growth in different patterns of industrialization is related to the relative degree of backwardness and innovative abilities of an economy to create new sources of capital finance. Despite the lack of precision of the classifications of relative states of backwardness, the Gerschenkron analysis suggests that in "extremely backward economies" the contribution of the banking system to capital formation is negligible. Only in "moderately backward" economies, where the level of business trust increases and banks' risk aversion decreases, will the banks have an impact. Once an advanced economy is attained, the structure of the economy and the approach to development determine the actual contribution of the banks, often with the development of alternative sources of capital finance. In Gerschenkron's terminology, the sources of capital finances at the different stages of backwardness may be summarized as the factories in advanced economies, the banks in moderately backward economies, and the state in extremely backward economies.

Implicit in this characterization is the notion that banks are either unnecessary or ineffectual in the extreme stages of development and could be utilized as a source of capital only in the intermediate stages. Also implicit is a stage theory of finance, even though Gerschenkron disavows any efforts at "stage making." In fact, he is explicit in his views of the deficiencies and simplifications of the standard stage theories. According to him, the process of industrialization depends on institutional innovations and substitutions, instead of "necessary preconditions." Nevertheless, in his analysis of the role of banks in industrial finance, there are distinct stages that determine bank operation and, possibly, effectiveness. For example, in describing the different stages of the Russian banking system, he concludes:

> A great transformation has taken place with regard to the banks . . . . Since it was the government that had fulfilled the function of industrial banks, the Russian banks, precisely because of the backwardness of the country, were organized as "deposit banks," thus resembling very much the type of banking in England. But as industrial development proceeded apace and as capital accumulation increased, the standards of business behavior were growingly Westernized. The paralyzing atmosphere of distrust began to vanish, and the foundation was laid for the emergence of a different type of bank. Gradually, the Moscow deposit banks were overshadowed by the development of the St. Petersburg banks that were conducted upon principles that were characteristic not of English but of German banking. In short, after the economic backwardness of Russia had been reduced by state-sponsored industrialization processes, use of a different instrument of industrialization, suitable to the new "stage of backwardness," became applicable.[42]

NOTES

1. R. W. Goldsmith, *Financial Structure and Development* (New Haven: Yale University Press, 1969), p. 390.

2. J. A. Schumpeter, *The Theory of Economic Development* (Cambridge, Mass: Harvard University Press, 1949).

3. Irma Adelman and Cynthia Morris, *Society, Politics, and Economic Development: A Quantitative Approach* (Baltimore: Johns Hopkins Press, 1967), pp. 118–23; Rando Cameron, ed., *Banking and Economic Development: Some Lessons of History* (New York: Oxford University Press, 1972), p. 25; Alexander Gerschenkron, *Economic Backwardness in Historical Perspective: A Book of Essays* (Cambridge, Mass.: Harvard University Press, 1962), pp. 12–45; Raymond Goldsmith, *Financial Structure and Development* (New Haven: Yale University Press, 1969) ("[Economic theory and economic history] both assure us that the existence and development of a super structure of financial instruments and financial institutions is a necessary, though not a sufficient, condition of economic development" p. 408); Ronald McKinnon, *Money and Capital*

in Economic Development (Washington, D.C.: Brookings Institution, 1973), pp. 89–117; Hugh Patrick, "Financial Development and Economic Growth in Undeveloped Countries," *Economic Development and Cultural Change* 14, no. 2 (January 1966): 101–14; and Edward Shaw, *Financial Deepening in Economic Development* (London: Oxford University Press, 1973). The theme of Shaw's book is "that the financial sector of an economy does matter in the economic development. It can assist in the breakaway from plodding repetition of repressed economic performance to accelerated growth" (p. 3).

4. Schumpeter, op. cit., p. 95 (emphasis his).

5. Ibid., p. 70.

6. Adelman and Morris, op. cit. Also idem, "An Econometric Model of Socio-Economic and Political Change in Underdeveloped Countries," *American Economic Review* 58, no. 5 (1968): 1188.

7. Adelman and Morris, "An Econometric Model," op. cit., p. 1211.

8. J. G. Gurley, "Financial Structures in Developing Economies," in *Fiscal and Monetary Problems in Developing States,* ed. D. Krivine (New York: Praeger, 1967).

9. Ibid., p. 104.

10. J. Gurley, review of *Banking in the Early Stages of Industrialization,* ed. Rando Cameron, *American Economic Review* 57, no. 4 (September 1967): 950–53.

11. Richard Porter, "The Promotion of the 'Banking Habit' and Economic Development," *Journal of Development Studies* 2, no. 4 (1966): 347.

12. "I have heard it asserted that the trade of the city of Glasgow doubled in about fifteen years after the first erection of the banks there; and that the trade of Scotland has more than quadrupled since the first erection of the two public banks in Edinburgh . . . that the banks have contributed a good deal to this increase, cannot be doubted." Adam Smith, *Wealth of Nations* (New York: Modern Library, 1937), p. 281.

13. Goldsmith, op. cit., p. 40.

14. Ibid., p. 45.

15. Patrick, op. cit., pp. 1974–81.

16. Peter Mathias, "Capital, Credit and Enterprise in the Industrial Revolution," *Journal of European Economic History* 2 (1973): 135.

17. Patrick, op. cit., p. 176.

18. Richard Tilly, *Financial Institutions and Industrialization in the German Rhineland, 1815–1870* (Madison: University of Wisconsin Press, 1966), p. 107.

19. Mathias, op. cit., p. 122.

20. J. M. Keynes, *The General Theory of Employment, Interest, and Money* (New York: Harcourt, Brace and World, Inc., 1936), and "The General Theory of Employment," *The Quarterly Journal of Economics,* February 1937, pp. 209–23.

21. Hyman P. Minsky, "An Exposition of a Keynesian Theory of Investment," in *Mathematical Methods in Investment and Finance,* ed. Karl Shell (London: North Holland, 1972), pp. 207–33.

22. J. M. Keynes, "General Theory," op. cit., p. 221.

23. Evsey Domar, "Capital Expansion, Rate of Growth and Employment," *Econometrica* 14 (1946): 137–47; "The Problem of Capital Formation," *American Economic Review* 12 (1948): 777–94; R. F. Harrod, "An Essay in Dynamic Theory," *Economic Journal* 49 (1939): 14–33.

24. Evsey Domar, "Capital Expansion," p. 139. The capacity expansion $= v.I$, with $v =$ the average capital and $I =$ investment/productivity, given other factors. The income expansion $= 1/s.\Delta I$, with $S =$ marginal propensity to save. The equilibrium condition is

$$1/s.\Delta I = v.I$$

That is;

$$\Delta I/I = s.v$$

and

$$\Delta I/I = G = s.v$$

25. W. Arthur Lewis, "Economic Development with Unlimited Supplies of Labor," *The Manchester School of Economics and Social Studies* 22 (May 1954): 155; *The Theory of Economic Growth* (New York: Harper & Row, 1970), p. 226.

26. W. W. Rostow, *The Stages of Economic Growth* (London: Cambridge University Press, 1960), pp. 39–45.

27. For a review of the reservations, see Theodore Morgan, "Investment versus Economic Growth," *Economic Development and Cultural Change* 17, no. 3 (April 1969): 392–414. And for empirical estimates showing positive correlation between investment and growth (even though it does not indicate causation), see Paul Sommers and Daniel B. Suits, "A Cross-Section Model of Economic Growth," *Review of Economics and Statistics* 53, (May 1971): 121–28.

28. Julius K. Nyerere, *Uhuru na Ujaama—Freedom and Socialism: A Selection from Writings and Speeches, 1965–67* (Dar-es-Salaam: Oxford University Press, 1969), p. 165.

29. Cameron, op. cit., McKinnon, op. cit., and Shaw, op. cit.

30. Shaw, op. cit., p. 3.

31. Cameron, op. cit., p. 24.

32. McKinnon, op. cit., pp. 51–61.

A modification of the familiar demand function for real balances with rate of investment as a proxy for the average real rate of return will be:

$$(M/P)^d = L(Y, I/Y, r_m, \dots)$$

with $\partial L/\partial Y > 0$, $\partial L/\partial(I/Y) > 0$, and $\partial L/\partial r_m > 0$
standard assumption: $\partial L/\partial r_k < 0$

33. Shaw, op. cit., p. 73.

34. Ibid., p. 81.

35. McKinnon, op. cit., pp. 68–69.

36. Shaw, op. cit., p. 86.

37. McKinnon, op. cit., p. 73.

38. Gerschenkron, op. cit., pp. 5–51, 353–64.

39. Ibid., pp. 353–54.

40. Ibid., p. 14.

41. Ibid., pp. 19–20.

42. Ibid., p. 22.

3

THE ECONOMIC
SETTING OF
EASTERN AFRICA

The current state of capital formation, the role of banks in its finance, and the real rate of growth in the Eastern African economies can only be meaningfully analyzed if their recent and not so recent history is explored. The brief review attempted in the first part of this chapter falls short of a comprehensive historical analysis; however, in the light of the limited information available about the past structure of these economies, true economic historians may liken it to a short journey into an unknown territory. The rates of growth, capital formation, and the financial techniques used in the Eastern African economies for the greater part of their history are unknown or not readily quantifiable. At least as far as the rate of economic development is concerned, it is fashionable to assume that there has not been any. The real magnitude of capital formation in the traditional economies of Eastern Africa cannot be estimated with any reasonable accuracy. The recent national accounting systems aside—where they exist—even at present statisticians concern themselves primarily with the monetary or cash sector.*

Financial techniques and, in particular, the sources and uses of capital finance in the traditional Eastern African societies have generally been rudimentary. Producers normally depended on internal finance for whatever capital improvements were necessary; in fact, external finance beyond family and friends did not exist. The only other forms of credit used were commodity loans that were repaid in kind or exchanged later for other commodities. This

---

*As of 1977, Somalia had no complete system of national accounts, while in Kenya and Tanzania the only capital formation estimated within the nonmonetary sectors is the change in the stock of traditional dwellings.

exchange extended to labor in the case of house building, land improvement, and other forms of cultivation assistance. This general lack of an indigenous money-lending class explains the eventual extension of expatriate financial institutions and "merchant bankers" in the region. Indeed, the emergence of the merchant money lenders and other types of credit institutions in the region is of a recent and foreign origin.

Even in the recent colonial history of these economies, the availability of statistical and other evidence is a limiting factor. As a result, the only period that can be reviewed with any reasonable accuracy is the last two decades of colonialism and the postindependence years. This chapter seeks, therefore, to analyze the extent of capital formation, its rate of composition, and sources of finance in selected Eastern African economies. The characteristics of these economies which directly or indirectly explain the state of capital formation and its finance are given particular attention.

THE PREINDEPENDENCE ECONOMIC SETTING OF EASTERN AFRICA

The Eastern African economies have been categorized as underdeveloped throughout their colonial history, and they are still grouped with other countries euphemistically termed developing. Despite basic differences even among the three economies with which we are concerned, in terms of structure and level of development they all fall at the bottom—regardless of the scale of economic development used.

The Eastern African economies relied substantially on subsistence production with low levels of productivity throughout most of the colonial years. The proportion of gross domestic product produced in the subsistence sectors or even in the nonmonetary sectors just before independence was substantial. The exact contribution of subsistence agricultural production alone in the Kenyan economy averaged around 24 to 25 percent between 1954 and 1963. Total agricultural production, both subsistence and market, contributed 42.4 percent of the gross domestic product for the same period. Since agricultural products are much more prominent in the Tanzanian economy, the proportion of gross domestic product outside the monetary sector is estimated to have averaged 39.1 percent for the eight years preceding independence, 1954–61. Within the same period, total agriculture and related production (fishing, forestry, and hunting) contributed 65 percent of the gross domestic product.

The importance of subsistence production in these economies is further illustrated by the proportion of the population of each country that is directly dependent on it. The case of the Somali economy, though the least commercialized, is still suggestive. The proportion of the population of Somalia that directly derives its livelihood from livestock raising is estimated at 65 percent. A further 23 percent of the population is considered to depend on agricultural activities and fishing.[1] The proportion of the population of Kenya and Tanzania that directly or indirectly depends on agriculture is estimated at about 60 percent. In Kenya and Tanzania the average percentages of the African labor force that were exclusively occupied in subsistence agriculture and related production in the preindependence decade were 45.7 percent and 55 percent, respectively (for annual rates see Statistical Appendix Table A.1).

More evident testimony to the state of underdevelopment of the Eastern African economies was the allocation of resources, physical and financial, via a colonial structure and mechanism. This pervasive influence of colonial allocation dictated the direction of trade, investments, and credit. More significantly, it affected the behavior of economic institutions. Though explanations of the state of underdevelopment of these economies emphasize different factors, depending on the theory of economic development,[2] any comprehensive analysis would have to account for the impact of colonial control and colonial institutions. The Eastern African economies were transformed into "dependent economies,"[3] which precluded any indigenous dynamic growth. All development in this period within these economies depended on external impulses. This resulted, as demonstrated below, in a classical form of dualistic development: a stagnant traditional sector and an export sector benefiting mostly the metropole.

The composition and direction of external trade in the Eastern African economies demonstrated a direct form of dependence on the metropolitan economies (in this case, British and Italian). This form of dependence is characterized by the high ratios of imports and exports within the monetized sectors of these economies. Since a high ratio of imports and exports alone may not be a sufficient condition, it is significant to point out that these economies were trading in a limited number of commodities with a single economy. Thus, the external trade dependence of the Eastern African economies on the respective metropoles was further aggravated by the composition of the products exchanged. As shown in Tables A.2–A.4, the larger portion of the exports of Eastern Africa consisted of primary products, while their imports were on the whole manufactured and other processed consumer-type products. Coffee, sisal, and tea exports accounted for 49 percent to 63 percent of the total exports of Kenya in the decade before independence. On the average, 64 percent of Tanzania's exports originated in sisal, coffee, and cotton for the 12 years before independence. Such dependence on a few products is obvious in Somalia, where bananas and livestock constituted as much as 86 percent of total exports.

Trade dependence is more evident if one looks at the direction of trade over the period. In the 12 years before independence, Kenya sent 50 percent of its exports and received 68 percent of its imports from the British Commonwealth. Within the same period, the exports of Tanzania to the Commonwealth ranged from 51 to 63 percent of its total exports, while the imports originating in the Commonwealth averaged 61 percent. Although no such breakdown is avaialble for Somalia in the preindependence period, one can reasonably assume that her trading partners were England and Italy, who had control over the northern and southern regions of the Somali Democratic Republic.

Analysis of the state of capital formation in preindependence Eastern Africa also demonstrates other forms of dependence. Capital formation in these economies was tied to their external trade positions.[4] As exports were a dominant and highly visible component of the national income and its real rate of growth, any unfavorable trends within this sector were eventually manifested as a decline in investments. Even though we could not quantify the proportion of total capital formation directly utilized in the production and promotion of exports, we could reasonably assume that it was substantial. Furthermore, any decline in the levels of capital formation for external trade purposes itself dampened investment in the rest of the economy.

A breakdown of the actual capital formation within the decade before independence demonstrates a more obvious form of dependence, reflected in the ownership, control, and direction of the reproducible capital within these economies. Investments in machinery and equipment, which averaged over 52 percent in Kenya and 40 percent in Tanzania, were the largest component in the private, productive capital categories. These investments were utilized neither in the traditional sectors nor in the public sectors but primarily in the private, modern sectors. The dependence attributed to capital ownership may be evident as one realizes that the modern sectors of these economies were exclusively in the hands of expatriates. The external trade, wholesale trade, and most retail trade, the few manufacturing firms, and all financial industries were owned and operated by European settlers and expatriate minorities.

This capital dependence has influenced the rate and composition of investments, and possibly the contribution of capital formation to the real growth of these countries. The rates of capital formation as a percentage of gross domestic product declined in Kenya and Tanzania in the years before independence. This slower rate of capital formation as political independence approached may be explained by reasons other than pure disinvestments by the expatriate community that controlled the modern sector. A change in the attitudes of expatriate investors due to independence uncertainties did, however, play a significant role. A relative increase in the production of the indigenous economy, which is traditionally less capital-intensive, could also have contributed to this decline.

The above analysis indicates that the larger portion of gross capital formation was undertaken in the private, "modern" sectors. It also indicates that, despite the high levels of investment rates (the minimum rate was 11.9 percent for Kenya in 1963), the associated rates of growth of gross domestic product were low. The average rates of growth of GDP at current prices were under

5 percent for all the Eastern African economies. Thus, the rates of growth of real GDP per capita are believed to have been rather small, if positive at all. Whether such low growth rates associated with the high private investment rate are directly attributable to the composition of investments alone is subject to dispute.

The rate and composition of capital formation in preindependence period demonstrate the absence of any systematic governmental or other efforts to manipulate them. There were no deliberate efforts to encourage or discourage investment in any particular sectors, such as agriculture and industry on the one hand, and real estate speculation on the other. Unlike the postindependence period, there were no systematic attempts to expand the base of capital formation by upgrading the indigenous economy.

COLONIAL BANKING IN EASTERN AFRICA

The structure of the economy and the rate and distribution of capital formation in Eastern Africa demonstrate the dominant influence of economic dependence. However, the structure and operations of the system of financial institutions and commercial banks in particular also illustrate this fundamental phenomenon. In the case of the banking system, the dependence is direct, in the form of ownership and management, and less direct, in institutional behavior, as evidenced by their operations.

Modern financial institutions were introduced around the advent of colonialism in the region. The first recorded full-fledged bank was the Bank of India—now the National and Grindlays Bank—established in Kenya in 1896.[5] In Tanzania the first bank was the Deutsch-Ostafrikanische Bank in 1905. Soon after, another private German bank—Handelsbank fuer Ostafrika—opened a branch there.[6] Only after World War I was a broad system of commercial banks developed. Besides the National and Grindlays Bank, the Standard Bank of South Africa (later the Standard Bank) and the National Bank of South Africa later taken over by Barclays D.C.O.) established branches in the major trade centers. In Tanzania the newly established British banks took over the assets of the original German banks. In the case of Northern Somalia, the National and Grindlays Bank established the first commercial bank branch in 1952; before that there had been one government savings bank introduced in 1930. The first institution that engaged in credit business in Southern Somalia was the Bank of Italy, established in 1920. It was not until much later, when the Banca di Roma (1936) and Banca di Napoli (1938) were established, that complete banking facilities were introduced.

The origins of the Eastern African banks thus lie in the promotion of trade between the metropole and periphery of the colonial empires. In Tanzania the first banks were set up to promote and facilitate trade between the new colony and the German economy. In similar fashion, the original purpose of the Kenyan banks was to enhance and connect the separate parts of the British overseas economy, while the Somali banks were established to join the Somali coastal economy to that of Italy. Hence, from their early history, modern financial institutions were established for the primary purpose of developing and supporting foreign trade. This early association with external trade created an "outward-looking" policy within the banks. Unlike banking systems developed through indigenous entrepreneurship, the colonial banks maintained this myopic view of the Eastern African economies as export-import sectors only.

In more general terms, colonial banking systems[7] and other dependent financial systems[8] have been indicted for having contributed little to indigenous economic development. Though thorough appraisals of the operations and impact of the colonial banking system in Eastern Africa are scarce, it has been shown that they exhibit some of the limitations common to other colonial banking systems.[9] Criticisms of colonial and other dependent financial systems center on the absence of innovation in their operations and, in particular, their standardized bank portfolio choices. I will therefore briefly examine the operations of the colonial Eastern African banks, emphasizing their bank liability management and assets allocation. From historical perspective, such an evaluation should be helpful in analyzing the current operations of the Eastern African banks.

The colonial banking systems of the region have failed even in the most basic of banking functions. In order to intermediate successfully between the surplus and deficit units of an economy, banks must mobilize sufficient financial and other resources. The failure of these banking systems cannot be explained by the small base of the economic surplus, since the "banking habit" itself has remained exclusively in the domain of the few urban merchants and traders. This limitation of the colonial banks is implicit in Newlyn's remarks:

> The major part of the national product is produced by African peasant farmers who do not use the deposit facilities of the banks. In Kenya the greater part of the marketed production is in European hands and the majority of trade is in Indian hands; both of these groups use banking services extensively. . . . In general, it can be stated quite simply that the use of commercial bank facilities by Africans is almost entirely restricted to savings bank business.[10]

As can be seen from Tables 3.1-3.3, the extent of financial intermediation in these economies was very small, and its rate of development unimpressive. The ability of the commercial banks to mobilize savings is measured by a number of complementary criteria as detailed in Chapter 5. Suffice it to say,

TABLE 3.1

Kenya: Commercial Bank Assets and Liabilities, 1950-60
(millions of Kenyan pounds)

	1950	1951	1952	1953	1954	1955	1956	1957	1958	1959	1960
Liabilities											
Demand deposits	30.1	38.7	39.4	37.6	46.8	51.9	43.4	42.9	39.9	44.0	40.3
Time and savings deposits	3.5	3.1	4.5	4.4	6.1	6.0	8.0	10.1	12.2	12.9	10.0
Balances due to banks abroad	9.7	11.5	13.1	14.2	12.0	14.8	20.2	23.2	23.5	23.9	32.6
Other liabilities	1.1	2.1	1.3	1.6	2.9	5.3	5.9	6.9	7.0	7.1	7.5
Total liabilities	44.4	55.4	58.3	57.8	67.8	78.0	77.5	83.0	82.6	88.0	90.3
Assets											
Cash	1.8	2.1	3.1	2.3	2.0	1.9	2.2	2.5	3.0	2.3	3.1
Balances due from banks abroad	27.3	29.4	31.2	31.3	28.6	26.4	30.7	31.2	31.8	35.6	32.4
Loans, advances, and bills discounted											
Industry	1.6	3.6	3.8	2.8	4.1	4.3	3.7	4.2	4.7	4.8	5.0
Agriculture	1.8	2.1	2.8	4.8	5.3	5.7	4.9	5.9	6.2	6.1	6.5
Commerce	6.5	12.5	11.0	10.2	17.7	25.3	21.9	23.0	18.3	21.5	26.2
Other	1.7	2.2	2.8	2.5	3.9	6.0	5.3	6.2	5.1	5.1	4.6
Investments in East Africa	2.5	1.4	1.3	1.6	1.6	1.6	2.1	1.7	1.8	2.5	2.2
Other assets	1.3	1.9	2.5	2.5	4.6	6.9	6.8	8.4	11.7	10.1	10.3
Total assets*	44.5	55.2	58.5	58.0	67.8	78.1	77.6	83.1	82.6	88.0	90.3
Ratios											
External earning assets as percentage of total assets	61.5	53.1	53.5	54.2	42.2	33.8	39.6	37.6	38.5	40.5	35.9
Commercial loans as percentage of total loans	56.8	61.0	54.2	50.0	57.1	61.4	61.3	58.7	53.4	57.3	62.1

*Discrepancies in totals due to rounding.

Sources: Statistical Abstract (Kenya: Ministry of Finance and Economic Planning, 1964), Statistical Abstract (East African Statistical Department, 1958).

TABLE 3.2

Tanzania: Commercial Bank Assets and Liabilities, 1950-60
(millions of Tanzanian pounds)

	1950	1951	1952	1953	1954	1955	1956	1957	1958	1959	1960
Liabilities											
Demand deposits	15.8	17.9	18.1	19.0	19.3	16.9	14.6	13.8	14.9	16.0	14.8
Time and savings deposits	1.7	2.2	3.0	4.0	3.7	4.3	5.6	5.5	5.6	5.9	4.7
Balances due to banks abroad	1.0	2.6	1.7	2.9	3.2	5.8	4.9	5.5	5.3	7.7	10.9
Other liabilities	.2	.5	.6	.6	.7	1.2	1.4	1.3	1.6	2.0	2.1
Total liabilities	18.7	23.2	23.4	26.5	26.9	28.2	26.5	26.1	27.0	31.6	32.5
Assets											
Cash	1.3	1.6	2.0	1.8	2.2	1.7	1.5	1.3	1.6	1.4	2.1
Balances due from banks abroad	12.8	13.6	14.7	16.6	13.6	14.3	14.2	11.3	12.8	13.2	11.3
Loans and advances to											
Industry	1.0	2.1	1.1	2.6	2.2	1.5	2.2	4.2	2.0	2.5	2.3
Agriculture	1.2	2.0	1.8	1.9	3.8	2.6	2.0	2.4	2.6	4.0	5.1
Commerce	2.1	3.4	3.3	3.1	4.4	5.6	3.5	4.1	4.2	6.3	7.3
Other	–	–	–	–	–	1.1	1.5	1.3	1.3	1.0	1.0
Investments in East Africa	0.0	0.0	0.0	.1	.1	.1	.1	.1	.1	.1	.3
Other assets	.3	.4	.7	.5	.7	1.6	1.6	1.4	2.5	3.1	3.2
Total assets*	18.7	23.1	23.6	26.6	27.0	28.5	26.4	26.1	27.1	31.6	32.6
Ratios											
External earning assets as percentage of total assets	68.4	58.6	62.8	62.6	50.6	50.7	53.6	43.3	47.4	41.8	34.8
Commercial loans as percentage of total loans	48.8	45.3	53.2	40.8	42.3	51.9	38.4	34.2	41.6	45.7	46.5

*Discrepancies in totals due to rounding.

Source: *Statistical Abstract* (Tanzania: Central Statistical Bureau, 1957, 1964).

TABLE 3.3

Somalia: Commercial Bank Deposits and Distribution of Loans, 1950-59
(millions of Somali shillings)

	1950	1951	1952	1953	1954	1955	1956	1957	1958	1959
Deposits										
Demand	21.9	22.6	31.5	33.4	37.2	42.6	39.7	48.8	47.2	46.7
Time and savings	3.8	6.2	8.6	9.0	9.8	12.0	12.3	12.6	15.9	14.2
Loans by branch of economic activity										
Agriculture	2.0	8.7	27.6	15.0	10.8	12.8	11.5	12.9	11.8	9.0
Industry	1.4	7.0	13.7	9.9	6.3	7.1	6.0	5.0	8.2	6.7
Commerce	11.9	26.4	104.7	65.7	41.4	34.5	32.4	36.2	40.6	47.8
Other	1.9	3.9	29.4	18.0	6.3	6.5	4.4	4.4	8.5	16.1
Ratios										
Banking lending as percentage of bank deposits	66.9	159.7	437.4	256.1	137.9	111.5	104.4	95.3	109.5	130.7
Commercial loans as percentage of total loans	69.2	57.4	59.7	60.5	63.9	56.7	59.7	61.9	58.8	60.1

Source: Somalia National Bank Bulletin, 1962.

45

however, that the utilization of bank money and banking services in general was restricted to the expatriate communities. More revealing is the rate of growth of bank assets as a proportion of gross domestic product. Between 1954 and 1960, the ratio of the change in total bank assets to gross domestic product in Kenya and Tanzania averaged 2.5 percent and 0.4 percent, respectively.

The distribution of bank assets in Eastern Africa as illustrated in these tables, furthermore, indicates two common limitations of colonial banking. Throughout the period, the banks held a high proportion of foreign and often liquid assets. They also maintained a high proportion of bank credits flowing to the commercial sectors and smaller amounts to agriculture and industry. External trade credits have remained the largest component of the total loans and advances by the Eastern African commercial banks; for some countries, it is in excess of all other loans and advances.

A disadvantage of colonial banking was that it allocated the larger part of its meager resources to holding liquid and often foreign assets. Besides the cash deposits with their central offices and other correspondent banks, the colonial banks repatriated substantial funds for investment abroad. Thus, the Eastern African colonial banks held as much as two-thirds of their total assets in foreign obligations; in 1950 the ratio for Tanzania was 68 percent and for Kenya, 62 percent. The balances due from banks abroad and in other territories in Eastern Africa from 1950 to 1960 for Tanzania and Kenya were 57 percent and 45 percent, respectively.

This external preoccupation of the colonial banks (as opposed to concern with the internal indigenous economy) is also evident in their loan portfolios. The largest component of loans and advances granted by these banks has consistently been associated with external trade and internal distribution of imports. During the 11 years before 1960, loans and advances to commerce averaged about 61 percent for Somalia, 58 percent for Kenya, and 44 percent for Tanzania. A less disaggregated breakdown of these data is often interpreted to demonstrate not only the dominant role of commercial loans, but also that the loans were collateralized, short-term, and often to expatriate firms.

Furthermore, the contribution of the colonial banks to indigenous economic development was very small. The major impact of the colonial credit institutions was to transform some limited production (such commodities as bananas in Somalia, sisal in Tanzania, and coffee in Kenya) from subsistence to cash crops. However, the net benefits from such cash crops, at least during this period, were limited to the expatriate community. Instead of supporting indigenous economic development, the net effect of the colonial banking systems was to integrate small sectors of the dependent economies into the more advanced metropolitan economies of Western Europe. This process of integration varied within the region; it was most successful in Kenya and least successful in Somalia.

THE POSTINDEPENDENCE ECONOMIC SETTING OF EASTERN AFRICA

The economies of Eastern Africa during the postindependence decade (Kenya, 1963–73; Tanzania, 1961–71; and Somalia, 1960–70) experienced institutional and structural changes, some of which were significant. The composition of the gross domestic products of the Eastern African economies did not change significantly from its preindependence levels. The predominant reliance of the Eastern African households on agricultural production—and subsistence agriculture at that—was maintained during the independence decade. The contribution of subsistence and other agriculture to the respective gross domestic products of the countries indicates the prime role it continued to play (Tables A.5 and A.6).

The Kenyan economy, which started from a more advanced stage, experienced moderate transformations. Besides a 6 percent annual average rate of growth of the gross domestic product at constant prices between 1964 and 1973, it achieved a higher level of industrialization. Even in this case, however, the contribution of the manufacturing sector to GDP remained around 11 percent during the period. The largest single sector contributing to gross domestic product continued to be subsistence agriculture, averaging 24 percent over this period, while total agricultural production inside and outside the market economy contributed 39 percent. In comparison with the preindependence period, the contribution of total agricultural production declined, while the portion due to subsistence production stayed constant.

Nevertheless, the magnitude of the changes in the structure of the Kenyan economy within the postindependence period is not impressive, as indicated by the composition of foreign trade. The main export commodities, coffee and tea, still accounted for 45 percent of total export earnings. The other leading crop of the colonial period, sisal, declined considerably within the scale of commodities exported. The United Kingdom remained the major trading partner of Kenya, though trade dependence diminished. In the postindependence period, the original six European Economic Community countries received 21 percent of Kenya's exports, while the United Kingdom received 22.2 percent.

The Tanzanian economy underwent comparatively fewer structural changes, especially in the composition of the gross domestic product. As explored in the next chapter, the Tanzanian and Somali economies have experienced radical attempts to reorient their structure and performance, yet the Tanzanian economy remains subsistence-based with export cash crop enclaves interposed. The estimated subsistence production accounted for 30 percent of the gross domestic product of Tanzania in 1964–73. More than half of the gross domestic product originated in agricultural production, subsistence and market. There was a slight increase in monetary nonagricultural production from preindependence levels. Nevertheless, the average annual rate of growth of gross domestic product, at constant prices (4.6 percent) and its annual variation can be explained by the agrarian base of the economy. The changes in the main export commodities of Tanzania were less impressive: cotton, coffee, and sisal fluctuated as the top three export commodities, as had been the case before independence. Furthermore, the key reliance on the foreign sector remained unabated: over the decade, both imports and exports as a proportion of GDP increased. The agrarian base of the Tanzanian economy is also evident in that the bulk of the Tanzanian population remained employed in the subsistence sector; the reported wage-labor force accounted for only about 4 percent of the population.

The structure of the Somali economy and its development from 1960 to 1973 can be discerned from the rate and value of the main export commodities. Somalia's exports consisted primarily of bananas and livestock. The share of bananas in total exports declined, while that of livestock and related products increased in the postindependence period. As a result of the prominence of livestock products in the later independence years, Italy was replaced by the People's Democratic Republic of Yemen and Saudi Arabia as the largest source of demand for Somali exports. It is still obvious that the trade dependence of Somalia on too few markets continued during the first ten years of independence.

In summary, the basic structures and performances of the Eastern African economies in the postindependence decade did not depart significantly from those of the last decade of the colonial era. (However, this does not preclude some explicit policies of the present regimes, especially in Tanzania after 1967 and Somalia after 1969, to establish new structures and institutions.) The conclusion of the IBRD economic survey that "Somalia is still a very poor country and it is probably true that most of its people are little better off in 1970 than they were when Somalia gained her independence in 1960" accurately reflects the postindependence economic setting of Eastern Africa.[11]

CAPITAL FORMATION AND FINANCE IN POSTINDEPENDENCE EASTERN AFRICA

The limitations on the real growth and structural transformation of postindependence Eastern African economies cannot be attributed to one factor alone. Among the more relevant variables are the rate and distribution of capital formation and the sources of finance. The role of capital formation and finance in the growth process was surveyed in the last chapter. Structural economic changes are also associated with the distribution of investments and the allocation of finance among sectors.

The rates of capital formation in the postindependence Eastern African economies did not depart significantly from their levels of the last colonial decade. As the pre- and postindependence capital formation data indicate, the proportions of the gross domestic product invested did not dramatically increase before the 1970s. In the case of Kenya, the average rate of gross fixed capital formation as a proportion of GDP increased from 19 percent to 21.7 percent between 1954–63 and 1964–73. In Tanzania the same ratios increased from 18 percent for 1954–61 to 21.8 percent for 1964–73. Since the similarities of average investment ratios over such a long period can be misleading, one should stress the divergence of the last years from the past trends. In the last recorded years, the annual rate of capital formation increased to about 30 percent of the GDP of each country.

The maintenance of the status quo in the initial years of independence is also evident in the distribution of aggregate fixed capital formation by type of asset use. The share of machines and other equipment in capital formation (probably the most reliable component, as it can be derived from import listings) shows a limited increase in the case of Kenya and no change in the case of Tanzania. Kenyan investments in equipment, as a percentage of the total, averaged 43 percent between 1954 and 1963 and 48.4 percent between 1964 and 1973. For the last years of the preindependence period and the initial years of independence, approximately half of all investments were in equipment and machines. The Tanzanian investments in equipment and other machines as a proportion of their total investments show no change over the two periods. With the exception of a few years, Tanzania consistently allocated approximately 39 percent of its capital formation to equipment; the annual averages were 39.9 percent and 39.3 percent for the pre- and postindependence years, respectively. The bulk of Eastern African investments was in buildings and other construction throughout these years. Investments in dwellings and other commercial buildings maintained a steady increase in the postindependence period; however, government expenditures on infrastructure have recently expanded to the extent that they caught up with or exceeded the expenditures on buildings.

The most marked changes in the composition of capital formation are in its uses by economic sectors. Contrary to the stated policies of the Eastern African governments, the only successful shift has occurred in sectoral distribution, and not in asset uses of investments. The proportion of recorded capital formation used in the nonmonetary subsistence sectors of these economies not only remained small, but also declined over the period. In Kenya the recorded share of the nonmonetary sector in capital formation declined from a high of 12.4 percent in 1965 to an estimated 6.1 percent in 1973. In like manner, the share of the Tanzanian subsistence sector's investments was reduced from 25.2 percent in 1964 to 8.1 percent in 1973.

The other major shift in the allocation of capital formation among sectors occurred in Tanzania. As explained in the next chapter, there has been a planned effort to shift resources from the private to the public sector in Tanzania. At the formalization of these plans in 1966, under one-third of investments originated in the public sector. Through acquisitions, nationalizations, and the planned increase of the public sector, the proportion of public investments to total reached 72 percent in 1973. In Kenya, where private investments have been encouraged, the share of public investments increased from 25 percent to 42 percent during the first decade of independence.

The statistical evidence on the sources of capital formation is fragmentary for the Eastern African countries. A comparison of these sources in the pre- and postindependence periods cannot be made, since no quantitative estimates were kept in the earlier period. Even in the postindependence years, a large portion of capital finance has been unrecorded, primarily in the nonmonetary sectors. As of 1977, none of these economies had a flow-of-funds accounting system. The domestic private sector's savings can only be derived as a residual from actual capital formation less other sources of finance.* With these limitations in mind, I will examine the contributions of the domestic public and foreign sectors to capital finance.

The only source of domestic finance which is independently derived in the Eastern African economies and for which reasonably accurate statistics are available is that of government savings. The receipts of the government are cash documented, as are their expenditures, both current and capital. It was shown above that a large proportion of capital formation originates in the public sector of Tanzania. Irrespective of the magnitude of public investments in the Eastern African economies, all the governments have remained in a net debtor position to the rest of the domestic sectors and to the rest of the world. The net balance position of all these governments after the deduction of capital expenditures has consistently resulted in a deficit.

The steady annual budgetary deficits of the Eastern African governments are no surprise to students of post-colonial Africa. The majority of these countries have chronic deficits and have to rely on external resources for the total finance of their development expenditures. The attempted explanations of the excess of public expenditures, current and capital, over receipts are many and varied. Among the more prominent theses are the small tax base, generally

---

*The gross domestic private saving (Sp) is obtained as the difference between the gross capital formation (I) and the government savings (Sg) and balance-of-payments deficits or surpluses (X-M); that is,

$$Sp = I - Sg - (X - M)$$

low rates of effective taxation (due to malpractice, inefficiencies, or other factors), and obviously the higher relative growth rates of expenditures.

The magnitude of each government's deficit and its reliance on borrowing either from domestic or foreign sources are made eminently clear by the respective development plans. In evaluating the first completed five-year plans of these economies, one is impressed by the discrepancy between formulated plans and their execution. An important cause of this discrepancy is often the difference between projected and available financing. The actual realization of these plans is, however, of secondary importance to us. What is relevant is that the initial planning process itself demonstrates the inability of these governments to rely on domestic sources of finance, and particularly government surpluses.

The Kenyan development plan of 1964–70 envisaged a total gross fixed investment of 6,340 million Kenyan shillings (Ksh). The plan further estimated that 39.2 percent of the total would originate in the public sector and the rest in the private sector, inclusive of public enterprises. According to estimated sources of finance, almost half of the total planned investment by both sectors was to be financed from foreign sources and the other half from domestic savings. One should further note that these estimates were on the conservative side, since the experiences of the few years preceding the plan would have implied complete dependence on foreign aid and loans for all government capital expenditures.

The Tanzanian development plan of 1964–69 also projected a large financial gap to be filled from foreign sources. The planned expenditures for the entire economy were 4,970 million Tanzanian Shillings (Tsh). The public sector, including public enterprises, was expected to contribute 61 percent of the planned investments. All domestic sources of finance combined were estimated to contribute under half of the desired financing. In particular, 78 percent of the government's investments were expected to be externally financed, with another 14 percent to come from domestic borrowing. Due to unforeseen circumstances, primarily political (discontinuance of aid from major donors), the Tanzanians were forced to raise a higher percentage of the finance domestically (approximately 60 percent).

The most pronounced case of domestic finance shortages was exhibited in the Somali plan of 1963–67. In its revised form, the plan projected capital expenditures of 2,427 million. Somali Shillings (So.Sh), to be made almost entirely by the public sector. Less than half of the financing for the planned expenditures was available or was from known sources. At the initial plan stage, Somalia could have counted on So.Sh 150 million from domestic sources, public and private.

It is obvious that, for the period covered, the fiscal mechanisms did not mobilize sufficient domestic resources for reinvestment purposes. We can also conclude that in the volume and distribution of capital formation there have been no major departures from preindependence performance, with the exception of Tanzania's shift to public ownership. Finally, the euphoria coupled with independence has not been rewarded: the growth rates have not been impressive, and there have been no structural shifts to favor the rural, subsistence "African" population. In response to these problems, the Eastern African governments have adopted different strategies. These strategies and the role of the financial institutions in the development of these economies during the first decade of independence are examined next.

NOTES

1. Mark Karp, *The Economics of Trusteeship in Somalia* (Boston: Boston University Press, 1960).

2. For a comprehensive survey of both Marxist and non-Marxist theories of underdevelopment, see Tamas Szentes, *The Political Economy of Underdevelopment* (Budapest: Akademiai Kiado, 1972).

3. The prevailing views on the impact of colonial control on the dependent economies are expressed by Mill and Rweyemamu:

> The colonies were to be looked upon more properly as outlying agricultural or manufacturing establishments belonging to a larger community, and were not to be regarded as countries with a productive capital of their own ... [but] the place where England finds it convenient to carry on the production of sugar, coffee and a few other tropical commodities. (J. S. Mill, *Principles of Political Economy*, ed. W. J. Ashley [London, 1929], pp. 685–86)

> A clear understanding of the colonial structure, however, impels us to look at a colony in the context of an 'overseas economy', consisting of a metropole and periphery. The metropolis was the locus of product elaboration and disposal and the source from which the system was provisioned with capital, managerial skill and the ancillary services needed for production.... The colony was merely an entity for supplying raw materials, land and labor, propelled by specific demands from its metropole. (J. Rweyemamu, *Underdevelopment and Industrialization in Tanzania,* (Nairobi: Oxford University Press, 1973), pp. 12–13.

4. Paul G. Clark, *Development Planning in East Africa* (Nairobi: East African Publishing House, 1965), pp. 18–19.

5. W. T. Newlyn, *Money in an African Context* (London: Oxford University Press, 1967), p. 41.

6. H. H. Binhammer, *Commercial Banking in Tanzania,* Economic Research Bureau, University of Dar-es-Salaam, paper no. 69.11, p. 1.

7. On the nature of colonial banking, see Edward Nevin, *Capital Funds in Underdeveloped Countries* (New York: St. Martin's, 1961), pp. 45–50. For a case study, see R. A. Sowelem, *Towards Financial Independence in a Developing Economy* (London: Allen and Unwin, 1967).

8. Several recent studies have concluded that, despite political independence, continuing financial dependence has resulted in banking systems with "poor" records in assisting economic development and emancipation. See for example, Irving Gerchenberg, "Banking in Uganda Since Independence," *Economic Development and Cultural Change* 20, no. 3 (April 1972): 505–23.

9. W. T. Newlyn and D. C. Rowan, *Money and Banking in British Colonial Africa* (London: Oxford University Press, 1954). They spend all of five pages discussing expatriate banking in Eastern Africa.

10. Ibid., p. 85.

11. IBRD, *Economic Development Prospects in Somalia, January 1971, p. 35;* IBRD, *World Bank Atlas,* 1974 population, per capita product, and growth rates. The estimated GNP per capita for the three countries in 1973 was Kenya, US$170 per annum; Somalia, US$80 per annum; and Tanzania, US$120 per annum.

4

DEVELOPMENT STRATEGIES AND
THE FINANCIAL SYSTEMS OF
EASTERN AFRICA

As noted in Chapter 3, the effects of the approach to economic development on the operations of financial institutions have not been sufficiently explored. The structure of the financial system and its functions, as well as its contribution to real growth, reflect the strategy of economic development adopted. The banking systems of socialist states differ in large measure from those of the developed capitalist economies in that the functions of the banks, monetary and intermediary, are subordinate to the state economic plan. The plan, which is drawn up mainly in physical units, assigns to the state banks the task of providing the financial means to satisfy predetermined production and investment targets. Financial flows in are planned in accordance with the physical plan and are adjusted accordingly. In the capitalist economies, on the other hand, financial resources are transferred through the market mechanism, with the monetary authorities' indirect influence channeled through macro policy measures. The proliferation of financial institutions and the associated specialization of their functions in capitalist economies are not required in planned economies.

Because of the low levels of financial and real development in the developing countries, the differences in the structure and functions of the financial systems between planned and capitalist economies may be less pronounced than expected. Nevertheless, the effect of the differing approaches to economic development on the banking systems of Eastern Africa are worth exploring. The three Eastern African economies chosen here are appropriate, since Kenya and Tanzania have followed divergent strategies in recent years, while Somalia followed no discernible strategy for the first ten years of independence.

The first section of this chapter reviews the development strategies of the Eastern African economies, starting with the year the strategies were formalized. The second section explores the changes that have occurred in the structure of the banking systems to make their functions and operations consistent with the selected development strategies. The final section reviews the role of specialized financial institutions in the attainment of development objectives. Particular attention is paid here to the institutions that were established to implement the respective development strategies.

DEVELOPMENT STRATEGIES

For a number of years after independence, the Eastern African countries lacked anything resembling a development strategy. This period of undefined programs and conflicting policies has gradually been replaced by a coherent strategy for each country—and at least for one country, by a specific plan within which development will be pursued. However, some semblance of planning was undertaken even in the earlier years of independence, with most of these plans put together either by the departing senior colonial officers or by visiting experts and scholars. The earlier attempts can best be described as a collection of unrelated projects that might be undertaken profitably. A national strategy of development was formulated in Tanzania about 1964, if the first position papers of the Tanzanian authorities are considered. The Kenyan strategy was clearly evident in 1965–66, as the disintegration of the East African Common Market demonstrated. It took Somalia almost the whole decade of the 1960s to move from a maintenance of the status quo to a national economic policy in any form. As a result of the absence of any meaningful strategy in Somalia during the first decade of independence, only the strategies of Tanzania and Kenya will be reviewed.

The Tanzanian strategy of development is by far the more specific in both objectives and implementation. It was first formalized in the Arusha Declaration of February 1967, and further defined and extended in subsequent papers and declarations by the ruling party (TANU) and by Julius K. Nyerere.[1] Despite the concern of these papers with sociopolitical affairs, they also set a basic frame within which economic development could be pursued.

The subtitle of the Arusha Declaration, "Socialism and Self-reliance," indicates the Tanzanian strategy of economic development. The foundations of this program are the minimization of economic dependence and the elimination of foreign penetration. It deemphasizes the pursuit of industrialization and subsequent urbanization, calling instead for development based on communal agricultural production. In particular, it emphasizes *ujamaa* production, in cooperatives among shareholders relying primarily on labor-intensive techniques. The Arusha Declaration states these policies in unmistakable language:

> We have made a mistake to choose money, something which we do not have,
> to be our major instrument of development. We are mistaken when we
> imagine that we shall get money from foreign countries, firstly, because to
> say the truth we cannot get enough money for our development, and, sec-
> ondly, because even if we could get it, such complete dependence on outside
> help would have endangered our independence and the other policies of our
> country.[2]

On the choice of small-holder agricultural development and deemphasis of
industrialization it declares:

> We have put too much emphasis on industries . . . we seem to say "industries
> are the basis of development." This is true [but] the mistake we are making
> is to think that development begins with industries.[3]

The type of industrialization it encourages uses simple technology and relies
minimally on foreign resources. It continues to point out the conflicts between
dependence and socialism, and the conflicts between the urban few and the
rural masses. According to TANU, the program has been designed to eliminate not only foreign penetration but also "economic dualism."

The Kenyan strategy, though less clearly defined, is at any rate distinct
from that of Tanzania. The Kenyan authorities profess to adhere to a form of
African socialism.[4] Ideological niceties aside, the Kenyan program in essence
follows the familiar strategy of encouraging exports, primarily cash crops, and
import-substituting industrialization irrespective of domestic or foreign ownership. Although the agricultural sector is of paramount interest, by virtue of
its current importance, the strategy sets a high priority on industrialization
through private domestic and foreign investment. In spite of the contradiction
between relying on private foreign investment for industrialization and promoting a favorable distribution of income between Africans and non-Africans,
the authorities have set the latter as an objective. Unlike the Tanzanians,
however, the Kenyan economic planners have shown little or no alarm over
the inequities between rural and urban incomes.

The Kenyan strategy of development is well summarized by the only
government position paper on the subject. The main lines of the strategy are
as follows:

   (i)   To attack directly the two principal limitations on growth, i.e.,
      shortages of domestic capital and skilled manpower.
  (ii)   To revolutionize agriculture for Kenya by developing unused and
      underutilized land through consolidation, development credit . . .
 (iii)   To develop industry as rapidly as opportunities are created.
 (iv)   To develop [infrastructure], to lay the basis for a rapid acceleration of
      industrial growth.
  (v)   To provide for a more equitable distribution of the benefits achieved.[5]

These summaries of the development strategies of Tanzania and Kenya provide at least a hierarchy of priorities. This book is less concerned with the implementations of these programs than with their essence and comparative nature. We can therefore state with reasonable accuracy that Kenya and Tanzania are following two distinct strategies, while Somalia followed no discernible strategy for the first ten years of independence. This distinction is highly relevant for the hypothesis to be explored in the next two chapters on the determinants of the role of financial institutions in Eastern African development. These hierarchies of economic objectives, as we will detail in Chapter 5, are useful in lieu of a specific social preference function. In fact, these objectives and the constraints outlined earlier must be considered in evaluating and explaining the performance of the financial institutions.

The distinctions drawn between the different strategies of economic development in these economies should be qualified by stressing the lack of any form of systematic physical or financial planning. Except for the annual and medium-term development plans, which set the desired levels of development expenditures in the public sector, and which project targets for private investment expenditures, there is no central mechanism to mobilize and allocate financial and real resources. Since 1971–72 Tanzania has initiated annual financial plans, which are no more than formal presentations of the expected sources of financing for the annual development plans. Thus, Caselli points out that the financial plans "deal only indirectly with credit problems with reference to specific sectors such as agriculture, industry, housing, etc. . . . Nothing at all is said about the growth of the money supply and the volume of credit, either in quantitative or in qualitative terms."[6]

Financial planning, even in the case of Tanzania, is therefore indicative in nature. As much as the established development priorities, the new financial plans assist in directing the performance of financial institutions. Thus, while it may be easy to find statements and official declarations about the desired development goals and the strategy to be followed, it is a good deal less easy to see how they would be implemented. It is even more difficult to trace how these pronouncements are translated into practice through government economic and financial policies. The declaration of Tanzania's second five-year plan that the planned investment level will require "an increased channeling of savings to the public and parastatal sector through the various public financial institutions,"[7] without any associated financial policy changes, is an example.

Despite this lack of specificity in the proposed execution of these development strategies and in the vague implications for financial policies, the divergent strategies have had a significant impact on the structure of the banks and other financial institutions.

CHANGES IN THE STRUCTURE OF COMMERCIAL BANKING SINCE INDEPENDENCE

Compared to the banking systems of Tanzania and Somalia, the Kenyan system has undergone only moderate changes since independence. During the first two years of independence (from December 12, 1963) there were no major institutional changes in Kenya's financial system. The commercial banking system continued to be dominated by the big three British banks (Barclays, Standard, and National and Grindlays). The first institutional change affecting the structure of the commercial banks occurred in May 1966, when the Central Bank of Kenya was established. The decision of the three East African countries to break up the common currency area also broke the linkage that tied the banking systems of the region. Since the three British banks were regional offices for the whole of East Africa, adjustments were required to set up an independent system in each country. The size of the Kenyan commercial banking system was reduced, as the branches outside Kenya transferred their balances to London instead of Nairobi. Also, direct loans to enterprises resident in the other two countries ceased. In line with the development strategy of Kenya, the same three British institutions and other foreign bank branches formed the nucleus of the banking system. Recently, though, some concessions have been granted to critics of the dominance of the foreign banks. The Banking Act of 1969, replacing that of 1956, provides that the banks are subject to government licensing and are required to maintain a paid-up capital of Kenya pounds (K£) 100,000, or up to 5 percent of deposits, whichever is greater. Further, as of December 1970 the government has initiated a policy of participation in the largest three foreign banks. The government acquired a 40 percent share in the international department of the National and Grindlays Bank, which was set up as a separate institution, the Grindlays Bank International (Kenya) Ltd. At the same time it acquired a 60 percent share in the Kenya Commercial Bank, which took over the local branch system of the National and Grindlays Bank. After a two-year lag (in 1972), the government purchased 50 percent of the shares of the Standard Bank and Barclays Bank. Finally, the monetary authorities have used both monetary instruments and moral suasion to enlist the banks in the realization of development objectives. (For details, see Chapter 5.)

From independence* to the end of 1966, the Tanzanian banking system was similar to that of Kenya—predominantly foreign bank branches led by the British big three. At about the end of 1966, 70 bank branches and agencies

---

*The United Republic of Tanzania was formed on April 27, 1964, when Tanganyika (which became independent on December 9, 1961) and Zanzibar (which became independent on December 9, 1963) were united.

were operating in Tanzania, including 4 in Zanzibar, and the three British banks owned 48 of them. The other branches were divided among smaller foreign banks such as the Bank of Baroda and the National Bank of Pakistan, and three newly formed indigenous banks: the National Cooperative Bank (1964), the Tanzanian Bank of Commerce (1965), and the People's Bank of Zanzibar (1966). The breakup of the East Africa currency union and the creation of the separate central banks did not have so dramatic an effect on the Tanzanian system as on the Kenyan. However, some East African firms outside Tanzania switched most of their banking transactions to the Tanzanian commercial banks.

Under the Arusha Declaration of February 1967, the commercial banking system was completely reorganized. All the expatriate banks were nationalized, a new National Bank of Commerce was set up, and the branches of the nationalized banks merged with the new bank. Besides the new National Bank of Commerce, the reorganization left the Bank of Zanzibar and the National Cooperative Bank, which were already government-owned. In 1970, the National Cooperative Bank was taken over by the National Bank of Commerce, leaving Tanzania with two commercial banks.

The decision to nationalize and reorganize the banking system follows from the Arusha Declaration and the adoption of a development strategy with socialism and self-reliance as its cornerstones. In the words of the Arusha Declaration, "To build and maintain socialism it is essential that all the major means of production and exchange in the nation [including the banks] are controlled and owned by the peasants through the machinery of their government and their cooperatives."[8] Nationalization was considered a requirement of the development strategy. It was also expected to improve radically the poor performance of the financial system. Among the major changes expected from nationalization of the banks were:

A more efficient mobilization and redistribution of savings geared to the requirements of economic development.

A speed-up of the rate of formation of household saving both in urban and rural areas, and a dense network of banking facilities throughout the country.

A banking system which, while not oblivious to the need to earn profits, would give priority to service to the community.[9]

At independence,* the Somali commercial banking system was composed of the branches of four foreign banks: Banca di Roma, Banca di Napoli, the

---

*The Somali Republic was founded on July 1, 1960, when the northern and southern parts of Somalia were united.

Bank of Port Said in the southern region, and the National and Grindlays in the northern region. The Somali National Bank, which started operations on the first day of independence, opened both central and commercial banking departments. Including the commercial department of the Somali National Bank, the total branches, scattered in four towns, numbered no more than nine. Although the structure of this system remained the same throughout the first decade of independence, the National Bank increased its involvement in commercial bank activities: in 1969 it accounted for over 70 percent of the loans to the private sector, and its share of the private-sector deposits was 42 percent. During this period, the National Bank also extended branches and agencies to a large number of towns.

The new government that took over on October 21, 1969, introduced dramatic changes in economic and financial policies. Among these were the nationalization of the foreign banks and the reorganization of the banking system. In May 1970, the government created the Somali Commercial Bank, which took over the branches and agencies of the four nationalized foreign banks. Simultaneously, the commercial banking department of the National Bank was set up in a separate institution to form the Somali Savings and Credit Bank. This system, comprising two commercial banks and the central bank, was maintained up to the beginning of 1975, when the two commercial banks were merged. In line with the socialism adopted by the new regime, the commercial banking system was transformed from a multiple banking system to a unitary system. The nationalization of the foreign banks and the creation of a single commercial bank were considered to be mandatory for an economy aspiring to socialism. The dependence created by the foreign bank branches and the competition among the two domestic banks were found to be inconsistent with the strategy of development. Furthermore, it was hoped this new structure would result in improved mobilization and allocation of savings and the rationalization of the location of bank branches.

SPECIALIZED FINANCIAL INSTITUTIONS

As indicated by the respective development strategies, agricultural production and the promotion of industries and African entrepreneurship are given high priority. Owing to the lack of substantial private capital, and the unacceptability of foreign financing in the cases of Tanzania and Somalia, the governments were obliged to search for alternative financing sources. A first measure, as we have seen, was to change the structure of the commercial banking systems so that their operations would be in accordance with the selected strategies. Another measure was to set up special financial institutions and to reorganize the operation of existing ones so as to provide the necessary funds for development. The special financial institutions operating in Eastern

Africa, their sources of finance, and their activities will now be discussed briefly.

Since independence, the Kenyan government has established six major development finance institutions to expand credit to the agricultural, industrial, and housing sectors. The specialized institutions, all established within the public sector, include the Agricultural Finance Corporation and the Agricultural Development Corporation; the Industrial and Commerce Development Corporation and the Development Finance Company of Kenya for industry; and the National Housing Corporation and the Housing Finance Company of Kenya, Ltd.

The most important institution dealing with agricultural financing in Kenya is the Agricultural Finance Corporation (AFC), established in 1963. The AFC serves the agricultural sector through a variety of lending programs that provide medium- and long-term credits to both the small and large farmers. It grants credit for the purchase of equipment and livestock, and since its merger with the Land and Agricultural Bank in 1969 it has also financed land purchases and improvements. The government provides most of the AFC's funds through capital subscription and long-term loans. As of the end of 1971, about 85 percent of its total resources (K£ 10.1 million) had come from the government, while the rest consisted of retained profits and current liabilities.

The Agricultural Development Corporation, established in 1965, is fully government-owned. Its primary function is to transfer large farms to Africans and to participate in commercial ventures in the agricultural sector. Most of the funds are therefore earmarked for specific purposes. For example, in 1972 about 50 percent of its resources (K£ 3.7 million) went to the land transfer program.

Among the specialized financial institutions engaged in promoting industries in collaboration with private domestic or foreign interests, the Industrial and Commercial Development Corporation (ICDC) is the largest. The first Industrial Development Corporation was established in 1954, but it was in 1964 that the ICDC was directed to facilitate the participation of Africans in industry and commerce. By equity participation, the extension of medium- and long-term loans, and the establishment of its own subsidiaries, the ICDC was to encourage industrialization in Kenya. The corporation relies on loans and grants from government (K£ 7.4 million at the end of 1972) and loans from foreign governments and institutions (K£ 1.2 million). Most loans have been small and have been issued to assist Africans in acquiring existing businesses or developing new ones. The ICDC also invests in plants and other facilities which are in turn leased to viable enterprises.

The Development Finance Company of Kenya (DFCK), established in 1963, is a subsidiary of ICDC, which holds 25 percent of its shares. Other shareholders are development corporations in Great Britain, West Germany, and Holland. The DFCK also promotes industrialization via equity participation and by providing medium- and long-term loans.

Specialized financial assistance to the building and construction sector is provided by the National Housing Corporation of Kenya, which was established in 1967 to replace a central housing board. Its original objective was to grant loans to local authorities for financing housing schemes. Recently, however, a large share of its operations have gone for construction of low-cost housing. Since 1965, direct mortgage lending has been offered by the Housing Finance Company of Kenya, Ltd. It offers financing both for new construction and for the purchase of existing housing. Both institutions rely on government loans and on loans from abroad, that is, from the Commonwealth Development Corporation.

Tanzania has also created specialized development finance institutions since independence. The specialized, public financial institutions include the National Development Credit Agency, concerned with agricultural loans; the National Development Corporation, responsible for industrial projects; and the Permanent Housing Company of Tanzania, which grants housing credits. More recently the Tanzanian government also established two development banks, the Tanzania Investment Bank (1970), which caters to the needs of industry, and the Tanzania Rural Development Bank (1971), which provides funds to the rural sector.

The National Development Credit Agency (NDCA), established in 1964, was to provide credit for agricultural production, marketing, and processing. In line with the emerging strategy of Tanzania, it was to use the cooperative movement as a channel for its funds, and gradually to discontinue all individual loans. The NDCA relied on government funds, even though it was supposed to mobilize private savings for direct employment in agricultural development. Besides government and parastatal deposits, the NDCA utilized domestic and international financial institution loans guaranteed by the government. In 1969, the NDCA loans outstanding were TSh 31.7 million, of which TSh 12.3 million were IDA loans re-lent. Other specialized institutions providing medium- and long-term finance to agricultural development include the Tanzania Rural Development Bank, established in 1971. The TRDB also utilizes funds from the government and international agencies.

The National Development Corporation (NDC) performs the functions of both an industrial development bank and a holding company. In 1964, the NDC started with TSh 34 million provided by the government. The corporation started taking an equity share of not less than 50 percent in all new companies it helped to established. However, after the Arusha Declaration it became an instrument of the government's policy to take over most of the large industrial enterprises. As of the end of 1971, the NDC held investments totaling TSh 1.5 billion in industrial enterprises including food production, textiles, mining, and chemicals. Though it has had a department that lent to these enterprises, intercompany borrowing was discontinued as of the end of 1971. The NDC thus remains more of an industrial holding company than an industrial development bank.

In 1970, however, the Tanzanian Investment Bank (TIB) was created. The TIB was to grant medium- and long-term loans to the expanding public-sector industries. It started operations with a paid capital of TSh 50 million, 60 percent of which was held by the Tanzanian government and the remainder by domestic financial institutions (the National Bank of Commerce and the National Insurance Corporation).

Specialized financial institutions for housing finance in Tanzania had existed for a number of years before independence. The Permanent Housing Finance Company of Tanzania, Ltd., which began operations in 1968, has the longest record. It started with TSh 1.2 million subscribed by the government and the Commonwealth Development Corporation. However, it raised the bulk of its resources from private depositors. Though it was expected to construct medium- to low-cost housing, its success was limited. As a result:

> The Permanent Housing Finance Company ceased to exist on 31 December 1972, and on 1 January 1973 was replaced by the New Tanzania Housing Bank. The new bank is trying to make good the worst shortcomings of its predecessor, to wit, its failure to finance enough low-cost houses, the rigidity of the mechanism of loan security, and the concentration of its activities in urban areas.[10]

Somalia's experience with specialized financial institutions is limited. The first development finance institution of any sort was the Development Loan Section of Credito Somalo, established on February 18, 1959, with an equity capital of So.Sh 1 million, wholly subscribed by the government. Other sources of funds included government loans, increases in equity participation, and a U.S. development loan of So.Sh 14.3 million. The Credito Somalo Development Loan Section was created to provide financing for agricultural and industrial production in the private sector. After exhausting its original resources, the institution was reorganized and replaced by the Somali Development Bank (SDB), jointly owned by the government and the Central Bank. The SDB is committed to promoting and financing viable development projects in the private and public sectors. As of the end of 1972, it held assets of So.Sh 33 million, of which about 57 percent were in development loans and a large share of the remainder in direct investments in enterprises. During 1972, the largest share of disbursed funds, loans as well as equity participation, was to industries (So.Sh 10.2 million) and to agriculture (So.Sh 5.5 million).

This list of specialized development finance institutions created since independence indicates that there were numerous efforts to facilitate the financing of priority sectors like agriculture, industry, and housing. (The list excludes the contribution of the regional and international development finance institutions in which the Eastern African countries participate.) The brief description nevertheless indicates as well the limitation of relying exclusively or predominantly on these financial institutions. Among such limitations are the large losses suffered by most of these institutions, which have resulted in frequent replacements and reorganizations. The general weaknesses of development finance institutions in these countries relate to both their sources of finance and the disbursal of loans.

The development finance institutions of Eastern Africa, almost without exception, rely on government contributions: equity subscription, long-term loans, and government-guaranteed loans from international institutions and foreign governments. The disadvantages of relying on such sources are evident in the size of each institution. As shown in Table 4.1, the leading development finance institutions were able to raise limited amounts of funds through government grants, loans, and guarantees. These institutions neither tap domestic capital markets, nor borrow directly from international sources. It should be obvious that such institutions are, therefore, in competition with direct govern-

TABLE 4.1

Summary of Accounts of the Leading Development Finance Institutions in Eastern Africa, 1973

	Kenya, ICDC (thousands of Kenyan pounds)	Tanzania (TIB) (millions of Tanzanian shillings)	Somalia (SDB) (millions of Somali shillings)
Current assets			
Cash, deposits	133	16.1	10.7
Development loans	7,274	86.8	50.0
Investments	5,017	1.8	4.9
Fixed and other assets	1,197	1.6	3.5
Total Assets = Total			
Liabilities	13,621	106.3	69.1
Current liabilities	196	1.1	9.2
Government loans	2,333	1.6	8.3
Other long-term loans	4,388	50.4	2.0
Grants and authorized			
capital	5,319	52.1	48.6
Retained earnings	1,385	1.1	1.0

Sources: Annual statements of the respective institutions, 1973.

ment development expenditures. As shown earlier, government development expenditures are not covered by domestic revenue mobilizations but are financed for the most part through external borrowing. Thus, only insofar as the projects financed by the development finance institutions are more productive or socially preferable to direct government investments would the development institutions matter to these economies.

Besides the constraints of the sources of funds, the specialized development institutions of Eastern Africa have shown some weaknesses in disbursing loans. These weaknesses have been attributed to deficiencies in project preparation, selection, and follow-up which have resulted in substantial bad debts. The experiences of the Tanzanian Investment Bank and the Credito Somalo in loan disbursements are instructive and by no means isolated. The management of both institutions clearly stated the difficulties faced in forming and financing development projects. The manager of the Tanzanian Investment Bank (TIB) stated that:

> The TIB operates in a difficult general setting, which impedes the chances both of accelerated industrial growth and of the bank's expansion, but which it can do little to alter. There is no organized capital market, the markets for industrial products are small . . . and investment opportunities are few and far in between.[11]

The director of the Development Loan Section of Credito Somalo was even more emphatic in attributing the unsatisfactory utilization of loans to:

> (1) lack of minimum understanding of what could be the stages through which any investment proposal should travel before it becomes eligible for obtaining financing facilities, (2) and lack of opportunity-seeking and risk-minded entrepreneurs.[12]

Finally, the operations of the specialized development finance institutions, despite their proliferation in both Kenya and Tanzania, are still small in comparison with the commercial banking systems. In the next chapter we will examine the operations of the commercial banks in the three economies since independence.

NOTES

1. Julius K. Nyerere, "Education for Self Reliance," *Ujamaa—Essays on Socialism* (Dar-es-Salaam: Oxford University Press, 1968), pp. 44–75. See also Nyerere, *Uhuru na Ujamaa—Freedom and Socialism* (Dar-es-Salaam: Oxford University Press, 1968), pp. 104–106.

2. TANU, *The Arusha Declaration and TANU's Policy on Socialism and Self-reliance* (Dar-es-Salaam, February 1967).

3. Ibid., p. 11.

4. W. Friedland and C. Rosenberg, *African Socialism* (Palo Alto: Stanford University Press, 1964).

5. Republic of Kenya Official Documents, *African Socialism and Its Application to Planning in Kenya* (Nairobi, 1965), p. 48.

6. Clara Caselli, *The Banking System of Tanzania* (Milan: Cassa di Risparmio delle Provincie Lombarde, 1975), p. 189.

7. United Republic of Tanzania, *Tanzania Second Five-Year Plan—1969–74* (Dar-es-Salaam: Government Printer, 1969), p. 216.

8. Nyerere, *Freedom and Socialism,* op. cit., pp. 233–34.

9. National Bank of Commerce, *Annual Report and Accounts,* 1971, p. 16.

10. Caselli, op. cit., p. 316.

11. C. Kahangi, "Tanzanian Investment Outlook," *Rasilimali,* January 1973, p. 16.

12. Mohamed O. Jama, "A Review of the Development Loan Section," *Somali National Bank Bulletin,* December 1965, p. 7.

5

EASTERN AFRICAN BANKING EXPERIENCE SINCE INDEPENDENCE

As we saw in Chapter 2, there are no generally accepted criteria to determine the contribution of financial institutions to economic development. However, the attempts to explain the role of financial institutions in industrialized market economies have emphasized their impact on the savings-investment process.[1] Furthermore, the few recent studies of financial institutions in developing economies have also emphasized their role in the mobilization of savings.[2] The occasional case study of total financial and monetary systems considers their impact on the balance of payments, and in particular on the foreign exchange reserve position. In developing countries, however, the more traditional line of inquiry has emphasized the impact of financial institutions, or certain types of financial institutions, on some specified sector of the economy, such as housing, subsistence agriculture, or industrial development.[3]

In evaluating the performances of the postindependence banking systems of Eastern Africa, I have adopted a set of criteria that extends and improves on these considerations. The primary concern of this book is with the role of commercial banks in the savings-investment process, and I have attempted to quantify the ability of these banks to mobilize domestics savings and to allocate them efficiently. I have also extended the analysis of past studies by introducing an evaluation of the role of the banks in eliminating the financial dualism that is prevalent in Eastern Africa as well as in many other developing countries. This last performance criterion, which depends on the process of monetizing these economies, is not of critical importance where there are no dual money markets.

The development of each Eastern African banking system, its actual allocation of existing savings, and "monetization" of the economy are discussed first. Each country's pre- and postindependence experiences are then briefly compared, and the performances of all three Eastern African banking systems are compared among themselves.

THE DEVELOPMENT OF BANKING INSTITUTIONS

In developing countries, banking institutions are the leading mechanism through which financial resources are transferred. The significance of bank liabilities as a vehicle of this transmission is not clear in financially developed economies, where they are one among an array of assets with nearly perfect substitutability. In financially developing economies, where financial holdings are limited to cash and bank liabilities, the growth of the latter takes on added importance. The development of the banking system is hence representative of the general development of the money and capital markets and of the success of this transfer operation.*

The development of the banking systems of Eastern Africa, and the development of financial institutions in general, may be measured in a number of ways. Most of the statistical measures suggested to test for the relative development of financial institutions, or a subsector thereof, in any economy are, in fact, complementary. As listed below, though, these measures all determine the relative size of the financial institutions with respect to the real sector of the economy.

The most generally accepted measure of financial development is the financial interrelations ratio (FIR), defined as the value of all financial assets in existence at one time divided by the value of all tangible assets, that is, national wealth.[4] Another measure is the ratio of financial instruments issued by financial institutions to those issued by nonfinancial units, which indicates the degree of the institutionalization of savings. Irrespective of the other shortcomings of these measures as indicators of financial development, it is obvious that they are not applicable to Eastern Africa. The financial interrelations ratio, for instance, assumes the existence of detailed accounts of not only the financial assets held but also the national wealth. Similarly, the measure of the "new issues" of financial institutions relative to those of other economic units assumes the existence of flow-of-funds accounts. Moreover, this indicator is of limited use in economies where the banking system's closest competitors are rural money lenders who keep no reliable records of new or old debt issues.

Most indicators of the development of financial institutions suggested in the literature are too broad for a study of commercial bank development. In this category other indicators, such as the financial ratio or the ratio of all financial assets to GNP, a slight modification of the FIR, are also included.

---

*The existence in Kenya of other financial institutions, some government securities and even a stock exchange, where a few corporate shares are traded, should be acknowledged. The existing financial assets outside the banking systems, however, are negligible. The second largest deposit institutions are the post office savings banks, which in 1972 held 3.2 percent of the bank deposits in Kenya and 2.1 percent in Tanzania.

Accordingly, to evaluate the effectiveness of the banks in mobilizing savings, I have limited the scope of these standard indicators of financial development, refined them, and introduced other appropriate indicators where necessary.

The level of development of the banking systems is indicated by the "banking ratio," or the ratio of total bank liabilities (assets) to GNP. As an indicator of the rate of growth of the banking systems over a period, I have used the net changes in the value of total bank liabilities (assets) divided by GNP. The banking ratio may be flawed in the case of financially mature economies, where a shift in asset holders' preferences may determine the size of the banking system relative to other financial intermediaries. Such a redistribution, however, is negligible in economies where the banking system for all purposes *is* the financial system. Thus, in the Eastern African economies, this ratio closely approximates the financial ratio of developed economies.

Other indicators of the operational effectiveness of the banking systems furnish more detailed measures of the relative institutionalization of savings in the Eastern African economies. We use the ratios of bank deposit liabilities (demand and time deposits) to total money supply (DD/M and TD/M), narrowly defined, as indicators of the level of savings channeled through the banking systems. These indicators are of further interest in that they are considered reliable measures of confidence in deposit banks in developing economies. In utilizing these complementary indicators (DD/M and TD/M), we are also concerned with the actual distribution of bank liabilities between short- and medium- or longer-term deposits. Also, one could get a distorted picture of banking growth if reliance were placed on either of these two measures; indeed, they could be moving in opposite directions as the changed preferences of depositors substitute one for the other.

Banking Growth in Kenya (1964–73), Tanzania (1962–73), and Somalia (1960–73)

The rates of growth of the Eastern African banking systems since independence have been uneven for each country over the period, and among the three countries. A common feature of all three countries' banking systems, however, is their low level of development at independence and in the early 1970s. This can best be illustrated by comparison with the development of other banking systems, in both developed and developing economies. Before such a comparative analysis is undertaken, in Chapter 6, some of the basic characteristics of the Eastern African banking systems during this period must be underscored.

The Kenyan banking system, despite some reversals attributed to a shift in the composition of the clientele and to the break-up of the East African currency union, has shown a moderate rate of growth during the 1964–73 period. At independence, the Kenyan banking system was more advanced than those of the other Eastern African countries. As a result of the formation of the separate national banking systems in the East African Community member countries in 1965–66, liabilities of the Kenyan banking system either declined or showed no substantial growth up to 1969. Thus, in 1966, total bank liabilities registered a net reduction amounting to 1.6 million K£. The annual rates of growth in the years following the break-up were substantially lower than the average annual growth rates of the last colonial decade. The Kenyan banking system, however, survived this early shock and showed an average growth rate of about 4.5 percent for the first nine years after independence.

As shown in Table 5.1, the Kenyan banking system has been more successful in attracting savings and time deposits. While the ratio of demand deposits to money supply, narrowly defined, remained at about 70 percent, savings and time deposits increased from 39 percent to 57 percent of the money supply. The higher growth of the term deposits is partially attributable to the shift in the composition of depositors. Before independence and up to the first few years of independence, the deposit holders were predominantly expatriates. In more recent years, however, a large number of urban Africans has replaced these expatriate deposit holders. Also, as the majority of Africans held savings deposits with the post office savings banks, and even with the commercial banks, an increase in their numbers may explain the higher growth rate of term deposits as compared to that of demand deposits.

Despite the impact of the creation of independent monetary authorities in East Africa, which shifted funds from Nairobi to Kampala and Dar-es-Salaam, and the net effect of independence, which may have shifted the composition of deposit holders, the Kenyan banking system grew faster than the gross national product. Thus, the total liabilities of the banking system as a percentage of GNP rose from 25.7 in 1964 to 43.4 in 1973. The determinants of the mobilized savings and the relative success of Kenya in comparison with other developing countries outside Eastern Africa, at the same levels of development, are taken up in Chapter 6.

The rate of development of the commercial banks of Tanzania since 1962, the first full year of independence, has been less than spectacular (see Table 5.2). The total bank liabilities as a percentage of GNP (the banking ratio) averaged 20.8 percent between 1962 and 1973. The annual changes in bank liabilities as a proportion of GNP did not exceed 5.6 percent and declined by 0.4 percent when the commercial banks were nationalized in 1967. The percentage of demand deposits in the money stock fluctuated from as high as 69 percent in 1969 to as low as 51 percent in 1972; it averaged about 58 percent through the period. Using this indicator as the barometer of confidence in the banking system, it would seem that bank utilization did not change substantially between 1962 and 1973. Except for demand deposits held, all indicators

TABLE 5.1

Commercial Bank Growth in Kenya, 1964-73
(millions of Kenyan pounds)

End of Year	Demand Deposits	Time and Savings Deposits	Total Liabilities	Money Supply (M$_1$)	GNP	Total Liability as Percentage of GNP	Change in Total Bank Liabilities as Percentage of GNP	Demand Deposits as Percentage of Money Supply (M$_1$)	Time and Savings Deposits as Percentage of Money Supply (M$_1$)
1964	48.5	16.5	90.5	—	352.0	25.7	—	—	—
1965	50.2	19.4	109.3	—	351.0	31.1	.054	—	—
1966*	49.8	27.6	107.7	70.2	409.0	26.3	-.004	70.9	39.3
1967	51.2	33.9	119.1	73.9	432.0	27.6	.026	69.3	45.9
1968	56.2	39.2	121.4	80.8	459.0	28.6	.027	69.6	48.5
1969	64.4	48.5	161.1	93.4	511.1	31.5	.058	69.0	51.9
1970	80.3	65.9	199.0	115.6	613.5	32.4	.061	69.5	57.0
1971	86.6	72.7	225.6	124.0	632.9	35.6	.042	69.8	58.6
1972	99.7	77.6	252.6	144.8	690.1	36.6	.039	68.9	53.6
1973	127.8	100.2	334.2	177.3	770.9	43.4	.106	72.1	56.5
1964-73 (average)	—	—	—	—	—	35.4	.045	69.9	51.4

*In 1966 the services of the East African Currency Board were terminated, and Kenyan, Tanzanian, and Ugandan central banks were created.
Source: Central Bank of Kenya, *Economic and Financial Review*, various issues.

TABLE 5.2

Commercial Bank Growth in Tanzania, 1962-73
(millions of Tanzanian shillings)

End of Period	Demand Deposits	Time and Savings Deposits	Total Liabilities	Money Supply (M₁)	GNP	Total Liability as Percentage of GNP	Change in Total Bank Liabilities as Percentage of GNP	Demand Deposits as Percentage of Money Supply (M₁)	Time and Savings Deposits as Percentage of Money Supply (M₁)
1962	484	157	691	828	4,392	15.7	.013	58.5	18.9
1963	498	205	754	898	4,860	15.5	.013	55.5	22.8
1964	564	191	911	980	6,017	15.2	.026	57.6	19.5
1965	663	235	1,009	1,043	6,141	16.4	.016	63.5	22.5
1966a	622	306	1,328	889	6,984	19.0	.046	69.9	34.4
1967b	680	353	1,297	1,192	7,398	17.5	-.004	57.1	29.6
1968	769	520	1,559	1,297	8,047	19.4	.036	59.2	40.1
1969	932	664	1,958	1,537	8,332	23.5	.048	60.0	43.2
1970	980	829	2,219	1,799	9,125	24.3	.029	54.5	46.1
1971	1,192	1,011	2,761	2,179	9,749	28.3	.056	54.7	46.4
1972	1,258	1,232	3,063	2,459	11,252	27.2	.027	51.2	50.1
1973	1,662	1,358	3,556	2,861	13,107	27.1	.038	58.1	47.5
1962-66 (average)	–	–	–	–	–	16.4	.025	60.9	23.6
1967-73 (average)	–	–	–	–	–	23.9	.033	56.4	43.3
1962-73 (average)	–	–	–	–	–	20.8	.030	58.3	35.1

ᵃMoney supply statistics up to 1966 are not separately available for any of the East Africa Currency Board member countries. The currency portion is based on the redemption of EACB currency by the Bank of Tanzania, which was 38 percent.

ᵇThe commercial banks in Tanzania, with the exception of two previously public-owned institutions, were nationalized in February 1967.

Source: Bank of Tanzania, *Economic Bulletin*, various issues.

show that the increase in bank liabilities, annual growth rates, and savings mobilization through term deposits were higher for the post-1967 years.

The Tanzanian banks, especially in the postnationalization period, have been more successful in encouraging medium- to long-term savings. Such savings were very small at independence, under 20 percent of the money stock. They have grown at a substantial pace since, to the extent that about equal amounts of demand and term deposits were held with the banks in the early 1970s. These expanded savings deposits not only demonstrate the increased confidence that could not be discerned unambiguously from changes in demand deposits held, but are also preferable in terms of the banks' developmental impact. The increase in term deposits allows the banks an added flexibility to lend for purposes other than working capital and short-term, self-liquidating commercial transactions. Further attention should be directed to the expansion in term deposits in Tanzania, as it is the only component of the bank liabilities that is subject to discretionary policies. As the demand deposits are held primarily for transactions needs and only secondarily as a portfolio asset, the monetary authorities or the banks themselves have a more direct influence on what happens to these savings deposits.

The increase in term deposits, particularly since nationalization, reflects the attempts of the National Bank of Commerce, which has instituted intra-branch savings accounts competition "with the aim of providing an added booster to the savings mobilization effort. The Bank has also recently established a deposit promotion decision in order to propagate 'financial education' to the masses as a means of promoting [the] savings habit and as a way of soliciting hoarded money into the banking system."[5]

The development of the banking system of Somalia between 1960 and 1969 has been the least impressive among the three systems (see Table 5.3). Even allowing for the relatively low levels they started from at independence, the commercial banks have not shown any significant growth. The four expatriate banks operating in Somalia have shown little interest in expanding their facilities behond the coastal establishments of 30 years back. The limited increase in bank liabilities may thus be attributed to the development of the commercial banking branch of the Somali National Bank. Within the decade, it had surpassed the four other banks combined in facilities and in deposits held.

The financial development indicators available for Somalia also demonstrate this stagnant financial position, if one can separately account for the increased savings with the "new" commercial bank. The proportion of the money stock held in the form of demand deposits decreased from 48.3 percent in 1960 to 43.6 percent in 1969. The lowest ratio (36.6 percent) was attained in 1970, when the expatriate banks were nationalized. In 1973, the level of demand deposits as a proportion of money supply did not even approach its preindependence levels.

TABLE 5.3

Commercial Bank Growth in Somalia, 1960-73
(millions of Somali shillings)

Year	Demand Deposits	Time and Savings Deposits	Money Supply (M_1)	Demand Deposits as Percentage of Money Supply (M_1)	Time and Savings Deposits as Percentage of Money Supply (M_1)
1960	45.7	12.2	94.7	48.3	12.9
1961	70.6	17.8	150.7	46.8	11.8
1962	81.4	20.8	165.3	49.2	12.6
1963	96.2	24.6	198.0	48.6	12.4
1964	89.9	27.6	196.4	45.8	14.1
1965	96.0	29.1	191.5	50.1	15.2
1966	84.0	30.4	202.0	41.6	15.1
1967	97.8	37.2	225.2	43.4	16.5
1968	110.1	45.1	250.8	43.9	17.9
1969	122.0	47.6	279.7	43.6	17.0
1970*	114.9	50.2	314.2	36.6	16.0
1971	154.4	57.9	333.9	46.2	17.3
1972	176.4	77.2	440.5	40.0	17.5
1973	219.3	100.8	507.0	43.3	19.9
1960-69	–	–	–	46.1	14.6
1970-73	–	–	–	41.5	17.7

*The private commercial banks operating in Somalia in 1970 were nationalized and replaced by the Somali Commercial Bank and the Saving and Credit Bank of Somalia, both wholly government-owned.

Source: Somali National Bank Bulletin, various issues.

The rate of growth of time and saving deposits has not known much growth either, in the first eight years. Again the primary jump occurred after 1970, or after nationalization, as was the case with the Tanzanian nationalization. The short duration of public control of the Somali commercial banks, however, prevents its inclusion in comparing the relative merits of private and public ownership of banks in developing economies. Thus, our evaluation of the commercial banks of Somalia will refer to the first decade of independence, 1960–69, and the private commercial banking system.

THE ALLOCATION OF FINANCIAL RESOURCES

The ability of banking systems to stimulate new savings and to attract existing amounts from alternative uses (cash or commodity holdings) is considered an appropriate indicator of their contribution to economic growth. However, the impact of the banks on the direction and levels of economic growth depends crucially on their allocation of the financial resources thus mobilized. Invariably the proponents of the financial development hypotheses subscribe to the critical importance of this transmission of the economic surplus to alternative uses. The assumption leading to the critical role assigned to this transmission process is that the banks (financial intermediaries) allocate scarce financial resources to the most productive uses.[6] In economies where direct securities placement is not feasible, and where financial intermediation is not sufficiently advanced, the resulting system for the allocation of funds is considered inefficient.[7] Despite the traditional emphasis on the efficiency of financial institutions in allociting savings to their most productive uses, there are some conditions under which major qualifications are required, particularly in developing economies. Some of these limitations are explored in the evaluation of the alternative hypotheses of financial development (Chapter 6).

The next few paragraphs summarize some of the major questions posed about the assumption that banks' allocation of funds is necessarily the most efficient. Among these are whether the allocation of financial resources and the inherent transfer of real resources are based on market criteria, whether the market allocation is the most efficient in development terms, and whether private marginal productivity and social productivity criteria coincide.

Among the possible reasons a banking system's allocation of savings may be inefficient is that market criteria alone do not determine bank portfolio composition. In the ordering of loan applications, subjective judgments may be substituted for an objective evaluation of risks and returns. Looking at some specific cases, the primary reason given by the authorities of developing countries for disenchantment with private commercial banks is that they are biased against one sector of the economy or one segment of the population. An extreme form of this subjective ordering was attributed to the colonial commercial banks of Eastern Africa, which for a substantial period did not grant any loans to indigenous enterprises. Other institutional constraints of the market process include the types of assets acceptable for collateral, which may be based on convenience or familiarity rather than critical evaluation of risk insurance. In a comment on the preindependence East African banks, Engberg concludes that "they have tended to insist on credit standards which few indigenous enterprises—agricultural, commercial, or industrial—are able to reach, and to demand collateral which is often non-existent." He continues that traditional conventions are unquestionably inadequate if the banks are to make a more positive contribution to economic development.[8]

A more serious objection to assuming efficient allocation of bank assets is based on possible shortcomings of the market allocative mechanism. Such a limitation is attributed to imperfections in the input markets or fragmentations of the output markets, to name but two of the distortions that can result in inefficient allocation. Once the existence of these or similar distortions in developing economies is granted, irrespective of their causes, bank allocation efficiency is dubious at best. In such a distorted market, prevailing prices would not normally signal those sectors which are most productive. Credit allocation by the banking system on the basis of distorted prices would aggravate the initial misallocation of real resources.

Another serious limitation of market allocation of bank assets is the possible divergence between private and social costs and benefits. The banks pursue private benefit maximization, which may not coincide with social benefits. Such a lack of coincidence could result from market imperfections, but it could be attributed to other factors as well: for example, financial institutions may be greater risk avoiders than is socially desirable. Some specific results relevant to the Eastern African experiences are due to unexploited economic externalities and worsening income distribution inequalities. The bank portfolio managers, in choosing the assets with the highest private yield, underestimate the social returns by the amount of the existing external economies. In evaluating new productive investments, the banks' criteria do not include benefits accruing to other enterprises as a result of interdependences and labor skill improvements. The magnitude of these externalities at firm or industry levels may not be explicitly estimated. However, a bank's portfolio, disregarding such externalities, is not likely to be the most socially productive allocation of resources. Furthermore, in the pursuit of the portfolio with the highest yield, the banks may perpetuate, if not aggravate, inequalities in the distribution of income. In their risk minimization, the banks favor firms and entrepreneurs with an initially "healthy" financial position; in both the granting of new credits and the retirement of outstanding loans, the victims are often the small and aspiring enterprises.

In Eastern Africa, income distribution inequities are compounded by the ownership of the major production units by the expatriate communities, so that the indigenous African population, primarily subsistence farmers and small merchants, has not had equal access to bank facilities. To ameliorate the disparities between expatriate and indigenous population earnings, a number of African countries have introduced portfolio ceilings or other forms of restrictions on credit to some sectors of these economies, or specifically to non-African enterprises.[9] Thus, if explicit public policies set an equitable income distribution goals, as has been done in the Eastern African countries, the private optimal allocation of bank resources could have undesirable results.

The allocation efficiency criteria I have used in evaluating the performances of the Eastern African banks are distinct from the conventional "market optimality" criteria. The basic test here of the banks' allocational performances in the postindependence period is their ability to finance credit needs of the development priority sectors of these economies as determined by the contribution of such sectors to economic growth and social equity. According to the strategies of development of the respective economies, the bank credits were to be increased for those sectors of the economies considered essential for growth and social equity and to be limited for sectors considered less essential. Therefore, adjustments in the banks' portfolios in conformance with the development plans and strategies of these economies will be considered indicative of their performance.

Among the basic objectives implicit in the development strategies of postindependence Eastern Africa was that deliberate efforts were to be made to improve the relative position of indigenous entrepreneurs via the allocation of a higher share of bank credit to firms under their control. Furthermore, bank credits were to be diverted to specified sectors of these economies, such as industries in Kenya and cooperative agriculture in Tanzania.

The purpose of this section is, therefore, to determine whether any changes have occurred since independence in the composition of the Eastern African banks' portfolios. A further concern is to ascertain the changes, if any, that were consistent with the development strategies of the respective economies. Any evidence that may illustrate a continuation of earlier bank lending practices or changes in bank lending policies will also be recorded. Analysis of any changes will be undertaken in the next chapter.

Analysis of Bank Assets Allocations in Kenya (1965–73), Tanzania (1964–73), and Somalia (1960–72)

At the gross level of aggregation of the data as presented in Tables 5.4–5.6, definitive judgments cannot be made about how well the Eastern African banks have allocated their loans and advances with respect to each country's development priorities. It is especially difficult to evaluate the responsiveness of the banks to indigenous entrepreneurs since independence, as no estimates or actual data are available on credit distribution according to final users. The same inadequacy of relevant data limits analysis of bank assets allocation according to maturity or the type of securities or collateral requested. However, except for Tanzania after 1967 and Somalia after 1969, we will not question the traditional view that commerce, both internal and external, and the major productive industries of the region were controlled by local minority interests or by expatriates. In this view, credit to the productive agricultural sector, within which the overwhelming majority of the indigenous population is occupied, is considered essential for both growth and social equity, the twin objectives of the development strategies of these countries. Also, in the priorities of the development strategy of Kenya, credit to the industrial sector, irrespective of ownership, is rated essential.

In evaluating allocation and each system's performance, I first examine the aggregate data of bank assets and credit distribution of the three countries, reaching some general conclusions. Then where the data permit, as in the cases of Kenya and Tanzania, the distribution of bank loans, advances, and bills discounted by economic sector is explored. First, the overall assets allocation is classified into cash and liquid assets, loans and advances, and other assets. Once the magnitudes and trends of each system's loans and advances are obtained, such loans are further subdivided. The four major sectors of economic activity considered initially are agriculture, industry or manufacturing, trade, and other sectors (including transportation, construction, and private households).

In the postindependence period for which uniform and reliable data are available, the composition of the portfolio of Kenya's commercial banking system changed only moderately. In the period 1965–73, substantial liquid assets were maintained (which averaged about 24 percent of deposits), and other investments increased by almost the same amount as loans and advances. As presented in Table 5.4, total loans and advances more than doubled in this period. The largest expansion occurred in loans to private households and other business (31 million K£), loans to manufacturing (22 million K£), and trade (19 million K£). Among the major sectors categorized, the lowest expansion was in the share of agricultural credit (10 million K£). It is especially noteworthy that the share of agriculture in total loans never exceeded the 12 percent attained in 1969, while its contribution to GDP over the 1965–73 period averaged about 40 percent. However, industrial production, the other priority sector, increased its relative position within the period. The share of loans and advances to the manufacturing sector expanded from 10 percent to 18 percent between 1965 and 1973. Nevertheless, throughout most of the period trade accounted for more than the total shares of agriculture and industry combined. Despite an uneven but declining trend in the trade loans as a percentage of total credits, it remained the single most important component in the distribution of bank credits in Kenya.

The Tanzanian commercial banking system, as shown in Table 5.5, expanded substantially its liquid asset holdings as well as its total credits to the major economic sectors. Loans, advances, and bills discounted increased from TSh 600 million in 1964 to about TSh 1,821 million in 1973. At this gross level of aggregation, estimation of the actual distribution of loans according to the major priority sectors is not feasible. Nevertheless, agricultural production fared well in the allocation of Tanzanian bank credits; 38 percent of the increase in credits went to this sector. Trade received 34 percent, and manufacturing and mining, 25 percent. As discussed shortly, however, not all the

TABLE 5.4

Kenya: Commercial Bank Assets and Allocation of Loans and Advances by Economic Sector, 1965-73
(millions of Kenyan pounds)

	1965	1966	1967	1968	1969	1970	1971	1972	1973	Change, 1965-73
Cash and other liquid assets	20.8	16.7	15.7	22.3	37.2	44.2	31.0	39.1	50.5	29.7
Loans, advances, and bills discounted	57.6	55.5	68.0	66.8	70.0	86.9	120.1	121.4	161.4	103.8
Agriculture	(7.0)	(6.3)	(6.6)	(7.8)	(8.6)	(9.3)	(12.6)	(12.0)	(17.8)	(10.8)
Manufacturing	(5.9)	(8.3)	(12.2)	(12.7)	(15.1)	(15.6)	(24.8)	(24.3)	(27.9)	(22.0)
Trade	(22.2)	(23.0)	(30.6)	(28.2)	(26.1)	(33.8)	(38.5)	(33.9)	(40.7)	(18.5)
Other	(22.5)	(17.9)	(18.6)	(18.1)	(20.2)	(28.2)	(44.2)	(51.2)	(75.0)	(52.5)
of which: other buisness and private households*	8.7	10.5	9.1	8.5	9.9	14.1	22.9	27.7	40.3	31.7
Investments and other assets	30.8	35.5	35.4	42.4	54.0	67.8	74.4	92.1	122.0	91.2
										Average
Total loans as percentage of total deposits	82.8	71.7	79.9	70.0	62.0	59.4	75.4	68.5	70.8	71.2
Liquid assets as percentage of total deposits	29.9	21.6	18.6	23.4	32.9	30.2	19.5	22.1	22.1	24.4
Trade loans as percentage of total loans	38.5	41.4	45.0	42.2	37.3	38.9	32.1	27.9	25.2	36.5

*This category also includes loans to the public sector, to transportation, and to other financial institutions. For further breakdown see Table 5.8.
Source: Central Bank of Kenya, Economic and Financial Review, various issues.

TABLE 5.5

Tanzania: Commercial Bank Assets and Domestic Lending by Economic Sector, 1964-73
(millions of Tanzanian shillings)

	1964	1965	1966	1967	1968	1969	1970	1971	1972	1973	Change, 1964-73
Cash and other liquid assets	–	–	182	212	347	525	555	935	1,212	1,388	1,211
Loans, advances and bills discounted	610	702	848	818	899	1,093	1,347	1,505	1,549	1,821	
Agriculture	(194)	(278)	(318)	(293)	(293)	(380)	(452)	(479)	(628)	(657)	463
Manufacturing and mining	(55)	(65)	(100)	(115)	(142)	(196)	(214)	(233)	(258)	(360)	305
Trade	(168)	(254)	(313)	(285)	(338)	(368)	(495)	(600)	(442)	(584)	416
Other	(193)	(105)	(117)	(125)	(126)	(149)	(186)	(193)	(223)	(220)	27
of which: construction and transportation*	–	–	–	36	57	59	81	68	73	76	
Investments and other assets	–	–	348	268	313	340	318	321	302	347	
											Average
Total loans as percent of total domestic deposits	80.7	78.2	92.0	79.2	69.7	68.5	74.5	68.3	62.2	60.6	73.4
Liquid assets as percent of total domestic deposits	–	–	19.7	20.9	27.5	33.4	31.1	43.3	50.0	47.0	34.1
Trade loans as percent of total loans	27.5	36.2	36.9	34.8	37.6	33.7	36.7	39.9	28.5	32.1	34.4

*For a breakdown of loans included in "other" category, see Table 5.7.
Source: Bank of Tanzania, Economic Bulletin, various issues (annual).

increase in agricultural credits went to agricultural production and hence to a priority category.

The experiences of Somalia (1960–72) in the expansion of bank credits were, in fact, the most phenomenal. Starting originally from a lower base (So.Sh 31 million in 1960), it reached a high of So.Sh 403 million in 1972. In fact, credits allocated to each branch of economic activity increased sixfold or more. However, more than 70 percent of the expansion in bank loans and advances (So.Sh 264 million) was allocated to trade, while agriculture's share accounted for only 11 percent; the remainder was divided between industry and crafts, and other loans.

The experiences of Somalia, though in some ways unique, point to the prominent position of short-term commercial loans and advances in the asset portfolios of the Eastern African commercial banks. In Somalia the banks

TABLE 5.6

Somalia: Commercial Bank Loans to the Private Sector by Branch of Economic Activity
(millions of Somali shillings)

Period	Total Loans	Agri-culture	Industry and Crafts	Trade	Other Loans	Loans as Percentage of Total Deposits	Trade loans as Percentage of Total Loans
1960	31.2	4.5	6.6	17.5	2.6	153.9	56.1
1961	42.5	4.5	6.2	27.1	4.7	48.1	63.8
1962	75.7	8.3	10.5	48.8	8.2	74.1	64.5
1963	90.0	5.3	13.6	50.4	20.7	74.5	56.0
1964	142.5	7.6	19.4	94.5	21.0	121.3	66.3
1965	159.8	13.9	23.9	95.0	27.0	127.7	59.4
1966	169.1	20.6	26.2	105.3	17.0	147.8	62.3
1967	191.0	22.4	37.2	113.5	17.8	141.5	59.4
1968	213.5	28.1	45.8	117.0	22.5	137.6	54.8
1969	237.0	22.2	62.8	115.8	36.1	139.7	48.9
1970	250.6	9.1	53.2	166.0	22.3	151.8	66.2
1971	297.4	18.3	69.0	181.2	28.9	140.0	60.9
1972	403.1	46.1	48.2	281.6	27.2	161.9	69.9
Change, 1960-72	371.9	41.6	41.6	264.1	24.6	–	–

Source: *Somali National Bank Bulletin*, various issues, 1972 and 1973.

allocated about two-thirds of their loans and advances to trade, and not less than 49 percent each year, averaging about 60 percent in the period 1960–72. The average ratios were lower for Kenya and Tanzania in the postindependence period, yet there too the largest component of bank loans and advances remained short-term, self-liquidating commercial loans.

Bank Credits Allocation and Development Priorities in Kenya and Tanzania

The above presentation of bank portfolio composition indicates the broad trends of sectoral credit distribution in Eastern Africa. To offer a more detailed picture of the credit allocation, I will now present the bank loans and advances according to industrial use, subject to the constraints of data availability and completeness.* Detailed analysis of bank credit allocation in Eastern Africa is limited by lack of specific credit allocation targets during the initial years of independence and the absence of specific financial planning for the postindependence period.[10] Though there were no specific financial plans, the development strategies of the Kenyan and Tanzanian authorities set general guidelines for the direction of bank credit. The objectives of the Kenyan and Tanzanian strategies do not set any magnitude shifts of bank credit allocation, but the direction of the shifts is dictated by the development priorities set. Any increases in credits to the development priority sectors of the respective economies (small-holder agriculture in Tanzania and Kenyan industrial enterprises) is considered favorable. Simultaneously, any absolute or relative decline in the share of trade credits in the bank portfolio will be considered to improve the allocative efficiency of the Eastern African banks. Such ordinal ranking of the loans to economic sectors or industries is based on what the respective development strategies consider "essential" and "less essential" for development and social equity.

The essential and less essential categories of loans and advances are reflected by the relative priority assigned to the recipient sector in these economies. Primary among the sectoral loans that were considered less essential are trade loans. It is evident that not all trade credits are less essential, since imports of capital goods and development of export commodities are considered necessary for the transformation of the Eastern African economies. As noted, however, the development strategy of each economy was to emphasize

---

*Detailed statistics on commercial bank loans by industry were found only for Kenya and Tanzania in the post-1967 period. For Somalia, the National Commercial Bank has made available some detailed records covering the first 18 months of its operations (January 1975–June 1976).

self-reliance and reduce dependence on imported capital goods and exports of raw products. Furthermore, the share of capital goods in total imports is so small that all trade credits are included in the less essential category. Other credits considered less essential within these criteria include the financing of buildings and construction, which is undertaken mostly by the private sector, other loans directed to households for consumption purposes, and loans to public administration entities.

Though no "essential sectors" list, as given here, has been decreed, the commercial banks have been instructed as to the sectors to which they should give priority in their loan distribution. In discussing the operational guidelines of the National Bank of Commerce, Tanzania, the chairman stated that although the usual commercial lending principles, such as analysis of the borrower's resources and liabilities and the purpose of the loan, are applied, the bank must go beyond the orthodox type of lending and be guided by the country's plan:

> This shift of emphasis from the orthodox types of lending is also evident in the areas and sectors that we give priority to when lending. We seek to give priority, where the criteria are met, to Tanzania's indigenous institutions, business promoting exports, industries providing employment [and] import substituting industries. We also give priority on rather premium terms, to those geographical areas which are economically still lagging behind.[11]

The commercial banking system of Kenya has also been instructed as to those sectors considered essential. Numerous Central Bank credit policy statements refer to the necessity of shifting loans from trade to the productive sectors of the economy (agriculture and industry), and of increasing their lending to African borrowers. Thus, in 1971 the commercial banks were instructed to reduce the amount of credit provided for the purchase of consumer durables and to switch credit from the import sector to the domestic production sector of the economy in agriculture and manufacturing.[12] Most of these institutions, however, do not set the magnitude of the required shifts or reductions.

Table 5.7 presents the distribution of Tanzanian commercial bank credits by industry, classified as essential and less essential. Those classified as essential, based on the objective priorities of the authorities and their policy statements, include all agricultural production and marketing loans; mining, manufacturing, and transportation loans; and loans to other financial institutions. A survey of Tanzanian commercial bank credit distribution after 1967 indicates a steady increase in loans and advances to the essential categories. Loans and advances to essential sectors have increased from TSh 427 million in 1967 to TSh 1,139 million in 1973; while in the same period, less essential categories have expanded from TSh 391 to TSh 682 million. Within the period,

TABLE 5.7

Tanzania: Commercial Bank Domestic Lending by Industrial Sector, 1967-73
(millions of Tanzanian shillings)

	1967	1968	1969	1970	1971	1972	1973
Total loans and advances	818.1	898.6	1,092.6	1,347.1	1,504.6	1,548.6	1,820.9
Public sector loans, of which:	77.9	153.4	326.0	713.0	984.0	919.5	1,078.0
Government	(4.0)	(5.6)	(3.3)	(2.8)	(2.4)	(1.9)	(1.9)
Agriculture*	293.0	292.5	380.3	452.0	478.9	627.7	656.6
Production	102.1	99.5	109.6	171.6	81.3	96.2	88.4
Marketing	190.9	193.0	270.7	280.4	397.6	531.5	568.1
Mining and manufacturing*	114.8	142.0	196.1	214.1	223.0	255.5	360.4
Trade	285.2	337.6	367.7	495.1	599.7	441.6	584.3
Export	148.4	159.2	141.2	138.8	107.2	115.0	69.3
Other	136.8	178.4	226.5	356.3	492.5	326.6	515.0
Building and construction	25.2	41.3	40.8	35.6	27.9	31.1	35.8
Transportation*	10.4	15.6	18.5	45.3	40.3	41.6	40.3
Financial institutions*	9.0	8.2	21.3	31.7	74.7	68.2	81.3
Other (including private households)	76.5	55.8	64.6	70.5	57.7	81.4	60.4
"Essential" loans and advances	427.2	458.3	616.2	743.1	816.9	993.0	1,138.5
"Less essential" loans and advances	390.9	440.3	476.4	604.0	687.7	555.9	682.4
"Essential" loans as percentage of total loans	(52.2)	(51.0)	(56.4)	(55.2)	(54.3)	(64.1)	(62.5)
Public-sector loans as percentage of total loans	(9.5)	(15.5)	(29.8)	(52.9)	(65.4)	(59.4)	(59.2)

*"Essential" categories.
Source: Bank of Tanzania, Economic Bulletin, various issues.

credits to the essential categories have increased from 52 percent to 63 percent of total loans.

Looking at the relatively large gains in essential category credits, one might conclude that the Tanzanian authorities have succeeded somewhat in reorienting commercial bank lending policies in accordance with their development objectives. However, further scrutiny shows that agricultural production and, through it, rural development—the sector allotted the highest priority in the Tanzanian strategy—did not receive any emphasis in bank credit allocation. Though agricultural production loans demonstrated wide fluctuations from year to year, there was an actual decline (from TSh 102 million in 1967 to TSh 88 million in 1973) within the period. Furthermore, it is evident that the largest increase in the essential loan and advance categories has been in agricultural marketing, which steadily increased from TSh 191 million to TSh 568 million within the seven years ended in 1973. Inasmuch as such credits were used to encourage the commercialization of *Ujamaa* villages and small-holder agricultural production, they will be considered essential. These loans could easily have been used by state trading and other marketing boards at the local or national level and with limited benefits to the small producers.

Credits to the mining and manufacturing industries, which are primarily directed to the latter since the mining sector is relatively small and not dependent on commercial bank credits, more than doubled. With the credits granted indirectly through other financial institutions, the total outlays to manufacturing increased from TSh 124 million in 1967 to TSh 442 million in 1973.* Because of the small base from which the loans to manufacturing industries started, the steady increase in the credits allocated to this sector, particularly the share granted to small or traditional cottage industries, is in accordance with the development priorities of Tanzania. Unlike the credits to agricultural production, the statistical evidence demonstrates unambiguously that the small but growing industrial sector of Tanzania in the period since bank nationalization has been accommodated, as the rate of growth of credit to this sector was higher than the increase in its relative contribution to GDP during the period.

With the exception of export loans and advances, credits to trade and other less essential categories, including construction and other household loans, increased substantially. Credits to exports within the period 1967–73 declined by TSh 79 million, while loans to all other trade increased by TSh

---

*Since the other financial institutions that receive credits from the commercial banks of Tanzania are specialized development institutions, particularly the Tanzania Investment Bank (TIB), I incorporated these credits in loans to manufacturing enterprises.

389 million. Over the period the rate of increase in all trade credits was about 100 percent, while that of the other components of the less essential loans was more modest; hence the decline in the relative share of less essential loans and advances in total bank credit, from 48 percent to 37 percent. In the first five years, however, the shift of bank credit distribution from less essential categories was neither continuous nor sharp.

Table 5.8 sets out the credit allocation by the Kenyan commercial banks for the period 1967–73, as classified between essential and less essential loans and advances. Essential credits, which exclude all trade and household credits as well as private building and public-sector loans, increased their share of the total only marginally (from 35 percent to 38 percent) over the period. The essential categories were allocated 38 million K£ of the total credit expansion of 93 million K£. Furthermore, a breakdown of the loans and advances to essential categories indicates that most of the growth occurred in industrial sector loans (16 million K£). A further 8 million K£ credit extension to financial institutions may be added to the share of the industrial sector, considering that the overwhelming portion of other financial institutions' credit was directed to industrial enterprises. A substantial increase was also made to the agricultural sector, inclusive of agricultural marketing operations. Agricultural loans were increased by 11 million K£, an amount that almost tripled the credits allocated to this sector in 1967. Nevertheless, the share of agriculture in total loans amounted to 11 percent in 1973 even though its contribution to GDP was about 30 percent. Credits to other essential categories such as transportation were also augmented, but they still accounted for only a small share of total credits at the end of the period.

In the period between 1967 and 1973 a high rate of growth in the credits to the less essential categories was maintained in Kenya. Trade loans, excluding agricultural marketing credits, rose by 10 million K£. As to the components of trade loans, a net small decline was registered in loans to exports, while that of other trade expanded. The large expansion in credit to the less essential categories was granted to public administrative entities, private construction, and households, which increased their share of total loans from 20 percent to 34 percent over the period. Overall, the rate of increase in loans to the less essential categories was substantially higher than that of loans to essential sectors.

The distribution of bank credit with respect to the essential sectors of the Kenyan and Tanzanian economies only partially indicates how well the banks conformed to the development strategies of the two countries. The development strategies of Tanzania, and to some extent those of Kenya, have attempted to increase the public sector's effective participation in their economies. The desire to restructure the Eastern African economies has been manifested in the nationalization of banks, trade, and major industries in Tanzania since 1967, and in government participation in some of the commer-

TABLE 5.8

Kenya: Commercial Bank Domestic Lending by Industrial Sector, 1967-73
(millions of Kenyan pounds)

	1967	1968	1969	1970	1971	1972	1973
Total loans and advances	68.0	66.8	70.0	86.9	120.1	121.4	161.4
Public sector loans, of which:	3.2	3.1	1.7	5.1	8.8	9.2	11.2
Government	(1.2)	(1.1)	(0.6)	(2.7)	(6.0)	(5.9)	(6.7)
Agriculture*							
Production	6.6	7.8	8.6	9.3	12.6	12.0	17.8
Mining and manufacturing*	12.2	12.7	15.1	15.6	24.8	24.3	27.9
Trade	30.6	28.2	26.1	33.8	28.5	33.9	40.7
Export	10.3	8.7	8.0	10.0	11.3	8.9	9.4
Other	20.3	19.5	18.1	23.8	27.2	25.0	31.3
Building and construction	1.5	1.8	2.2	3.4	5.3	7.1	8.0
Transportation*	1.1	1.4	2.9	3.0	3.9	3.1	3.7
Financial institutions*	3.6	3.4	3.4	2.7	3.4	4.1	11.8
Other (including private households)	9.1	8.5	9.9	14.1	22.9	27.7	40.3
"Essential" loans and advances	23.5	25.3	30.0	30.6	44.7	43.5	61.2
"Less essential" loans and advances	44.5	41.5	40.0	56.3	75.4	77.9	100.2
"Essential" loans as percentage of total loans	(34.6)	(37.9)	(42.9)	(35.2)	(37.2)	(35.8)	(37.9)
Public-sector loans as percentage of total loans	(4.7)	(4.6)	(2.4)	(5.9)	(7.3)	(7.6)	(6.9)

*"Essential" categories.

Source: Central Bank of Kenya, *Economic and Financial Review*, various issues.

cial banks and initiation of numerous public enterprises in Kenya. The owner-ships or partial control of the banks was to facilitate the use of credit to encourage public enterprises and, in the case of Tanzania, to restrict the growth of the private sector.

In the period 1967–73 the distribution of credit between public and pri-vate sectors in Kenya and Tanzania portrays two distinct trends. The share of the public sector (including public enterprises) in bank credit remained under 8 percent throughout the period. Between 1967 and 1973, public-sector loans in Kenya increased from 3 to 11 million K£, with no significant shifts of credit allocation from the private to the public sector. Contrary to the Kenyan experience, though, the allocation of bank credit in Tanzania shifted dramatically in favor of the government and other public enterprises. The public-sector loans, including the parastatals, increased sharply, from TSh 80 million to TSh 1,078 million during the period. This dramatic shift in favor of the public sector (from 10 percent to 59 percent of total loans) is explained primarily by the government takeover of major industries and the encourage-ment given since to public enterprises.

FINANCIAL DUALISM IN EASTERN AFRICA

The existence of nearly complete dualism between the modern and rural sectors of the Eastern African economies has been widely acknowledged.[13] This dualism has generally been attributed to technological and sociological factors, and the phenomenon of financial dualism with which we are concerned has received less attention. There is undeniable evidence that a significant constraint on the integration of the rural and urban sectors of these economies has been the dualism of the financial markets, notwithstanding the overall low level of development of financial institutions. There are at least two parallel financial markets with distinctive characteristics in each of these economies. These markets are often geographically separate, and only rarely does arbi-trage take place between them. The smaller and more organized market utilizes bank deposits and other financial institutions' liabilities besides currency; the unorganized market utilizes currency for the most part, and in some areas the use of barter is not uncommon.

The two markets also differ in the types and terms of credit granted. The only form of loans available outside family and friends in the unorganized money market may well be from merchant money lenders. This type of finan-cial dualism has persisted in Eastern Africa in spite of a substantial decline in the relative share of subsistence production in recent years. The development of modern financial institutions and other forms of organized money markets indicates the existence of an advanced financial technology in an economy or its subsectors. In particular, for the Eastern African economies, where most financial instruments and institutions were associated with external trade and colonial branch banks, the distinction between the financially developed and undeveloped sectors has been clear in the past. The lack of any identifiable local money-lending class prior to the emergence of expatriate merchants further made this dichotomy explicit. Therefore, in considering the existence and magnitude of financial dualism in the postindependence period, the trends in the extension of banking facilities in the rural sector of these economies are emphasized. Also, changes in the extension of other modern financial services to this sector (as distinct from bank branch expansion) and the availability of organized institutional credit from all sources to the rural sector are evaluated.

Integration of the rural and often subsistence sectors with the more modern and urban sectors has been given high priority by all three countries since independence. The emphasis on improving the techniques and productivity of the traditional sector is most obvious in Tanzania. Nevertheless, in all countries there have been attempts to introduce modern financial institutions and instruments to these traditional sectors. Implicit in all these policies has been the belief that the level of savings in the traditional sector is constrained by the absence of assets that are attractive in terms of safety, yield, and liquidity. It is further expected that integration of the financial markets would reduce if not eliminate the distortion in resource allocation between the traditional and modern sectors. Furthermore, equal access to the resources mobilized by these institutions is expected to lead to more equitable distribution of the growth dividend as the process of capital formation is spread across all sectors of the economy and across all strata of the population. Besides the integration of the fragmented savings and investment markets, the extension of bank operations to the traditional sectors and the actual monetization of these subsectors encourage some basic structural transformations. Some of the gains occurring as a result of the transformation of a barter economy to a monetary economy, such as efficient transactions and production specialization, are obvious.

The Elimination of Financial Dualism in Eastern Africa, 1962–73

Even though it was a stated objective of the authorities, the elimination of financial dualism in the Eastern African economies has progressed slowly. Within these economies, however, the rate of integration of the rural and urban financial markets progressed at different rates. Tanzania, particularly after 1967, experienced a more rational allocation of the branch banks. Kenya, the most financially developed, maintained a concentrated urban-oriented banking system, while Somalia, because of the extremely low development of its financial system, did not experience any dramatic extension of banking facilities in either the urban or the rural sector.

As presented in Table 5.9, the number of bank branches, sub-branches, and agencies increased in Kenya and Tanzania between 1963 and 1971. The increase, however, does not necessarily indicate any major shift in the extension of bank branches and services to the rural sectors. in fact, a closer look at the data reveals a tendency to locate new branches in areas that already had banking facilities. It is particularly instructive to note that in Kenya the two largest urban centers accounted for about half of all complete branches during the period.* In Somalia the only increase in the number of branches was registered in Mogadishu, the largest urban center; the largest two urban centers accounted for 36 to 44 percent of all bank branches. Tanzania shows the only decline in the relative density of bank branches in the two major urban centers: the actual number declined from 14 to 13 branches, and their share of total branches fell from 35 percent to 26 percent during the same period. The dispersal of bank facilities and the decline in their urban concentration were due to the bank branch rationalization undertaken right after the take-over of the commercial banks. After the merger of the nationalized banks into the National Bank of Commerce, a number of branches were closed and others were opened, so as to attain a better geographical coverage, to bring in more small towns, and to serve the rural areas.

The urban concentration and orientation of the Eastern African banking systems are further indicated by the distribution of deposits and loans by region. In Somalia, as illustrated by Table 5.10, the overwhelming portion of bank deposits originates in Mogadishu and Hargeisa, and loans are directed to these two urban centers. More important, the loans distributed to the rest of the regions have been systematically below the deposits originating in these regions; except in Mogadishu during 1962–63, the banks have lent to units at the urban centers in excess of the deposits collected there. One cannot conclude definitively, but this distribution lends credence to the view that the banks transfer rural savings to the urban centers. The data are not available for Kenya and Tanzania, but similar bank behavior is postulated in a recent World Bank report:

> Although adequate statistics were not available, it appears that commercial banks direct their funds from rural to urban areas and, above all, to foreign owned firms in the formal sector. An indication of this is that, by December 1971, loans to Africans, although rising rapidly, were only 13 per cent of all loans.[14]

---

*Agencies and sub-branches, which include mobile agencies, are not full-fledged banking offices but offer limited services, primarily the collection of savings.

TABLE 5.9

Location of Commercial Bank Branches

	Kenya		Tanzania		Somalia	
	Nairobi and Mombasa	Other	Dar-es-Salaam and Mushi	Other	Mogadishu and Hargeisa	Other
1963						
Branches	29	26	14	26	5	9
Agencies and						
sub-branches	1	42	–	18	–	–
1971						
Branches	51	58	13	37	7	9
Agencies and						
sub-branches	10	100	39	80	–	–

Sources: Thomas Skinner Directories, The Bankers Almanac and Year Book, 1963, 1971; Central Bank economic bulletins.

TABLE 5.10

Somalia: Private-Sector Deposits and Loans by Region, 1962-71 (millions of Somali shillings)

	Mogadishu		Hargeisa		Rest of Country	
	Deposits	Loans	Deposits	Loans	Deposits	Loans
1962	90.7	58.4	6.6	13.8	2.5	3.4
1963	101.1	60.5	7.3	25.8	7.8	3.8
1964	91.0	97.4	13.7	39.5	9.7	5.5
1965	93.6	124.6	16.3	27.5	10.5	7.7
1966	85.1	139.6	14.8	22.3	11.2	7.8
1967	97.9	146.3	18.7	22.1	14.7	9.9
1968	110.0	172.2	22.4	23.1	18.2	10.6
1969	123.7	169.7	21.4	22.4	20.7	14.7
1970	141.3	144.5	24.2	23.2	23.8	17.5
1971	163.1	225.3	24.9	24.6	24.7	9.6

Source: Somali National Bank Bulletin, various issues.

POSTINDEPENDENCE BANKING TRENDS IN EASTERN AFRICA

The postindependence banking experiences of the Eastern African countries suggest that the banking systems have not strongly contributed to their growth. The next two chapters discuss whether these banks have indeed constrained the real growth of the respective economies, and how effective they have been. Trends in the development of these systems, as manifested by the mobilization of domestic savings, have been unimpressive. Furthermore, their allocation of financial resources exhibits some of the basic characteristics of the much maligned colonial banking systems that preceded them.* Also, the extension of bank services to the rural sectors has been slow, where it has occurred.

Recent trends indicate a continuing rudimentary level of financial development and a low rate of savings mobilization. Though Kenya's banking system remains more developed than those of the other two countries, the banking ratios of all three countries are within the ranges associated with financially underdeveloped economies. Another indicator of the stagnation of the systems is the relatively low growth of the ratio of change in total bank liabilities to GNP. The average annual rates of growth of this ratio, about 5.4 percent in Kenya and 3 percent in Tanzania, were substantially below the rates associated with high-financial-growth systems (for details see Chapter 6). As to the mobilization of savings, improvements are shown in total deposits primarily as a result of increases in term deposits. Demand deposits as a percentage of money supply, narrowly defined, remained at about 70 percent in Kenya, about 58 percent in Tanzania, and about 48 percent in Somalia. The other components of bank deposits (time and savings) as a percentage of money supply increased in all three banking systems. The increase has been most dramatic in Tanzania, where the ratio rose from 6.0 percent to about 50 percent. It is especially noteworthy that the large increase in the term deposits occurred after the bank nationalization and the rationalization of the branch banks in Tanzania. However, even the upward trends in the term deposit ratios in Eastern Africa were moderate compared to the trends experienced by high-financial-growth systems.

The allocation of bank assets in the postindependence period has continued to show the emphasis on loans to trade and other less essential sectors.

---

*The view of the colonial banking system of Eastern Africa in summary is that the banks, which were predominantly branches of foreign banks, concentrated on short-term self-liquidating loans to exports of raw materials and imports of consumer goods. Credit extension not related to the international movement of goods was small, as preference was given to investing surplus funds in the developed capital markets of the home countries—in this case, England, Germany, and Italy.

The shares of industrial loans in Kenya and of agricultural loans in Tanzania have increased; however, the largest component of bank loans and advances has remained short-term, self-liquidating commercial loans in all three countries. The commercial loan bias has been manifested most clearly in the Somali banking system, where more than 60 percent of total loans were allocated to the trade sector alone. In the other two countries, where more disaggregated data exist, the share of less essential loans (primarily trade loans) has averaged about 63 percent for Kenya and 44 percent for Tanzania in 1967–73. The evidence on the recent financial history of the region, therefore, shows that the traditional distribution of bank assets has not significantly shifted in favor of the priority sectors of these economies. A major exception has been the steady increase in the share of loans and advances to the government and public enterprises of Tanzania since the nationalization of the banks and other large firms. Such a shift is consistent with the development strategy of Tanzania, even though the public enterprises may have used the increased credits for less essential purposes.

The attempts of the authorities to reduce financial dualism have met with limited but varied success. The limitation is obvious, as the concentration of banking facilities in the urban centers has continued. Thus, in 1971 the two major urban centers of each country contained at least 25 percent of the total bank branches: Kenya, 47 percent; Somalia, 44 percent; and Tanzania, 26 percent. More indicative of this concentration, however, is that the banking density in the urban centers was consistently higher than that for each country as a whole, throughout the period under review. Furthermore, the share of bank deposits originating in, and loans directed to, units in the rural sectors is still fairly small. As for the varied effectiveness of the policies to eliminate financial dualism, we have found that the extension of bank offices to the rural sectors has been most successful in Tanzania, particularly since nationalization.

In comparing the postindependence banking systems of Eastern Africa and their performances, the position of foreign branch banks in each system has special relevance. The foreign branch banks dominated the Tanzanian system up to 1966, the Somali system up to 1969, and the Kenyan system up to the present. As expected, these systems have not departed significantly from their preindependence operations. The major change in their operations has been the holding of domestic earning assets instead of foreign governments' paper. However, portfolio composition and, in particular, the large share of short-term commercial loans have not changed. Furthermore, where foreign branch banks predominate, the extension of bank branches and services outside the urban centers is limited.

As to the effects of nationalization and the creation of unitary commercial banking systems in Tanzania and in Somalia since 1970, no significant differences in the rates of growth of financial assets were recorded. Despite an increase in the mobilization of term deposits, an increase in agricultural and rural credits, and the rationalization of bank branch location in Tanzania, the public banks held portfolios no different from those of the colonial banks or of banking systems dominated by foreign branches. The maintenance of large cash and liquid assets and a large proportion of trade and other less essential loans were thus common features of all the banking systems of Eastern Africa, irrespective of ownership and structure.

The performance of the National Commercial Bank (NCB) of Somalia* during the first 18 months of its operations attests to the lack of innovation in the Eastern African banking systems, whether publicly owned or private and foreign-owned. During this period, the only favorable trend that can be distinguished in the operations of the NCB was a moderate rise in savings and time deposits. In June 1976, the bank's term deposit liabilities amounted to 24 percent of the money supply (M_1) as compared to a 15 percent average during 1960–69. All other indicators point to a slow growth in the bank's liabilities. Indeed there was a net decline in bank total liabilities (assets) between the first and last quarters of 1975, and there was only a moderate increase in the year ended June 1976.

Although the bank exhibited interest in lending to nontraditional production activities such as fishing and cooperative farming, about 60 percent of all bank loans were still allocated to the trade sector. Including loans to the export trade category, about two-thirds of all loans and advances were to commercial activites. Available data also indicate that the bias of the banking system of Somalia toward short-term and often small loans to commerce has been maintained by the NCB. Almost all the loans granted by the bank in the first half of 1975 were for periods of 12 months or less; a sizable number were for less than 6 months. Furthermore, the bank rarely granted loans in excess of SSh 5,000. In August 1975 less than 5 percent of all loans were above the SSh 5,000 limit, and during the year only 7 percent of all loans exceeded SSh 15,000 (US$2,500 at the official exchange rate).

The similarities in the operations of the NCB and the earlier banking systems of Somalia are indicated by the fact that the NCB reduced its total branches outside the capital city and did not even improve the location of its six branches in that city. All six branches are located in an area no larger than a few square miles, a locational design that had some merit when five different banking institutions owned the branches. Also, as in previous years, a large proportion of the banking operations in Somalia are still maintained within the capital city and a few other urban centers.

---

*On February 6, 1975, the two government-owned commercial banks were unified to form the NCB as the only commercial bank in Somalia.

Even though the final direction of the operations of the NCB cannot be judged at this early date, the available evidence shows that there has been no departure from the performance of the preceding banking system. These operational similarities also indicate that the changes introduced in the ownership and structure of the banking systems of Eastern Africa did not per se guarantee a more development-oriented banking performance.

NOTES

1. J. Gurley and E. Shaw, "Financial Structure and Economic Development," *Economic Development and Cultural Change* 15, No. 3 (1967):257–68.

2. U Tun Wai, *Financial Intermediaries and National Savings in Developing Economies* (New York: Praeger, 1972).

3. Saeed Osman, "Financial Institutions and Industrial Finance in the Sudan" (Ph.D. thesis, University of California at Los Angeles, 1968).

4. R. W. Goldsmith, *Financial Structure and Development* (New Haven: Yale University Press, 1969), p. 49.

5. National Bank of Commerce, "Chairman's Statement," *Annual Report and Accounts,* June 1973, p. 42.

6. H. T. Patrick, "Financial Development and Economic Growth in Under-Developed Countries," *Economic Development and Cultural Change* 14, No. 2 (January 1966): 182.

7. J. Gurley and E. Shaw, *Money in a Theory of Finance* (Washington, D.C.: Brookings Institution, 1960), pp. 48–50.

8. H. L. Engberg, "Commercial Banking in East Africa—1950–63," in *The Applied Economics of Africa,* ed. Edith Whetham and Jean Currie (Cambridge: Cambridge University Press, 1967), pp. 68–69.

9. Andrew Brimmer, "Central Banking and Economic Development: The Record of Innovations," *Journal of Money, Credit and Banking* 3, No. 4 (November 1971): 786–90.

10. Central Bank of Kenya, *Economic and Financial Review* 4(1971): 5. In 1971 the Kenyan Central Bank invoked, for the first time, its statutory powers to conduct selective credit controls by imposing a 12 percent ceiling on the increase in commercial bank credit to the private sector.

11. National Bank of Commerce, "Chairman's Statement," *Annual Report and Accounts,* June 1971, pp. 17–18.

12. Central Bank of Kenya, op. cit., p. 5.

13. Giordano Dell' Amore, *Banking Policy and Saving Policy in African Countries: Proceedings of a Conference on the Mobilization of Savings in African Countries* (Milan, September 1971), p. 4

14. IBRD Mission to Kenya, *Kenya: Into the Second Decade* (Baltimore: Johns Hopkins University Press, 1975), pp. 274–75; D. N. Ndegua, "Banking in Kenya," *Economic and Financial Review* 5 (1972): 14. Ndegua, the governor of the Central Bank of Kenya, also shows that only 2.6 percent of the loans and advances of the commercial banks in May 1967 were made to African borrowers, and that in 1972 the percentage of total loans to the same borrowers was 14.1.

6

THE DETERMINANTS OF
BANK PERFORMANCE IN
DEVELOPING ECONOMIES

The poor performance of the postindependence banking systems of Eastern Africa, as surveyed in the last chapter, is consistent with the experiences of most developing countries. With the exception of a few recent and now famous cases, the banking systems of the developing countries have not significantly contributed to real development. Therefore, recent studies of the role of the banking systems in the mobilization and allocation of domestic savings in the developing countries have also attempted to explain the generally unimpressive performance of these banking systems. In this chapter the determinants of the performance of the banking systems of Eastern Africa and other developing economies are analyzed. In order to emphasize the relative position of the Eastern African banking systems, the development of these systems since independence is first compared with the recent development of selected high-financial-growth economies. In the second section, the relevance to the Eastern African experiences of one hypothesis that explains the determinants of banking developments in the developing countries is evaluated. In the third and final section, alternative determinants of the recent development of these banking systems are presented.

BANKING DEVELOPMENT IN EASTERN AFRICA: A
COMPARATIVE ANALYSIS

In assessing recent banking developments in Eastern Africa, it is instructive to compare them with the high financial growth associated with Korea and Taiwan among the developing countries, and with Germany and Japan among the industrial countries.* Such a comparison is particularly useful in high-lighting the relative levels of development and the growth paths of the selected banking systems. Moreover, the level of development of each system could prove, for the most part, the efficacy of the policies recommended to improve its performance. Also, the rate and level of development of the banking system could affect the behavior of nonfinancial enterprises. Thus, we will compare the experiences of the Eastern African countries, from independence up to 1973, to those of the high-financial-growth countries in the same period.

The level of development of the banking systems is indicated by the ratio of total bank liabilities to GNP, and the ratio of total savings and time deposits to the money supply narrowly defined. The growth path of each banking system is illustrated by the rate of change in total bank liabilities relative to GNP. As shown by Tables A.14–A.19, the Eastern African banking systems started from a relatively small base, and their rates of growth were relatively low throughout the period. A summary of these bank development indicators is presented in Table 6.1.

The Eastern African banking systems experienced a moderate upward trend in the volume of term deposits relative to money supply, narrowly defined (see Tables A.14–A.19), from 39 percent to 57 percent in Kenya and from 19 percent to 48 percent in Tanzania. The rate of growth of bank liabilities relative to GNP averaged 4.5 percent in Kenya during 1966–73, and 3.0 percent in Tanzania during 1962–73. The limited growth of the banking systems of Eastern Africa and their low level of development throughout the period may be judged in comparison to the high-financial-growth systems. It is particularly noteworthy that there are many similarities between the Eastern African banking systems and that of Korea before the 1966 reforms and the high financial growth that followed. Thus, the rate of growth and the level of development of the Korean banking system, 3.6 percent between 1962 and 1965, were within the same range as those of the Eastern African banking systems.

However, comparing developments in the banking systems of Eastern Africa to those in post-1965 Korea and Taiwan, as well as with the industrial country systems, the disparities in the rate and level of growth are highlighted. As the Korean banking system shifted to a more accelerated rate of growth, the term deposit ratio reached a high of 200 percent, the ratio of total bank liabilities to GNP rose to about 50 percent, and the rate of growth of bank liabilities relative to GNP averaged about 11.4 percent. Taiwan also experi-

---

*The selected countries are portrayed as successful case studies of financial development, and their experiences, as models to be emulated in developing economies.

TABLE 6.1

Average Growth of Deposit Banks and Other Financial Development Ratios in Selected Countries

		Time and Saving Deposits/M_1	Total Bank Liabilities/GNP	Change in Total Bank Liabilities/GNP
Kenya	1962-73	0.514	0.354	0.045
Tanzania	1962-73	0.351	0.208	0.030
Korea	1962-65	0.345	0.115	0.036
	1966-73	1.618	0.392	0.114
	1962-73	1.194	0.313	1.088
Taiwan	1962-73	1.408	0.456	0.135
Germany	1962-73	2.075	0.826	0.100
Japan	1962-73	1.497	0.979	0.150

Sources: Central Bank of Kenya, *Economic and Financial Review*, March 1974; Bank of Tamzania, *Economic Bulletin*, December 1973; IMF, *International Financial Statistics*, various issues.

enced a substantial increase in time and saving deposits, which averaged 141 percent of money supply. Its total bank liabilities amounted to about 48 percent of GNP, and financial assets grew at 13.5 percent. The systems of Germany and Japan, within this period, were particularly large and grew at substantially higher rates than those of the Eastern African countries. Thus, time deposits were about one and a half times M_1 in Japan throughout the period, while they increased from 136 to 294 percent in Germany. The enormous size of the banking systems of the industrial countries is further exhibited by the ratio of total bank liabilities to GNP, which increased from 66 percent to 107 percent in Germany and from 88 percent to 105 percent in Japan between 1962 and 1973. Within the same period the rates of growth of bank liabilities relative to GNP were also much higher than those prevailing in Eastern Africa, averaging 10 percent in Germany and 15 percent in Japan.

Therefore, as compared to the levels of development and the rates of growth of the high-financial-growth banking systems, including those of post-1965 Korea, the Eastern African banking systems were all at a rudimentary stage of development and their rates of growth low. The ratio of the total liabilities of the Eastern African banking systems to GNP are less than one-fourth, and their average rates of growth are about one-third those of the high-financial-growth systems. These levels of development and the limited rates of growth in the Eastern African banking systems indicate the relatively small size of the financial sector in these economies (see Figure 6.1).

The Eastern African banks' credit distribution has also been found unsatisfactory, particularly as it relates to the distribution of credit between indigenous rural production and the urban commercial sectors. The allocation of bank assets in the postindependence period has emphasized loans to trade and other less essential sectors. The shares of industrial loans in Kenya and agricultural loans in Tanzania have increased; however, the largest component of bank loans and advances in all three countries has remained short-term, self-liquidating commercial loans. The overall evidence on the recent financial history of the region shows that the traditional distribution of bank assets has not significantly shifted in favor of the priority sectors of these economies.

Comparison of the Eastern African banking systems, their levels, and their rates of development, with the high-financial-growth economies does not indicate how high their levels or rates of growth should be at some future date. It merely guides the evaluation of their recent relative development positions and the search for the determinants of these diverse developments. Thus, in the next few sections, the factors affecting the growth and development of the Eastern African banking systems and other developing countries, as distinct from those at the other end of the pole, are explored. The most comprehensive theory of financial development that explores the determinants of the development of banking systems of the developing countries is the financial repression hypothesis. I will now review this hypothesis, its policy implications, and its relevance to the Eastern African experiences.

RELEVANCE OF THE FINANCIAL REPRESSION HYPOTHESIS TO EASTERN AFRICA

A Restatement of the Hypothesis and Policy Implications

The financial repression hypothesis offers a comprehensive analysis of the role of the banks and other institutions of the money and capital markets in developing economies.[1] It concludes that financial development contributes significantly to economic growth; that unfettered financial markets offer the best results; and that repressed financial markets act as an obstacle to economic development. It further emphasizes that financial development and its positive contribution to growth have not been realized in most developing countries because of pervasive interference by the authorities in the operation of their financial systems. The poor performances of banks and other financial institutions are therefore attributed to interest-rate regulation and other forms of intervention in bank lending policies. In the developing countries a frequent

FIGURE 6.1

Growth of Commercial Banks in Selected Countries
(Change in total bank liabilities/GNP)

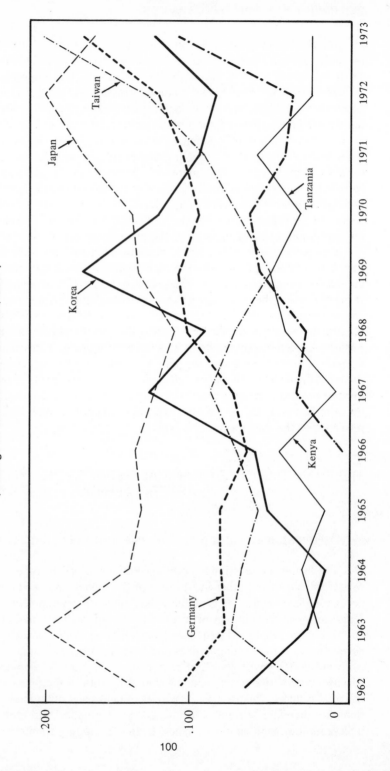

100

element in a financial intervention package is stipulation of ceilings on deposit and loan rates. Such ceilings, which are in nominal terms, result in low and often negative real rates of return on financial assets. Thus, the financial repression hypothesis postulates that a positive-interest-rate policy is necessary for financial development, particularly for the effective mobilization of domestic savings and their efficient allocation.

By incorporating the peculiar characteristics of developing countries (fragmented markets, indivisible investments, and predominance of self-finance), the advocates of financial liberalization argue that a positive-interest-rate policy encourages savings mobilization without discouraging new capital formation. Contrary to accepted portfolio theory, they argue that because of these peculiarities, an increase in the rate of return on real balances leads to an increase in physical capital assets held in private portfolios. Furthermore, besides increasing the levels of savings and capital formation, a high-interest-rate policy leads to an efficient allocation of savings and an efficient use of real resources. The high interest rates encourage savings in financial earning assets rather than in currency, inventory holding, and hoarding of precious metals. Furthermore, increases in the interest rate, which reflect the actual scarcity of capital in these economies, tend to shift financial and real resources from low-yield to high-yield investments. This manifestly more efficient allocation of resources contributes to a more judicious utilization of capital and a more intensive utilization of labor.

Also, where there are traditional curb markets and problems of financial dualism, a high-interest-rate policy contributes to the integration of the organized and unorganized financial markets. An increase in loan rates in the organized markets would normally reduce the costs to and dependence of traditional borrowers in the unorganized financial markets, as the prevailing interest rates in the organized markets remain below those in the unorganized financial markets. Thus, the narrow base of the banks and other financial institutions in developing economies, while the credit needs of the economy are met primarily by money lenders, epitomizes the phenomenon of financial repression.

The basic theses of the financial repression hypothesis are that the prevailing interest-rate policies determine banking developments in developing countries; that it is within the capabilities of these countries to use high nominal interest rates for the effective mobilization and allocation of savings; and that the optimal real rates of interest on deposits and loans, for which capital scarce economies should strive, are surprisingly high. Thus, the repression of the financial markets and, in particular, low interest rates due to statutory ceilings are offered as the causes of low financial development and the associated misallocation of resources. I will, therefore, examine the interest-rate policies and levels in postindependence Eastern Africa. Where the availability of data permits, the interest-rate experiences of these countries will be compared with the "successful" interest-rate experiment of Korea, which is one of the few examples of a developing economy where finance has been liberalized.

Interest-Rate Levels

In Eastern Africa the interest-rate levels and their structure have been almost static during most of the period for which data are available. During the 1967–73 period, neither the level nor the structure of the principal interest rates of the commercial banks has changed in Kenya. The same lack of flexibility in interest-rate policy is shown for Tanzania, where fixed rates were maintained during 1963–66 and 1967–73.* As presented in Table 6.2, interest rates on savings deposits were in the range of 3 to 3.5 percent, while interest rates on time deposits of up to 12 months ranged from 3 to 4.5 percent. Minimum rates on prime loans were fixed at 6.5 to 7.0 percent throughout the period for all countries. Even though maximum ceilings of 10 to 12 percent are indicated, there is reason to believe that the actual loan rates have varied within the period. Exceptions also exist where some preferred essential loans were granted at rates below the announced minimum rates.

Furthermore, the static interest rates maintained in these economies were low, as compared to the rates in Korea after 1965 and in the other developing countries that have followed an active interest policy. In response to an increase in the rate of inflation, Korea made a dramatic change in its interest rates and other financial policies, resulting in a change of real return on time deposits from –13 percent to 18 percent between 1964 and 1966. The experiences of Eastern Africa indicate that price increases were moderate throughout most of this period, and that real rates on time deposits were low but only rarely negative. Thus, by deflating the deposit rates by the respective consumer price index, we find that deposits with Kenyan banks had a negative return in 1966 and since 1972; while in Tanzania deposits registered negative returns in 1965–66 as well as in 1972–73. As shown by the figures, these relatively low yields on time deposits in Eastern Africa may be further generalized across all bank deposits and loan rates (see Table 6.3).

The interest-rate developments in Eastern African indicated that there were some statutory ceilings throughout the period after independence. As illustrated in earlier chapters, the central banks of these countries have only rarely utilized monetary tools to manage the economy. The low interest rates

---

*The static deposit and loan rates are generalized throughout the financial system; almost no variation is shown by discount rates of commercial bills or the deposit and loan rates of other financial institutions.

TABLE 6.2

Commercial Banks' Principal Interest Rates

	Tanzania		Kenya		Somalia
	1963-66	1967-73	1964-66	1967-73	1972
Savings deposits	3.00	3.50	3.00	3.0	0.75
Time deposits					
Minimum 30 days					
(7 days notice)	n.a.	3-3.5	3.00	3.0[a]	2.00
3-6 months	3.50	4.00	n.a.	3.50	2-3.5
6-9 months	3.75	4.25	n.a.	3.75	n.a.
1 year	4.00	4.50	4.00	4.00[b]	3.50[c]
Loans and advances					
(minimum)	7.00	6.50	7.00	7.00	7.00

[a]For deposits of Sh 0.5 million and over, the rate increases by 1/8 of 1 percent.

[b]For deposits of Sh 0.5 million and for periods in excess of 18 months, rate increases by 0.5 percent.

[c]For deposits of up to 24 months, the rate increases by 0.5 percent, and for over 24 months by 1.0 percent.

Source: Country central bank economic bulletins, various issues.

have thus been maintained long after the currency board monetary managements were eliminated. By not decreeing any changes and by maintaining the existing interest levels and structure, the central banks have demonstrated their concurrence with such a low-interest-rate strategy. In the few instances when the monetary authorities have addressed the appropriate deposit and interest-rate levels, the maintenance of reduced loan rates to encourage investments appear to have taken precedence over offering incentives to savers. Soon after the formation of the Kenyan Central Bank, the governor of the bank raised this apparent conflict:

There is a feeling that in a developing region like East Africa, the interest rate to savers should be high enough to encourage the small man to put aside some of his resources for the future. But at the same time, it is felt that the lending rates should not be so high as to frighten away the emerging entrepreneur who needs all the encouragement to start his own business.[2]

TABLE 6.3

Estimated Real Rates of Interest on One-Year Time Deposits
(percent per annum)

End of Period	Kenya			Tanzania			Korea		
	Percentage Change in CPI	Interest Nominal	Real Return	Percentage Change in CPI	Interest Nominal	Real Return	Percentage Change in CPI	Interest Nominal	Real Return
1964	-0.1	4.0	4.1	1.7	4.0	2.3	27.9	15.0	-12.9
1965	3.6	4.0	0.4	6.6	4.0	-2.6	13.6	18.8	5.2
1966	4.9	4.0	-0.9	4.6	4.0	-0.6	12.0	30.0	18.0
1967	2.3	4.0	1.7	2.3	4.5·	2.2	10.8	30.0	19.2
1968	0.7	4.0	3.3	3.6	4.5	0.9	11.2	27.2	16.4
1969	-1.0	4.0	5.0	1.3	4.5	3.2	10.1	24.0	13.9
1970	2.2	4.0	1.8	2.8	4.5	1.7	12.7	22.8	10.1
1971	3.8	4.0	0.2	4.1	4.5	0.4	12.4	20.4	8.0
1972	5.9	4.0	-1.9	8.6	4.5	-4.1	11.8	12.0	0.2
1973	9.3	4.0	-5.3	9.2	4.5	-4.7	3.0	11.0	8.0

Sources: IMF, International Financial Statistics, various issues; and country central bank economic bulletins.

This review of recent interest-rate developments in Eastern Africa shows that with the exception of a few minor adjustments, interest rates have remained unchanged since independence, with deposit rates ranging from 3 to 4.5 percent and lending rates from 6.5 to 10 percent. The impact of these static interest-rate levels and structure on the Eastern African banking system, and the implication of financial liberalization, particularly a high-interest strategy, in the Eastern African and other developing countries are examined next.

Effects of Interest Rates on the Mobilization and Allocation of Savings

The effects of an active interest-rate policy, in the case of the Eastern African and other developing countries, depend primarily on its impact on the mobilization and allocation of domestic savings. Such a policy also affects the allocation of real resources, the distribution of income, and the management of international capital movements and aggregate demand. The present analysis will concentrate on the impact of a high-interest-rate policy on financial development and the efficient allocation of resources.

The case for a high and active interest-rate policy is based on the availability and efficient allocation of savings, particularly savings through the financial intermediaries (financial savings), as the main constraint on economic development. Formation of new capital is thus postulated to be constrained by the low aggregate level and unfavorable composition of savings; other constraints such as foreign exchange and entrepreneurship limitations are not considered to be as critical. An active interest-rate policy is expected to relax or eliminate this only constraint via increases in the level of domestic savings and improvement in its composition.

A priori, however, the effect of a high-interest-rate policy on the level of aggregate domestic savings in developing countries is ambiguous. The amount of savings originating in the government and business sectors is considered insensitive to the level of interest rates. Even where the government is a net large borrower in the domestic market and the retained earnings of business are subject to opportunity cost evaluation, the effects of interest rates are expected to be small. The major impact of interest rates on domestic aggregate savings depends on the interest responsiveness of household savings. An increase in the nominal deposit rates and in the real return on savings leads to higher preference for future consumption and increased savings. However, the increase in interest rates also results in income effects that lead to higher preference for current consumption. It is not clear, therefore, whether a high-interest-rate policy will lead to increased net savings or decreased net savings as the income effects dominate the price effects. The net impact of interest-rate changes on household savings might be ascertained from empirical evidence.

However, where research findings are available, the evidence is inconclusive. In a recent survey of the theoretical and empircal literature, [3] Mikesell and Zinser found that the research conclusions, which were based exclusively on observations from Asian countries, have been contradictory. In a study of six Asian countries, Williamson[4] found the real interest rates negatively correlated with national savings, while in more detailed investigations in India high interest rates were found to lead to increased savings.[5] Virtually no quantitative studies of household savings in relation to any measure of interest rates exist for the Eastern African economies. Furthermore, in the light of their recent experiences, such attempts would be unproductive, since, as illustrated in the last section, variations in the levels of interest rates were minimal.

A high-interest-rate policy in developing economies has a positive and unambiguous effect on household financial savings. An increase in bank deposit rates shifts the holdings of surplus units from excess inventory and commodities to financial assets, in this case, bank term deposits. This process of the financialization of domestic private savings, as the opportunity costs of holding barren assets increases, is primarily determined by the rate of increase in the deposit rates. In these economies, where the development of the money and capital markets is rudimentary, a sharp increase in bank deposit rates is expected to improve the relative development of the banking systems.

Allowing for a positive interest-rate elasticity of financial savings, we can summarize the implications of low or negative interest-rate ceilings for individual banks and other economic units in the imperfect money markets of the developing economies. If the aggregate domestic savings are also interest-elastic, the effects of interest ceiling are more pronounced; however, the response of each unit is not changed. Considering that each bank in these economies operates on an imperfectly competitive market as a result of fragmentations in the financial markets, it is limited in the issue of its liabilities and in the demand for its services. Contrary to perfect money and capital markets, where bank liability management is feasible, the banks in the developing economies rely predominantly on the response of the depositors. A low deposit rate that depresses the demand for financial assets and term deposits of the banks, in particular, would not only limit the supply of loanable funds but would introduce some discretionary rationing by the banks.

The net result of a low interest-rate ceiling is, therefore, to stunt the development of the banking system; where the ceilings are set on nominal rates, and the real rates are negative, a smaller amount of involuntary savings is maintained with the banks. Because of the low yield or the penalty on holding bank deposits, the surplus units are induced to retain their earnings, or to lend them in the unorganized markets. The development of the unorganized parallel markets cannot be explained by interest-rate differentials alone. However, the low yield on assets and the limited credit availability in the organized sector encourage direct transactions between the surplus and deficit units. Thus, the response of lenders and borrowers to low interest-rate ceilings may not cause but will nevertheless accentuate the financial dualism the developing economies are trying to eliminate.

As to the allocation of financial savings, the efficacy of a high-interest-rate strategy depends on the resulting behavior of the individual financial and nonfinancial productive enterprises in each economy. If one were to assume, as the proponents of the financial liberalization hypothesis do, that the banks distribute credit so as to maximize profits, that they lend according to the highest rates of return on investment, and that investment is constrained only by savings,[6] then it could be shown that such a strategy would lead to a more productive and socially optimal allocation of savings and real resources.

The banks, irrespective of ownership, are considered to maximize their profitability subject to the expected returns and risks of the loan-investment alternatives available. If the utility function of the portfolio manager or the banker, which is directly related to the expected returns and inversely to risk (we assume portfolio managers are risk averters), is superimposed on the investment-loan locus preferred at each point in time, then we can show that a low interest-rate ceiling will reduce the amount of funds allocated to high-risk, high-return investments and loans. Specifically, the investment opportunities of each individual bank in the developing economies consist of cash holdings, small amounts of government securities, short-term self-liquidating commercial loans, and loans and advances to productive activities (agriculture, industry, and mining). In the Eastern African economies, the choice is limited to holding low-return, almost risk-free reserve assets, low-return, low-risk, collateralized short-term loans, and high-risk, high-return loans to indigenous entrepreneurs (in the case of no shortage of viable projects).

As shown in Figure 6.2, the ability of the bank to allocate loans to the higher-return and higher-risk categories is constrained by low ceilings on interest rates. The point of tangency between the utility indifference curve and investment opportunity locus L_e shows that the preferred bank portfolio composition would include higher-return and higher-risk investments and loans. However, once the interest rate ceiling is imposed, the bank portfolio managers would settle for a less profitable and less risky investment-loan mix, L_c.

It would appear, therefore, that the financial repression hypothesis is only partially relevant to the experiences of the Eastern African economies. Insofar as the imposed deposit-rate ceilings have discouraged savings held in the form of financial assets, the development of the banking systems was repressed. The proponents of the financial repression hypothesis, however, argue not merely that a high-interest-rate strategy will bring forth increased financial savings, but that it will also lead to an efficient allocation of financial and real resources. As Figure 6.2 illustrates, this conclusion is based on a narrow assumption which is invalid for Eastern Africa and other developing countries—that there is an abundance of viable projects and that investments are constrained by

FIGURE 6.2

Effect of Interest Rate Ceilings on Bank Assets Allocation

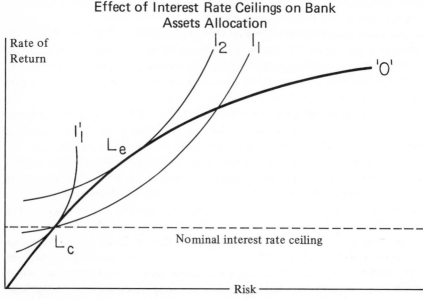

Source: Compiled by the author.

availabilities of finance alone. As argued in the next section, such an assumption is inconsistent with the realities of the Eastern African and most other developing economies.

The relevance of this hypothesis to the Eastern African economies is also questionable in that it concludes from a limited number of case studies (prominent among which are the recent experiences of Korea and Taiwan, as well as Indonesia) that a high-interest-rate strategy would lead to efficient financial development in the developing economies. This may be tenable under limited stages of development, but it cannot be generalized across all developing economies. The experiences of the moderately developed Asian countries listed above, which share more in common with each other than any one of them does with the Eastern African countries, are of limited relevance to the larger number of African and other developing economies. Without dwelling on the institutional diversity and the relative economic standards of the developing nations, I will highlight some major economic characteristics that distinguish the problems facing Eastern Africa from those of Korea (since 1965) and Taiwan (since 1960).

A particularly relevant distinction, though an obvious one, is that the financial institutions and policies adopted in any economy are expected to reflect the strategy of development and ideology of the authorities in question.

This factor alone invalidates the financial development path selected by the three Asian countries for some of the Eastern African countries. Implicit in this distinction also is that one strategy may elicit international capital inflows in the form of aid or private investments, which are directly reflected in domestic financial development, while an alternative strategy may not.

Other relevant distinctions include the differing purposes of financial reform. In the Asian countries, interest-rate reforms were to contribute primarily to economic stabilization and only secondarily to mobilizing and allocating financial resources. Each of these countries has undergone a period of rapid inflation preceding its interest-rate increases. The purpose was to restore the comparability of financial assets with other competing investments and consumption for discriminating surplus units. The purpose of financial liberalization and interest-rate reforms in Eastern Africa, however, would be to enlist new savers and to encourage those holding nonearning assets to switch to earning financial assets. And as shown earlier, the need for economic stabilization in Eastern Africa, in the period covered, has not been a paramount issue. As to the allocation of financial resources, the Asian countries were faced with sustaining their productive industries and farms, while the issue in Eastern Africa is primarily one of establishing them.

Finally, the experiences of a number of the developing economies have shown that neither liberalization alone nor a high-interest-rate strategy coupled with a liberal financial regime would guarantee an improved allocation of savings. The experiences of Eastern Africa in the preindependence years indicate that liberalization would not automatically result in more competition and a more efficient allocation of savings. During this period, since there was no effective control on bank operations by the colonial authorities, a common agreement was signed by the major foreign branch banks in the region to regulate the rates of deposits, loans, and other acceptable practices.[7] During this relatively liberal period, there was no noticeable effort by the banks to solicit any business outside the acceptable domain of short-term commercial finance. Another characteristic of the banking system of this period in Africa was the high liquidity maintained despite the lack of reserve requirements and other forms of liquidity management.

In the high-interest-rate strategy followed by Ghana during a period of general liberalization (after 1966), the banks experienced a substantial inflow of savings which, however, was not associated with similar expansion in credit to the productive indigenous enterprises. The high-interest-rate strategy has since been supplanted by selective credit ceilings to the major economic sectors and according to enterprise ownership. The latter policy has terminated loans and advances to firms owned and controlled by expatriates.

In summary, let me reemphasize that where an adequate financial structure and demand for financial services exist, a high-interest-rate policy may lead to a better allocation of savings; but where the financial system operates imperfectly or where the effective demand for finance is limited, a high-interest-rate strategy would not necessarily result in improved allocation of savings.

A STRUCTURALIST VIEW OF FINANCIAL DEVELOPMENT IN DEVELOPING ECONOMIES

The alternative explanation of the determinants of financial developments in the developing countries is based on different assumptions about the behavior of individual banks and investors in these economies. This approach emphasizes imperfections in the banking systems and deficiencies in the demand side for financial services at the initial stages of development. The foundations of this approach are in Gerschenkron's analysis of the role of the banking systems in the early industrialization of Western European countries and the Soviet Union.[8] He concluded that as the relative backwardness of an economy increases, the role of the banks in industrial capital formation declines. For extremely backward economies, the need for capital is estimated to be so large, and the confidence in the banking system so low, that sufficient financing of industrial capital formation cannot be accomplished through the banking system. For this type of economy, the structuralist holds that the mobilization and allocation of savings would have to be accomplished through substitute institutions such as the state.

The Gerschenkron scenario is not totally applicable to the recent experiences of the Eastern African countries. He views a mode of development in which latecomers are catching up with the original industrialized countries, with their methods of production and consequent capital needs dictated by the available technology. The development strategies of the Eastern African economies (including to some extent that of Kenya, which is promoting industrialization via import substitution) are, however, to achieve agricultural modernization and to stress the development of small-scale industries based on domestic inputs. Though these are problems of technological limitation based on economies of scale exploited by established firms and technological transfer, the current capital requirements of the Eastern African economies remain much smaller than those envisioned in Gerschenkron's more backward economies. The Gerschenkron analysis also, not unlike the financial repression hypothesis, emphasizes the supply side of financing industrial capital formation.

Thus, recent developments in the Eastern African banking systems are attributed to the structure of these economies. The imperfections in these banking systems may have limited the flow of funds to investment, but deficiencies in the demand side for financial services are the main constraining factor. As a result of nonmarket credit rationing by the banks, which emphasized their traditional association with trading firms and the availability of collateral, highly profitable and productive investments may have been excluded. Figure 6.2 also illustrates the case where higher-risk, high-return investments are not funded depending upon the preferences (I'_1) of the bank portfolio managers. In such a case the conservative decision rates of the portfolio manager are sufficient to explain the limited credit flowing to the priority sectors of these economies. As these priority sectors often entail investment in new activities and by new entrepreneurs, a lack of prior credit standing limits the flow of credit.

The single most important determinant of recent banking development in Eastern African is the deficiency in effective demand for bank financing. Both the low development of the banking system and the emphasis on trade loans are attributed to lack of demand. This effective demand deficiency is clearly indicated in the operations of specialized development finance institutions which, despite their limited funds, experienced difficulties in locating productive viable investments. As discussed in Chapter 4, these institutions were faced with few investment opportunities, few well-prepared projects, and few well-trained entrepreneurs.

For the Eastern African and other developing countries, where there is a shortage of viable investment opportunities, it is easy to show that bank asset allocation is primarily determined by the low or deficient effective demand for bank services. The entry of new and viable indigenously owned enterprises to the Eastern African and other developing economies may be limited by prior entrepreneurial, technological, and equity finance constraints.[9] Irrespective of the levels and structure of interest rates, bank credit allocation to capital formation, particularly to the indigenous productive sectors, will be small under these constraints. The initial low profitability and high risks associated with new ventures in the indigenous sectors would preclude substantial bank finance. The essential issue, then, is not how to allocate credit to the more socially profitable uses at the time, but how to allocate bank credit to uses which, although not profitable in the short run, are preferred for development and social equity reasons. In the simple framework of Figure 6.2, the potential loans to and investments in these sectors are not on the efficient opportunity locus facing the banking system, since the liabilities of these sectors are associated with higher risks and lower returns than the alternative uses of the limited financial savings. An extreme but obvious example is that the commercial-sector loans dominate those of the indigenous productive sector in both returns and risk.

In this alternative analysis, the limited amount of financial savings allocated to the priority sectors of the developing economies is attributed primarily to demand deficiency and only secondarily to lenders' decisions. An objectively measured low profitability of new or emerging enterprises would preclude bank financing—unless, of course, the bank principal and yield are guaranteed, as some governments have attempted to do. Therefore, considering the effective demand for bank financing of productive investments as indicative of the level of economic development, one may distinguish at least three different types. First, new capital formation is limited by prior nonexternal, nonfinancial constraints, in which case the contribution of the banks and other financial intermediaries would be minimal. Second, the prior constraints are reduced, but the sources of noninstitutional external finance are limited, in which case external bank finance is highly significant. And finally, the prior nonfinancial constraints are reduced, and alternative sources of noninstitutional external finance are developed, in which case the contribution of the banks is negligible again. In this view, therefore, the efficient allocation of financial savings and the contribution of the banks to capital formation, particularly in the indigenous sectors, reflect the relative level of development of an economy.

Furthermore, for the developing economies, including those of Eastern Africa, the above deficiencies rule out the prospect of demand-following financial development. Demand-following financial development is termed "as the phenomenon in which the creation of modern financial institutions, their assets and liabilities, and related financial services, is in response to demand for these services by investors and savers in the real economy."[10] It is because of the low development levels of these economies and their low rates of growth, which constrain demand-following financial development, that I have suggested innovations in the financial and real sectors of these economies. The recommendations include measures for both the banking system and the state that will induce financial development to lead real economic growth. These measures are expected to reduce the deficiencies in the demand for financial services and also to reduce the imperfection in the financial markets.

NOTES

1. Both, McKinnon and Shaw deal with financial instruments and institutions in general, while Cameron restricts his comments to developments in commercial banking systems. See Ronald McKinnon, *Money and Capital in Economic Development* (Washington, D.C.: Brookings Institution, 1973); Edward Shaw; *Financial Deepening in Economic Development* (London, Oxford University Press, 1973); and R. Cameron, ed., *Banking and Economic Development: Some Lessons of History* (London: Oxford University Press, 1967).

2. D. N. Ndegwa, "Monetary Cooperation Between Tanzania, Kenya and Uganda," *Economic and Financial Review* 1 (1968): 10.

3. Raymond F. Mikesell and James E. Zinser, "The Nature of the Savings Function in Developing Countries: A Survey of the Theoretical and the Empirical Literature," *Journal of Economic Literature* (March 1973): 194–210.

4. J. G. Williamson, "Personal Savings in Developing Nations: An Intertemporal Cross-Section from Asia," *Economic Record* 44 (1968): 194–210.

5. K. L. Gupta, "Personal Savings in Developing Nations: Further Evidence," *Economic Record* 46 (1970): 243–49

6. Shaw emphatically states that "the typical lagging economy short of physical and human wealth, is long of investment opportunities, . . . there is no shortage of investment opportunities, there is a shortage of savings for their finance, especially for the best ones among them" (op. cit., p. 81).

7. Ernest-Josef Pauw, "Banking in East Africa," in *Financial Aspect of Development in East Africa,* ed. Peter Marlin (Munich: WeltForum Verlag, 1969), pp. 176–77.

8. Alexander Gerschenkron, *Economic Backwardness in Historical Perspective: A Book of Essays* (Cambridge: Harvard University Press, 1962).

9. Sayre P. Schatz, *Development Bank Lending in Nigeria* (Ibadan: Oxford University Press, 1964), p. 89.

10. Hugh Patrick, "Financial Development and Economic Growth in Underdeveloped Countries," *Economic Development and Cultural Change* 14 (January 1966): 174.

CHAPTER

7

SUMMARY, CONCLUSIONS,
AND IMPLICATIONS
FOR POLICY

SUMMARY AND CONCLUSIONS

The theoretical foundations of this study are that domestic mobilization of financial resources is essential for capital formation and growth, that an efficient allocation of the available domestic resources is imperative, and that commercial banks offer an appropriate institutional vehicle through which savings can be directed from less essential expenditures to productive investments. As the survey of the literature indicates, an emerging consensus holds that financial development facilitates real growth and that financial underdevelopment constrains the growth process. More significantly, the thesis that financial development matters for real growth is based on the measurable increase in financial assets associated with a real increase in GNP and tangible wealth, for some countries over time and across countries. An examination of the growth of commercial banks and other deposit banks as economies develop also shows a significant association, which is less pronounced across developing economies.

Before exploring the interaction of commercial banks and real development in recent years, the economic setting and the strategies of development of the Eastern African countries were surveyed. Among the variables highlighted was the low level of development, real and financial, of these economies, associated with pervasive economic dependencies in trade, technology, and finance that were more visible during the preindependence years. These dependencies have affected both the operations of the commercial banking systems and the development of an entrepreneurial class in Eastern Africa.

A more important factor for the recent performance of these banking systems is, however, the introduction and initial development of modern commercial banking. In all these countries, full-service banking originated when the colonial banks set up branches in the coastal and, later, urban areas. This lack of indigenously developed modern financial institutions operating where indigenous production was most successful was the genesis of future bank performance. During the preindependence years, the expatriate banking systems concentrated on financing the movement of goods between the metropoles and the colonies and hence contributed little to indigenous economic development. Credit extension not related to the movement of goods was small, and preference was given to the holding of liquid foreign assets or other investments in the developed capital markets of the home countries. Furthermore, from the standardized portfolios held throughout the period, one may conclude that the colonial banks did not undertake any financial innovation and were satisfied with merely greasing the wheels of trade.

To no one's surprise, no major transformations took place in the initial years of independence. This era of maintaining the status quo at a relatively low level of development lasted for about a decade in Somalia, Kenya, and Tanzania. Only after 1966 were distinct strategies of development formulated in Kenya and Tanzania. The earliest attempt at systematic development strategy in Somalia occurred only in the final months of 1969.

In surveying the postindependence economic setting, I concluded that the basic structure and performance of the Eastern African economies did not depart significantly from those of the last decade of the colonial era. The modes of production, employment, and capital formation and composition did not change dramatically. A higher level of industrialization has been achieved in Kenya than in the two other countries, but this differential was equally marked during the last decade of colonial occupation. A characterization of these economies as "dependent" and developing still applied a decade after political independence.

During the postindependence years, the operations of the banking systems are of importance, especially since the alternative techniques of mobilizing and allocating domestic savings were deficient. This deficiency in all the Eastern African economies is evident in the failure of the fiscal mechanism to mobilize domestic savings for reinvestment purposes. In order to finance public development expenditures, the authorities had to rely for the most part on foreign loans and assistance, as well as on central bank and other domestic borrowing. Only rarely have government revenues exceeded the recurrent government expenditures in sufficient magnitude to cover development expenditures. Moreover, in a large number of cases part of the current government expenditures had to be financed by external budgetary support. Whatever the true causes of the deficits, these governments were unable to rely on domestic sources of finance, and particularly on budgetary surpluses, for the desired capital formation. This financial gap is most clearly demonstrated by the process of development planning over the period, which often listed prospective sources of external assistance in lieu of financial programs.

Another alternative technique for mobilizing and allocating domestic financial resources was the creation of specialized development finance institutions. These institutions were set up to meet the medium- and long-term financial needs of enterprises in agriculture, industry, and construction. As these institutions relied on the respective governments for capitalization, and as their overall sources of finance were limited, their contribution was small. The specialized development finance institutions also experienced difficulties in the dispersal of loans, which led to numerous cases of insolvency. In comparison with the influence of the budget and the commercial banking system, the specialized development finance institutions have played a minor role in the financial systems of Eastern Africa.

In order to evaluate the role of the commercial banks and to examine their postindependence operations, I adopted a simple taxonomy that emphasizes the three main channels through which the banks affect real growth: first, the trends in bank deposits relative to money supply and total bank liabilities relative to gross national product as indicators of the effectiveness of the mobilization of financial savings were examined; second, the banks' asset portfolios were scrutinized to evaluate how well their assets composition conformed to the priorities set by the development strategies finally adopted; third, the extension of the banking systems and services beyond the confines of the urban centers was investigated. The issues were analyzed with a view to comparing the performance of each country's banking system with its most recent colonial experience, and to comparing each system's performance with those of the others. The intersystem comparison is of particular interest since the development strategies of Kenya and Tanzania are different, while Somalia followed no systematic strategy within the first decade of its independence. After 1966, the parallel development of the private (later mixed) banking system of Kenya and the nationalized banking system of Tanzania were compared.

The performance of the Eastern African banking systems in terms of the mobilization of domestic savings has been inadequate. Considering that the commercial banks account for almost all the savings in the modern financial institutions, the growth rates of the banks and thus of financial savings were low. Even though the banks were eliciting savings from populations whose majority is either reluctant or unable to hold bank deposits, the static share of demand deposits in the money supply in all the systems is indicative of stagnation in financial development. The banks were more successful in attracting term deposits; the levels of savings and time deposits as a proportion of money supply increased moderately in both Kenya and Somalia and almost doubled in Tanzania. Overall, however, the evidence indicates a rudimentary level of financial development and a low rate of financial savings mobilization in the postindependence period.

The performance of the banking systems in allocating their assets in accordance with development priorities has not been successful either. Although the liquid assets held in the banking systems were exceptionally large at times, the volume of loans and advances grew rapidly over the period. Nonetheless, the impact of the expanded bank credit was minimal, since the largest share of bank loans and advances in all three countries was directed to commerce. The shares of bank loans to industry in Kenya and to agriculture in Tanzania increased, but an emphasis on trade and other less essential loans is indicated by analysis of the disaggregated data, even in these countries. This emphasis is clearest in Somalia, where trade loans account for more than 60 percent of the total bank credits.

Contrary to the explicit objectives of the strategies adopted, the direction of the bank loans to productive capital formation and particularly to indigenous enterprises has not been achieved. Disaggregation of the main categories to which bank credits are issued shows that the categories considered less essential with respect to development priorities have maintained an average of about 63 percent of the total loans and advances in Kenya (1967-73), and about 44 percent in Tanzania for the same period.

As to the elimination of financial dualism, the full-service banking systems are still concentrated in the largest urban centers and a few other major trading centers. This concentration is most severe in Kenya and least so in Tanzania, which has achieved a fair amount of success in rationalizing bank branch locations since the National Bank of Commerce took over the branches of the private banks. Also, where data were available, we concluded that the share of bank deposits originating at and loans distributed to the rural sectors was very small.

In comparing the performances of the postindependence banking systems with their most recent colonial operations, very few distinguishing characteristics can be ascertained. Disregarding the cosmetic changes of local incorporation of foreign branch banks, where this has occurred, and the personnel changes, there is little to suggest that political indepence has had an impact on bank operations. An exception is that in the postindependence years few foreign earning assets have been held by the commercial banks. The rest of the banks' asset composition has not changed over the period, as the continuing emphasis on short-term loans and advances to the commercial sector and other less essential sectors indicates.

In comparing the performances of the predominantly private banks of Kenya and the public banks of Tanzania in the seven years ended 1973, there are few differences of magnitude. First, the Kenyan banks, on the average, grew at a faster rate than those of Tanzania, even though the proportional increase in term deposits was much higher in Tanzania. More significantly, the Tanzanian banks distributed a greater proportion of their loans and advances in accordance with development priorities: essential loans as a percentage of total loans was 56 percent in Tanzania as compared to 37 percent in Kenya. Second, the National Bank of Commerce (of Tanzania) also successfully directed a large share of its loans and advances to the parastatals and cooperatives, a shift which was again consistent with government strategy. The share of private loans in Tanzania thus declined from 90 percent of the total in 1967 to about 41 percent in 1973. Finally, the National Bank of Commerce undertook the most successful attempt at bank branch dispersal, eliminating the concentration of branches in the urban centers and extending new branches, sub-branches, or agencies to areas originally unserved. Sufficiently disaggregated data are not available to determine the term structure of loans and advances, but the National Bank of Commerce has initiated medium-term loans of three to five years' duration to indigenous producers. The effectiveness of this program and the magnitude of medium- to long-term loans in the rest of Eastern Africa cannot be estimated with accuracy.

The divergences in the performances of the Eastern African banking systems are, however, minor compared to the gap between the rudimentary level of development of these systems and the high financial growth of some more advanced banking systems. In a comparative analysis of the rates of growth of the Eastern African banks and those of Korea, the average rate of growth in the Eastern African systems is about one-third of those of the high-financial-growth countries. The average rates of growth ranged from Tanzania at 2.9 percent, to Kenya at 4.5 percent, to Korea at 11.2 percent. For all other indicators of the importance of the banking systems, the gap between the Eastern African countries and the high-financial-growth economies is also wide.

Given these general characteristics of the Eastern African banking systems and their performance in the postindependence years, the validity of the financial repression hypothesis as it relates to their performances was explored. Indeed, the low level of development of the banking systems was associated with a low and static interest-rate structure. Though positive real interest rates were maintained for most of the period, the real levels of deposit rates were not sufficiently high to elicit or to encourage large savings. Some justification could be made for a high-interest-rate strategy on this ground alone. As to the impact of high interest rates on the allocation of financial savings, I have argued that it has no universal validity and that its advantages are unlikely to be realized within the Eastern African economies. I have discounted the prescription of a liberal financial regime and a high-interest-rate strategy to attain the best allocation of financial resources on the basis of some features of the developing economies. These features include the effective demand deficiency of the indigenous entrepreneurs, the traditional banking attitudes which limit the domain of banking services, and the divergences between private and social costs and benefits in these economies.

It should be reemphasized that the poor performances of the Eastern African banks in directing funds to indigenous productive uses is attributable, for the most part, to identifiable economic constraints. These constraints are inherent in the structure and relative level of the development of these economies and will not be eliminated or reduced by liberalization and high-interest-rate strategies alone. It is conceivable, however, that in economies where demand for bank services is high and the production technology is highly developed, these high-interest-rate policies will have an impact in screening the projects financed.

Social control of the banks will not, by itself, resolve the central problem either. Government participation in bank ownership or nationalization of these institutions, although possibly desirable on other grounds, will not per se guarantee an increased share of productive investment loans in bank portfolios. As the experiences of Kenya, Tanzania (to some extent), and other developing countries show, the banks, irrespective of ownership, dance to their own tune. The choices of the bankers, be they private businessmen or public employees, have not so far met the needs of the indigenous entrepreneurs.

TOWARD FINANCIAL DEVELOPMENT IN EASTERN AFRICA

As a result of the differences in the current development strategies of Somalia, Tanzania, and Kenya, one would expect a different program of financial development for each country. On the one hand, Somalia since 1969 and Tanzania since 1967 have elected to let the state take the lead in development efforts. This has been manifested in the takeover of the banks and most other large enterprises. However, agricultural production in both countries remains in private hands, with the governments desirous of converting it to cooperative farming. The prospective contribution of the National Bank of Commerce (Tanzania) and the Somali Commercial Bank would have to be maximized within these predominantly "socialized" economies. Kenya, on the other hand, follows the path of a mixed economy in which private entrepreneurship in all sectors is encouraged. The commercial banks have also remained predominantly private institutions and mostly expatriate, with some government participation. Nevertheless, owing to the lack of any detailed physical and financial planning in the case of Somalia and Tanzania, the banks in all three countries are autonomous in their operations and particularly in deciding their portfolio composition and their distribution of loans and advances.* Thus, with the exception of the desired priority allocations suggested in the development strategies, the bankers in all three countries follow no higher authority in deciding the most efficient allocation of their assets and all

---

*In some years the banks have been required to hold certain amounts of their reserves in government bills. Since the practice has been limited in magnitude and duration it is not considered a major regulation.

other aspects of their operations. It is in this spirit, therefore, that the policies prescribed below are considered to be applicable to all these countries and other developing economies in similar circumstances in their effort to mobilize domestic savings, to direct a high proportion of bank credits to productive investments, and to eliminate financial dualism.

The obstacles to satisfactory performance of the banking systems are attributable to fundamental structural characteristics of these economies. A principal attribute that accounts for the limitations of the banks' operations is the deficiency in the effective demand for their services. Within this deficiency, however, a number of specific factors may be identified and accordingly corrected. Below I divide these factors between those that innovative banking may tackle and those that would require the state's attention.

Toward Innovative Banking

A basic characteristic of commercial banking in the Eastern African countries is the limited scope of modern institutions in every facet of their operations. Such a limitation was shown in types of assets held, in the maturities of their loans, and in their geographical base. Regardless of how this is identified, whether as traditional British banking or even armchair banking, the net result is minimal financial development and negligible contribution to economic development. For policy discussions this phenomenon may best be characterized as an absence of financial linkages and a lack of innovative banking. The absence of financial linkages in Eastern Africa and other developing countries is due to the desire to have their efforts determined by the receipt of profitable, secure, and preferably self-liquidating loan applications submitted for approval. It is evident that at each stage of the process numerous pitfalls have frustrated indigenous entrepreneurs, but these could be transcended with some innovative banking. Indeed, if contact channels were available between the bank and the entrepreneur, some of the services would be within the presently acceptable banking practices in the region.

In recognition of the absence of these linkages and the resulting financial gap, the governments of these countries have set up specialized institutions to lend for productive investments on a medium- and long-term basis. The experiences with industrial and agricultural development banks have been mixed with some relative success and some major failures, as indicated by the case of Credito Somalo, where a SSh 20 million loss on the total portfolio had to be absorbed by the government, and the experience of the Tanzanian Investment Bank. Even within these specialized banks, however, assistance offered to indigenous entrepreneurs was limited to loan approval. In project selection, preparation, and eventual management, the banks were often unprepared or possibly unequipped to assist. Irrespective of the terms of the loans and of the nature of the granting institution, a successful productive lending program for the new generation of entrepreneurs in Eastern Africa would require more attention than a computation of the ability to repay and the existence of collateral.

The suggested linkages would thus include "personalized" banking operations that may eventually require the creation of supplementary channels to serve the needs of the typical Eastern African entrepreneur. Personalized banking operations would include bank involvement with the investor's prospects from inception to maturity. It would entail direct assistance in project preparation and financing, as well as in management. It should be acknowledged, however, that if the skills required are unavailable in the general population, they are also at a premium within the bank staff. Such an involvement of the banks with the major productive sector (agriculture) would require special expertise for the banks to appraise or discriminate among the competing projects intelligently in the first place. Therefore, it is the banks' responsibility to upgrade their staff in the required skills. Furthermore, the experiences of some of the more advanced countries, even in recent years, show that the adaptability of the banks to the changing needs of their business clientele is a fairly good indicator of their success as ongoing concerns. As I have also shown (Chapter 2), historical precedents exist where commercial banks have participated in both the financing and management of the early industrialization of what are now developed economies.

Such innovative or personalized banking would, however, require some supplementary or new financial channels. Even if the current banking systems were to extend their services beyond the traditional domain, the direct beneficiaries would be limited to those presently utilizing the banks' services, and the bulk of the populations of Eastern Africa would be unaffected. Supplementary banking facilities or alternative full-service agencies to reach the large part of these populations would have to be initiated. The utilization of agricultural cooperatives by the commercial bank of Tanzania in order to disperse loans where its facilties are otherwise unavailable points to a promising trend. The supplementary channels or agencies that are most effective in each economy would depend on the high-priority sectors to be reached.

The introduction of both innovative support services and supplementary channels is thwarted by cost considerations. It is doubtful, indeed, whether innovative or extended services could be justified by analysis of the short-term, direct economic costs and benefits to private banks. Traditionally, the small base and urban orientation of commercial banks in the region have been attributed to these short-term, direct economic costs outweighing the benefits to the individual banks. The validity of the above argument aside, a proper evaluation should take into account the indirect and long-term benefits to society, besides the direct and short-term effects on the individual bank. These indirect social benefits include the positive economic externalities attainable from high-priority investments, as well as the long-term educational gains to savers and investors alike. This classical divergence between the private and social net benefits, among other factors, would indicate that the "interference" of the authorities of the developing economies in bank operations is unavoidable.

Toward Improved Effective Demand and Implications for Public Policy

In these final remarks, I have suggested policies the authorities should adopt to induce the commercial banks to make a greater contribution to economic development, and particularly the development of indigenous production. In order not to distract from this essential issue, I have deemphasized the differences introduced by the structure and ownership of commercial banks in Eastern Africa. In fact, whether the commercial banks are capable of encouraging indigenous production may partially depend on their structure and ownership. On this point, the performance of the unitary state banking system of Tanzania was found superior in some ways to that of Kenya's system, which is dominated by foreign branch banks. However, in their portfolio selection and loan distribution the two systems face similar constraints. Those public policy measures that will reduce the effective demand constraints facing the Eastern African banking systems, irrespective of structure and ownership, are suggested below.

The limited contribution of the commercial banks to indigenous economic development in Eastern Africa is attributable to deficient effective demand for bank services in the targeted high-priority sectors and enterprises. Such a deficiency may best be illustrated by assuming "perfection" in the financial markets and then considering the actual constraints on the flow of finance to the high-priority sectors. The simplifying assumption of perfect financial operations would entail adequate institutions for the mobilization of savings and objective bank decision making in classifying prospects. The problem, then, is how to find profitable investments at acceptable risks in the high-priority sectors. It is essential, therefore, that in both profitability and riskiness the indigenous enterprises be transformed before they could compete with alternative uses of bank resources on equal terms.

The role of government in the improvement of profitability of high-priority indigenous production is central to the pursuit of economic development. Detailed analysis of what role the state should play in upgrading traditional activities and what tools it should use is outside the scope of this study. Once the state's responsibility for the improvement of the productivity and profitability of lagging indigenous enterprises is accepted, the tools could be determined by their relative cost and benefits to society. In the case of the transformation of traditional agriculture, improved productivity may require the state to offer subsidized fertilizer, equipment leasing, and storage and marketing assistance, as well as farmer education and other extension services. Some of these services are already being provided by the Eastern African governments, but effective demand for credit and bank accommodation of this high-priority sector depends on the impact of these other public policies on the productivity of traditional agriculture.

In the case of indigenous industrial development, improvements in productivity and profitability would require similar attention. However, besides the nonfinancial constraints to be reduced, the initial financial requirements for the large part of viable industries is beyond the capabilities of most indigenous entrepreneurs. Therefore, without making any definitive judgments about the relative efficiency of private and public industrial enterprises in the region, the initial capitalization alone makes government involvement in larger and medium-scale enterprises in this sector imperative. Where major private industrial development is feasible, as in the case of Kenya, and for the smaller firms, in the case of the other countries,* and where some economic externalities are involved, the governments should be prepared to assist both financially and otherwise. The governments would have to review their overall policies affecting industrial productivity in order to realize the desired flow of bank credits to these enterprises.

Finally, besides the actual profitability of the indigenous productive enterprises, we have concluded that the risks involved in lending to these sectors are a significant constraint on the flow of bank credit to them. The objective component of these risks may be partially compensated for by higher loan returns that could be feasible within an improved productivity environment. Other subjective risks, which are predominantly attributable to lack of linkage between the financial institutions and the productive enterprises, could be reduced via the bank innovations recommended. However, some risks are inherent in the present characteristics of the typical African entrepreneur and cannot be eliminated either by higher interest charges or by improved linkages. These risks may be associated with the level of managerial development and the instability in the earnings of such enterprises. This phenomenon is much clearer in the case of small farmers, whose level of earnings is subject to the vagaries of weather. Such instability in earnings is by no means unique to the farmers' income, as drastic fluctuations are exhibited in industrial enterprises as well. Therefore, it is in reducing these risk of loan default and bankruptcies that a governmental policy change is expected to have the greatest effect.

---

*In Tanzania, large industrial investments are undertaken by the state, but much effort is being put into the Small Industries Development Organization (SIDO), which started in 1974. The idea is to stimulate, train, teach, and assist all rurally based small industries, using local raw materials and a minimum of capital.

According to the information available, no government in Eastern Africa has attempted specific loan guarantees for any lending program within its high-priority sectors. Such a loan guarantee scheme might be costly if applied across all the enterprises within these high-priority sectors. However, the governments could effect substantial change via a limited coverage initially, to be extended eventually to the maximum coverage affordable. The recommended governmental role in reducing the risks associated with bank loans to the high-priority sectors would be determined by the severity of the problem in the respective economies. Whether partial or complete coverage is required, and for what enterprises, cannot be determined without a review of the actual cases. Nor would I determine the appropriate channels of this risk insurance —whether the monetary authorities should rediscount these loans and absorb the losses when they occur, whether independent reinsurance of such loans should be set up, or, for that matter, whether direct subsidies should be offered to the banks proportional to losses incurred. These and other factors would have to be selected within the dictates of each economy and what each government finds consistent with its other policies.

In conclusion, direct government involvement with the operations of the commercial banking systems of the region would have to be expanded, and not reduced as some suggest, in order to realize the desired bank credit distribution. Besides adopting more flexible interest-rate policies to encourage savings, and financial savings in particular, the governments would have to be involved in improving the profitability and reducing the risks of indigenous enterprises. Increased bank credit to the priority sectors depends on the creation of effective credit demand within these sectors.

TABLE A.1

Contribution of Agriculture to GDP and Employment in Kenya (1954-63) and Tanzania (1954-61)

	1954	1955	1956	1957	1958	1959	1960	1961	1962	1963	Average
Kenya											
Agricultural production as percentage of GDP	46.8	41.7	43.0	41.4	41.9	41.2	40.0	38.5	42.2	42.9	42.0
Of which: subsistence	(28.8)	(25.6)	(24.8)	(25.1)	(25.3)	(24.7)	(22.3)	(21.3)	(25.9)	(25.7)	(25.0)
Share of agriculture in total employment	44.6	44.0	43.2	45.2	46.2	46.4	47.9	47.2	46.3	45.3	45.6
Tanzania											
Agricultural production as percentage of GDP	64.9	65.3	68.6	67.6	65.0	65.2	64.4	59.0	—	—	65.0
Of which: subsistence	(36.8)	(37.2)	(41.4)	(42.8)	(41.4)	(40.0)	(38.6)	(34.8)	—	—	(39.1)
Share of agriculture in total employment	54.4	56.4	53.5	55.6	54.7	55.9	55.7	53.8	—	—	55.0

Sources: Republic of Kenya, Ministry of Planning, *Statistical Abstract*, 1965; United Republic of Tanzania, Central Statistical Bureau, *Statistical Abstract*, 1963.

TABLE A.2

Kenya: Direction and Composition of External Trade, 1950-60
(percent)

Year	X_{BC}/X_T	M_{BC}/M_T	Principal Export Commodities as Percentage of Total			
			Coffee	Sisal	Tea	CST
1950	60.8	77.3	20.7	23.6	7.8	52.1
1951	56.1	63.1	17.0	28.9	5.8	51.7
1952	51.2	66.0	27.6	17.3	5.1	50.0
1953	53.3	68.9	34.4	12.7	4.8	51.9
1954	56.9	63.8	28.2	10.1	10.2	48.5
1955	50.5	61.7	34.7	7.6	10.7	53.0
1956	45.3	74.3	47.1	7.2	9.0	63.3
1957	46.9	68.2	40.9	7.9	10.8	59.6
1958	45.8	67.8	35.5	7.6	11.0	54.1
1959	43.5	72.1	31.8	10.4	10.8	53.0
1960	44.9	62.9	29.2	13.0	12.5	.54.7

X_{BC} = Exports to British Commonwealth.
X_T = Total exports of Kenya.
M_{BC} = Imports from British Commonwealth.
M_T = Total imports of Kenya.
CST = Total of coffee, sisal, and tea.
Source: Republic of Kenya, Ministry of Economic Planning and Development, *Statistical Abstract*.

TABLE A.3

Tanzania: Direction and Composition of External Trade, 1950-61
(percent)

Year	X_{BC}/X_T	M_{BC}/M_T	Principal Export Commodities as Percentage of Total			
			Sisal	Coffee	Cotton	SCC
1950	63.8	73.1	48.1	14.4	5.9	68.4
1951	61.6	64.6	58.5	11.3	6.8	76.6
1952	57.4	67.7	47.7	11.9	10.1	69.7
1953	57.3	71.1	37.4	17.0	14.1	68.5
1954	54.6	71.2	30.1	27.6	9.3	67.0
1955	57.4	60.0	27.5	19.1	15.3	61.9
1956	51.3	62.3	24.1	20.6	16.7	61.4
1957	53.6	53.1	24.1	18.1	16.7	58.9
1958	52.8	53.1	24.8	18.2	17.4	60.4
1959	56.5	55.6	28.8	12.7	14.7	56.2
1960	54.9	49.3	28.1	13.3	16.1	57.5
1961	57.9	53.3	28.8	13.9	14.0	56.7

X_{BC} = Exports to British Commonwealth.
X_T = Total exports of Tanzania.
M_{BC} = Imports from British Commonwealth.
M_T = Total imports of Tanzania.
SCC = Total of sisal, coffee, and cotton.
Source: Central Statistical Bureau, Tanzania, *Statistical Abstract*.

TABLE A.4

Somalia: Major Exports and Exports to Italy and Arabia as Percentage of Total Exports, 1951-59 and 1961-73

Year	Bananas	Livestock Products	Exports to Italy	Exports to Arabia*
1951-59	38.4	38.4	—	—
1961	48.0	35.4	—	—
1962	44.5	44.6	51.4	39.2
1963	44.6	46.6	49.4	40.3
1964	32.6	56.8	45.6	38.9
1965	32.8	51.0	48.8	38.8
1966	36.7	50.7	45.5	44.9
1967	34.4	55.0	37.5	56.2
1968	28.1	65.6	30.6	62.8
1969	24.1	65.6	26.0	67.0
1970	27.9	62.9	26.1	62.7
1971	26.1	66.1	22.4	56.1
1972	26.1	67.2	18.3	57.9
1973	19.8	68.3	16.5	64.7

*Arabia includes only Saudi Arabia and the People's Democratic Republic of Yemen (Aden).

Source: *Somali National Bank Bulletin*, 1964, 1972.

TABLE A.5

Kenya: Gross Domestic Product at Factor Cost
1964-73
(millions of Kenyan pounds, percentages in parentheses)

Sector	1964	1965	1966	1967	1968	1969	1970	1971	1972	1973
Outside monetary economy	88.9	79.7	97.6	101.4	105.1	109.0	112.6	116.0	119.9	123.5
	(27.1)	(24.1)	(25.7)	(25.6)	(24.6)	(24.0)	(23.2)	(22.4)	(21.8)	(21.1)
Monetary economy										
Agriculture, forestry, etc.	52.0	49.3	58.9	57.4	61.9	69.2	72.9	77.6	87.6	94.2
	(15.8)	(14.9)	(15.5)	(14.5)	(14.5)	(15.2)	(15.0)	(15.0)	(15.9)	(16.1)
Manufacturing and other										
monetary	187.6	201.9	222.7	237.6	260.1	276.1	300.0	323.4	343.2	368.9
Total gross domestic product	328.5	330.9	379.2	396.4	427.1	454.3	485.5	517.0	550.7	586.6
Rate of growth of GDP	—	(.7)	(14.6)	(4.6)	(7.7)	(6.4)	(6.9)	(6.5)	(6.5)	(6.5)

Note: Constant 1964 prices.
Source: Central Bureau of Statistics, Ministry of Finance and Planning, Republic of Kenya, *Statistical Abstracts*, 1972, 1974.

TABLE A.6

Tanzania: Gross Domestic Product at Factor Cost, 1964-73
(millions of Tanzanian shillings, percentages in parentheses)

Sector	1964	1965	1966	1967	1968	1969	1970	1971	1972	1973
Total subsistence production	1,854 (33.0)	1,872 (32.4)	2,054 (31.5)	2,126 (31.2)	2,192 (30.5)	2,135 (29.1)	2,178 (28.0)	2,241 (27.7)	2,348 (27.6)	2,462 (27.9)
Total monetary economy Agriculture, forestry, etc.	1,246 (22.2)	1,194 (20.7)	1,402 (21.5)	1,346 (19.7)	1,402 (19.5)	1,492 (20.3)	1,574 (20.2)	1,545 (19.1)	1,614 (19.0)	1,573 (17.8)
Other monetary production, secondary and tertiary	2,519	2,707	3,062	3,353	3,580	3,711	4,027	4,290	4,542	4,779
Total gross domestic product	5,619	5,773	6,518	6,825	7,174	7,338	7,779	8,076	8,504	8,814
Rate of growth of GDP	—	(2.7)	(12.9)	(4.7)	(5.1)	(2.3)	(6.0)	(3.8)	(5.3)	(3.6)

Note: 1966 prices.

Source: Tanzania, Ministry of Economic Affairs and Development Planning, *National Accounts of Tanzania*, February 1972, and *Economic Survey*, 1974.

TABLE A.7

Kenya: Uses of Domestic Fixed Capital Formation, 1964-73
(millions of Kenyan pounds)

	1964	1965	1966	1967	1968	1969	1970	1971	1972	1973
Uses by type of asset										
Buildings	12.2	12.9	15.3	22.8	28.6	30.4	32.7	40.7	44.9	42.6
Other construction	8.6	9.3	13.0	17.5	19.9	20.2	22.8	32.5	39.9	54.0
Equipment and machinery	23.9	23.3	31.6	40.6	39.8	41.9	55.1	70.6	72.9	83.5
Other capital	.4	.3	1.4	1.3	1.3	1.3	2.0	0.4	2.7	1.4
Gross domestic capital formation (GCF)	44.3	45.8	61.3	82.2	89.6	93.8	112.6	144.2	160.4	181.5
Uses by sector										
Public	11.1	11.9	19.4	28.5	32.9	30.7	34.2	55.5	60.9	77.8
Private—monetary	28.0	28.1	35.4	46.2	48.3	54.4	69.3	78.8	89.1	92.7
Private—nonmonetary	5.2	5.7	6.5	7.5	8.4	8.7	9.2	9.9	10.4	11.0
Important ratios*										
(GCF/GDP)	13.5%	13.8	16.2	20.7	21.0	20.6	23.2	27.9	29.1	30.9
Private GCF/total GCF	74.9	74.0	68.4	65.3	63.3	67.3	69.7	61.5	62.0	57.1
Equipment/total GCF	54.0	50.9	51.5	49.4	44.4	44.7	48.9	49.0	45.4	46.0
Nonmonetary GCF/total GCF	11.8	12.4	10.6	9.1	9.4	9.3	8.2	6.9	6.5	6.1

*During the years 1954-63, the GCF/GDP ratio averaged 18.9 percent, private GCF/total GCF, 62.4 percent, and the share of equipment in total GCF, 43.1 percent.

Source: Republic of Kenya, Central Bureau of Statistics, Ministry of Finance and Planning, Statistical Abstracts, 1973, 1974.

TABLE A.8

Tanzania: Uses of Domestic Capital Formation, 1964-73
(millions of Tanzanian shillings)

	1964	1965	1966	1967	1968	1969	1970	1971	1972	1973
Uses by type of asset										
Buildings	251	294	307	375	402	386	518	—	—	—
Other construction	106	107	163	313	326	322	558	—	—	—
Equipment and machinery	271	344	489	533	552	486	847	—	—	—
Other capital	46	44	32	50	38	23	24	—	—	—
Increase in stocks	93	107	111	80	94	90	100	—	—	—
Gross capital formation (GCF)	767	896	1,102	1,351	1,412	1,307	2,047	2,368	2,376	2,728
Uses by sector										
Total public	234	253	400	642	683	601	1,291	1,674	1,713	1,958
Parastatals	77	62	180	379	357	215	760	1,084	1,167	1,148
Private—monetary	339	441	520	483	516	522	568	517	461	550
Private—nonmonetary	193	203	182	226	214	184	188	177	202	220
Important ratios*										
(GCF/GDP)	13.7%	15.5	16.9	19.8	19.7	17.8	26.3	29.3	27.9	31.0
Private GCF/total GCF	69.4	71.9	63.7	52.5	51.7	54.0	36.9	29.3	27.9	28.2
Equipment/total GCF	35.3	38.4	44.4	39.5	39.1	37.2	41.4	—	—	—
Nonmonetary GCF/total GCF	25.2	22.7	16.5	15.9	15.1	14.1	9.2	7.5	8.5	8.1

*During the years 1954-61, GCF as a percentage of GDP averaged 17.9 percent, private capital as a percentage of GCF averaged 66.3 percent, and the share of equipment in GCF averaged 39.9 percent.

Sources: Tanzania, Ministry of Economic Affairs, National Accounts of Tanzania, 1972, and Economic Survey, 1974.

TABLE A.9

Eastern African Government Expenditures and Revenues

	1964-65	1965-66	1966-67	1967-68	1968-69	1969-70	1970-71	1971-72	1972-73	1973-74
Tanzania (millions of TSh)										
Revenues	676	754	1,024	1,130	1,270	1,577	1,654	1,897	2,419	3,216
Recurrent expenditures	613	708	980	1,065	1,186	1,527	1,623	1,717	2,134	2,685
Development expenditures	157	191	220	263	326	386	531	870	956	1,629
Deficit and surplus	-93	-145	-176	-198	-242	-336	-500	-690	-671	-1,098
Kenya (millions of Kenyan pounds)										
Revenues	57.0	62.6	71.1	80.8	91.3	99.8	117.9	142.0	149.6	187.5
Recurrent expenditures	56.9	63.3	68.5	74.4	80.5	91.1	109.1	128.7	139.6	166.2
Development expenditures	11.1	11.9	19.4	28.5	32.9	30.7	34.2	39.8	44.8	69.8
Deficit or surplus	-11.0	-14.5	-16.8	-22.1	-22.1	-22.0	-25.4	-26.5	-34.8	-48.5

	1961	1962	1963	1964	1965	1966	1967	1968	1969	1970	1971
Somalia (millions of So.Sh)											
Revenues	124	143	153	178	178	224	248	257	272	289	337
Recurrent expenditures	165	158	180	198	199	237	272	282	280	295	318
Development expenditures	–	–	21	33	19	20	–	–	145	134	134
Deficit	-41	-15	-48	-53	-40	-33	-24	-25	-153	-140	-115

Sources: Tanzania, Ministry of Economic Affairs, *National Accounts, 1970*, and *Economic Survey*, various issues; Kenya, Ministry of Finance, *Economic Survey*, 1971, and *Statistical Abstract, 1974*; and *Somali National Bank Bulletins*.

TABLE A.10

Somalia: National Commercial Bank Growth, 1975-76
(millions of Somali shillings)

	Demand Deposits	Savings and Time Deposits	Money Supply (M_1)	Demand Deposits as Percentage of M_1	Savings and Time Deposits as Percentage of M_1	Total Assets
March 1975	243.8	158.8	570.6	42.7	27.8	2,054.1
June 1975	289.0	167.2	595.1	48.6	28.1	2,030.1
September 1975	312.0	172.4	673.9	46.3	25.6	1,975.2
December 1975	385.2	179.0	774.7	49.7	23.1	2,042.7
March 1976	339.5	181.7	774.0	43.9	23.5	2,086.3
June 1976	366.1	189.6	780.6	46.8	24.3	2,051.3

Source: National Commercial Bank, Research Department.

TABLE A.11

Somalia: National Commercial Bank, Distribution of
Loans and Advances by Economic Activity
(millions of Somali shillings at end of period)

	1974	1975	June 1975	June 1976
Agriculture	36.2	81.4	113.4	109.4
Industry	118.7	200.6	177.6	172.9
Fishing	8.5	16.6	12.1	22.0
Livestock*	21.7	38.3	36.1	56.7
Trade*	269.8	592.4	486.3	509.1
of which: external trade	(233.4)	(542.8)	(442.9)	(—)
Total	454.9	929.3	825.4	870.2
Trade loans as percentage of total	59.3	63.7	58.9	58.5
Less essential loans as percentage of total	64.1	67.9	63.3	65.0

*Less essential loans include loans granted to livestock exporters to finance "holding ground" and other incidental expenses.

Source: National Commercial Bank, Research Department.

TABLE A.12

Somalia: National Commercial Bank Size Distribution of Loans, 1975
(percentage of total)

	Below 2,500 So.Sh	Below 5,000 So.Sh	5,000-9,999 So.Sh	Above 10,000 So.Sh	Above 15,000 So.Sh
January	50.8	63.1	16.9	20.0	6.2
February	58.6	67.1	18.6	14.3	4.3
March	77.4	88.7	3.2	8.1	3.2
April	33.3	50.0	29.2	20.8	4.2
May	47.5	62.5	7.5	30.0	15.0
June	45.2	54.8	29.0	16.1	9.7
July	50.9	66.0	17.0	17.0	9.4
August	90.8	95.8	1.7	2.5	1.4
September	65.5	72.4	8.6	19.0	6.9
October	51.7	58.6	17.2	24.1	6.9
November	36.0	56.0	20.0	24.0	16.0
December	66.7	75.0	16.7	8.3	—

Note: The loans exclude advances and letters of credit to which the bulk of bank resources are directed.

Source: National Commercial Bank, Research Department.

TABLE A.13

Somalia: National Commercial Bank (Branch No. 1), Term Structure of Loans Issued in the First Half of 1975

	Loans for 3 Months or Less	Loans for 3-6 Months	Loans for 6-12 Months	Loans for More than 12 Months
March 1975	5	11	47	2
As percentage of total loans	(7.7)	(16.9)	(72.3)	(3.1)
June 1975	12	6	50	2
As percentage of total loans	(17.1)	(8.6)	(71.4)	(2.9)

Source: National Commercial Bank, Research Department.

TABLE A.14

Kenya: Growth of Commercial Banks, 1966-73 (millions of Kenyan pounds)

End of Year	Money Supply (M_1)	Time and Savings Deposits	Total Bank Liabilities	GNP	Time and Savings Deposits/ (M_1)	Total Bank Liabilities/ GNP	Change in Total Bank Liabilities/ GNP
1966	70.2	27.6	107.7	409.0	.393	.263	−.004
1967	73.9	33.9	119.1	432.0	.459	.276	.026
1968	80.8	39.2	131.4	459.0	.485	.286	.027
1969	93.4	48.5	161.1	511.1	.519	.315	.058
1970	115.6	65.9	199.0	613.5	.570	.324	.061
1971	124.0	72.7	225.6	632.9	.586	.356	.042
1972	144.8	77.6	252.6	690.1	.536	.366	.039
1973	177.3	100.2	334.2	770.9	.565	.434	.106
1966-73	—	—	—	—	.514	.354	.045

Source: Central Bank of Kenya, *Economic and Financial Review*, March 1974.

TABLE A.15

Tanzania: Growth of Commercial Banks, 1962-73
(millions of Tanzanian shillings)

End of Year	Money Supply (M_1)	Time and Savings Deposits	Total Bank Liabilities	GNP	Time and Savings Deposits/ (M_1)	Total Bank Liabilities/ GNP	Change in Total Bank Liabilities/ GNP
1962	828	157	691	4,392	.189	.157	–
1963	898	205	753	4,860	.228	.155	.013
1964	980	191	912	6,017	.195	.152	.026
1965	1,043	235	1,009	6,141	.225	.164	.016
1966	889	306	1,328	6,984	.344	.190	.046
1967	1,192	353	1,297	7,398	.296	.175	-.004
1968	1,297	520	1,559	8,047	.401	.194	.036
1969	1,537	664	1,958	8,332	.432	.235	.048
1970	1,799	829	2,219	9,125	.461	.243	.029
1971	2,179	1,011	2,761	9,749	.464	.283	.056
1972	2,459	1,232	3,062	11,252	.501	.272	.027
1973	2,861	1,358	3,556	13,107	.475	.271	.028
1962-73	–	–	–	–	.351	.208	.030
1967-73	–	–	–	–	.433	.239	.033

Source: Bank of Tanzania, *Economic Bulletin*, December 1973.

138

TABLE A.16

Korea: Growth of Commercial Banks, 1962-73
(billions of won)

End of Year	Money Supply (M₁)	Time and Savings Deposits	Total Bank Liabilities	GNP	Time and Savings Deposits/ (M₁)	Total Bank Liabilities/ GNP	Change in Total Bank Liabilities/ GNP
1962	39.4	12.2	66.8	348.5	.310	.192	.065
1963	41.9	12.9	77.9	488.0	.308	.160	.023
1964	48.9	14.5	81.3	696.7	.297	.117	.005
1965	65.6	30.6	121.9	805.8	.466	.151	.050
1966	85.2	70.1	190.4	1,032.1	.823	.184	.066
1967	122.0	128.9	354.2	1,242.4	1.057	.285	.132
1968	153.6	255.5	515.4	1,575.7	1.663	.327	.102
1969	218.2	451.5	869.2	2,047.1	2.069	.425	.173
1970	305.6	573.3	1,182.2	2,545.9	1.876	.464	.123
1971	357.4	705.1	1,476.0	3,085.8	1.973	.478	.095
1972	519.4	928.6	1,829.9	3,860.0	1.788	.474	.091
1973	730.3	1,237.8	2,449.5	4,928.7	1.695	.497	.126
1962-65	–	–	–	–	.345	.155	.036
1966-73	–	–	–	–	1.618	.392	.114
1962-73	–	–	–	–	1.194	.313	.088

Source: IMF, *International Financial Statistics*, various issues.

139

TABLE A.17

Taiwan: Growth of Commercial Banks, 1962-73
(billions of NT dollars)

End of Year	Money Supply (M_1)	Time and Savings Deposits	Total Bank Liabilities	GNP	Time and Savings Deposits/ (M_1)	Total Bank Liabilities/ GNP	Change in Total Bank Liabilities/ GNP
1962	7.8	9.6	25.9	77.5	1.231	.334	.030
1963	10.1	12.5	32.2	87.7	1.238	.367	.072
1964	13.3	15.8	39.5	102.7	1.188	.385	.071
1965	14.7	18.6	46.3	113.4	1.265	.408	.060
1966	17.0	24.2	55.0	126.3	1.424	.435	.069
1967	21.9	29.6	67.8	145.9	1.352	.465	.088
1968	24.7	33.2	80.4	170.9	1.344	.470	.074
1969	28.6	41.0	89.7	195.6	1.434	.459	.048
1970	34.5	51.9	105.5	226.4	1.504	.466	.070
1971	40.9	71.4	129.4	261.4	1.746	.495	.091
1972	55.1	95.7	168.5	307.4	1.737	.548	.127
1973	80.9	116.0	247.8	388.6	1.434	.638	.203
1962-73	–	–	–	–	1.408	0.456	0.135

Source: IMF, International Financial Statistics, various issues.

140

TABLE A.18

Germany: Growth of Commercial Banks, 1962-73
(billions of Deutsche Marks)

End of Year	Money Supply (M_1)	Time and Savings Deposits	Total Bank Liabilities	GNP	Time and Savings Deposits/ (M_1)	Total Bank Liabilities/ GNP	Change in Total Bank Liabilities/ GNP
1962	56.9	77.3	238.7	360.1	1.359	.663	.106
1963	61.0	89.4	267.6	384.0	1.466	.697	.075
1964	67.8	103.1	301.8	420.9	1.521	.717	.081
1965	72.5	120.4	340.2	460.4	1.661	.739	.083
1966	74.2	140.3	371.1	490.8	1.891	.756	.063
1967	81.6	163.8	407.0	494.7	2.007	.823	.073
1968	88.4	196.2	465.5	538.9	2.219	.864	.109
1969	93.7	223.8	523.8	602.6	2.338	.884	.112
1970	102.7	250.3	596.8	682.9	2.437	.874	.094
1971	115.8	291.0	674.2	756.1	2.513	.892	.102
1972	131.9	337.4	776.3	833.9	2.558	.931	.122
1973	132.9	390.0	926.9	863.5	2.935	1.073	.174
1962-73	—	—	—	—	2.075	.826	.100

Source: IMF, *International Financial Statistics*, various issues.

TABLE A.19

Japan: Growth of Commercial Banks, 1962-73
(billions of yen)

End of Year	Money Supply (M_1)	Time and Savings Deposits	Total Bank Liabilities	GNP	Time and Savings Deposits/ (M_1)	Total Bank Liabilities/ GNP	Change in Total Bank Liabilities/ GNP
1962	5,725	8,968	18,576	21,199	1.576	.876	.131
1963	7,703	10,965	23,567	24,465	1.424	.963	.204
1964	8,704	12,818	27,503	28,839	1.473	.954	.136
1965	10,287	15,107	31,730	31,787	1.46	.998	.133
1966	11,716	17,806	36,891	36,544	1.52	1.010	.141
1967	13,369	20,729	42,432	43,097	1.551	.987	.131
1968	15,155	23,999	48,580	51,709	1.584	.940	.117
1969	18,282	28,117	56,601	60,244	1.538	.940	.133
1970	21,358	32,877	66,405	70,985	1.539	.936	.138
1971	27,692	39,705	80,123	78,960	1.434	1.015	.174
1972	34,526	49,514	98,222	90,320	1.434	1.087	.200
1973	40,311	57,877	116,652	111,061	1.436	1.050	.166
1962-73	—	—	—	—	1.497	.979	.150

Source: IMF, International Financial Statistics, various issues.

BOOKS AND ARTICLES

Abdi, A. "Banking in Uganda Since Independence: Comment." *Economic Development and Cultural Change* 24, no. 2 (January 1976): 417–19.

Aboyade, O. *Capital Formation and Development Theory: Foundations of an African Economy.* New York: Praeger, 1970.

Adelman, Irma, and Cynthia Morris. "An Econometric Model of Socio-Economic and Political Change in Underdeveloped Countries." *American Economic Review* 58, no. 5 (December 1968): 1184–1218.

———. *Society, Politics, and Economic Development: A Quantitative Approach.* Baltimore: Johns Hopkins Press, 1967.

Ali, Anwar. "Banking in the Middle East." *IMF Staff Papers* 6, no. 1 (November 1957): 51–79.

Balinky, Alexander. *Marx's Economics—Origin and Development.* Lexington, Mass.: D. C. Heath, 1970.

Bennett, Robert. *The Financial Sector and Economic Development: The Mexican Case.* Baltimore: Johns Hopkins Press, 1965.

Ben-Shahar, Haim. "The Structure of Capital Markets and Economic Growth—The Case of Israel." In *Financial Development and Economic Growth,* ed. Arnold Sametz. New York: New York University Press, 1972.

Bhatia, Rattan, and Deena Khatkhate. "Financial Intermediation, Savings Mobilization and Entrepreneurial Development: The African Experience." *IMF Staff Papers* 22 (March 1975): 132–59.

Binhammer, H. H. *Commercial Banking in Tanzania.* Economic Research Bureau Paper no. 69.11. Dar-es-Salaam: University of Dar-es-Salaam, 1969.

Brimmer, Andrew. "Central Banking and Economic Development: The Record of Innovations." *Journal of Money, Credit and Banking* 3, no. 4 (November 1971): 786–89.

Cameron, R., ed. *Banking and Economic Development: Some Lessons of History.* New York: Oxford University Press, 1972.

———. *Banking in the Early Stages of Industrialization.* London: Oxford University Press, 1967.

Caselli, Ciara. *The Banking System of Tanzania.* Milan: Cassa di Risparmio delle provincie, 1975.

Chandavakar, Anand G. "Some Aspects of Interest Rate Policies in Less Developed Economies: The Experience of Selected Asian Countries." *IMF Staff Papers* 18 (March 1971): 48–110.

Chenery, Hollis, ed. *Studies in Development Planning.* Cambridge, Mass.: Harvard University Press, 1971.

Christian, James, and Emilio Pagoulatos. "Domestic Financial Markets in Developing Countries." *Kylos* 26, no. 1 (1973): 75–90.

Clark, Paul G. *Development Planning in East Africa,* Nairobi: East Africa Publishing House, 1965.

Dell'Amore, Giordano. *Banking Policy and Saving Policy in African Countries.* Proceedings of a Conference on the Mobilization of Savings in the African Countries, Milan, 1971.

Demas, William. *The Economics of Development in Small Countries.* Montreal: McGill University Press, 1965.

Domar, Evsey. "Capital Expansion, Rate of Growth, and Employment," *Econometrica* 14, no. 1 (1946): 137–47.

———. "The Problem of Capital Formation." *American Economic Review* 38, no. 5 (December 1948): 777–94.

Engberg, Holger L. "Commercial Banking in East Africa." *Journal of Modern African Studies* 3, no. 2 (1965): 177–99.

Felix, David. "Technological Dualism in Late Industrializers: On Theory, History and Policy." *Journal of Economic History* 34, no. 1 (March 1974): 194–238.

Gerschenberg, Irving. "Banking in Uganda Since Independence." *Economic Development and Cultural Change* 20, no. 3 (April 1972): 504–23.

Gerschenkron, A. *Economic Backwardness in Historical Perspective: A Book of Essays.* Cambridge, Mass.: Harvard University Press, 1962.

Goldsmith, R. W. *Financial Structure and Development.* New Haven: Yale University Press, 1969.

Gurley, J. "Financial Structure in Developing Economies." In *Fiscal and Monetary Problems in Developing States,* ed. D. Krivine. New York: Praeger, 1967.

Gurley, J. Review of *Banking in the Early Stages of Industrialization,* ed. R. Cameron. *American Economic Review,* 57, no. 4 (1967): 951–53.

Gurley, J. and E. S. Shaw. "Financial Aspects of Economic Development." *American Economic Review* 45, no. 4 (December 1955): 515–38.

———. "Financial Structure and Economic Development." *Economic Development and Cultural Change* 15, no. 3 (April 1967): 257–68.

———. *Money in a Theory of Finance.* Washington, D. C.: Brookings Institution, 1960.

Harvey, Charles. "The Control of Credit in Zambia." Institute of Development Studies, Sussex, February 1973.

Hirschman, A. *The Strategy of Economic Development.* New Haven: Yale University Press, 1958.

International Monetary Fund (IMF). *Survey of African Economies,* vol. 2. Washington, D.C.: IMF, 1969.

Johnson, Harry G. *Money, Trade and Economic Growth.* Cambridge, Mass.: Harvard University Press, 1962.

Jucker-Fleetwood, E. E. *Money and Finance in Africa.* London: George Allen and Unwin, 1964.

Karp, Mark. *The Economics of Trusteeship in Somalia.* Boston: Boston University Press, 1960.

Landau, Luis. "Savings Functions for Latin America." *Studies in Development Planning,* ed. Hollis B. Chenery. Cambridge, Mass.: Harvard University Press, 1971.

Lewis, W. A. *The Theory of Economic Growth.* New York: Harper & Row, 1970.

Loxley, John. *The Domestic Finance of Development Projects in Tanzania.* Economic Research Paper, August 1971. Dar-es-Salaam: University of Dar-es-Salaam, 1971.

Maldonado, Rita M. *The Role of the Financial Sector in the Economic Development of Puerto Rico.* Washington, D.C.: Federal Deposit Insurance Corporation, 1970.

McKinnon, Ronald. *Money and Capital in Economic Development.* Washington, D. C.: Brookings Institution, 1973.

Meier, Gerald M. *Leading Issues in Development Economics.* New York: Oxford University Press, 1964.

Michaelsen, Jacob B. *The Term Structure of Interest Rates.* New York: Intext Educational Publishers, 1973.

Mikesell, R., and J. Zinzer. "The Nature of the Savings Function in Developing Countries: A Survey of the Theoretical and Empirical Literature," *Journal of Economic Literature* 11, no. 1 (March 1973): 1–27.

Minsky, Hyman. "The Capital Market Route for Monetary Policy." Unpublished paper, 1968.

———. "Financial Intermediation in the Money and Capital Markets." In *Issues in Banking and Monetary Analysis,* ed. G. Pontecovo, R. Shay, and A. Hart. New York: Holt, Rinehart and Winston, 1967.

Morgan, T. "Investment versus Economic Growth." *Economic Development and Cultural Change* 17, no. 3 (April 1969): 392–414.

Myint, H. *Economic Theory and the Underdeveloped Countries.* New York: Oxford University Press, 1971.

Narasimbam, M., ed. *Proceedings of the International Seminar on Banking and Development.* Bombay, February 1970.

Nevin, Edward. *Capital Funds in Underdeveloped Countries.* New York: St. Martins Press, 1961.

Newlyn, W. T. *Money in an African Context.* London: Oxford University Press, 1967.

Newlyn, W. T. and D. C. Rowen. *Money and Banking in British Colonial Africa.* London: Oxford University Press, 1954.

Nyerere, Julius K. *Ujamaa—Essays on Socialism.* Dar-es-Salaam: Oxford University Press, 1968.

———. *Uhuru na Ujamaa—Freedom and Socialism: A Selection from Writings and Speeches, 1965–7.* Dar-es-Salaam: Oxford University Press, 1968.

Osman, Saeed. "Financial Institutions and Industrial Finance in the Sudan." Ph.D. dissertation, University of California, Los Angeles, 1968.

Papanek, Gustav F. "Aid, Foreign Private Investment, Savings and Growth in LDC's." *Journal of Political Economy* 81, no. 1 (January 1973): 120–30.

Patel, I. F. "Selective Credit Controls in Underdeveloped Economies." *IMF Staff Papers* 4, no. 1 (September 1954): 73–85.

Patrick, Hugh. "Financial Development and Economic Growth in Under-Developed Countries." *Economic Development and Cultural Change* 14, no. 2 (January 1966): 174–89.

Pauw, Ernst-Josef. "Banking in East Africa." In *Financial Aspects of Development in East Africa,* ed. Peter Marlin. Munich: Weltforum Verlag, 1970.

Perera, Phillips. *Development Finance: Institutions, Problems and Prospects.* New York: Praeger, 1968.

Porter, Richard. "The Promotion of the 'Banking Habit' and Economic Development." *Journal of Development Studies* 2, no. 4 (August 1966): 347–56.

Rosen, George. *Some Aspects of Industrial Finance in India.* Glencoe, Ill.: Free Press, 1962.

Rostow, W. W. *The Stages of Economic Growth.* London: Cambridge University Press, 1960.

Rweyemamu, Justinian. *Underdevelopment and Industrialization in Tanzania: A Case Study of Perverse Capitalist Development.* Nairobi: Oxford University Press, 1973.

Sameltz, Arnold, ed. *Financial Development and Economic Growth.* New York: New York University Press, 1973.

Schatz, Sayre P. *Development Banking Lending in Nigeria.* Ibadan: Oxford University Press, 1964.

Shaw, Edward. *Financial Deepening in Economic Development.* London: Oxford University Press, 1973.

Szentes, Tamas. *The Political Economy of Underdevelopment.* Budapest: Akademiai Kiado, 1972.

Thomas, Clive. *Monetary and Financial Arrangements in a Dependent Monetary Economy* [Mona]. Jamaica: Institute of Social and Economic Research Studies, University of West Indies, 1965.

Tilly, Richard. *Financial Institutions and Industrialization in the German Rhineland, 1815–1870.* Madison: University of Wisconsin Press, 1966.

Tremblay, Rodriques, ed. *Africa and Monetary Integration.* Montreal: University of Montreal Press, 1972.

Wai, U Tun. *Financial Intermediaries and National Savings in Developing Countries.* New York: Praeger, 1972.

―――. "Interest Rates Outside the Organized Money Markets of Underdeveloped Countries." *IMF Staff Papers* 6, no. 1 (November 1957): 80–142.

GOVERNMENT REPORTS AND PUBLICATIONS

Bank of Tanzania. *Economic Bulletin* 5, nos. 2–3. Dar-es-Salaam, 1973–74.

―――. *Economics and Operations Report.* Dar-es-Salaam, 1969–73.

Central Bank of Kenya. *Economic and Financial Review* 1–4. Nairobi, 1968–72.

Central Bank of Somalia, Research and Statistics Department. *Bulletin,* no. 38. Mogadishu, 1974.

East African Economic and Statistical Review, various issues. Nairobi, 1956–64.

Republic of Kenya. *African Socialism and Its Application to Planning in Kenya.* Nairobi, 1965.

―――. *Development Plan, 1964–70.* Nairobi, 1964.

Republic of Kenya, Ministry of Finance and Planning, Central Bureau of Statistics. *Statistical Abstracts.* Nairobi, 1965–73.

―――. *Economic Survey.* Nairobi, 1973.

Somali Democratic Republic, Department of Central Statistics. *Industrial Production 1970.* Mogadishu, March 1972.

Somali National Bank. *Annual Report and Statement of Accounts.* Mogadishu 1973.

―――. *Bulletin,* various issues in vols. 15–25. Mogadishu, 1961–69.

―――. *Economic Report.* Mogadishu, 1963–64.

Somali Republic, Planning Commission. *Short-Term Development Program, 1968–70.* Mogadishu, 1968.

Somali Republic, Planning and Coordinating Committee for Economic and Social Development. *First Five-Year Plan, 1963–67.* Mogadishu, 1963.

United Republic of Tanzania. *The Arusha Declaration and TANU's Policy on Socialism and Self-Reliance.* Dar-es-Salaam, February 1967.

United Republic of Tanzania, Ministry of Economic Affairs and Development Planning. *Five-Year Plan for Economic and Social Development, 1964–69.* Dar-es-Salaam 1964.

United Republic of Tanzania, Ministry of Economic Affairs and Development Planning, Bureau of Statistics. *National Accounts of Tanzania 1964–70.* Dar-es-Salaam, February, 1972.

United Republic of Tanzania, National Bank of Commerce. *Annual Report and Accounts.* Dar-es-Salaam, June 1974.

ALI ISSA ABDI is an economist in the Western Hemisphere Department of the International Monetary Fund. A citizen of Somalia, Dr. Abdi has been associated with commercial banks in North America and in Eastern Africa, working briefly with First National City Bank of New York, and Banca Di Roma, Mogadishu branch. He has also worked with the Central Bank of Somalia. His previous publications include journal articles in the field of finance and economic development, which appeared in the *Economic Development and Cultural Change.*

Dr. Abdi holds an MBA in finance from Washington University, St. Louis, Missouri, and a Ph.D. in economics from the same university. He has taught at the Bankers Training Institute, Mogadishu and at universities and colleges in St. Louis.

RELATED TITLES
Published by
Praeger Special Studies

THE COMPUTER AND AFRICA: Applications, Problems and Potential
edited by
D. R. F. Taylor
R. A. Obudho

IMPORTING TECHNOLOGY INTO AFRICA: Foreign Investment and the Supply of Technological Innovations
D. Babatunde Thomas

MANAGING COMMERCIAL BANK FUNDS
Emmanuel N. Roussakis

NATIONAL CONTROL OF FOREIGN BUSINESS ENTRY: A Survey of Fifteen Countries
Richard D. Robinson

The Praeger Special Studies program, through a selective worldwide distribution network, makes available to the academic, government, and business communities significant and timely research in U.S. and international economic, social, and political issues.